PARNELL

A Novel

PARNELL

A Novel

Brian Cregan

First published 2013, this edition 2014

The History Press Ireland
50 City Quay
Dublin 2
Ireland
www.thehistorypress.ie

British Library Cataloguing in Publication Data.
A catalogue record for this book is available from the British Library.

ISBN 978 1 84588 858 9

Typesetting and origination by The History Press

To

Catherine

Prologue

London, October 1895

Several years after Mr Parnell's death, I met with Mr Gladstone at his home in London. I had not seen him since his retirement some years earlier, but he was not much changed. His face was perhaps more lined, his slight figure more stooped and he was now a little hard of hearing, but his grey eyes still pierced, and the great voice which had dominated the House of Commons for decades was still mellifluous and resonant. He welcomed me affectionately, ever eager to hear the news from Ireland, from one whom he had befriended many years earlier when he had been Prime Minister and I a young associate of Parnell.

We talked for some hours about those troubled times and towards the end of our interview I asked Mr Gladstone how he would compare Mr Parnell to other men he knew in public life, how he would compare him to Disraeli and Salisbury, Palmerston, Peel and O'Connell and all the other titans of that era.

He paused for a moment, reflecting on the verdict he was about to deliver. 'I have thought on this for some time,' he said, 'and I would say that Mr Parnell was the most remarkable man I ever met. I don't think I ever met a man to compare with him. I do not say he was the ablest man but he was certainly the most remarkable. He was a phenomenon. He did things quite unlike other men. He said things quite unlike other men.'

He looked at me directly. 'You and I, Mr Harrison, have had a better opportunity of knowing Mr Parnell than any other men in

England. We have seen him at his work and I would say that he was a genius – a genius of a most uncommon order.'

As he said these words he seemed to fall into a reverie, as if thinking back to the days when Parnell and he had confronted each other in the House of Commons and in the country. But after a moment or so, he resumed.

'He was your greatest leader. I have no doubt on that. I knew O'Connell also but Parnell was the greater man. You were with him from the start, Mr Harrison, but I was there before the start. I saw his inheritance when O'Connell died.'

The pale sun of the late autumn afternoon suffused the room with a mellow light and there was no sound save for the soft collapsing of some logs in the fire.

Gladstone leaned back into his chair and stared mournfully at the embers. 'Your nation broken by that terrible famine, its spirit crushed. Its people wholly dispossessed, bereft of hope, bereft of leadership.' Gladstone raised his voice and his hand in unison, the long-repeated habits of the public orator. 'You must remember that, Mr Harrison – you must judge his achievements by what he inherited. And twenty-five years after the famine, it was still the same.'

I was about to ask him another question but he waved me down gently.

'And then Parnell appeared in the House of Commons. Alone. And within three years he had made our parliament unworkable; within six years he had destroyed the landlords in Ireland and within a decade he controlled the House of Commons and put English Prime Ministers in and out of Government, at will.' He opened his veinous, gnarled hands towards me in a gesture of helplessness. 'And there was nothing we could do. Nothing. He forced us to confront him; he forced us to solve the land problem; he forced us to grant him a Home Rule bill.'

Gladstone paused to ensure I followed his every word. 'And he achieved all this – in the face of total English opposition – without an army or a navy – without even a rebellion. That is genius, Mr Harrison. Political genius.'

I put down my pen and listened to his strong flow of words, this paean of praise from our greatest adversary.

'And do you know, Mr Harrison, how many times he spoke to me throughout that period?' he asked.

'Countless – I presume,' I said, smiling.

'Twice!' exclaimed Gladstone. 'Twice in sixteen years! Even though we were days, months together in the House.'

Gladstone shook his head and then continued as if communing with himself. 'There was about him a strength of purpose which I always admired. He was like granite. He would not be moved from his position and so we had to flow around him. We had to *deal* with him. There is no doubt in my mind that were it not for his end there would be a parliament in Ireland today. That is his tragedy. And mine too ... '

He fell silent for a few moments and then asked me about Parnell's last days. When I told him the details of the end, I could see that he was deeply moved. He bowed his head and rested it on his folded hands.

'Poor fellow. Poor fellow,' he said sadly. 'I cannot tell you how much I think about him and what an interest I take in everything concerning him. A marvellous man, a terrible fall.'

But all that lay ahead.

My story begins in the summer of 1872, when, at the age of twenty-three, having finished university and unsure of my career, I decided to take a position as secretary to a young landowner in County Wicklow. I knew little of him or of his family and the position had been offered and accepted in polite correspondence.

On the day appointed for the commencement of my employment, I took the train from Dublin to Rathdrum and a carriage from there to Avondale. As the carriage rounded the avenue on the final approach to the house, I saw, against the glare of the mid-morning sun, a group of men playing cricket on the front lawn amidst a small knot of onlookers. When I stepped down and enquired where I might find Mr Parnell, I was directed over to the lawn and as I approached, Parnell raised his bat to stop the game and came over to greet me: a tall, lean figure with a trimmed beard and a high brow, now beaded with perspiration.

'You are welcome, Mr Harrison,' he said, smiling. He shook my hand with a firm, warm handshake. 'Do you bowl?'

I nodded hesitantly.

'Excellent. We are a man short.'

And in those hours of vigorous sport on a glorious summer's day almost twenty-five years ago a bond was formed between us which lasted until the end.

At that time Parnell was only twenty-six years old and there was about him no hint of the greatness he would subsequently achieve. Indeed, the Parnell I first knew was, apparently, only interested in playing cricket at Avondale and managing his estates and in those early years I never heard him utter a single word about Ireland. It was only two years later, when Gladstone called an election, that Parnell suddenly announced over dinner, to his startled family – and myself – that he intended to stand for Parliament, for the new Home Rule Party. He had, he told us, written to Isaac Butt, its leader, to seek a nomination and Butt in reply had asked him to attend a meeting in Dublin at which a new candidate would be chosen for the Party.

How could we have known then what destiny awaited him? Or what destiny he would create for himself and for our nation?

Throughout the turbulent and extraordinary years which followed, I kept a journal in which I recorded my impressions and recollections of the events and conversations of those times. This journal, this memoir, is my account of the life of Parnell as I witnessed it.

And so I will begin this memoir of my friend, at the beginning, on an evening on which he took his first tentative steps into public life – an evening which I thought at the time would end his career before it had even begun.

Part One

Part One

One

An Inauspicious Start

Dublin, March 1874

It was just after seven o'clock in the evening when Parnell and I set out from Morrison's Hotel on Dawson Street, for the short walk across Dublin to the Rotunda on Little Britain Street. We crossed College Green, past the old Parliament, then, as now, a windowless counting house, its rusting and redundant cannon jutting out from the colonnades defending a citadel which had long since fallen. It was almost dusk and the broad avenue of Westmoreland Street was noisy with the cries of hawkers seeking the last bargain of the day and pedlars packing up their carts and pushing them home. As we crossed the narrow Carlisle Bridge, an icy blast of wind funnelled upriver, causing me to shiver and huddle into my coat. Just over the bridge the corporation labourers were finishing up their day's work on the never-ending O'Connell monument, clattering their shovels into a makeshift shelter.

We walked along Sackville Street in silence for most of the way. Parnell was not a man for small talk and if he had nothing to say, he remained silent. At first, I had found these silences unsettling and I had talked away nervously to fill them, but now I had grown more used to them and whiled away the walk with my own thoughts. I was uncertain what the evening would hold. Parnell certainly had not discussed it with me or, to my knowledge, prepared a speech. But as I glanced over at him, he appeared resolute and unconcerned.

We arrived at the squat, grey building of the Rotunda and went inside. The assembly hall was cold and forlorn, lined with empty chairs. A motley group of men were standing around; some, merchants and lawyers, with hats and gloves still on; others more plainly dressed, talking and smoking, stamping their feet on the worn wooden floor to keep warm.

As we stood there uncertainly, Isaac Butt detached himself from the group and came towards us. He was then over sixty years old; a large man, grown portly after years of overindulgence, and his fleshy face flowed over his tight starched wing collar like pastry on a pie. His thick white hair stuck out in unruly clumps on all sides, giving an impression of an eccentric genial grandfather.

'Parnell, Parnell. How good to see you again.' He came forward to greet Parnell with a full smile and an extended hand.

Parnell smiled, shaking his hand. 'It has been a long time.'

'It certainly has,' Butt replied. 'How is your dear mother? And your charming sister Fanny?'

'Both very well,' said Parnell, and then courteously introduced me.

'Mr Butt, this is my secretary, James Harrison.'

'Pleased to meet you, Harrison,' said Butt and, putting his arm around Parnell's shoulder, he ushered us towards the group standing by. 'Come on in, gentlemen. I want you to meet some members of the Party.'

He introduced us briskly to John Martin, the Member of Parliament for Meath, Alexander Sullivan, the editor of *The Nation*, and the O'Gorman Mahon, an elder of the Party and a friend of the great Daniel O'Connell.

After some moments of desultory conversation between us, Butt took out his watch.

'It's almost time,' he said. 'I shall speak first and introduce you, Parnell, and then you can address your voters.'

We walked into the hall. The crowd had increased over the last few minutes and as they saw us coming in they took their seats expectantly.

Isaac Butt, the O'Gorman Mahon and Parnell went up the steps of the raised dais at the front of the hall; Parnell looked as if he were climbing the scaffold, his head down, his hands held stiffly by his sides. They took their seats at a table covered with a green baize cloth. The O'Gorman Mahon called the meeting to order and as he introduced the speakers I took a seat about halfway back in the half-empty hall, near the wall.

Isaac Butt spoke first. He was a fine orator and he spoke fluently, eloquently – and at some length – about the misrule of Ireland by the English; about the urgent need for an Irish parliament; about the Home Rule Party; about its successes in the recent election and how they would press Disraeli and the Tories in the House of Commons for Home Rule at every turn. Although I had read his speeches in the newspapers, this was the first time I had heard him in person.

'We now have, gentlemen,' he said, 'no less than fifty-nine Irish Members of Parliament to seek Home Rule, to seek a parliament in Dublin. We need only prove to the English that we are capable of self-government and the English will see the justice of the case, the merits of our argument. It will not happen next week or next month, but it will happen.'

The crowd roared and shouted their approval, playing their part as they were expected to do. Every mention of Ireland, freedom and the Home Rule Party was accompanied by loud cheers and piercing whistles; every mention of the English, Disraeli and the Tories was greeted with boos, derision and catcalls. Isaac Butt stood like a great conductor before this orchestra of noise and continued on with enthusiasm.

'And today we have found a new candidate for the Party ... a brilliant young man with an illustrious name ...'

He gestured towards Parnell who still looked tense and ill at ease, his eyes fixed on the floor.

'A young man of great promise,' continued Butt, 'a man whose great-grandfather was Chancellor in Grattan's parliament ... over seventy-four years ago ... a great man ... incorruptible' – Butt made the last word sound like a sentence in itself – '... who refused to bend the knee to Westminster and who voted against the Union with Britain when it was not profitable for him to do so. A man of great principle – dedicated to Home Rule – as his great-grandson is now.'

Eventually, Butt brought his peroration to a circuitous end.

'But, gentlemen, you have not come here this evening to hear me but to meet the Home Rule Party candidate who will fight this election on our behalf. We have recruited a handsome young man to fight our cause but one whom the Saxon will, no doubt, find to be an ugly customer. Gentlemen, I give you Mr Charles Stewart Parnell.'

Butt delivered this introduction in a voice rising to a crescendo, like an impresario introducing a new act. On cue the audience cheered and clapped and welcomed Parnell as they had been invited to do.

As he heard Butt's final words of introduction Parnell raised a glass of water to his mouth. To my dismay, I could see, even at a distance, that his hand was shaking as he raised the glass; he brought his left hand over quickly to hold the glass steady as he drank. He then rose and, moving around the table to the front of the platform, he stood before the crowd, stiff and tense, his hands held behind his back.

He was taller than Isaac and more fastidiously dressed, with a tailored frock coat, and a neck tie, adorned with a pearl tie-pin.

'My name is Charles Stewart Parnell,' he began in a low voice. His accent was English, an immediate difference to Butt's. However, after Isaac's stout, confident gravitas he seemed callow and unsure.

'I ...', he trailed off.

'I ... would like to thank Mr Butt for his kind words.' He finished a sentence.

'I am not an orator like Mr Butt,' he said, a moment or so later.

His nervousness rippled like a wave across the quietening crowd.

'I am here tonight because ...' – he looked out at the crowd, as if expecting them to answer – 'because I want to stand for election for this party. Because I want Home Rule for Ireland.'

This was said in such a quiet, sombre manner that the crowd could not have cheered, even if they had wanted to.

The silences between sentences seemed to increase and after a few moments I could hear murmurs from people around me.

'Quiet, quiet.' Voices in the crowd urged others to quieten down.

Parnell looked out at the crowd, hushed now, looking at him.

'I ... I ... intend to stand for election for the Home Rule Party.'

Parnell repeated his sentence slowly, hesitantly, each word ground out, syllable by syllable.

'I am here to ask for your vote ... for your support,' he began. His voice was dry. He coughed. 'I support Home Rule and I support the Party.'

This was supposed to raise a cheer but none came.

Parnell stood there, like a rock, his hands now by his sides, clenching and unclenching in his tension.

The crowd waited for him to continue. On the platform, Isaac Butt and the O'Gorman Mahon waited for him to continue. I waited for him to continue. I could feel my stomach tightening with tension. Just when it became almost unbearable, Parnell would deliver himself of another sentence.

'What has Disraeli ever done for Home Rule?' he stuttered.

'Aye. Nothing. Nothing.' A man in the audience tried to chivvy him along.

The crowd gave a strangled cheer and then quietened down, ominously, and as Parnell's unease grew, the crowd's sympathy dissolved and they turned on him like a pack of whelping hounds.

'Say something,' a voice shouted, 'anything.'

The first catcalls were not long in coming and soon I could hear jeers and boos echoing all over the hall.

'And so with your support, I shall win this election. Thank you.' Parnell brought his speech to an abrupt end and, bowing slightly, walked back to the table and resumed his seat.

Isaac Butt jumped to his feet and began clapping, urging the crowd to do likewise; the impresario whose star act has failed to live up to his advance billing must cover up his embarrassment and bring the curtain down as smoothly – and as quickly – as possible. Butt thanked them for their support, called on them to vote and bade them good evening.

I stayed where I was to allow the crowd shuffle out of the hall before me. Both Alexander Sullivan and John Martin passed by, on the aisle, without noticing me.

'... a dreadful speech.' I only heard Martin's final words.

'Shocking,' agreed Sullivan.

'Why bother with a seat in Parliament if you can't speak?' said Martin.

'I daresay we'll never hear from him again,' replied Sullivan.

It was clear that the rest of the crowd shared their opinion, except in less polite language, and I let them pass before I joined Butt and Parnell at the front of the stage.

Butt paused to light a cigar. 'Don't worry, Parnell,' he said, unconcerned. 'People are often nervous on the first speech. I've seen it many times. It will get better – mark my words. After a hundred speeches, you'll look back at tonight ...' He didn't finish the sentence but puffed hard on his cigar to get it smoking.

Parnell didn't respond. He seemed pale and withdrawn.

'A stiff brandy and a good night's sleep,' said Butt kindly. 'It will look better tomorrow.'

Parnell nodded his farewells and he and I walked back up Sackville Street. It was after ten o'clock now and the street was quiet. When we got to the bridge, Parnell stopped and leaned over the stone parapet staring at the dark, slow-moving river below. I waited with him. A low-lying barge, its lantern swaying, passed underneath the arch of the bridge, bringing hogsheads of stout and ale from the breweries at Kingsbridge to the Guinness ships moored downriver at the Custom House dock. I could hear the plop and splash of the pole as the bargeman let it slip though his hands to the shallow riverbed and watched as he levered on it to push the barge further on. A schooner drifted along the crowded quays searching for a mooring place.

'I had nothing to say,' Parnell murmured, to himself as much as to me. 'Nothing at all.'

He drew in lungfuls of the cold, damp air.

I tried to reassure him but I knew that his sensitive pride had been wounded by the abuse of the vulgar crowd.

As we stood there, a small troop of English soldiers marched past, rifles against their shoulders, their hobnail boots ringing rhythmically on the hard ground. We watched as they crossed the bridge, and headed west along the river back to their barracks. Parnell stared at them for a long time until they disappeared into the gloom.

'They have no right to be here,' he said suddenly and with an unexpected venom.

'You should have said that earlier,' I said drily. 'They'd have cheered you to the rafters.'

'I *will* say it,' he said softly, 'and they *will* hear me.'

Two

The Member for Meath

I DID THINK, after the ignominy of the inevitable defeat in the
Dublin campaign, that Parnell might retire to Avondale and
resume the life of a country gentleman. But he was determined
he would enter Parliament and a year later, with the immense support of Isaac Butt, who adopted him as a protégé, he was elected as
the Honourable Member of Parliament for the County of Meath.

The day after his victory Parnell arrived back to Avondale
to a hero's welcome. Estate workers and tenants, friends and
neighbours, all turned out to cheer him home. He jumped down
from the carriage at the gate and shook hands with every one of
them, all the way up the avenue to the front door.

As we stepped into the front hall, he was greeted by another great
gathering of family and friends, many leaning over the balustrades
on the gallery above. Someone cried out 'Three cheers for Charlie'
and the cheers were lustily delivered, reverberating off the dark
oaken rafters as Parnell went around the hall hugging each brother
and sister and shaking hands with each relative and friend in turn.

That evening, a celebratory dinner had been organised in his
honour by his mother. Mrs Delia Stewart Parnell, as she always
introduced herself, was a formidable and loquacious woman
of American birth. Tall and vivacious, with dark hair and blue
eyes, she had married Parnell's father when she was only eighteen
years old and had been abducted from the dazzling social scene of
Washington to the forlorn wilds of Wicklow – as she told us on many
occasions. Her father – as she also told us on many occasions – had
been a celebrated American naval hero who had defeated the British
Navy in a number of engagements, for which a grateful Congress

had bestowed on him an estate and a pension and a jingoistic press had bestowed on him the title of 'Old Ironsides'. She had strident anti-English views which she never tired of sharing, particularly at the Viceroy's banquets and garden parties in Dublin, a habit which made her less than popular in these circles.

As we stood around before dinner, I saw Mrs Parnell pointing out the portrait of her father in the hall, to a captive Isaac Butt.

'And this is my father,' I heard her say.

I joined Isaac and we both stared up at the portrait.

'A great American hero. My son is following in his footsteps, Mr Butt.'

'I have no doubt, Mrs Parnell,' said Butt playfully. 'No doubt at all.'

As we stood there, Charles' sister Fanny came over to us.

'Mother, you are not boring Mr Butt about grandfather, are you?' she asked.

Of all Parnell's family, his beautiful sister Fanny was his favourite. She was some years younger than her brother but the physical resemblance between them was striking: each had brown hair, brown eyes and a sallow complexion. They delighted in each other's company and Parnell had an ease with her that I never saw him have with anyone else – until he met Katharine. Fanny was an ardent, romantic soul who wrote stirring, revolutionary poems about Cathleen Ni Houlihan winning her freedom from her English oppressor. She gave readings of her poetry – prompted and unprompted – until Parnell begged for mercy. I could have listened to her all evening. Her beauty and confident poise, however, made me diffident and awkward in her presence.

As we sat down to dinner, she came over to Parnell and, standing at the back of his chair, she threw her arms around his neck, and drew her face close to his. 'I'm so proud of you, Charlie,' she said.

There was a loud 'Hear, hear' from around the table.

'You have been elected to the House of Commons to fight for Irish independence,' Fanny continued dreamily, 'and I know you will become famous. You will be the next Daniel O'Connell.'

There were further cheers and Fanny, picking up the glass of wine nearest to her, called for a toast.

'To Charlie and to Freedom,' she cried, smiling triumphantly.

'To Charlie and to Freedom,' we cried, all rising to our feet, and the cheers resounded through the dining-room until everyone resumed their seats.

Parnell nodded in acknowledgement, smiling that rare, sweet smile of his.

'Just remember, Charles,' said his mother sternly. 'You are not just a Parnell – you are also a Stewart. Remember your grandfather. And remember what he said. You are dealing with the English now. Not the Irish. You will not persuade them by appealing to their better nature. They don't have one. At least, not where Ireland is concerned.'

Parnell listened impassively. He had heard it before, many times.

'My father was always outgunned and outnumbered,' continued Mrs Parnell to a now silent table. 'The only things he *could* control, he told us, were the choice of time and the choice of tactics for battle. Time and tactics! You pick your fights and you make sure to win them. That was his strategy and it served him well.'

'But Charlie can't carry guns into the House of Commons,' said Fanny.

'And even if he could,' said her brother John, 'Charlie couldn't hit a single Member of Parliament – even if the House of Commons was packed to the rafters.'

This jibe provoked uproarious laughter from everyone, even Parnell. His poor marksmanship was a family joke of long standing.

Fanny raised a glass. 'To our grandfather,' she said, and we all drank another toast to Admiral Stewart and then another and then another. It was a very long night, although as usual Parnell left his first glass unfinished.

෨෧෩

The following morning Parnell and I were up at dawn to catch the first train to Dublin. As we stood at the door, suitcases in hand, about to leave, we heard a noise of someone running upstairs and Fanny appeared above the gallery balustrade.

'Wait for me, Charlie,' she called. 'I'm coming with you.'

She ran downstairs, dressed for travelling, her black overcoat already on and carrying a small suitcase and hat. She walked over to Charles and linked her arm in his.

'I am not going to miss my brother taking his seat in the House of Commons,' she said, 'and' – she put her hand up to Parnell – 'don't try to stop me. My mind is quite made up.'

'I wouldn't dream of it,' said Parnell, laughing. 'I know better.'

In a moment we were in the carriage travelling to Rathdrum, where we caught the train to Dublin, and by nine o'clock we were sailing out of Kingstown harbour.

⁓

It was a bright spring morning as the ship set sail, if I may use such a misplaced image for the dirty steam packet that funnelled its black smoke into the clear morning air. The days of elegant sailing ships were long gone: destroyed by the age of steam – all in the name of progress!

We sailed out past the grey, granite harbour where, even at that hour, the morning strollers were on the pier, waving us goodbye. As I stood on deck, like thousands of people before me and after, I looked back at the huddled houses and gentle spires of Kingstown and thought about leaving Ireland for the first time, sailing for England and what the future would hold. But I was privileged: I had a position and I could return to Ireland whenever I wished. I was not an exile and I did not feel the loneliness of an exile as so many of my countrymen did – only the excitement of an adventurer. I watched as the houses of Kingstown faded away in the distance, then the harbour, and soon all I could see was the curve of Dublin Bay. Then that too dissolved and there was nothing to see in any direction except the dark green-grey waters of the Irish Sea, the white-grey foam of the ship's wake and the black smoke from the ship's funnels in the blue morning sky.

It was the first of many journeys I would carry out with Parnell – and afterwards without him. It was then, as now, a tiring thirteen-hour journey: four hours sailing to Holyhead and a nine-hour train journey to London. But all was new to me that morning and I had the giddy excitement of spending all day with Fanny. We spent much of the crossing on deck, breathing in the sea air, and it seemed almost too soon when we arrived at the rocky outcrops and promontories of North Wales.

The train journey took us uneventfully along the Welsh coast, into Cheshire, then down through Staffordshire and Buckinghamshire. All afternoon I looked out on the English landscape, so ordered and prosperous compared to the unruly, unkempt disorder of the Irish countryside. It was hard not to think that the English were blessed to keep the harvests of their own lands over the centuries, to build prosperity over generations and to hand down wealth from father to son – and not be forced, as the Irish had been, to pay all their harvests in rents to English absentee landlords, to divide and subdivide land from father to son, with each generation becoming poorer than the last.

In the late evening, we arrived in London, hailed a cab and travelled to the Westminster Palace Hotel, close to the Houses of Parliament.

After supper, at Fanny's suggestion, we took an evening stroll. Parnell had visited the city many times whilst a student at Cambridge but this was my first time walking around London. It was a city already alive in my imagination: the city of Shakespeare and of Dickens; the city of a thousand streets, a thousand scenes and a thousand characters. We walked along streets whose names I had heard so often in my childhood, they seemed almost magical to me: along Piccadilly, down Haymarket, into Trafalgar Square and through Whitehall to Westminster Bridge. Even though it was late in the evening the streets were thronged with people, carriages and conveyances of every description.

Fanny walked between us, linking both our arms in hers.

'It's not often I have the chance to be on the arms of two such handsome men,' she said, laughing and looking at us both.

I wanted to repay the compliment but I thought it inappropriate in Parnell's presence. He might regard it as presumptuous.

We walked along Westminster Bridge, almost to the far side of the river, and then stopped and looked back to the Houses of Parliament.

'What will happen to you here, Charlie?' said Fanny. 'I do wonder. You are the third Parnell to be elected here.'

'And hopefully the last,' laughed Parnell, 'or else I shall have failed.'

It was difficult not to be struck, if not overawed, by the sheer magnificence of the Palace of Westminster. At this hour the great gothic spires were silhouetted against the darkening sky; Parliament was in session now and the warm yellow gas-lamps inside made it glow like an amber jewel. This was the House of Commons, the Mother of Parliaments, the great Imperial Parliament of the British Empire. This was the parliament which had ruled Ireland for centuries and which we were now seeking to repudiate. I had expected to feel resentment – or even anger – on first seeing this great Palace but instead, to my surprise, I was silenced by its grandeur, its grace, the power of it all. It commanded, demanded respect, even obeisance. Strange feelings these and, needless to say, I kept them to myself.

Three

Joseph Biggar

THE FOLLOWING MORNING was taken up in deciding which dress Fanny would wear. She sought our opinion on no less than three. The first, a green dress, was immediately vetoed by Parnell: he would not have, he said, his day tainted by ill-luck; Fanny teased him about his superstition but he was unyielding. Eventually a blue dress was selected and Fanny was ready. Once attired, Fanny turned her attention to us, straightening my necktie and fastening Parnell's tie-pin.

'Now, gentlemen, we are ready,' she said and she led us out of the hotel and across to Westminster.

We walked across Palace Yard, past the graceful and imposing statue of Oliver Cromwell on horseback guarding the entrance to Parliament.

'They view things differently here,' I thought ruefully. I had never seen a statue of Cromwell in Ireland and I never would.

We passed through the arches and then into the cavernous lobbies and corridors of the Palace of Westminster. It was like entering a great cathedral and as we walked through I looked around at the vaulted arches, the stone statues of former kings and eminent ministers, and the enormous tapestries of memorable scenes in England's history. After some moments, we came to the Chamber of the House of Commons, where Fanny and I left Parnell and climbed the stairs to the Strangers' Gallery.

The Chamber of the House of Commons is familiar to many people now from newspaper illustrations, but as I had never seen it before, it was a dazzling sight. The Strangers' Gallery runs above the Chamber on both sides and at both ends so that a visitor has a perfect sight of everything in the Chamber, except for those persons sitting directly beneath. Fanny and I sat at the front of the gallery looking towards the Speaker and so we had an uninterrupted view of the scene below. At the front of the Chamber was the Speaker's chair; below him sat his Registrars. In front of the Registrars there was a large oak table, on either side of which were placed two despatch boxes and the great Mace, the symbol of parliamentary authority. On both sides of the Chamber there were five rows of seats stepped up to the wall. A wide aisle separated the two sides of the Chamber, with the Government Members of Parliament and Ministers sitting on the Speaker's right and opposition Members of Parliament sitting in the rows of seats to his left. Although there were no windows, the Chamber was brightly lit with gas-lamps lowered from the great wooden ceilings high above.

As I looked down I could see a melée of members in the Chamber below: some searching for a place on the benches; others standing around talking and gossiping with their colleagues in the centre aisle.

As Big Ben tolled four o'clock, the Speaker appeared in the Chamber and the Members of Parliament in the centre aisle all took their seats expectantly.

The Speaker rose and waited for silence.

'The first order of business. We welcome the Right Honourable Charles Stewart Parnell, newly elected Member of Parliament for the County of Meath,' the Speaker intoned.

As Parnell walked in, escorted by Isaac Butt, all the Irish members on the opposition benches cheered and waved their order papers in the air to welcome him. Parnell bowed to the Speaker, recited his oath, and took his position alongside the other Irish members, just below the gangway on the second bench – a position he occupied thereafter whenever he was in the Commons. The Speaker formally welcomed him to the House and Parnell nodded courteously in reply.

Fanny squeezed my arm excitedly and looked over at me for a moment, her eyes bright with pride.

As I watched from the gallery, I found it hard to believe that only three days earlier I had been rushing around Trim getting out every last vote for Parnell, and now I was in the House of Commons watching him take his seat as a Member of Parliament. How quickly our lives turn.

But the romance and decorum of the moment quickly dissipated as the realities of the struggle cut through. The Chief Secretary for Ireland, Sir Michael Hicks Beach, took to the despatch box later that afternoon to introduce a new coercion bill for Ireland. 'Black Michael', as he was known because of his grim countenance and black beard, was a lean and severe figure, the very embodiment of an uncompromising, puritanical Tory squire. There was – according to Hicks Beach – a huge increase in rural crime in Ireland, with bands of farm labourers prowling around in fields and farms at night maiming cattle, burning out-buildings and destroying crops; there was, he said, a consequent need to give the police greater powers of arrest and also to increase the punishments for such wanton acts of destruction. I was surprised by his descriptions; they did not accord with the country I had just left, and the power to impose evening curfews in towns and villages seemed particularly excessive.

My attention to his speech wandered, I must confess, when the Prime Minister entered quietly from behind the Speaker's chair and took his seat on the front benches close to the despatch box. Benjamin Disraeli was even more unusual in his appearance than newspaper photographs made him appear. The deep creases under his eyes gave him a rather lugubrious appearance; his hair, still in ringlets, and worn longer than was the fashion, made him appear exotic, like a royal courtier from another country and another age; and the slow, deliberate movements of his head and the gracefulness of his hands gave him a delicate air. I had read so much about him that I stared at him for some time. Perhaps he sensed my stare, because his eyes moved up from the opposition benches to scan the Strangers' Gallery, and rested on myself and Fanny for a moment before reverting to the debate on the floor of the House. But then, Disraeli was well-used to being stared at; the British people had watched, entranced or appalled, depending on their political hue, as he had clambered up the political ladder – from his inauspicious start in parliamentary life to achieving his ambition of becoming the Queen's First Minister.

Later in the afternoon, the Speaker called on Isaac Butt to reply to the Chief Secretary. I leaned forward to listen more intently. Butt's speech was superb: lucid and forensic. He took the arguments apart one by one and undermined them all so comprehensively that it was a wonder Hicks Beach did not shamefacedly withdraw his bill immediately. This was an Isaac Butt I had not seen before – more parliamentarian, less demagogue – and his voice and presence filled the Chamber. I was sure it was only a matter of time before the bill was defeated.

Then suddenly, to my astonishment, I realised that no one was listening. Even in the middle of his speech, many Members of Parliament simply rose and left the Chamber; many who remained – even on the Government side – often yawned openly and loudly. Even Hicks Beach was not listening. Half-turned in his seat, he was carrying on a lengthy and animated conversation with one of his backbenchers. Disraeli, likewise, only listened for a short while and then slipped out of the Chamber behind the Speaker's chair, as quietly and unobtrusively as a ghost. The only persons who seemed to be listening to Butt were his own party colleagues, the very members he did not need to persuade.

By the time Butt had finished it was almost half-past seven, and the Speaker announced the adjournment for dinner.

I had not even noticed time passing, I was so utterly absorbed by it all – the spectacle, the personalities, the speeches, the great political theatre. Fanny, however, had to stifle more than an occasional yawn. We went downstairs and, amidst the crowds, eventually found Parnell and Butt in the lobby. They were going for supper in the House of Commons restaurant and invited me to join them.

I walked Fanny back to the hotel, and promised to return for her later that evening should Parnell be giving his maiden speech. I was back in the House of Commons within the half hour and found my way to the members' restaurant, a great vaulted space deep in the cellars of the Palace. I found Parnell and Butt in a small alcove at the end of a long corridor.

As we sat down to dinner Parnell introduced me to another Home Rule Member of Parliament whom he had just met in the Chamber, Joseph Biggar, the member for Cavan.

'Pleased to meet ye, Harrison,' Biggar rasped in his raw, guttural Belfast accent. 'Welcome to our small band of warriors.' I leaned forward to shake his hand and had difficulty in not yelping with pain, for he shook my hand with such force it was momentarily crushed. He had hands like hams, thick, red and blotchy. He must have seen me wincing; he laughed and slapped an arm on my shoulder.

'You clearly need nourishment, lad. Sit down. Sit down and eat up.' He gestured to me to sit down opposite him. He was a man of unusual stature – small and stout and with a curious posture. He seemed stooped, almost hunched over. As he sat down to dinner he took off his frock coat and placed it carefully on the back of his chair. As he turned, I saw he actually was a hunchback; his hunched, misshapen shoulder protruded through the back of his waistcoat in a solid bulge, causing his waistcoat to rise unevenly at the front, exposing a portion of stomach and shirt which gave him a somewhat unkempt appearance. Because of his hunch he seemed to have no neck, and his head seemed directly attached to his shoulders; he had a beard which he wore – as some did at the time – below the jaw line, so that it looked like a greying Elizabethan ruff. His hair was thick and grey and swept to the left side, giving his strong face a somewhat fearsome appearance. But for all his unusual demeanour, he looked at me directly in the eye and his fine, clear, grey eyes sparkled with humour. Then in his early fifties, Biggar had made his fortune as a pork merchant in Belfast, a social misfortune relentlessly exploited by his landed opponents in the House of Commons because he was 'in trade'. Like many northerners he spoke his mind directly, without dissembling but without malice.

Over supper, I could see that Parnell was anxious about his maiden speech. He asked Butt about the order of speakers.

'Biggar's next to speak,' said Butt. 'You can speak after him if you want.' Butt's speech was done and he intended to take his ease for the evening. He poured wine liberally for us all. With the bottle still in his hand, he finished his first glass and poured himself another immediately.

'Tonight?' said Parnell. 'No, I am not ready to speak tonight. I have only just arrived.'

'Don't worry, Parnell,' said Biggar. He held out a glass for Butt to fill. 'I have a speech that will take me all evening.' For a man who was about to speak in the House he showed no signs of nerves or apprehension. It was clear the House of Commons held no fears for him. It certainly did not affect his appetite and he tucked into the hill of pork chops, peas and potatoes on his plate with gusto.

'All evening?' said Parnell, surprised.

'Aye,' said Biggar. 'Well, certainly until midnight.'

'But it's only half-past seven,' I said.

'Aye, but the debate won't resume until half-past eight or so,' Biggar replied, chewing noisily on a chop.

'But that's still four hours. How long are you allowed to speak for?' I asked.

'As long as I want, Harrison,' said Biggar, 'there are no time limits at all.'

I was surprised.

'Well, Harrison,' said Biggar, 'that's the practice. There have been speeches in the Commons which have been six, seven, eight hours long. Now I can't say that I will take eight hours, but if a Member of Parliament is exercised by the great issues of the day then he has a right to say his piece.' He winked at me.

'And I can tell ye all,' he continued, cutting his meat with great force, 'that Joseph Gillis Biggar is very exercised by giving the peelers more powers to arrest people on no evidence and on trumped-up charges.'

'So you will be speaking all evening?' asked Parnell.

'I will, Parnell,' replied Biggar, leaning forward to nudge Butt for more wine. 'No doubt on it, so you can take things easy. You have plenty of time to write your speech. All night and all day tomorrow.'

Butt looked uneasy. He was just lighting his after-dinner cigar, a ritual on which he concentrated for some time.

'What are you planning, Biggar?' he asked.

'Nothing at all, my friend,' said Biggar, leaning back in his chair and looking hard at Butt. 'But even if I were, what of it? Maybe we should obstruct this bill.'

'No, Biggar,' said Butt, shaking out the match. 'You know if we are going to obstruct this bill, we should do it as a party.'

'Bah,' said Biggar sourly, 'the Party would never agree.'

'Why not?' asked Parnell.

'Because it would involve hard work,' said Biggar harshly.

'That's hardly fair,' said Butt, 'it would just be futile.'

'But how would you obstruct it?' I asked.

Butt patiently tried to explain. 'You try to talk away the time available to the bill so the Government can't proceed with it.'

'Aye, ye talk it to death,' laughed Biggar.

'But it's been done rarely,' said Butt. 'And then only by a whole party. We wouldn't have the numbers. And anyway,' he concluded as if this were the decisive argument, 'it's a breach of parliamentary privilege, it's very bad form.'

'Bad form!' exclaimed Biggar. 'You care too much about what they think of us, Butt.'

He fumbled in the pockets of his tight black waistcoat and brought out an enormous gold fob-watch, which he consulted ostentatiously.

'Now, gentlemen,' he said, getting to his feet and struggling into his frock coat, 'it's time for Biggar the Younger to give his oration.'

'Biggar the Younger!' I exclaimed.

'Yes, my boy,' he said, 'Biggar the Younger. My father was Biggar the Elder. At the start I wanted to be known as Biggar the Smaller but I thought better of it. Biggar the Younger has more gravitas, don't you agree?'

He gathered up his papers and left us to our laughter.

Four

A Seed is Sown

MOMENTS LATER, PARNELL and Butt walked back into the Chamber and I returned to the Strangers' Gallery. At this hour in the evening it was empty and I could sit anywhere to watch Biggar's speech – or perhaps performance would be a more appropriate word – in comfort.

Biggar was as good as his promise: he spoke all evening. It was a powerful speech too – well … perhaps, on reflection, that might be overstating it, but certainly at the start it was impressive; he accused the Chief Secretary of seeking to take dictatorial powers over Ireland and he challenged the figures showing an increase in crime. But the great joy of the speech was in the padding. Biggar had a collection of Official Reports – 'Blue Books' – on the bench beside him, from which he proceeded to read prodigiously long and utterly irrelevant extracts to the House. He had unearthed the Report of the Westmeath Commission on agrarian crime, written only five years earlier and he read out the conclusions of the report in their entirety. That, however, was not sufficient, he said; one could not understand the conclusions without understanding the evidence and so he also read out much of the evidence to the Commission. Parnell sat beside him throughout, his left arm outstretched on the back of the bench, and as Biggar finished one extract, he handed the volume back to Parnell, who handed him the next.

As the evening passed, many of the remaining members drifted out of the Chamber, but still Biggar droned on, his grating Belfast gutturals rebounding off the ceiling of the House and echoing throughout the Chamber. After some hours his voice became hoarse and somewhat indistinct and the Speaker intervened.

'Might I remind the Honourable Member that all his remarks should be addressed to the Speaker of the House, and I regret to say that it is difficult to hear everything that the Honourable Member is saying.'

This intervention was an unintended godsend.

'Oh, I am sorry, Mr Speaker, sir,' Biggar bellowed in mock contrition. 'I shall move, sir,' and he took his papers, his volumes of Hansard and his mounds of official reports and bustled up to an opposition bench above the gangway, closer to the Speaker.

'Mr Speaker, I hope that's clearer,' he resumed. 'Now, Mr Speaker, there were some very important passages in the reports which I have just read and, for fear that members may not have heard them properly, I had better read them all again.'

Biggar rustled through the volumes of the Westmeath Commission Report, looking for an appropriate section.

'Perhaps I might start halfway through.'

He proceeded to read the lengthy extracts for the second time. There were loud groans from the Government benches and even more members left the Chamber. Biggar was undeterred. He went through the report again – so hypnotised by the text that he didn't finish reading until he intoned the final words at the bottom of the final page, 'Printed in London by Eyre and Spottiswoode, printers to the Queen's Most Excellent Majesty for Her Majesty's Stationery Office'. He was like an old locomotive, which, although not going at any great speed, had failed to stop at the end of the tracks and gently went through the buffers. This incongruous sentence, however, awoke him from his trance.

'Hmm, ahem,' he coughed and spluttered, and produced an enormous red polka-dot handkerchief from his pocket, into which he blew his nose so noisily that it startled awake those members who had been gently dozing for the last two hours. 'Yes, Mr Speaker, well, that may suffice to give the provenance of this report.'

I laughed out loud at this and, in the stillness of the Chamber at midnight, my laughter rang out across the Chamber, much to my embarrassment, as it caused several members of the House to look up. Biggar also looked up at me and smiled.

Having depleted the House's resources, Biggar eventually finished. 'Well, as it's after midnight, Mr Speaker, and as I feel I have demonstrated beyond argument that this bill should not pass, I will close my speech.' He gathered up his papers and moved back to his original place beside Parnell.

The Speaker wearily adjourned the debate until the next day and, after bowing to the few remaining members, made his ceremonial exit. I went downstairs and joined Parnell and Butt in congratulating Biggar on his speech. It was, in truth, not a magnificent speech, or indeed a significant moment in the history of the Commons, but it was a significant moment for Parnell, as it planted the seed of an idea in his mind which would germinate within a short period of time.

The following afternoon, Fanny and I took our places in the Strangers' Gallery to listen to Parnell's maiden speech to the House.

Parnell stood at his bench below the gangway, both hands clenched tensely behind his back. Despite the hours of preparation, it was a leaden performance, delivered in a flat, mechanical and almost spasmodic manner, devoid of any colour or passion. But the manner of his delivery contrasted with the idealism of his speech, which declaimed that whenever a coercion bill against Ireland was mooted, Irish landlords supported it because they could not, they said, exercise their property rights without coercion; that he had heard a great deal of talk about property rights but very little about their attendant duties; and that the root of all Irish problems was a lack of self-government. He ended with a rhetorical flourish, saying that 'Ireland is not a geographical fragment of England. She is a Nation', but the cadences seemed to fall in all the wrong places and his speech went unnoticed.

It is a feature of the House of Commons that Members of Parliament do not applaud each other's speeches – ever. Otherwise they might spend their days in polite applause. But no one had informed Fanny of this, and she began to clap loudly when Parnell sat down, until she realised she was on her own. She stopped immediately, and put her hands to her face and blushed.

'I'm so embarrassed,' she hissed in mock anger. 'Why didn't you stop me, Mr Harrison?'

'I made a similar mistake last night,' I said, laughing.

We went downstairs and waited for Parnell. After a short time, he emerged from the Chamber, flanked by Isaac Butt and also Joseph Biggar, who was slapping him vigorously on the back. Fanny and I added our congratulations.

'I think I heard yours already, Fanny,' smiled Parnell.

'I'm so sorry, Charlie,' said Fanny, blushing again. 'I didn't mean to embarrass you.'

'I am just relieved to have it over,' said Parnell.

Isaac Butt suggested a ceremonial dinner and recommended a restaurant he knew on the Strand. Fanny excused herself, on the grounds that it would be an evening for gentlemen and she would be surplus. We remonstrated with her, but she was adamant and, after we escorted her back to the hotel, we walked on to Gotti's – an Italian restaurant to which we returned over and over again in the following years. Butt, by this time, was known to Mr Gotti personally, and we were shown to a quiet booth at the back of the restaurant, with red velvet upholstery, and a candle which barely illuminated our food. Butt ordered several bottles of Haut-Brion and we toasted Parnell's health and future speeches in the Commons.

'What will you do now, Parnell?' asked Butt over dinner. 'I mean, after the vote is taken. Will you go back to Ireland?'

Parnell was surprised at the question.

'But Parliament sits until the end of July, doesn't it?' he said.

'It certainly does,' said Butt, 'but there are no other Irish measures before the House – at least not until the Home Rule debate in July.'

'Is that organised already?' asked Parnell.

'Yes, indeed it is.' Butt beamed at his achievement. 'I have arranged with the Government that they will give us time every year for an annual debate on Home Rule. We had one last year.' He addressed this last remark to me.

'And it was a complete waste of time,' said Biggar gloomily.

'I don't agree, Biggar,' said Butt with some asperity, 'on the contrary, I thought it a fine debate in the great traditions of the House of Commons.'

'Which we lost by ... what ... 450 votes to 30,' said Biggar.

'Only thirty votes in favour,' said Parnell in disbelief. 'Why so few?'

'Half the Party didn't bother to turn up,' said Biggar.

'Well, I can't make them,' said Butt plaintively. 'I write to them all but some just refuse to come.'

'Makes you wonder why they wanted to be elected in the first place,' said Biggar. 'How can we make progress if they are not here?'

'Sooner or later, the Liberals will join us,' continued Butt.

'What makes you say that?' said Parnell.

'They are reasonable men. They will respond to reason.'

'Bah! Pure optimism, Butt,' said Biggar dourly. 'Not one Liberal joined us last year.'

'So, when is the debate?' asked Parnell.

'The date is not fixed but I am assured it will be in July or at the latest the first week of August.' Butt moved to pour us all more wine but Parnell as usual declined.

Butt lifted his glass and drained it before continuing. 'Personally, I hope it's August. I have a number of trials that look as if they will come on before the end of July and I would hate to hand them over. I've already spent the retainers.'

'How do you manage it, Butt?' I asked. 'Running a practice in Dublin and keeping up with the House of Commons?'

'It's not easy, Harrison,' Butt sighed as he contemplated his empty plate and full workload. 'It's not easy.'

At that moment an acquaintance of Butt's hailed him loudly from across the floor and Butt excused himself to go over to him.

'The truth is,' grunted Biggar in Butt's absence, 'he doesn't manage it at all. He should be here the whole time. He's no use to us fighting cases in the Four Courts.'

'So why does he do it?' I asked.

'Debts,' said Biggar matter-of-factly. He shrugged his shoulders, causing an upheaval in his clothing. 'His creditors have been after him for years and he is just one step ahead of them. Too much high living and fine wine.'

'So I noticed,' said Parnell, smiling.

'And a mistress with expensive tastes, I gather,' continued Biggar, grinning maliciously.

Before either of us could react, Biggar put his finger to his lips.

'Sshh,' he said. 'He's coming back.' Then to Butt, as he arrived back at our table and slumped back into his seat, 'Who was that?'

'That,' said Butt, beaming, 'was Gathorne-Hardy. Very well-connected! Rumour has it Disraeli is going to grant him a peerage.'

'And what did he want,' said Biggar with a grin, 'with a commoner like you?'

Butt scowled. 'Well, if you must know, he has invited me to a dinner party in his house next week.'

'I thought you were going back to Ireland,' said Biggar.

'Well, I was going …' said Butt, 'but I told Gathorne-Hardy I'd be delighted to attend. I can stay in London for a little longer.'

'Did he say how much longer this coercion bill would take?' growled Biggar.

'Oh …' Butt settled back into his seat. 'They thought they'd finish tomorrow but thanks to you, they now think it'll be early next week.'

Biggar laughed and raised his glass. 'To small victories,' he said.

Five

I Espy Strangers

SEVERAL DAYS LATER, at about six o'clock in the evening, Parnell, Biggar and I were chatting in the lobbies of the House during a short recess. Biggar lounged against a stone pillar, one foot nonchalantly crossed over another, his shirt-front hanging over his trouser band. Other Members of Parliament emerged from the Chamber in twos and threes, chatting idly among themselves. Isaac Butt joined us for a moment before going to the tea-rooms. Then, just before he went back into the Chamber, Biggar took my arm and walked me over to the side of the corridor where he could not be overheard.

'Look lively this evening,' he whispered gruffly.

When I enquired why, he gave me a conspiratorial grin and told me again to look to my post.

I went back upstairs and took my seat some rows back in the gallery – the first two rows being reserved – and waited for the debate to start. I looked down to see Parnell and Biggar lounging on the half-full benches below. After some moments I saw, and heard, an overweight, red-faced man wheezing his way up the gallery stairs.

'These stairs,' he breathed noisily to no one in particular, but as I was the only person in the gallery I assumed he was addressing them to me. 'I'm getting too old for these stairs.'

He paused for breath for a few moments and then approached me.

'What's this, young man, what's going on now?' he said peremptorily, staring down at the House.

I told him of the imminent debate on horse breeding.

'Fascinating,' he intoned sarcastically. He took out a dirty, crumpled handkerchief, wiped the beads of perspiration from his forehead, hawed on his spectacles and then proceeded to clear them or smear them, I couldn't tell which, with his handkerchief.

'I'm Henry Lucy – parliamentary correspondent for the *Daily News* and the *Observer*,' he said portentously. He held out his hand.

I shook the damp, limp hand, introduced myself and, trying to be polite, asked him if he had a special interest in the debate about to start.

Lucy snorted in derision. 'I'm here to cover the Prince of Wales. He is to attend the House this evening. What did you say your name was again?'

I repeated my name, for the second time in as many minutes.

'So, Harrison,' Lucy repeated in an overly familiar way. 'What are you doing here? Are you a journalist too?' He sat down heavily in the seat beside me.

'No, no,' I said. 'I am Mr Parnell's secretary.'

'And who, pray tell, is Mr Parnell?' asked Lucy.

'The Member of Parliament for Meath,' I said.

'Oh, an Irish blighter, is he?' said Lucy. 'Which one?'

I pointed Parnell out, but Lucy had no real interest and he continued to breathe heavily and to look around the Chamber below.

Moments later, I heard a group of people coming up the stairs.

'If Your Royal Highness will permit me to show you to your seat.' I heard the obsequious words of a courtier as he showed a person – whom I immediately recognised as the Prince of Wales – to his seat at the front of the gallery.

'That's Sir Richard Lawton, equerry to His Royal Highness,' Lucy whispered loudly to me. 'And that is Lord Ashton,' he said, pointing to a second man who glanced over to us. 'I don't know the rest.'

The Prince stepped forward and peered over the gallery at the scene below. The debate had not yet started and members were standing around in the central aisle, huddled in small groups or sitting talking to each other on the benches. The arrival of the Prince caused a stir and many looked upwards to the gallery and bowed to the Prince, who acknowledged them with a regal wave of his hand. Parnell and Biggar had their backs to the gallery; they seemed unaware of the Prince's presence.

Lord Ashton intoned: 'The debate on horse breeding is about to start, Your Highness.'

'Ah yes.' His Royal Highness feigned an interest and then resumed his conversation with one of his other courtiers.

The Speaker called the House to order and opened the debate and the Minister rose at the despatch box to speak on the vital necessity of new measures to regulate horse breeding.

After about five minutes, Biggar swivelled to his feet with an exaggerated struggle and a sigh.

'Mr Speaker, sir, on a point of order, sir,' he said in his harsh rasping northern accent.

'Mr Biggar,' intoned the Speaker.

The Minister at the despatch box gave way.

'Mr Speaker, sir,' said Biggar. 'I wish to say, sir, that I espy strangers in the public gallery.'

The Speaker frowned. 'I'm sorry, Mr Biggar, what did you say?'

'I said, Mr Speaker, that I espied strangers in the gallery.' Biggar repeated his words loudly.

The House quietened down as they heard these words.

'But, Mr Biggar,' – the Speaker was evidently surprised by Biggar's intervention – 'that is the Prince of Wales in the gallery.'

'I don't care who it is, Mr Speaker,' said Biggar brutally. 'I said I espy strangers in the public gallery.'

The Speaker was aghast. He looked for the Prime Minister, but Disraeli was not in the House at the time.

'What is happening?' the Prince enquired of one of his courtiers.

'I don't quite know, Your Highness,' the courtier replied hesitantly.

Biggar remained on his feet. 'Mr Speaker,' he said again, loudly, insistently. 'For the third time, I say that I espy strangers, and under the rules of the House I demand that you uphold the privileges of this House!'

The Speaker thought for a moment. Then he called over the Sergeant-at-Arms.

'Sergeant,' he said aloud. 'The member for Cavan has stated that he has espied strangers; and under the rules of the House I must immediately request all persons in the public gallery to leave so that the House can transact its business in private. I wish you to request all persons in the galleries to leave immediately. Is that clear?'

I gasped with astonishment and looked down at Parnell who sat, unmoved, watching the Speaker intently.

The Sergeant-at-Arms acknowledged his instruction and strode off. Within moments, he appeared at the top of the stairs in the gallery.

'I'm sorry, Your Highness,' he said sheepishly. 'Gentlemen.' He acknowledged the small court surrounding the Prince. 'But I have been asked by the Speaker to request all persons in the public gallery to leave.'

'Under whose authority?' demanded Sir Richard, jumping to his feet.

'I'm sorry, sir,' the Sergeant replied. 'Under the authority of the Speaker of the House of Commons.'

'This is an outrage,' said Lord Ashton.

'What's the matter?' said the Prince, looking over the gallery at the House below.

'I'm sorry, Your Highness,' said Sir Richard, 'but we have to leave.'

'Leave?' said the Prince. 'What do you mean? We've only just arrived.'

'Yes, my Lord,' mumbled the equerry. 'But one of the members has asked the Speaker to clear the public gallery.'

'Has he, by God?' said the Prince, and, without more ado and with considerable dignity, the Prince rose and descended the gallery stairs, followed by his entourage.

The members of the House – on both sides – had been following the scene with increasing anger and, when the Prince of Wales disappeared from view, their fury was unleashed and a storm of calumny and abuse swept over Biggar. I watched as many of the Tories leapt to their feet, shouting and roaring across the floor.

'You're a disgrace, Biggar.'

'Have you no shame, man?'

'Go back to your butcher shops, Biggar.'

'You too, gentlemen,' said the Sergeant to myself and Lucy. I rose hastily. I had been so absorbed in watching the drama that I had forgotten that I too would have to leave.

The Speaker banged the gavel, called for order in the House and bellowed above the raucous din that the House would stand adjourned for one hour.

As he witnessed the scenes below, Lucy's face went blotchy with indignation as his anger took hold.

'What an insult,' he hissed at me. 'What an insult to the Royal Prince. By – that guttersnipe, what's his name?'

'Joseph Biggar,' I said uneasily and immediately wondered if I should have volunteered his name.

'And that guttersnipe is an associate of your Mr Parnell, I see,' hissed Lucy.

I nodded.

'My readers will hear all about this,' he said, and without the civility of a goodbye he turned and puffed his way down the stairs.

I followed the Royal entourage, and Lucy, down the stairs and waited impatiently in the lobbies for Parnell and Biggar to appear. Within a few moments I saw them walking towards me, Biggar rubbing his hands and smiling gleefully.

'A fine evening's work I'd say!' he said to me.

'You did know the Prince of Wales was there?' I asked gingerly.

Biggar looked at me almost in disbelief.

'I wouldn't have done it otherwise,' he said. 'We were told he was coming a week ago. That's when I got the idea!'

Suddenly I saw Butt walking hurriedly towards us.

'Biggar, what on earth have you done?' Butt exclaimed breathlessly. 'There's uproar in the tea-rooms! They're saying you forced the Speaker to remove the Prince of Wales from the House.'

'I did indeed,' said Biggar proudly.

'Have you taken leave of your senses?' Butt was furious. 'This escapade will bring everything down around our ears.'

'Bring down what exactly?' said Biggar defiantly.

'Everything. Members of Parliament, the Government ... the press ... everyone,' expostulated Butt.

'Let them,' said Biggar. 'What do I care?'

'Oh, Biggar, how can you be so damn irresponsible? Parnell ...' He trailed off, looking to Parnell for support.

Parnell shrugged his shoulders but offered none.

I stood by, uncomfortable at this angry exchange.

'Why on earth did you do it?' asked Butt.

'I wanted to give Disraeli a bloody nose,' said Biggar. 'Now he'll know there are consequences for coercion.'

'And what about the consequences for our party?' said Butt.

'What more can he do? He ignores us entirely as it is,' Biggar replied.

After an hour or so, the Commons crier appeared, walking through the lobbies clanging the bell to announce that the House would shortly resume. Several Members of Parliament looked severely at Biggar as they passed; some even admonished him, but he was unconcerned. Eventually Parnell, Butt and Biggar walked back into the Chamber and I rushed back to the gallery, taking the steps two at a time. I was followed, more slowly and with considerable wheezing, by Lucy.

The Speaker called for order. 'The Prime Minister,' he intoned.

Disraeli rose to his feet. His face was creased with the lines of age and the strains of office, but there was no mistaking his anger at this insult to the Royal visitor. Disraeli knew the Queen would question him closely on it at his next audience and he would be forced into an embarrassing apology.

'The scene we have just witnessed, Mr Speaker,' he said, slowly and deliberately, 'is one of the most disgraceful outbursts in the history of this House. It was an affront to the very dignity of the House of Commons. This ancient and venerable rule – which exists for the protection of the councils of the Commons since the time of Cromwell – was abused by the member for Cavan in a manner wholly inconsistent with his position as an Honourable Member. The insult was not just to His Royal Highness but to this House which has invited him here. The actions of the member for Cavan are reprehensible. He has trampled on the dignities of this House and abused its privileges.' He paused and looked across the Chamber. 'Perhaps we have no right to expect any better from the member for Cavan, given his background …'

I gasped at the insult.

'But the member for Cavan is, or is supposed to be, a gentleman. A gentleman first and a Member of Parliament second. His actions were not those of a gentleman and he deserves the round criticism of every member of this House.'

There were cries of 'Hear, hear' from all sides of the Chamber.

It was a devastating personal criticism of Biggar, which would resound all over England and Ireland through the newspapers, in the ensuing weeks. The House was united in its condemnation of Biggar – and in terms which would have crushed the career of almost any other Member of Parliament.

But, as I looked on, I could see that Biggar himself was gloriously unconcerned. He lounged back on his seat with both arms outstretched on the back of the bench and chatted away to Parnell with a smile on his face, as if he enjoyed the attention.

Even over supper, Biggar was still in great spirits.

'Did you see Disraeli's face, Harrison?' he said. 'He was thunderous.'

I was concerned, however, that Biggar had miscalculated.

Parnell smiled at me. 'You're too impressed by royalty, Harrison. He is not our Prince.'

I said I thought there might be a rumpus for weeks to come.

'Let's hope so,' said Biggar. 'It'll liven things up here. Now, gentlemen, I propose we don't go back after dinner. Let them have time to cool off.'

I thought so too, but Parnell disagreed.

'No,' Parnell said firmly. 'We go back in and we will stay until midnight as usual. Otherwise they will think they can frighten us away.'

Biggar was persuaded and after supper Parnell and Biggar went back into the House and sat together, shoulder to shoulder, until every member had had his say. By eleven o'clock the storm had blown over and the House moved onto other business.

Afterwards I told them about Henry Lucy. Biggar knew him by repute.

'He's no friend of the Irish,' he said. 'He'll be scathing.' Then he thought for a moment and said brightly: 'Why don't we all have lunch tomorrow and read my reviews?'

༺ஒ༻

Thus began Biggar's lunchtime newspaper reviews, a tradition we continued for many years. The following afternoon, when Parnell and I walked into the tea-rooms in the Westminster Hotel, Biggar was stuffed into a small, worn armchair by the fire, his face hidden by the paper. At first I heard a snigger, then a snort, then a guffaw, and finally Biggar collapsed the paper noisily and laughed solidly for a full minute. He beckoned to us to come over.

'I've never read Lucy before,' he said. 'But he's good. I'll give him that. He's very good.'

Parnell and I took our seats beside him and listened intently.

'Heaven knows,' Biggar read, 'that I do not scorn a man because his path in life has led him to be a pig farmer. But though I may honour a pig farmer who is a Member of Parliament it is quite another feeling when I behold a Member of Parliament who acts like a pig farmer. Mr Biggar brings the manner of his business into this assembly and his manner, even for a Belfast provisions dealer, is very bad. When he rises to address the House, a whiff of pork seems to float upon the air ...'

Biggar's laughter was infectious and the three of us laughed heartily at Lucy's puny indignation.

'There's more, there's more,' he said excitedly.

'He might be forgiven,' Biggar read on, 'if he thought there had been a large failure in the bacon trade and that the House of Commons was a meeting of creditors and the gentlemen of the Government benches were suitable and safe subjects for the abuse of an ungenerous creditor.'

Biggar sat wedged in the armchair, his small, overweight frame heaving with laughter until he set Parnell and me laughing a second time. The other newspapers had written about the incident also, but none had Lucy's venom. I'm sure Lucy would have been distressed to see Biggar's laughter, but Biggar did not care what Members of Parliament or journalists thought of him. He was, as he said many times, answerable only to his mistress, his constituents, and God – in roughly that order, and depending on the circumstances – and he was sure that all three were delighted that he had given Disraeli a bloody nose for imposing coercion on Ireland.

Six

A Parliamentary Observer

THE NEXT DAY I was sent out to find lodgings – we clearly could not live in the hotel for weeks on end – and within days Parnell took a set of rooms, spartan and sparsely furnished, in Keppel Street, in Bloomsbury. It was not Avondale, but Parnell was not one to seek out luxuries and he pronounced it perfectly adequate for his needs. I found a smaller garret for myself in a boarding-house about ten minutes' walk further away.

As Butt had said, there were no further Irish matters before the House until the end of July, but Parnell had decided that he would attend Parliament each day until the end of the session.

He kept the Speaker's hours, arriving into the Chamber minutes before him each afternoon and staying until after midnight, at which time the Speaker adjourned the House until the following day. I had the mornings to myself and I wandered around the old bookshops on the Charing Cross Road, where I found cheap editions of Dickens' and Disraeli's novels, and I explored the coffee-houses of Covent Garden where I could read the newspapers free of charge. By such picturesque and self-indulgent routes I made my way to the House of Commons, where I met Parnell at four o'clock every afternoon. During these weeks, I had little enough work to do, and I whiled away my time in the Strangers' Gallery, watching the debates and reading. As I read Disraeli's novels and watched him in the Chamber I found myself increasingly fascinated by him. Biggar attended every day also, partly to keep us company, and partly because he enjoyed the banter and camaraderie of the House. For all its politics, the House of Commons in many ways resembled a gentlemen's club, and Biggar, despite his physical deformity, social background and political views, was at ease within its confines and, surprisingly, given his antics, with many of its members. Parnell, although friendly with Biggar and at ease in the company of the rough-hewn pork merchant, made no real effort at friendship with members of other parties and kept himself quite aloof.

During the following weeks and months, as I sat and watched the debates, I was struck by the marked contrast in their styles: Biggar reclined on the benches, lolling back with both arms resting on the bench behind him, his legs outstretched, his crumpled frock coat falling open to reveal his overly tight black waistcoat and his creased white shirt, which fell out untidily over his trousers. He watched the debates in an indolent manner, sometimes speaking to colleagues on nearby benches, or, more often, nodding off to sleep, particularly on hot stuffy afternoons.

Parnell, by contrast, tall, spare and fastidious, sat rigidly upright, looking intently at Government Ministers at the despatch box or listening to the speeches of opposition Members of Parliament; watching the interventions by backbenchers on points of order, or points of information; leaning forward to concentrate further when the Speaker intervened to give a ruling. He listened to Tories and Liberals with equal attention; he followed debates on issues of substance and on minor points of procedure with equal acuity; he watched as parliamentary questions were asked and noted the manner in which they were answered; he observed the etiquette of when members gave way and when they failed to give way; he learned about parliamentary privilege and the limits of parliamentary privilege. He absorbed the polite dialect of parliamentary language, and the jarring phrases of unparliamentary language.

I obtained a copy of the House of Commons rules of procedure, which I read in the gallery to while away the occasional boredom of an evening. I offered my copy to Parnell but, to my surprise, he declined. I thought if he were studying the House, he would at least read the rules, but that was not his way. Instead, he was absorbed in trying to understand its rhythms and arrangements, its methods and designs, its ebb and flow. His method – as I realised later – was resolutely scientific: he studied it as an engineer might survey a fortress to which he intends to lay siege; he considered its fortifications and its vulnerabilities, its watch-towers and its drawbridges, its points of impregnability and its points of weakness. There was an intensity of purpose about him which I had never seen before.

'I need to understand it,' he said, when I asked him about it, 'the people, the moods, the temper of the place. Disraeli has the high ground. And the numbers. We will have to pick our steps carefully.'

Parnell's schooling in the House of Commons went on throughout that year and the next. He went to the Commons every single day, and if he went, I went.

As I reflect on it now, I believe that Parnell was not only watching the outward forms and patterns of the House of Commons but observing its very spirit, which, over the centuries, had protected the liberties of English citizens from tyrannical kings, from arbitrary rule, from unjust laws and from unjustifiable arrest. This spirit was the touchstone of the great, unwritten English Constitution, and the terrible battles of previous generations had each left their mark and given rise to another unwritten convention, another venerated tradition. It was the wisdom and suffering of previous generations, accumulated layer by layer, stone by stone, which had built this House, not to any grand design, but as a gradual evolution of the defence of liberty. The spirit of the House was not to be found in its rulebook but in the ebb and flow of heated political debate, in the respect for differing positions, and the emergence – gradually – of new political rights and liberties. The House of Commons was the very tabernacle of this holy spirit of liberty.

∽◦∾

However, one lesson we all learned from our daily attendance in the House – and which was as unexpected as it was apparent – was how infrequently the Irish Members of Parliament appeared. Parnell and Biggar were exceptional in their attendance; Alexander Sullivan attended regularly, as did some others; but Butt's boast that there were now fifty-nine Irish Members of Parliament was a nonsense; what did it matter how many members he had, if none of them ever turned up?

One evening over supper in the House of Commons restaurant, when Parnell raised this with Biggar, Biggar's response was scathing.

'It's an absolute disgrace,' Biggar railed. 'All over Ireland people voted for a Home Rule Member of Parliament in the hope that it might make some difference. But how can it? Do you know' – he narrowed his eyes in that fierce look of his – 'that young buck McCarthy, from Kerry, has not even taken his seat yet? He was elected fifteen months ago and he has yet to set foot in the place, let alone make his maiden speech.'

Parnell raised an eyebrow in surprise.

'Why get elected?' he asked.

'Family seat, maybe,' said Biggar, 'who knows? Then you have members who turn up occasionally if they are in London on business, or for a social occasion, and deign to call into the House and grace us with their presence. I mean, can you believe' – Biggar was warming to his theme and getting more exasperated by the sentence – 'that only thirty of them actually turned up for the debate on Home Rule? On Home Rule!'

'Why didn't they all come?' I asked in surprise.

'They don't care,' said Biggar. 'They come and go as they like, if and when they like; they are answerable to no one.'

'Except their constituencies,' said Parnell.

'Bah, they don't know whether their members are in Parliament or not,' Biggar replied. 'And it's not helped by Butt being absent most of the time.'

Parnell pursed his lips but said nothing.

'And sooner or later we will lose patience,' continued Biggar. He didn't elaborate on who the 'we' referred to and Parnell did not ask.

'Mind you,' Biggar continued, 'what is the point of coming here? Disraeli has no intention of granting us Home Rule.'

'So what do you suggest we do?' said Parnell impatiently.

'You know Butt's strategy,' grunted Biggar, leaning back in his seat. 'Wait for another election, win more seats, hope the Liberals get in.'

'Relying on others is not a strategy,' said Parnell.

'Let's see what happens at the debate this year,' said Biggar. 'Maybe more of them will turn up. Maybe Disraeli will give in and say "I've thought it over and you can have your independence"'. Biggar grinned, that gargoyle grimace of his. 'But I wouldn't bet on it.'

๛

Throughout those months, Isaac Butt and the members of the Home Rule Party decided they would bring forward their own bills, to show Disraeli just how many matters required urgent attention in Ireland. I watched with increasing dismay as every single one of these bills – without exception – were rejected by Disraeli and Hicks Beach, without explanation or courtesy. It was a brutal exercise of parliamentary power. Government business always took priority and took up the greater part of each day. By the time the Speaker called for private members' bills it was usually around midnight, and in the House of Commons any measure which was still opposed after midnight could not proceed and was, in effect, abandoned for months on end. All Irish bills were rejected, peremptorily, without discussion or explanation, because they were opposed after midnight.

Despite these setbacks, Butt retained his eternal optimism that, sooner or later, the tide would turn in our favour. 'Just wait until the Home Rule debate,' was his refrain. 'We'll make progress then.'

๛

One evening during this spring session, as I sat in the lobby waiting for the evening debate to resume, I saw Butt walking towards me, his arm thrown jovially over the shoulder of a friend.

'Ah, Harrison, the very man,' he said. 'I've just been talking about you to McCarthy.'

Before he could introduce us, his companion extended a hand.

'Justin McCarthy,' he said, beaming. He was a slight man of medium height, with spectacles and a refined face, a grey trimmed beard with streaks of black, and black trimmed hair with streaks of grey; gentle in speech, gentle in temperament and gentle in manner. He was at the time parliamentary correspondent for the *Daily News*, a liberal newspaper, radical in its views, a great friend of Butt's and a firm supporter of the Home Rule Party.

I spent a delightful evening with McCarthy, gossiping and chatting in the gallery, and thus began a friendship between us that lasted throughout the difficult years that followed. When McCarthy discovered that Parnell had taken rooms in Keppel Street and that I lived in Fitzrovia – only minutes away from his home in Gower Street – he insisted we come to his home for dinner the following evening.

In the months – and indeed years – that followed, Parnell and I were regular guests at McCarthy's home: either for lunch on our way to the House of Commons or for dinner on any evening when Parliament was not sitting. I met his wife, Charlotte, and their two children, Charlotte and Justin. Their home was constantly open to us, and in those early, difficult and hostile years it was a blessing to enter the home of an Irish friend, to tell yarns and while away the evenings.

When McCarthy realised that I shared his literary interests, he exhorted me to read such-and-such a novelist or to attend such-and-such a poetry reading, and he talked at length about English writers, many of whom he knew, and their foibles. He had met Dickens at many of his public readings, and he regaled me on several occasions with stories he had heard Dickens recount – all the time apologising that he could not do them justice, as he did not have Dickens' great skills of mimicry. Not that McCarthy tried to assume a friendship which did not exist: he was scrupulous in emphasising that he only had the slightest acquaintance with the celebrated author.

After some weeks, McCarthy suggested that as I was present in the House night after night, I should write some articles for his newspaper. He promised to speak to his editor, and within days I was asked to submit a weekly article on parliamentary matters. I now watched the debates with a renewed excitement; I was no longer a passive spectator but an active witness. Each evening I took copious notes, and late into the night I worked them up into a draft; the following morning I reworked them again and again, until I could do no more. When I had quite exhausted what I wanted to say on the subject, I walked to McCarthy's house and presented it to him. He would welcome me in, usher me to his desk where he would read the piece quickly, praise it as a fine piece of work, take a pencil to edit it thoroughly on every line, and explain his amendments patiently to me. It was as complete an education in journalism as I could ever have obtained, and when I saw my own words published in the *Daily News* for the first time, under the by-line 'Our Parliamentary Correspondent', I was exultant. To this day, I have a copy of that edition in my papers.

As the months went by, I found that I could soon write an article in an hour or so, and it would be accepted by McCarthy with fewer and fewer amendments. Over time, he asked me to write on other matters also: to review a play, a novel or an exhibition, and, under his tutelage, the whole of London opened up before me.

I was even paid for these articles – only a penny a line, but I was indifferent to the rate. I mentioned it to Parnell and offered to take a corresponding reduction in my salary, but he laughed at my scruples. I was, however, concerned that there seemed less work for me to do for him in London than at Avondale.

'Have no fear on that account. That will soon change,' he said.

∞⊙⊙∞

Throughout these sessions, the long-promised debate on Home Rule became our intense focus, and we waited for it impatiently. Eventually, on a warm afternoon in August, after a number of false starts and postponements, the first Home Rule debate which I was to witness took place in the House of Commons.

Butt spoke first, holding his sheaf of notes in his right hand. The House of Commons was his natural theatre and he enjoyed every moment. Disraeli was present for the entire debate: indeed, I came to realise that there was a considerable sympathy, even a friendship, between the two men, and they seemed comfortable in each other's company. Butt's speech was listened to carefully, and with respect, by all sides of the House. There were no interruptions, no catcalls. Every now and then, he shuffled his papers, moving the top pages and putting them aside, but I don't believe he glanced at his notes even once in what was a three-hour oration. It's all in the structure, he told me afterwards. Once you have a clear structure, you can memorise it easily. It was an impressive speech: he had great presence and an easy eloquence, and he set out for an attentive House the reasons why Ireland should have its own parliament. I did think, however, that his tone was strange; he seemed to be almost pleading with Disraeli and his Government to grant Home

Rule; he seemed to emphasise how little Ireland wanted – not how much – and how the Irish earnestly desired to maintain the link with the British crown – a 'federal solution', as he called it – and he stressed that Ireland only sought minor powers to deal with minor matters, a local parliament for Dublin with strong links to London.

Butt's problem that day was not Disraeli – or even the Tories. In fact, the first blow came from behind, from within his own party. P.J. Smyth, the member for Westmeath, gave a blistering speech: short and sharp. He was not in favour of a federal solution: he wanted full repeal of the Act of Union and full independence for Ireland. There were other speeches too, from different members of the Irish party, all advocating different solutions.

After several hours of debate, Disraeli rose to reply. He waited at the despatch box, his hands delicately playing with the papers in front of him, until there was total silence in the House.

'Mr Speaker,' he said slowly, looking around the Chamber. 'I think the Irish complain too much. They speak as if all their ills emanate from English rule and from their conquest by Cromwell.' He paused, and leaned on the despatch box with his left arm. 'But Cromwell conquered all of England too – and you do not hear the English constantly complaining about it.'

His sarcasm was greeted with loud guffaws of laughter, particularly from the Tory benches, and Disraeli, encouraged, continued to ridicule and pour scorn on our demand for Home Rule.

'Nor do the Irish seem to know exactly what they want,' he said with mock seriousness. 'Some, like their leader Mr Butt, appear to want some form of local government but still have Members of Parliament at Westminster, and others – such as Mr Smyth – appear to want full repeal of the Union.'

Disraeli turned to his own supporters, shrugged his shoulders and held out his hands. 'So I am at a loss. What am I to do? It really is most difficult for Her Majesty's Government to consider a request which is so ill-thought-out. I do not think we should grant a demand which is so unclear, and which is not even demanded by all Irish members – not even by those who deign to turn up to the House for this debate, to say nothing at all of the Irish members who are not here. Are we to take it that their absence shows a lack of consent to their Leader's demands? I think we are.'

There were further loud cheers from the Tory benches.

I winced. Disraeli understood that, yet again, the absence of half the Irish members was a fatal weakness in our cause. They may have been elected as Home Rule Members of Parliament, but they were in reality Tories or Liberals, who saw which way the wind was blowing and had only adopted Home Rule as a flag of convenience to win their seats.

Disraeli sat down to a great ovation. He had not only rejected the demand, he had poured scorn on it, and, indeed, on the whole Home Rule Party. He had not answered a single one of Butt's arguments – he had simply ridiculed the entire case. It was an effective performance and one which Butt could not answer.

Some time later, Biggar was called upon to speak in the debate. He had barely started when Disraeli began to taunt him.

'Is that what in Ireland they would call a leprechaun?' said Disraeli loudly. There were guffaws of rude laughter from his backbenchers. It was time to avenge the insult to the Prince of Wales. Ridicule was often a weapon of choice for Disraeli, and the short, stout, hunchbacked figure of Biggar was an irresistible target.

I shifted uncomfortably in the gallery, feeling some sympathy for Biggar. But Biggar had been used to such taunts all his life – from the streets of Belfast as a child, to the Chamber of the House of Commons. It made little difference to him who taunted him, a street urchin or the Prime Minister of England. He had learned long ago that the best way to protect himself was to return all insults with interest.

'No, Prime Minister,' roared Biggar. 'I am not a leprechaun. But I am Irish and I can say at least that I am Irish. Whereas you ... you may be the Prime Minister of England but the English people cannot feel secure when they know that you, their Prime Minister, are a man alien in race and in religion to all of them.'

There was uproar in the House, and cries for Biggar to withdraw the insult, but he refused and stood, red-faced and furious, glaring at Disraeli. Disraeli was no longer smiling and he declined to answer the taunt; he knew it would be dangerous to provoke Biggar's wrath any more: the man could say anything.

Parnell rose to Biggar's defence.

'Mr Speaker,' he said, 'if the Prime Minister wished to see a leprechaun then I would suggest to him that he should visit Ireland, a country I believe he has never once set foot in, and one which he nevertheless presumes to govern.'

There was uproar again, and now all the Tory members were on their feet, shouting at Biggar and Parnell and demanding they withdraw their insults. But Biggar and Parnell just resumed their seats and talked to one another, as if they were oblivious to the rumpus they had just created. The Speaker adjourned the debate for a number of hours, to allow tempers to subside.

The vote, late in the evening, came as no surprise. The demand for Home Rule was rejected by another crushing majority of over 450 to 30 votes, and it was hard to see how that position could ever change.

It was a gloomy supper that evening – despite Butt's attempts to remain optimistic.

'I thought that went well,' he said.

'How did ye think that?' growled Biggar. 'It was a rout.'

'Well, yes, but ...' said Butt.

'You mean, you think you spoke well,' said Biggar.

Butt said nothing.

'Well, ye did, Butt, I grant you that,' grunted Biggar, somewhat less than graciously, 'but it's not doing us any good. We're not making any progress here. Why don't all our members turn up?'

'I don't know,' said Butt, crestfallen.

'It's just not good enough, Butt,' Biggar said loudly, slapping his hand on the table. 'The people vote them in; they are relying on them to represent them here and they don't bother even turning up ... it's monstrous.' Biggar was becoming red in the face.

'What can I do, Biggar?' said Butt helplessly. 'I can't force them to attend. They are Members of Parliament. They follow their own consciences.'

'Absentee landlords in Ireland and absentee Members of Parliament in the House of Commons,' said Biggar. 'The poor country is doomed.'

'What can we do?' asked Butt plaintively.

'Butt, you think if we all behave ourselves,' said Biggar, 'that if Disraeli sees we are all "the right sort", and we can be trusted to govern ourselves, he will be persuaded to grant us Home Rule.'

'Disraeli has mocked us,' said Parnell angrily. 'He has mocked the entire country.'

I saw his jaw clenching with repressed fury.

Biggar was red with anger, expostulating and roaring, bringing down curses on Disraeli, and roaming the lobbies like a caged animal. Parnell's anger, by contrast, was cold and silent; contained within him, it blazed out in his eyes, and was evident in his hands, which were clenched tightly behind him. Biggar's anger found an immediate outlet and was dissipated into the air, but Parnell's anger was harboured and nurtured. It would find an outlet later, and in a more deadly form.

'So, what is to be done?' Parnell said calmly to Biggar, out of earshot of Butt.

'We should do what we should have been doing all year,' shouted Biggar, 'obstruct, obstruct, obstruct. If they are not going to allow us a debate on Home Rule, we shouldn't allow them a debate on anything.'

'Why haven't you done that before?' Parnell asked.

'Butt was utterly opposed to it, and still is,' hissed Biggar. 'I think we should go in there this minute and just obstruct everything ourselves.' He started to go back into the Chamber immediately.

'No,' said Parnell firmly. 'Not now, Biggar. We will bide our time and make Disraeli pay a heavy price for his insolence.'

And so the sessions – which had started with high hopes – ended in another humiliating defeat. I read in the *Daily Telegraph* that the issue of Home Rule had now been decisively dealt with for another generation! It was difficult to see how any progress could be made in Westminster, and when the sessions finished in the summer Parnell returned to Avondale once again.

Seven

A Change of Strategy

AT THE END of January, we crossed to London for the new parliamentary session. It was a harsh winter that year, and there were fearsome storms in the Irish Sea. We were forced to sail to Liverpool, thence travel by train to London, and when we eventually arrived in London, many parts of the City were flooded and impassable.

On the opening of Parliament in early February, I arrived early to Westminster Square. For some reason, I did not want to miss the Queen's arrival: more like an arch-royalist, I thought, than an Irish nationalist. Even though it was only just gone ten o'clock in the morning and the Queen was not expected until two o'clock, the streets around Westminster were crowded with eager and excited onlookers. Even the balconies along Parliament Street were thronged, and, throughout the morning, carriages carrying peers and their wives passed along Parliament Street and through the gates of Westminster.

It was a bright but bitingly cold morning, and the street stones chilled my feet through the soles of my shoes. Arch-royalist or not, I could not stand in the cold for the next four hours. I walked into the Westminster Hotel, ordered some soup and sat down to read the newspapers, which were full of the opening of Parliament and the political stories of the day. In return for Disraeli making the Queen Empress of India, she had made him an Earl – the Earl of Beaconsfield – and he would now leave the House of Commons and take his seat in the House of Lords. It was, according to *The Times*, a glorious coda to a glorious career. But he was still Prime Minister, and his place in the House of Commons would fall to Sir Stafford Northcote.

The papers were also full of the Eastern question, the threat of war between Russia and Turkey, what might happen in the Balkans, and how Britain would run its empire in India. Not a word about Ireland. Indeed, an editorial in the *London Illustrated News* pronounced that there was no anticipation of any great public disputes in this session. According to the papers, all was quiet, and this green and pleasant land would now set to and govern its empire. I ate my soup and bread, finished the papers and, just after one o'clock, hearing the noise of cheering crowds, I went out again towards Westminster Yard.

The Royal carriage, drawn by eight greys in black plumage, had arrived at the Sovereign's entrance to the House of Lords. Although I was well back in the crowd, I could see the Queen descending from the carriage in her purple robes, followed by the Princesses Louise and Beatrice, being greeted by a royal flunkey. The crowds cheered her enthusiastically and a contingent of the Coldstream Guards played *God Save the Queen*; the royal standard fluttered on the flagstaff, and afterwards a Royal salute was fired. When the Queen had disappeared inside, I went back to the warmth of the hotel and resumed my newspapers.

About two hours later, I heard another burst of cheering and went out, just in time to see the Queen ascending into the carriage with her two daughters. As the carriage slowly turned and drove off, the crowds cheered loudly, throwing caps, handkerchiefs and God knows what else into the air. There was a pealing of church bells all over London, and I could hear the far-off, muffled sound of the artillery salute in St James' Park. I assume it was the same every year. I never went back again.

I did wonder, however, what the Queen had said in her speech to Parliament. Butt had been optimistic that it would contain some measure for Ireland – perhaps on the prisoners or on Catholic education. It was too much to expect anything on land reform, and nothing was expected on Home Rule. I went back into the foyer of the Westminster Hotel and waited.

After about an hour, the first members of the Party began to drift in, followed in short order by Parnell, Butt, Biggar and others. They had serious faces; there was no laughter. Butt looked dismayed and Biggar's face was thunderous. Parnell, by contrast, appeared curiously calm.

I asked Biggar what had happened.

'What happened, Harrison?' Biggar expostulated. 'I'll tell you what happened. Nothing. Nothing at all.' He walked ahead of me, in his stately, misshapen manner.

'Nothing?' I was astonished.

'Aye,' said Biggar grimly. 'Nothing. Ireland wasn't even mentioned by Her Royal Majesty.'

I followed Biggar to the small, stuffy meeting-room, but held back as the others entered the room.

Biggar looked back. 'Are you not joining us, Harrison?'

'I'm not sure I should,' I said. 'I presume it's just Members of Parliament.'

Biggar looked at me again. 'A stickler for etiquette, are you? Butt.' He turned, looking for the leader.

'Yes, Biggar.' Butt was just behind him. Biggar took hold of my forearm. 'Might I propose that Harrison here takes the minutes of the meeting?'

'A good idea,' said Butt, and then directly to me, kindly, 'A thankless task, Harrison, but one of the first importance, I assure you. If you would.'

'I would be honoured,' I said. Thus began my new role as unofficial secretary for the parliamentary party, a role I carried out for many years.

Butt sat at the side of a long oval table and, taking off his glasses to clean them, looked around the room at his colleagues.

'Well, gentlemen,' he began, 'a disappointment. Turkey, Russia, Serbia, Montenegro, India, the famine in Madras. The hostilities in the Transvaal. All mentioned.' He looked up from his notes.

'But not a single proposal on Ireland,' said Biggar sourly. He picked up the bottle of wine on the table and poured about six glasses in quick succession, leaving a stream of red stains on the tablecloth. Butt handed them around.

'It doesn't augur well,' said Frank Hugh O'Donnell, stretching to take one and wiping it fastidiously with his handkerchief. Like Parnell, O'Donnell was one of the younger members of the Party; unlike Parnell, he sought to assume a gravitas to which his age did not entitle him, and which made him appear pompous. It was as if the very act of being a Home Rule Member of Parliament was a serious matter which required his most serious attention. He had read Classics at Queen's University in Galway, and he wore his learning ostentatiously on his sleeve. He had a walrus-like moustache which drooped down on both sides of his mouth, giving him what looked like a perpetual scowl; and he wore a monocle wedged in his eye socket, even though there was nothing wrong with his eyesight – only his judgment, as I found out later.

'What can we do?' Butt shrugged his shoulders helplessly.

'My considered opinion is that we should withdraw from Westminster immediately,' said O'Donnell, looking around the table for support.

'Your considered opinion!' Butt glared at him. He had not campaigned hard for O'Donnell in Dungarvan – handing over some very lucrative briefs, as he told me later – only to be repaid by such outlandish ideas. 'We talked about that in Dublin only two weeks ago,' he said shortly.

O'Donnell was defensive. 'Yes,' he said, 'but the situation is different now. Disraeli has set his visage against Ireland. If we withdraw en masse – if we all withdrew to Dublin ...' He trailed off.

'And, pray tell, what good would that do?' said Butt impatiently. 'Where would we withdraw to? Have a meeting of sixty Irish Members of Parliament in a Dublin hotel?'

'Half of whom wouldn't even turn up,' said Biggar.

'Exactly,' said Butt, taking support where he found it. 'Thirty Irish Members of Parliament, all following this great policy of abstention, talking to ourselves in a hotel room. What would that achieve?'

'It would be a magnificent gesture,' said O'Donnell defiantly.

'It would be a complete waste of time. We'd be forced back to London with our tails between our legs within weeks. We'd become a laughing stock,' said Butt. 'So what other options do we have?'

'All we can do is continue what we did last year, Butt, bringing in our own bills,' said Shaw. Plump and self-satisfied, Shaw was Member of Parliament for Cork, the chairman of the Munster Bank, and he spoke with the practised, urbane affability of a bank manager.

'And a complete waste of time that was', said Biggar irritably. 'Do you know how many private members' bills we brought in last year? Fifteen? Twenty?'

'Twenty-two,' said Butt.

'Twenty-two. And how many were accepted?' said Biggar. He paused. 'None. Absolutely none.' He glared at Shaw.

'But we have no other choice, Biggar,' said Butt.

Parnell, sitting at the far end of the table, had remained quiet throughout the debate. He spoke now for the first time.

'We must obstruct them,' he said firmly. 'There is no other option.'

'Exactly,' said Biggar. He banged his clenched fist on the table.

'No, Parnell,' said Butt wearily. 'That is not the answer either. We must have patience.'

'How long must we have patience for, eh?' said Biggar impatiently, getting to his feet and prowling around the table. 'How long? I have run out of patience.'

'We tried to obstruct last year, Parnell, and it didn't get us very far,' said Shaw. 'Or have you forgotten?' he added dryly.

'It didn't get us very far,' said Parnell, 'because we didn't go far enough.'

'Didn't go far enough!' cried Shaw. 'We spent hours objecting to their bills.'

'Whatever it was, it wasn't enough,' said Parnell. 'We must obstruct them just as they are obstructing us. They will not grant us Home Rule; very well – we will not let them rule themselves; if they will not permit us to debate our bills, then we will not let them debate theirs. They are obstructing all our bills. Very well, we will obstruct all of theirs.'

'All of them!' exclaimed Shaw and Butt simultaneously.

'Yes,' said Parnell, 'all of them.'

'That's more like it,' said Biggar, a smile beginning to replace the scowl.

'We will obstruct every single bill Disraeli introduces between now and the Easter recess. Without exception,' said Parnell.

'What on earth will that achieve, Parnell?' said Shaw.

'It will achieve nothing,' said Butt, 'other than increased hostility to our cause. Just like that prank over the Prince of Wales!' He glared at Biggar.

'It will teach Disraeli a lesson,' said Parnell, 'that if he obstructs our cause, we will obstruct his. It will show him there is a price for his obduracy.'

'And how long do you suggest we keep up this obstruction?' said Shaw.

'Until Disraeli surrenders,' said Parnell in a quiet tone.

There were guffaws of laughter around the room.

'And when do you expect that to be?' said Shaw sarcastically. 'When he hoists a white flag in the House of Lords?'

'I do not know,' said Parnell. 'But if we do not surrender, he will have to. He will have no other option. It is a simple equation.'

'This is not the right time, Charles,' said Butt, shaking his head. 'Disraeli, the whole Cabinet, they're wholly preoccupied with what's happening in Constantinople.'

'It's the perfect time,' said Parnell. 'Disraeli is now in the Lords – he won't be able to deal with us directly.'

'You're not suggesting we take advantage of the fact that Disraeli has gone to the House of Lords,' said Butt, 'to obstruct the Commons?'

'That's precisely what we should do,' said Parnell.

'Brilliant,' said Biggar. 'I never thought of that.'

'But Sir Stafford Northcote will be leader in the House,' said Butt plaintively, 'and I promised him my full cooperation.'

'Why the devil did you do that?' said Biggar.

'I was at a dinner party with him some weeks ago and I congratulated him on his new role,' said Butt. 'He told me he needs time to settle in and I told him we would assist him in any way we could. He assured me in return that there would be another Home Rule debate in July.'

'Northcote is vulnerable,' said Parnell, ignoring concerns about Butt's social obligations. 'He doesn't command the House – unlike Disraeli.'

'But, Parnell,' Butt got quite heated as he considered his loss of face with Northcote, 'no one will support you in this ... this irresponsible scheme.'

'I will,' said Biggar.

'Well, of course you would, Biggar, but no one else will,' said Butt defiantly.

'No. I'm against it,' said Shaw.

'So am I,' said King-Harman, the member for Sligo and a representative of the many Protestant landlords in the Party at that time. 'I never heard such nonsense. It will cause chaos.'

'That's the whole point,' grinned Biggar. 'We must bring the English nose to the Irish grindstone and we must keep it there.'

'Parnell,' – Butt tried to persuade his protégé one last time – 'you can't obstruct everything. It's never been done before. I mean, I've seen the Liberals obstruct some bills for weeks. But that was with a whole party. I mean … what you're proposing, it's impossible.'

'I assure you, Butt,' said Parnell, looking directly at him, 'it is not impossible. But it will be difficult, and the more support I have, the easier it will be. It will be a test of wills and we must prevail.'

Then, suddenly, he stood up from the table, as if to draw the meeting to a close, as if any further debate were otiose. Imperiously, I thought, almost as if he were already leader of the Party. He did not seek to persuade them any further.

Butt, realising the meeting was going to break up, coughed and gathered up his papers.

'Yes, well, gentlemen,' he said. 'We will think about it. But I must say I am totally against it. It will work against us, mark my words.'

I scribbled down my notes on the last contributions and joined Parnell and the others as they left the room.

Eight

A Declaration of War

THE FOLLOWING DAY, just before he and Biggar were about to go into the Chamber, Parnell beckoned to me and to Biggar to follow him. He turned left at the central lobby and we followed him into St Stephen's Hall, a long, high-ceilinged gallery with stained-glass windows, flanked by statues of eminent Members of Parliament. Parnell walked very deliberately to the statue of Henry Grattan at the end of the gallery and waited for us to gather round.

'Harrison, I want you to file a Notice of Opposition in the parliamentary clerk's office today,' he said, 'to every bill proposed for this term.'

Biggar exhaled in a loud whistle.

'Why give them notice, Parnell?' I asked. 'Why not just oppose each bill as it comes up?'

'Harrison is right,' said Biggar. 'Let's ambush them every evening. Otherwise, they'll be prepared.'

But Parnell was adamant.

'I want them to be prepared,' he said. 'I intend to signal our opposition to every single bill in advance.'

'They'll think you're bluffing,' I said.

'They will think that at the start,' said Parnell. 'Every afternoon they will think I am bluffing. And every evening they will realise I am not. I want Disraeli to understand me clearly. He will soon realise I mean what I say.'

Without further argument, but still not convinced, I went up the stairs to the clerk's office. It was difficult to find. I had never been there before. There were no signs and no one seemed to know where it was. No one ever went there, apparently, apart from the clerks. Eventually, however, I found it, set high in the Palace of Westminster in a maze of dark oak corridors, with waxed floorboards and little light. I knocked on the door and a voice called out to come in.

I stepped into a dark cubby-hole of an office, which might have been illuminated by a small window were it not for the accumulated dirt on the window's panes. This small space was divided by a counter, on top of which were mountainous heaps of grey folders, overflowing with official papers, leaning against one another for support, like two uneven piles of bricks.

A bespectacled clerk, sitting at his desk, on the other side of the counter, with a pencil behind his ear, looked up at me expectantly. I told him I wished to file some opposition papers to certain bills before the House.

'Certainly, sir,' he said helpfully. He went to a shelf and pulled out a heavy brown ledger, and, sweeping aside some files with his elbow, put it on the counter.

'Let's see,' he said, turning the pages noisily. 'Ah, yes, here we are. I only have the bills from now until Easter.' He turned the book towards me. 'We won't get the others until after Easter. Now if you look here, sir,' he craned his neck to look at his own handwriting. 'On the left is the title of the bill, then the proposer and seconder, and on the right hand side, there's a space for the opposer.' He pointed to the different columns on the ledger.

His neat handwriting had written out the full title of each of the proposed bills.

'There needs to be a proposer and seconder for each Opposition Notice also,' he explained. 'Filed by Members of Parliament. May I enquire, sir, if you are a member?'

I explained that I was Mr Parnell's secretary, here at his request.

'Very well, sir,' he said. 'Then you simply put Mr Parnell's name opposite the bill. You have a seconder, sir?'

I said I did, and he turned away to let me write in their names.

I looked carefully at the page. Apart from one or two Liberal Members of Parliament opposing certain measures, it looked as if almost all the bills that term were unopposed. I quickly wrote 'Charles Stewart Parnell MP' and 'Joseph Gillis Biggar MP' in the columns opposite all the bills.

When I had finished, the clerk returned to the counter and swivelled the ledger towards him to review what I had written; like clerks everywhere, he assumed it was filled out incorrectly.

'I'm sorry, sir,' he coughed apologetically. 'I may not have explained myself properly.'

'Oh?' I enquired, with feigned surprise.

'Yes, sir,' he continued helpfully, 'you see, sir, there's no need to put the names in all the columns, just in the columns opposite the bills Mr Parnell wishes to oppose.'

He looked at me, sympathetically, as if I were a simpleton.

'Yes, yes,' I said. 'I understood you perfectly. Mr Parnell wishes to oppose all the bills this term.'

'All of them?' said the clerk, taking off his glasses, in astonishment, as if it might help him to hear correctly. 'That can't be right, sir. I mean, sir, are you sure, sir?'

I told him that I was perfectly sure.

'Well, I'll be …' he said. 'I've never heard of such a thing. You don't mind if I tell my head clerk?'

'Not in the slightest,' I said airily.

'And he may have to tell members of the Government,' he said.

'Naturally,' I said, unable to resist a smile breaking out.

I felt as if I had just delivered a declaration of war.

Nine

Obstruction

SOME DAYS LATER, the Government brought forward the first of its bills for the term – on much-needed public health improvements. The Minister did not finish his speech until just before midnight and, as the Liberals had assented, he had thought it might pass without a vote, despite Parnell's Notice of Opposition. Parnell, however, rose to say that he opposed the measure, and he spoke until after midnight.

'Now, Mr Speaker,' he said. 'I have just noticed the hour and, as I do not wish to detain this House any longer than is necessary, but as this measure is contested ...'

'Yes, Mr Parnell,' said the Speaker, 'we will adjourn this debate for now. The Government can bring the measure back to the House at a later date.'

Parnell nodded and resumed his seat. The Minister glared at him, gathered up his papers and left the Chamber.

The second bill, the next evening, was on the navy estimates. The debate had begun shortly after six o'clock in the evening and the Minister finished shortly after ten o'clock. Biggar spoke for two hours and, after midnight, it was his turn to inform the Speaker – mournfully – that, as the bill was opposed at this hour, it could not be dealt with by the House any further. The Secretary for the Navy remonstrated with the Speaker and with Biggar, who shrugged his hunched shoulders and smiled maliciously. There was no option, Biggar told the Speaker unctuously; the bill would have to be held over. The Speaker agreed.

The third bill to be obstructed was an electoral reform bill. I was anxious to help, and asked Parnell if there was anything I could do.

He handed me a sheaf of parliamentary bills to be debated in the coming weeks. 'I need you to read these bills and think of any arguments we could make against them.'

'What sort of arguments?' I asked.

'Anything at all,' said Parnell airily, 'to keep fuel on the fire until after midnight. Punctuation, grammar, no point is too small.'

'And, if I may, Parnell,' intervened Biggar. 'Harrison, could I ask you to look up some official reports, enquiries, Royal Commissions … that sort of thing?'

'On what?' I asked, puzzled at the vagueness of the request.

'On anything even remotely relevant,' said Biggar expansively. He paused. 'In fact, Harrison, it doesn't have to be relevant. It only has to be official. That way it can appear to be relevant. Anyway, by the time I have read out fifty pages of it everyone will have forgotten whether it is relevant or not.'

I started that very afternoon. The library in the House of Commons was empty and I had it to myself. I wandered through the stacks and shelves, filled with heavy leather-bound books, many of them hundreds of years old, containing Acts of Parliament, cases of the House of Lords or the Privy Council, books of evidence from hearings of Royal Commissions and such matters. I sat at one of the long oak writing tables placed in the alcoves of the library, beneath the mullioned windows, and pored over volumes of parliamentary reports, parliamentary enquiries, judicial enquiries, Royal Commissions – anything which looked relevant and official. The accumulated dust caused me to sniffle and sneeze, but I persevered, searching out reports which could be of any possible use.

By early evening, having obtained some reports which I thought might be of some help to Biggar, I returned to the gallery. The Minister of the Crown was on his feet, finishing his contribution, and the debate would have ended before dinner if Biggar had not got to his feet.

'Mr Speaker, sir,' he breathed heavily, 'unfortunately I have a number of difficulties with this bill. There are important issues of principle which go to the heart of this important measure, which I wish this House to consider.'

'Very well, Mr Biggar,' the Speaker said evenly, 'we will take it up again after dinner.'

'Thank you, Mr Speaker, sir,' Biggar said, and then joined his colleagues on the way out of the Chamber. 'Harrison,' he said, when he came out to the lobby, 'tell me you have found something. How in hell's name can I speak for three and one-half hours on franchise reform when I don't know the slightest thing about it?'

I produced a large parliamentary volume. 'Gladstone reformed the franchise some years ago after a full enquiry,' I told him.

Biggar seized the report greedily, as though it were a tray of Fry's chocolate creams.

'I've gone through it,' I said. 'There are sections at the start about the principles which should be considered before such reforms are carried out, and at the end, in the appendices, statistical tables.'

'Oh, this is marvellous, Harrison,' said Biggar. He licked his fingers as he flicked through the report. 'This should keep me upright for at least three hours. Who knows, Parnell, you mightn't even need to speak tonight.'

Parnell smiled at Biggar's enthusiasm.

'But I can do nothing on an empty stomach,' said Biggar. 'Gentlemen, will you please join me for supper whilst we consider these important matters of State?'

After supper, Biggar commenced his speech on the franchise reform bill. His judicious and careful review of the appropriate principles which should support any reform of the franchise was full. Very full, I thought, as I watched him from the gallery. Biggar read a paragraph from the Commission Report to the House, paraphrased it to explain what it meant to him, considered how it had been put into practice over the years, illustrated how it applied to the present case, contended that the present bill did not fully embrace this principle, exhorted the Minister to reconsider the bill to include this principle, moved on to the next principle, and repeated the entire exercise – all to a rapidly emptying House of Commons. Eventually, shortly after midnight, he suggested, most apologetically, to the Speaker that, as he had many hours left, and as the hour was past midnight, and as the House must be diligent in considering the extension of voting rights because the vote, once given, could never be taken back, the Speaker should consider adjourning the matter for further consideration by the House.

The Speaker, wearying of the concentration required in following Biggar's arcane yet seemingly erudite arguments, agreed and the Government's third bill was lost – much to the irritation of the Minister involved.

Biggar sat down, sighing heavily, as though the issues which he had been debating had been weighing on him for months and continued to burden him down, as a conscientious legislator for the nation. Then, when he had done sighing, he looked up at me and gave me his fearsome grin and a wink which caused his whole head to roll ninety degrees west.

∾ᘐᘐᘐᘐᘐᘐ∾

Day after day, night after night, throughout the following weeks, Parnell and Biggar went to work like foresters, wielding their axes with enthusiasm and Government bills were felled like timber. The prison bill, the courts bill, bills on public works, local government bills, public health bills, railway bills, factories bills were all lost. No matter what the Government proposed, it was always opposed by two people – Biggar and Parnell – and often these two alone.

On most evenings throughout those weeks, Parnell took the lead in obstructing the Government's path. On such occasions, he rose silently in his place and stood rigidly, his hands clenched tightly by his sides or behind his back, staring not at the Government benches or at the Speaker but, apparently, at a fixed immovable spot directly across the floor of the House.

When the Speaker eventually called on him to speak, as he had to do, Parnell's voice was firm and his accent as English as any of the Tory landlords in the benches opposite him, in sharp contrast to his colleagues, who spoke with a range of Irish accents from the lilting singsong sounds of West Cork to the harsh, metallic gratings of East Ulster. But Parnell's accent was unmistakably English, acquired from his English ancestors and his English education, and one which his fellow landlords in the House of Commons could understand, even if the substance of his remarks was offensive to their ears. It was this unfamiliar rhetoric delivered in a familiar accent which assured him of the close attention of the House whenever he spoke. And yet, as I watched him, night after night, it was not only his accent or what he was saying, but also his curious mode of saying it, which commanded attention. He would speak deliberately, but not at all fluently, and his spasmodic speeches often shuddered to a silence as he considered inwardly the next word or phrase; this silence forced the listener to attention, until the speaker would find the word – never an expected one – and resume his speech until the next halting interlude.

There was something mesmeric about Parnell's performances in the Commons at that time. It was not on account of his oratory, because he was still no orator. But it was as if he had found a new way of speaking which suited his character perfectly. It was not the florid oratorical style of Isaac Butt, nor the languid sardonic style of Disraeli, or even the weighty Old Testament moralistic style of Gladstone. It was a cold, declamatory, baleful, almost malevolent style. For students of rhetoric – which all Members of Parliament were – it was a unique style, almost bizarre, and yet one which held them riveted – particularly if Parnell allied passion to his words. He did not do this often in those days – the navy estimates were hardly matters about which he could be passionate – but on issues about which he *was* concerned, his speeches were intriguing, even fascinating.

On alternate nights, it was Biggar's turn. His openings were always impressive. He prepared what he intended to say, and his speeches were carefully structured in advance. His notes, made in his scrawling handwriting on sheets of House of Commons stationery, were drawn from inside his jacket pocket when the Speaker called on him. His opening remarks always aimed to repeat, to précis – if that is not too misleading a word – the arguments of the Minister, one by one. Then he would review all the arguments, one by one, and put forward a lengthy counter-argument. Then having adroitly summarised all the arguments and counter-arguments, he would start all over again with the first argument and then begin his references to the official reports on the matter. He introduced his official reports ostensibly with great reverence, as if contained therein was the accumulated wisdom of previous generations of parliamentarians; wisdom which should not be departed from lightly but should be read out reverently, weighed carefully and applied respectfully.

'Now, Mr Speaker, the report which I would like the House to consider is the report of the Royal Commission on ...' – he intoned his words like an elderly parish priest reciting the solemn liturgy – 'But before I even bring your attention, Mr Speaker and members of this House, to the important passages in this report, we must, I believe, understand the terms of reference of the report, and I would like to read these so that the passages of the report can be seen in the context in which they were written.'

Loud groans of what seemed like physical pain could be heard from the Government benches.

Biggar stopped in mid-inhalation, pretending to be shocked by the interruption, and looked over to the other side, daring further interruption. Having shuffled through the terms of reference, he would then urge the members to consider the eminent Members of Parliament who served on these Commissions.

'And in dealing with these complex terms of reference, Her Majesty's Government ...' The term was always bellowed out, sonorously, magnificently, with his head held high, tilted back as far as his hunch would allow, to ensure that Her Majesty's Government received its fullest measure of respect at least from the Right Honourable Joseph Gillis Biggar MP.

'Her Majesty's Government, Mr Speaker,' he intoned, 'appointed gentlemen of exemplary judgment, of great learning and of the deepest wisdom, men of experience, men of property, men who graced this fine House, men who ... who ... who ...' – at times his powers of description failed him and he would glide inelegantly into their actual names. 'Ahem, well, Mr Speaker, the following men,' and he proceeded to list the members of the Royal Commission with their full names, titles and awards.

When he had finished the preliminaries, Biggar then launched himself into the text of the official report and, burrowing into it like a mole, read extracts from it for hours on end. Occasionally, when he read aloud a sentiment with which he agreed, he paused to draw attention to it – 'And that is precisely the point I was making to this House, Mr Speaker' – before resuming his reading.

Of course, these tactics were bound to provoke a reaction from the furious Tories and, as the days and nights wore on, there were catcalls of abuse aimed at Biggar.

'Go back to Cavan, you butcher.'

'Mr Speaker, I can smell pork.'

'Is that the hunchback of Notre Dame?'

'I've seen enough pigs in my time to recognise the porkers on those benches,' Biggar bluntly retorted, using his sheaf of papers to gesture across the aisle to the Tories.

This, of course, elicited another howl of execration from the Tories, but Biggar ignored it. Often, whilst the shouts continued from the other side, he would lean down to consult with Parnell, and then when they subsided he would resume his speech.

I watched, night after night, as the scenes on the floor of the House grew more and more heated with each passing week. Night after night, as Parnell rose to speak, he was excoriated by the House, his voice overwhelmed by a chorus of jeers, catcalls and abuse from the Government benches. This was not a good-natured barracking but a snarling, angry, baleful group of senators, full of fury that one of their own should so abuse his privileges. On some occasions he could get no further than uttering 'Mr Speaker' before the blizzard of sound began.

There was no disguising the increasingly noisy and angry shouts from the Tory benches. They ascended the scales: from impatient humour to cross words, to strident cries, to vulgar abuse, to full-throated roars of anger at these two interlopers who had dared to abuse their privileges. They were like a pack of hounds in full pursuit of their prey. But the moment they strayed, Parnell immediately complained to the Speaker about the use of unparliamentary language by an opponent, and demanded that the offending Member of Parliament be named and the comment withdrawn. The Speaker of the House had no choice but to acquiesce, and that crack of the whip usually brought the hounds to heel for another few hours.

Many speakers might have tried to battle through this blizzard of noise, starting and restarting their sentences until they were heard, but that was not Parnell's way. He let the storm blow itself out, let the voices shout themselves hoarse, and all the while paid no attention to them whatsoever. He stood in his place, perfectly calm, almost motionless, his hands clasped behind his back, like an elegant bronze statue, all the time waiting for the tempest to pass. Occasionally, Parnell would look to the Speaker and shrug his shoulders as if to say, 'It is for you, Mr Speaker, to control this assembly. I have the floor and I shall not surrender it.'

Then, when the tirade of abuse had quieted, Parnell would resume his speech and his observations on the bill. This, in turn, seemed to incite his opponents to new furies, but at the first sound Parnell would stop again and wait until a total silence took hold in the Chamber. On many such occasions a tense, taut silence gripped the Commons as both sides waited for the other to speak. Then, when he had asserted himself in the House, Parnell would resume his observations on the bill under consideration.

The Tories sought to intimidate Parnell, but he was not a man to be intimidated. Their imprecations and abuse broke over him like waves on a rock, and made about as much of an impression. If anything, their hostility to him made him despise them even more; instead of breaking him as they intended, it seemed to strengthen him.

But at the end of it all, after all the jeering, all the catcalls, Parnell was left standing; he was in control of the floor. He did not buckle and he would not bend. He never surrendered the floor of the House to his enemies. In this way, the normal weapons of the House were useless against him – indeed, they were turned and used against the Tories. Their tirades all used up valuable time, and time was the only weapon Parnell and Biggar had; each interruption took them closer to midnight and to the abandonment of a bill for another term. In this way, Parnell confronted not only the House of Commons but also, perhaps, his inner demons as a speaker; his fear of hostility, of rejection, of derision: all were encountered, challenged, faced down and vanquished.

Ten

Cat and Mouse

O F COURSE, IT must not be supposed that all these evenings were nights of high drama. Even Shakespeare wrote comedies and with a player like Biggar a farce was always possible.

A Tory Member of Parliament, Henry Chaplin, a firm opponent of Home Rule, sought to bring in a bill to regulate machines for the threshing of corn. Chaplin was a heavy-set man, much inclined to stand on his own dignity and to lecture pompously to all on the appropriate procedures of the House. Biggar was assigned to deal with this bill; Chaplin knew he was assigned to it and Biggar knew that Chaplin knew. As the evening wore on, Chaplin eyed Biggar as warily as a mouse would a cat; he waited to see if Biggar would leave the Chamber, even for a moment, so that he could introduce the bill and take it down without a division; but Biggar just dawdled in the Chamber all evening, feigning boredom, languishing, stretched back on the benches looking to all the world as if he were asleep.

Then, at about ten o'clock, Chaplin rose ponderously to his feet and suddenly Biggar opened one eye and was alert. After a brief comment about the merits of threshing machines, Chaplin commended the bill to the House. Biggar was faced with the awesome task of speaking for over two-and-a-half hours on threshing machines. There were no Commissions of Enquiry into threshing machines; there were no previous debates from which to quote large extracts from Hansard. But Biggar did not flinch or falter. He spoke at great length about the comparative merits of corn and wheat, barley and oats, as arable crops; he

spoke about the agricultural and climatic conditions necessary
for each of these important crops to thrive; he spoke about the
husbandry practices required for all types of crops, beginning a
complicated matrix of comparisons between corn and turnips,
corn and carrots, corn and potatoes, barley and turnips, barley
and carrots, barley and potatoes; he compared farming crops to
farming livestock. This led on seamlessly to a comparison with
pig farming, his own particular area of speciality; he delivered an
impressive exegesis of the pig industry, lasting at least an hour,
dealing with every detail of the business from piglet to pork chop;
he bemoaned the increasing industrialisation of agriculture and
harkened back to the pastoral practices of previous generations;
he warned about the dangers caused by using machines for
threshing corn; he talked about all manner and means of
threshing corn, about the importance of separating the grain
from the husk; and he reviewed all the agricultural instruments
which had been used. All this led inexorably on to a review of
other agricultural implements and other agricultural practices,
and took him through until midnight. As Big Ben chimed the
midnight hour, Biggar intoned: 'Which time, Mr Speaker, is
a good time to discuss why there is a need at all for threshing
machines. What's wrong with the good old flail?'

Even the Speaker could not suppress his laughter at the
awesome sight of Biggar talking on for half an hour on the joys
of the hand plough and his father's favourite ploughing horses,
his detailed exposition of the value of horses to agriculture and
the relationship between horses and threshing machines. Everyone
saw the joke – except Chaplin, of course, his face thunderous as
he watched his favoured project deferred for another term. It was
as good a night's entertainment as anything in the Haymarket or
Drury Lane.

∽৩৩৹

Their behaviour caused outrage among Government Members of
Parliament, and even among some Liberals. It was, however, the
Tories who were most livid. Perhaps they looked on Parnell as one
of their own. Whilst Biggar or Isaac Butt were – from their accents

alone – clearly members from Ireland, Parnell, with his aristocratic background, his estates in Ireland and his education in Cambridge, was, they thought, one of them.

Of course, they could not have been more wrong. But there was no doubt in my mind that Parnell regarded himself as the social equal of all the men opposed to him on the Government benches, and, indeed, superior to many of them. His ancestors had had great estates in England and he could trace them back to the great English barons, as they could; his great-grandfather had been Chancellor of the Exchequer in Ireland and had turned down a peerage in the House of Lords. Parnell, with that sensitive pride in himself and in his family name, suffered no social inferiority either in the Commons or in the Lords; he felt as if he were among his own class, but that he was simply on a different side of the political argument. It allowed him to ignore all the gibes about class and station which were often directed towards the Irish Members of Parliament.

It was the remorseless, implacable and sustained application of the strategy which made it effective. And soon it brought recruits. As O'Connor Power, Frank O'Donnell, Dwyer Grey, Captain Nolan and Harley Kirk saw what was happening, and as they realised that Parnell was absolutely in earnest, they joined him. Within weeks, the band of two had swelled to seven. Seven loquacious Irishmen could do significant damage in the House of Commons. Actually, to be accurate, six loquacious Irishmen and a mute: Harley Kirk was incapable of addressing the House on any issue, but he assured Parnell of his full support. And he was true to his pledge: he stayed at his post all night with them and he acted as teller for all the votes, thus relieving the others of at least one tiresome duty.

Northcote, a large, fleshy man with a bulbous nose and fleshy jowls hidden by a luxurious growth of white beard, looked completely bewildered by Parnell's tactics. It was as if he simply could not fathom the sheer unreasonableness of the man. His cautious and gentle character made him slow to attack, and his bewilderment at Parnell's tactics made him slow to defend. He was a ponderous and poor speaker, and a poor relation to many of his richer Tory colleagues, which made him diffident, and his diffidence was evident to all when Parnell began to assert himself. Parnell was right: Northcote did not command the House, and Parnell pounded away, exploiting the weakness.

❦

As the end of term drew near, and as Biggar, Parnell and I were having our evening supper in the Commons restaurant, a junior member of the Government, Mr Monks, approached us. A stocky, barrel-chested man in a green tweed suit and a yellow waistcoat, with fat red cheeks and great folds of flesh under his chin, he seemed apoplectic with indignation.

'What the hell do you think you're playing at with these bloody antics of yours?' he practically shouted at Parnell and Biggar.

'Which antics are these?' asked Biggar sweetly.

'You know bloody well what I'm talking about.' Monks raised his voice still further.

'We are simply trying to improve your legislation,' said Biggar, even more sweetly.

This response made Monks yet more apoplectic. His eyes bulged with fury.

'We have an empire to run and you are making monkeys out of us and you, Parnell,' – Monks jabbed a fleshy finger towards Parnell – 'you're the worst of them.'

Parnell raised a napkin to his mouth and took a slow, deliberate sip of wine.

'Did Disraeli send you?' he asked.

'Of course not,' said Monks, surprised at the question. 'I'm here of my own accord. But everyone in the Government thinks the same as I do.'

'As you can see, we are at dinner,' said Parnell. 'You can reply to us in the Chamber. Good evening.'

He drew the exchange to a close and Monks, dismissed like a servant, scowled and moved on.

❦

February passed into March and March passed into April, and with it came the Easter recess. The parliamentary term came to an end without a single bill of any significance being passed. For Parnell and Biggar, their new policy of obstructionism was a triumph of tactics and endurance. But for Disraeli and his government, it was a disaster of significant proportions; in his third year in office, with an empire to govern, and a litany of measures to pass, they were faced, not with an opposition which they could outvote, or an army which they could conquer by force of arms, but by two men determined to obstruct their path for weeks and months on end.

It was now up to Disraeli to respond.

Eleven

The Battle Rages

THERE WAS A wary, expectant air about the House when it resumed after Easter and Northcote looked more determined than before. The list of bills to be put forward that term had been published and I had returned to my friend, the clerk in the parliamentary bills office (to a frosty reception, I should add), to register Parnell's opposition to all the bills for this term also.

On the first day of the new session, Northcote lumbered to the despatch box, grasping both ends of it for support.

'Mr Speaker,' he said, looking at his backbenchers for approval. 'In the light of the behaviour, the unprecedented and ill-mannered behaviour, of certain members of this Parliament – some of whom should know better … ' He looked pointedly towards Parnell. 'I have consulted with the Prime Minister and Her Majesty's Government has decided that the venerable rule of this House – that pertaining to all measures opposed after midnight – should be suspended.'

'Hear, hear,' went the shouts of the serried masses behind him.

I looked down at Parnell, who continued to look directly at Northcote. Northcote stroked his beard hesitantly.

'And we would hope that, even now, our friends in the Home Rule Party know that we have not taken this step lightly.'

He spluttered on to other business.

Butt looked around, and gestured to his members to meet him outside.

I hurried downstairs from the gallery, and I found them gathered in a circle in the members' lobby, directly outside the Chamber.

'I say we continue until midnight as before,' said Frank O'Donnell. 'We will then have maintained our protest.'

'That's completely senseless,' said Shaw. He glared at Parnell. 'Are you a member of this party or do you just want to destroy it?' He appealed to Butt. 'For heaven's sake, Butt, let's have some common sense here and abandon this stupid ploy. It's … it's … childish.'

Butt glanced around at the ten or fifteen members. Many nodded in agreement with Shaw's view. But before Butt could say anything, Parnell intervened.

'Nothing has changed. Disraeli has not surrendered.' He spoke quickly, but in a low voice so that he could not be overheard. 'We will continue to oppose every bill – throughout the night if necessary.'

'That will be difficult,' Biggar mused.

'It will be difficult for the Tories also,' said Parnell. 'They won't want to stay up every night. Let's see if they have the stomach for the fight.'

'Oh, for heaven's sake, Parnell,' said Shaw, and he strode off impatiently.

'Be reasonable, Parnell,' Butt pleaded.

'The battle is not yet over,' said Parnell, and with that he broke off and walked back into the Chamber.

Several days later the mutiny bill was before the House and Parnell started speaking just after eleven o'clock in the evening. Clause after clause was disputed, voted on and passed. Midnight – the old hour of respite – came and went unmarked. Parnell carried on with his slow, relentless analysis of the measure. It was clear the debate would continue long into the night. I remained in the gallery to watch the drama and also to share in his travails.

Then, just after one o'clock in the morning, without notice or warning, Isaac Butt appeared in the House and raised a point of order. Parnell immediately yielded to him.

'Mr Speaker,' Butt declaimed. 'I am sorry that the House is still sitting at this hour. I am sorry that the House still *has* to sit at this hour. I regret – and I say this with great sadness – that my Honourable Friend, the Member for Meath, has seen fit to waste the time of this House in this miserable and wretched discussion, this arid and futile debate. I am not responsible for the Member for Meath and I do not, and cannot, control him. However, what he does, he does against my advice and against the policy of our Party. I have a duty to discharge to the great nation of Ireland and to do this I wish to state that I and my party entirely disapprove of the conduct of the Right Honourable Member for Meath and his obstructionist policy.'

I leaned forward in astonishment that Butt had sought to criticise Parnell in so public a fashion. The Government benches were, given the hour, thinly populated, but those present, including Northcote, cheered heartily and applauded Butt for his sentiments.

Butt sat down and wiped his brow with his handkerchief. Parnell, stony-faced, stood immediately to reclaim the floor. The Tories assumed, everyone assumed – I assumed – that Parnell would withdraw his objection and let the bill through. He paused for a moment, looking at his papers, flicking through some documents as if searching for something to say.

Eventually he looked up at the Speaker. 'Now, Mr Speaker, if I could resume at section 12, subsection 1 of the bill.'

I held my breath. Parnell had ignored Butt's intervention so completely that it was as if Butt were not there. There was no acknowledgement of him, no engagement with his argument, no deference towards him as a leader; just an implacable, cold determination to pursue his own course. It was a calculated and decisive rebuff, a moment which broke the link between them. Parnell intended to follow his own instincts and his own policy, regardless of his critics.

After some moments, Butt raised himself to his feet and left the Chamber without a word, his authority over Parnell – and his party – broken. I hurried downstairs and caught up with him.

'Isaac.' My voice echoed in the stillness of the early morning hours in the deserted lobby.

Butt turned. 'Ah, Harrison,' he said. He came back to meet me. 'I can't reach him, Harrison,' he said, putting a hand on my shoulder. 'He's intent on ruining himself and the Party.' He looked at me. 'I had great hopes for Parnell ... I really did. I thought he would advance our cause; but I misjudged him.'

'Yes,' I stammered, 'but to criticise him in front of the House, without warning ...' I left my rebuke unfinished.

'I know, I know, Harrison,' said Butt wearily, 'but I did try to warn him.'

'But ... why on the floor of the House?' I asked.

'Disraeli has to know that this is not how we do our business. Can't you see that, Harrison?' Butt looked at me directly. 'But tell Parnell I am sorry it has come to this.'

I watched him walk away, shoulders hunched, head down; he had the look of a weary old man.

I went back to the gallery. Parnell was still on his feet, with Biggar and O'Donnell keeping him company on the benches beside him. The debate went on until after three o'clock in the morning, when the Government spokesman capitulated and said the remainder of the amendments would be dealt with on another day. Another bill had fallen.

Parnell's obstruction continued relentlessly after Easter, and the Government's bills continued to fall. The education bill was deferred, the prisons bill was withdrawn, the patents bill was abandoned; the mutiny bill and the taxation bills were fought over, section by section, sentence by sentence, phrase by phrase, comma by comma. Matters that should have taken one hour took eight; matters that should have taken one day took one week. The business of the House ground to a halt.

Parnell stood, day after day, night after night, arguing with successive Ministers on every single bill. His approach, however, was irreproachably subtle: he did not just engage in mindless obstruction or in reading out irrelevant reports; he actually appeared to want to improve every single bill presented to the House; he sought to consider its policy and structure, to probe and consider the wording and to suggest improvements. He was, in other words, playing the part of the perfectly conscientious Member of Parliament. Although it was clear he was doing this to obstruct the Commons, such a charge could not be made against him. If it were, he denied it and said, quite seriously, that all he was doing was trying to improve the legislation. He did add that, of course, if Ireland had its own parliament then he would concern himself with these matters in Dublin, without having to bother the House of Commons in London, but as the Government believed that his presence was necessary in London then of course he would do his duty. Biggar soon followed his lead and refined his tactics, but with less patience than Parnell, and there were occasions when Biggar simply took out the blunderbuss of an official report and began reading it aloud from start to finish.

Throughout those days and weeks and months our lives were lived upside down: we stayed up all night – and kept the House up all night – and we slept until lunch time. Lunch became breakfast, dinner became lunch and supper was rarely taken before midnight.

At this time, we took to joining Parnell at his rooms in Keppel Street for breakfast at one o'clock in the afternoon. Parnell had two rooms on the first landing: his bedroom, and a drawing-room with two large windows looking out onto the street. His housekeeper, Mrs Clarkson, was a large lady with a speciality in kippers and scrambled eggs. These attractions were too much for Biggar, who made a circuitous diversion from his home in Clapham Common to join us daily, stopping off en route to pick up the newspapers. Thus our lunchtime reviews continued – over breakfast!

The greater the invective in the newspapers, the more hilarious Biggar found it, and, with his contagious laughter, he blunted the barbs and diverted the arrows aimed at Parnell. Without this, Parnell, with his deep sensitivity and fierce pride, might have been wounded by the attacks on him, for they were vicious and merciless.

'Listen to this, Parnell.' Biggar began reading another article by Lucy.

'The new Member for Meath, Mr Charles Parnell, seems to have no redeeming qualities at all, unless we regard it as an advantage to have in the House a man who unites in his own person all the childish unreasonableness, all the suspiciousness and all the astounding credulity of the Irish peasant.' Biggar started to chortle. 'He's got you to a tee, Parnell,' he said, and then resumed. 'He is the least loveable of all the Irish members.'

Biggar raised an eyebrow.

'Apparently Lucy finds me even more loveable than you, Parnell. You should certainly be offended by that.'

He continued reading, his newspaper shaking as he laughed out loud.

'Whether Heaven has blessed Mr Parnell with a full measure of intelligence or ... blah, blah ... whether something material was omitted are interesting speculations ... – they're saying you've lost your wits, Parnell – Something really must be done about Mr Parnell ... About Mr Parnell there is not the faintest glimmer of humour.'

Biggar put aside his paper. 'I told you, Parnell, you're losing your audience. You really must put more effort into holding your audience spellbound – like I do. Why doesn't he write these nice things about me?'

It was hard not to laugh at Biggar's mock injured pride.

Summer passed slowly that year, lost to us in the great cavernous halls of the House of Commons. There was a heatwave in June which was particularly oppressive: the Chamber and the galleries were stuffy and airless, and the second debate on Home Rule took place during this time. Isaac Butt was ill and unable to attend and so his place was taken by William Shaw, who gave the speech of a bank manager. After all the obstruction of recent months, the House was not in any humour to entertain a debate on Home Rule. The atmosphere was hostile and Shaw almost apologised to the House for taking up their time. Our request for Home Rule was of course defeated by an even bigger majority. It seemed as if we were going backwards. Neither Parnell nor Biggar spoke; they were saving their voices for the fights ahead.

Curiously, I noticed Gladstone returning to the House at around this time. He had retired from Government the previous year, at the grand old age of sixty-eight, leaving the leadership of the Liberal party to Hartington. But he couldn't stay away; the Eastern question worried him and he thought it necessary – or so he said – to share these worries with the House of Commons. Even at his age, he still looked strong and purposeful, and he commanded the

House effortlessly whenever he spoke. But I noticed that he came into the House on many occasions just to watch Parnell. He took his seat quietly at the end of the Liberal benches and he listened carefully to Parnell's speeches – certainly until midnight. He never stayed beyond midnight. Doubtless he had had enough of late-night sessions in the House.

Twelve

A Motion to Suspend

BUT THE STORM was gathering, the anger of the Tories was increasing and it was inevitable that the House would seek to suspend Parnell. For most Members of Parliament, suspension was a dreadful punishment, not because of the length of the suspension – which was usually only a matter of days – but because it betokened a condemnation by all of a member's conduct, a statement that the member had fallen below the standards required of a gentleman. It was the ultimate sanction, and thus rarely used.

But these were fractious times and Parnell had worn out the patience of all the English members of the House. We heard rumours in the lobbies and threats in the tea-rooms that if Parnell did not stop his behaviour then the Government would move to have him suspended. Butt heard of these threats – indeed, he was approached directly by a Tory whip – and he was appalled. For Butt, a suspension would have been a deep dishonour, and he presumed Parnell would feel the same. But he was wrong. He tried to warn Parnell; he remonstrated with him, but Parnell was unmoved.

From the Strangers' Gallery, I watched every day as Parnell increased the temperature of the House, putting more wood on the fire with his constant interruptions. The Tories were stewing with discontent in their cauldron on the Government benches, and there was something almost comical in seeing Parnell taking the lid off the cauldron and stirring the concoction one more time with one more defiant interruption, one more baleful look, one more lengthy speech, made with contemptuous disregard for their precious conventions. The pot was boiling over.

So the move, when it came, was not unexpected. One Wednesday, in mid-July, on a hot, humid afternoon, when the Chamber was stifling and airless and Parnell was at his irritating best, I could see Northcote, on the Tory front bench, half-rising on a number of occasions as if he wanted to speak but had thought better of it, his colleagues behind, twitching with impatience and anger, tapping him on the shoulder, remonstrating with him, urging him to do something to rein in Parnell. Other Tories were shouting at Parnell to finish. But Parnell was unyielding, still on his feet, his hands clasped behind his back, complaining to the Speaker – without even a trace of irony – that he was unable to make his speech because his opponents were obstructing him and wasting the House's time. He even accused Members of Parliament of seeking to intimidate him, saying it had now become dangerous for him to speak in the House. The Speaker, conscious of Tory anger, intervened to warn him of unparliamentary language, whereupon Parnell shamelessly changed tack and said he meant to refer to intimidation of him by members of the press. For hours on end, Parnell continued his lengthy contribution, all the time insisting he was trying to shorten the debate.

It was one of these contributions which triggered the attempt to suspend him.

'As an Irishman, coming from a country which has experienced to the fullest extent the consequences of English cruelty and tyranny,' Parnell said, 'I feel a special satisfaction in preventing and thwarting the intentions of the Government on this bill.'

On hearing these words, the Tories howled again, and Northcote rose immediately as if he had been stung by a wasp. In his ponderous and meandering way, he demanded that Parnell's words be taken down, that he be tried in the House for contempt and that he be suspended. The Tories cheered him on: they wanted this Irish troublemaker expelled.

The Speaker intervened.

'What do you say, Mr Parnell, to Mr Northcote's charge?'

Parnell paused for a moment and looked across the Chamber at the hundreds of Tories staring angrily at him.

'I wonder, Mr Speaker,' he said, 'whether my friend, Mr Northcote, is entitled to bring this motion without proper notice. It is not on the order of business for the day.'

Biggar sniggered; how typical of Parnell to ask whether a motion to expel him was procedurally correct.

'It is in order, Mr Parnell,' intoned the Speaker. 'Have you any other further remarks?'

'Perhaps the words I used could be read back to me,' Parnell said calmly.

'Certainly,' the Speaker said. He must have hoped Parnell would retract what he said.

One of the registrars looked back through his shorthand notes of Parnell's last contribution.

'I feel a special satisfaction in preventing and thwarting the intentions of the Government on this bill ...' the registrar read out to a suddenly hushed House.

When the registrar had finished, Parnell paused and looked upwards as if he might be thinking about retracting his words.

'I thought I had used the word "interest" instead of "satisfaction",' he said, 'but the substance is certainly correct.'

Biggar's frame started shaking as he tried to suppress his laughter.

How the Tories howled. Many of them stood up and, waving their fists or order papers at Parnell, shouted at him to go home to Ireland.

The Speaker was on his feet immediately.

'Mr Parnell,' he said, 'I must ask you to withdraw from the House, as is required under the rules, whilst the House debates this motion for contempt.'

Parnell nodded, bowed and left the Chamber. He reappeared, within minutes, beside me in the gallery.

We watched over the next few hours as Northcote and other Members of Parliament debated Parnell's utter disregard for the forms and traditions of the House and contended that he should be suspended. A boil had been lanced and the pus oozing from the Tory benches was unsightly, as they vied with one another in the insults they levelled against him.

Biggar and others defended Parnell as best they could, but the decisive intervention came from a wholly unexpected quarter.

Joseph Chamberlain, Member of Parliament for Birmingham and a new light in the Liberal party, had sauntered back into the

Chamber and had watched the whole incident with a look of wry amusement. Just before the vote was taken, he intervened.

'Mr Speaker,' he said, 'I must ask – before we vote – that Mr Parnell's words be read out again. I am afraid I was not here when they were spoken.'

The Speaker acquiesced and nodded to the registrar.

'As an Irishman,' the registrar read out again, 'I feel a special satisfaction in preventing and thwarting the intentions of the Government on this bill.'

'But so do I,' said Chamberlain loudly, to the surprise of the Tories. 'That is my fervent wish as an opponent of this Government. Mr Parnell has said he wishes to thwart the *Government* and I agree with him. That is our role as Her Majesty's opposition. My friend, Sir Stafford Northcote, has been in Government so long that he forgets himself. If Mr Parnell had sought to thwart this *House*, he would be in breach of his privileges, but in seeking to thwart the *Government*, he is only fulfilling his duty and his conscience as an elected member. He cannot be suspended for that.'

Northcote went pale, as the strength of Chamberlain's point struck home. He appeared almost winded and could not think quickly enough to cover up his discomfiture. He had blundered into a mistaken assault upon Parnell and it could not be sustained.

After some moments, the Speaker said, 'Mr Chamberlain's point would appear to be well-founded, Mr Northcote.'

Northcote nodded and mumbled that the motion to suspend Parnell could be withdrawn.

The Speaker called on his Sergeant-at-Arms to tell Mr Parnell he could return to the Chamber. Although this was clearly audible to us in the gallery, Parnell stayed in his place until – watched by every Member of Parliament – the Sergeant-at-Arms came up and announced that he could return. Parnell rose from the gallery, walked back down the stairs and re-entered the Chamber. He walked back to his place, below the gangway, and, without even sitting down, or adverting to the scenes just witnessed, he resumed his speech exactly where he had left off.

'Mr Speaker, I was on section 24 of this bill and the purpose of my proposed amendment was …'

He spoke calmly, as if he had never been interrupted. He never acknowledged Chamberlain or even thanked him for his contribution.

The House fell into a sullen and angry silence. It had done its best to expel him and it had failed.

Thirteen

A Fight to the Death

BUT THE GREATEST battle of all lay ahead. In mid-July, the Government sought to unite all its colonies in South Africa into a confederation. It was the centrepiece of Disraeli's imperial foreign policy and was supported by the Liberals. In normal times, it should have gone through in about an hour, after speeches by the Colonial Secretary explaining its purpose and some perfunctory speeches in reply by the opposition. But these, as Northcote and Disraeli now realised, were not normal times. Northcote announced in the Commons that the House would stay up as long as was necessary to pass the bill and that relays of Ministers had been organised for that purpose. It was a signal to Parnell that battle would be joined.

Isaac Butt immediately summoned a meeting of all Home Rule Members of Parliament in a committee-room within the House. He was solemn.

'Gentlemen, I have spoken to the Government,' he said. 'They have made it clear that this is the Government's main priority for the remainder of this term and they don't want any opposition to it.' He looked slowly around the table. 'For my part, I believe this is an imperial matter and we should not stand in their way.'

Shaw was the first to respond. He was now in full agreement with Butt on all matters, particularly in response to the tactics of Biggar and Parnell.

'If the Government wants to reorganise South Africa, let it do so,' he said. 'What is it to us? It has nothing to do with Ireland.'

There were a number of 'Hear, hears' from around the room.

Parnell made no attempt to speak or to persuade.

Butt turned to Parnell eventually, after everyone else had spoken. 'Parnell, what do you say?'

'I said I would oppose every single measure this term and that is precisely what I shall do,' Parnell said stonily.

'But, Parnell,' implored Butt, 'what has this got to do with Ireland, with Home Rule?'

'It's disgraceful,' said King-Harman, glaring at Parnell. 'How can you possibly think you're helping our cause by this ... this stupid policy?'

'Disraeli will not grant us Home Rule, Butt,' Parnell replied. 'Not now. Not ever. He's not going to create an empire in India, annex South Africa and then grant us Home Rule. And I am not going to sit here and do nothing. I shall oppose this bill as I have opposed every other bill this term.'

'I think we should put the matter to a vote,' said Shaw suavely. 'Let's see what support Parnell has for his view.' It was a pre-arranged ploy.

Butt called for a show of hands.

'All those in favour of letting the bill go through,' said Butt. He turned to me. 'Harrison, will you do the honours?'

I counted over forty.

'All those against.'

I counted two: Parnell and Biggar.

'The Party is completely against you on this, Parnell,' said Butt, as if that were the end of the matter.

'I don't care if the whole country is against me,' said Parnell. 'Disraeli will have to take this bill through me, line by line.'

There was a taut silence in the room as the line between the factions was pulled to breaking point.

'Now, gentlemen, if you will excuse me,' said Parnell and, standing up, he left the meeting.

Butt let out a deep sigh.

'There's nothing more I can do, gentlemen,' he said, 'nothing at all.'

The meeting broke up and Biggar and I joined Parnell in the tea-rooms.

'We are a house divided,' said Biggar portentously, leaning back in his chair and drumming his fingers on his stomach, 'and a house divided against itself cannot stand.'

'This party needs to be broken,' said Parnell fiercely. 'Broken and remade.' He looked at Biggar. 'If we had twenty or thirty members committed to obstruction, think what we could achieve.'

'A good night's sleep, for a start!' Biggar exclaimed.

෨෨෨

Parnell's exploits were exciting some interest in Ireland and Fanny had written to him a few days earlier, to say that she would like to be present at some great debate which he was seeking to obstruct. Parnell suggested she come over at once and so Fanny came to London and sat with me in the Strangers' Gallery to watch the forthcoming debate.

In an afternoon in late July, Northcote introduced the South Africa bill onto the floor of the House. His Government, he said, was determined to force it through that very evening. There would be no adjournments and no delays.

The debate opened just after four o'clock and Northcote spoke for over an hour. Hartingdon, the Liberal leader, replied for about an hour. So it was just after six o'clock when Parnell rose to his feet.

His opening remarks were an attack on the whole principle of the bill. The creation of a confederation in South Africa was not in South Africa's interest, he said; it was only in England's interest, which was not in the least surprising, as England always acted only in its own interest and never in the interests of her colonies. This raised the temperature immediately. It was perhaps needlessly provocative, but Parnell wanted to provoke. There were loud cries from the Tories to Parnell to sit down, shut up, and go back to Ireland.

Fanny looked over at me, wide-eyed and startled at the venom and hatred directed at her brother.

Parnell continued, paying no heed; he knew, he said, that England always followed her own interests and trampled on those of her colonies, because he knew what England had done to Ireland over the last 700 years. This increased the temperature even further and it became increasingly difficult for him to speak, as the cries and roars from the Tory benches seemed to grow louder with every passing sentence. Parnell stopped speaking and waited for the tumult to subside.

'Order, order,' the Speaker said. He knew it would be a trying evening. 'Let the Honourable Member for Meath finish his remarks.'

Parnell thanked him for his courtesy and resumed. He began to analyse the bill, line by line, pointing out problems or inconsistencies. The Government tried to rush him, to force him into a vote at once, but Parnell was not going to allow any matter be put to a vote until he had finished his comments. He had not even finished his preliminary comments when the Speaker announced the break for dinner.

After dinner, at about nine o'clock, Parnell resumed the debate: he had over forty amendments to the first section of the bill alone. Hour after hour ticked away, and by one o'clock in the morning, the House had still not even passed the first section. I lost count of the number of amendments put down by Parnell, but each had to be spoken on by him, replied to by the Minister and then voted on. The Government whips had ensured a full turnout and in some cases the vote was over 200 to 6 or 7.

The anger from the Tories was palpable and real. It was clear they hated Parnell – there was no other word for it. I watched as he rose to speak; that very movement forced many of them to their feet, bellowing and roaring at him to sit down, their fat, red faces getting redder, the wattles under their chins wobbling like agitated turkeys in a farmyard. At times I actually wondered whether fisticuffs might break out – such was the level of fury. The central floor of the Commons divided Government from Opposition and afforded a measure of protection, but the Speaker, aware of the mounting sense of outrage, had primed his Sergeants-at-Arms to be vigilant. He did not want a violent scene – which he knew would be immortalised in Commons sketches and folklore – to happen on his watch. If matters got overly heated, the Speaker promptly adjourned the House for an hour, a tactic which suited Parnell perfectly.

᠅

During one of the recesses – at about two o'clock in the morning – I took Fanny downstairs to the lobby, where we met Parnell. We needed some air and we stepped outside to walk around Parliament Square. It was a balmy, windless night and the streets around

Westminster were completely deserted. Fanny walked between myself and Parnell, linking our arms. She was visibly upset.

'I had no idea, Charlie,' she said, 'that they hated you so much. I've been reading it in the papers in Ireland but they haven't given any idea of what it is really like. It's hateful.'

Parnell tried to reassure her.

'And there are so many of them and so few of you,' she said.

'But we have Biggar,' I said.

'Yes,' Parnell laughed. 'I don't know what I would do without Biggar. He just makes us laugh at everything and suddenly what's malicious becomes … well … just ridiculous.'

'And you have Mr Harrison,' said Fanny.

'Exactly,' said Parnell, smiling at me. 'A loyal friend.'

'And you have me,' added Fanny, hugging her brother tightly.

'You see,' said Parnell. 'I have an army.'

We walked on for some moments in silence.

'But they do seem to hate you more than Mr Biggar,' said Fanny.

Parnell mused about this for a few steps. 'They think I am a traitor to my class,' he said.

'How could that be?' cried Fanny.

'They are all landlords, Fanny,' he said. 'They feel I should be on their side, not calling for Home Rule and land reform.'

We had walked around Parliament Square several times by now, and Parnell thought he should go back in. It was a strange moment, in the middle of the night, to step out of the deserted streets of London and back into the crowded lobbies of the House, bustling with people; hundreds of Members of Parliament and journalists all mingled around, talking and gossiping under the hissing gas-lamps hung high on the walls.

As we walked through the lobbies, some people stared at Parnell as they would at a curiosity; others pointedly turned their backs and ignored him. I became aware of conversations ceasing and a tense silence taking hold as we crossed the lobby. Out of deference – perhaps to Fanny – no unpleasant comments were exchanged, and I took her upstairs again to the Strangers' Gallery, whilst Parnell disappeared into the corridor leading to the Chamber.

Fourteen

A Visitor from the Lords

W HEN WE RETURNED, the Government was in the process of changing its relay team and the third Minister of the evening took to the despatch box to deal with the never-ending series of amendments put down by the small band of Irish Members of Parliament. Now Biggar took the lead. His first contribution was to tell the weary Tories opposite him that he had been resting in the Commons library.

'I fell asleep in one of your armchairs there,' he said cheerfully. 'It was even more comfortable than my own bed. And I would recommend it to ye all. You look as if ye need it. Now I am like a giant refreshed, ready for a full day's labour.'

Even at that unsociable hour of the morning, Biggar's comparison of himself to a giant raised a laugh.

'And I understand,' he continued, 'that the morning ferries have landed in Liverpool and Holyhead, bringing reinforcements for us, so you will find, gentlemen, that we can go on for hours yet. As there are 600 Englishmen against six Irishmen, I would say the conditions are evenly matched. Let the games continue.'

At that hour, in the deep well of the night and in a chamber illuminated by gas-light, Biggar, short, stout, bearded and hunchbacked, must have looked like a goblin from the underworld to the patrician Tories opposite him. Happy in his work, delighted to tug the beard of the English lion, he revelled in his role as an obstructionist. He had no shortage of amendments to suggest, improvements to make, matters to criticise; I had given him some good reading material from the library – previous debates on South Africa, books on Africa generally – and I did think there was a real possibility that Biggar might read out an entire book on Africa to the House. But he was learning some of Parnell's skills, and he had refined his tactics so that it could be said – at a considerable stretch – that he was acting as a conscientious legislator, anxious to protect the well-being of a colony. But no matter what he did, it was bound to provoke a huge storm, and the ferocious winds of abuse from the Tory benches would have been enough to blow an ordinary man off course. But Biggar, stout-hearted as well as stout-statured, trimmed his sails to continue sailing through the very eye of the storm. It was great theatre and Fanny and I looked on in admiration. Whenever he stalled, Parnell handed him another volume, which provided him with a fresh impetus to keep going; whenever he said something noteworthy, Parnell and his supporters cried 'Hear, hear', and whenever he needed a seconder for his amendments four or five voices immediately cried out: 'I second that.'

But Fanny was right: although the abuse aimed at Biggar was as loud as that directed at Parnell, it did not seem to be so hateful; Biggar, of course, had got to know many of his opponents, and perhaps they liked him, or perhaps they were afraid of his retorts. For whilst Parnell absorbed all the insults and simply ignored them, Biggar not only heard them – he hurled them back to the sender with such an accumulation of muck and dirt that it often shut the heckler up entirely for the night.

I had noticed in the past that on occasion a Tory Member of Parliament might approach Parnell or Biggar, perhaps in the lobby or in the tea-rooms, ostensibly to talk in a friendly manner, to try to get to know them outside the Chamber. Biggar always welcomed these approaches and, as often as not, would share a whisky with his opponent in the Commons bar. But that was not Parnell's way; such approaches were met by a polite but frosty hauteur, a perfunctory response and a moving-on. He was not a man who made friends easily and in the hostile, febrile atmosphere of the Commons, it was as if he had already decided that as all Members of Parliament were political enemies, they would be personal enemies too. It was not that he disliked them; it was simply that they were foreign troops on the battlefield and he did not intend to fraternise with them. This aloofness might have increased their animosity towards him but, if so, he shrugged it off with indifference. He did not seek their friendship. Indeed, I think he was more comfortable with their enmity; it allowed him to see matters more clearly.

Fanny retired some hours later and, although I took numerous naps throughout the night, I stayed at my post. At about five o'clock in the morning, just before dawn, I was sitting in the gallery on my own when Disraeli came up the stairs. He was now Lord Beaconsfield and, as he had taken his seat in the House of Lords, he could no longer take a seat in the Commons. But he wanted to see for himself the progress of the debate. For some reason, I stood up when he appeared – perhaps out of respect for a great statesman, even if he was an opponent. He bowed courteously to me and took a seat close by. After watching the debate for some time, he turned to me.

'You are an associate of Mr Parnell, are you not?' He spoke in a quiet, gentle voice.

I replied that I was, that I was his secretary.

'He has caused quite a stir for a member who has only been with us for three sessions,' he murmured. 'Quite a stir.' He smiled at me in a benevolent manner and asked me my name.

'James Harrison, sir,' I said.

'Mr Harrison, I am Benjamin Disraeli,' he said.

'Yes, sir,' I stammered. 'I know.'

He smiled gently at me and looked over the rail of the public gallery to the Chamber below.

He had come, like a general, to the heights, to survey the battlefield. It was a curious spectacle. There were over 200 Members of Parliament on the Government benches, and only two or three on the Liberal benches, but the knot of three or four Irish members on the opposition benches was the group which barred the pass.

'Your Mr Parnell is remarkable,' he said, inclining his head to one side, 'remarkable.' He rose and slowly looked at the floor of the House one last time, before saying 'Good night, Mr Harrison' and beginning his stately descent down the stairs.

It was the one and only time I was in his presence and I was mesmerised. It was only then that I understood how he had captivated his party, his monarch and even his opponents.

꜠꜡

At the next break, I told Parnell about the apparition of Disraeli. Parnell was instantly curious.

'Was he angry?' he asked.

'Not in the slightest,' I said. 'On the contrary, he seemed to be admiring your resistance.'

'How typical of Disraeli,' said Parnell.

'Did you think he might be angry?' I asked.

'He was angry earlier in the session because he thought we were just a nuisance ...' said Parnell, 'but when he realised it was a strategy, he knew he had to respond accordingly. Now we both know what will happen.'

'How do you mean?' I asked, puzzled.

'He knows now that we are capable of wrecking the next parliamentary sessions as well. And he knows that to avoid that he will have to give us something. He will release some of the Fenians.'

'But he said categorically he wouldn't release any prisoners.'

'He will wriggle off that hook,' said Parnell.

'How do you know?'

'Because he has sent his message through you,' said Parnell, smiling.

I was mystified. 'But he didn't say anything.'

'He didn't have to,' said Parnell. 'He knows you are an associate of mine. Why did he appear at all? In the middle of the night! I'm sure you'll find a scene in one of his novels where an elderly statesman befriends a young associate of a political opponent. It appeals to the romantic in him.'

I had to admit that the subtlety of this exchange in high politics had completely passed me by. I told him I had never read such a scene in any of his novels. 'Maybe you're making too much of it,' I said.

'Maybe,' he smiled. 'But I don't think so. Disraeli is seeking an accommodation, a truce.'

꜠꜡

In the hours after dawn, it was Frank Hugh O'Donnell's turn to guard the ramparts. I listened as he bored the House for hours with his affected accent and his pompous, overblown oratorical style. He had a far greater estimation of his own skills and talents than was accorded him by others. He tried to win the admiration of the House for his colossal learning but, unhappily for him, his monocle, his dress and his vanity made him an irresistible target and he had a torrid few hours. He wanted to ride two horses simultaneously: to be an obstructionist and also to win the admiration of the House – but, as these horses were galloping in different directions, he fell off both. The only way to win the admiration of the House, as I found out later, was not to seek it in the first place.

As the attacks on O'Donnell intensified, he began to weaken and to get flustered. Instead of sticking to the plan agreed with Parnell, he began to concede ground, to withdraw pages of proposed amendments on the grounds that they had already been argued, and to go through the remaining sections of the bill with alarming rapidity. Biggar caught my eye and gestured to me to meet him downstairs.

'Go and get Parnell,' said Biggar urgently, 'this idiot O'Donnell is surrendering too quickly. I'll hold the bridge as best I can.'

I rushed out to the Westminster Hotel, where Parnell had gone for a nap, and woke him. Within moments, we were walking back to the House, and he strode straight back into the Chamber. I watched as he signalled to O'Donnell to sit down, that he would resume the debate. Parnell tried to recover some of the lost ground and to reintroduce the conceded amendments on later sections, but the Speaker ruled him out of order.

When the Speaker broke for breakfast at eight o'clock, Parnell excoriated O'Donnell in the tea-rooms in front of Biggar, O'Connor Power, myself and others.

'Was it too much to ask, O'Donnell,' – he spoke with barely suppressed fury – 'that you would simply continue with all the amendments we had agreed?'

'They were completely unsustainable, Parnell,' said O'Donnell haughtily.

'Of course they were sustainable,' said Parnell. 'If you weren't so spineless.'

O'Donnell glared at Parnell, pushed back his chair and left the table abruptly. It was a breach which was never repaired, the first breach between Parnell and one of his followers.

❦

At half-past nine the debates resumed, with Parnell speaking on further amendments. By this stage no one in the House was listening, except perhaps the new Minister – the fourth of the relay team. The rest of the members were exhausted, slumped in their seats, their eyes heavy with sleep as they nodded off, their chins resting on their chests; others shook themselves awake and forced themselves to listen afresh. After Parnell, T.P. O'Connor made a sturdy contribution which continued the debate until almost midday.

At midday, the Speaker adjourned for lunch until one o'clock. When the House reassembled, even more of the Tories had gone home to bed, whilst many Liberals had come in to view the proceedings. Gladstone was back, sitting on the Liberal benches, looking intently at Parnell.

But after lunch, it was clear that Parnell and Biggar were near the end of their amendments, and by two o'clock the last sections had been put to the House, the last divisions had been taken and the Speaker, with a weary knock of his gavel, declared the bill carried.

I had expected a great cheer of jubilation from the Tory benches, but it never came. Instead, there was a strange hush as the Minister gathered up his papers from the despatch box and joined the other Members of Parliament filing out of the Chamber. Parnell and Biggar and the others let them go, before leaving the Chamber themselves, and when I saw them get up, I stirred myself to join them.

I had just witnessed the longest debate ever held in the House of Commons, a debate for ever afterwards known as 'the Long Sitting'. It was, even by the history of the House of Commons, a remarkable event. The Government claimed victory because they had passed their bill – but, in truth, the battle was an extraordinary victory for Parnell and Biggar and their obstructionist tactics.

❦

The following evening I met Parnell and Biggar for supper. I had obtained a copy of the *Illustrated London News* and they were, as always, eager to read their reviews.

'Read it aloud, Harrison,' grunted Biggar, 'whilst I have my dinner. It should help to settle my stomach!'

I flattened the paper on my knee. 'The country,' I read, 'has watched this conflict with a deep sense of humiliation. It has witnessed with a feeling of shame, an attempt to destroy a system in which it took pride ...'

I looked up.

'What do you think of it so far?' I asked.

'I'd say we're making progress,' grunted Biggar.

Towards the end of this campaign, we procured a new recruit – John Dillon, who had been elected for Tipperary, a seat once held by his father, the noble Young Irelander, John Blake Dillon. Like his father, Dillon looked more Spanish than Irish, with dark skin, black hair and heavy-lidded, brown eyes. He was tall and excessively thin, almost emaciated, a condition caused no doubt by his decision to eat as little as possible to avoid the agonies caused to him by his digestive system. I had known Dillon since we were boys; he had lived near me on Fitzwilliam Square when we were growing up, and we had been schoolboys together at Dr Quinn's School in Harcourt Street. Our paths separated when we went to university as Dillon went to the Catholic University to read medicine, whilst I went to Trinity to read literature. Medicine was, I thought, an appropriate choice of career for Dillon, who could now diagnose all his own maladies; I had never met anyone stricken with so many illnesses as he. He suffered grievously – as he told me in gory medical detail on too many occasions – from ulcers, dyspepsia, hernias, and all other manner of ailments; he also had a weak chest – two of his sisters had died of consumption – and he not unnaturally had a fear of all such infections.

But, from the start, Dillon put his worries about ill-health aside; he was a revolutionary firebrand and immediately joined Parnell and his band of obstructives, which welcomed every new recruit, and he took an active part in the final debates on the South African bill.

Several days later, we were back in the Commons. The Government was introducing a prisons bill for Ireland and Parnell had tabled a number of amendments – all to improve conditions for prisoners. As he stood up to begin his speech, Hicks Beach rose to intervene.

'Mr Speaker, if I may,' he said, 'the Government has examined the amendments put forward by my Honourable Friend, Mr Parnell, and we feel, having considered them, that they will improve the legislation. We intend therefore to accept each of them as proposed.'

Parnell nodded curtly and sat down, silent and watchful as a leopard, and stared straight ahead. The bill was put to the House and agreed without a vote. It had taken just over ten minutes.

Biggar looked up and nodded for me to meet them outside.

'Did I just see a surrender?' asked Biggar.

Parnell gave us a wry smile – the first in many weeks.

'What else could you call it?' he asked.

Biggar let out a whoop of a cry and slapped his leg.

'So Disraeli has hoisted a white flag in the House after all,' he said. 'What will Butt say to us now?'

And so the Government's entire programme for that year had fallen, stopped by the will of one man. Parnell alone had stood in the pass and, when he did so, others joined him. His actions could not be ruled out of order by the Speaker; he was within his privileges as a member and could not be stopped; the fiction was clear to all, yet it could not be assailed. It was now evident to Disraeli, to the Tories, to the Liberals and to the English that the rules of engagement had changed. They could no longer rely on a supine Irish party. Seven men had blocked their way but, of those seven, the most obdurate, the most implacable, the most stern was Parnell. He had used as his weapons the very rules of procedure which were so admired by his opponents and, in so doing, he had become the most infamous, the most notorious, the most hated man in England.

Fifteen

A New Leader

SOME DAYS LATER, after the bill had passed, we returned to Dublin. The Home Rule League had called a public meeting at which Butt and Parnell would speak. Parnell stayed in Morrison's Hotel that night and I returned to my home in Fitzwilliam Square.

The next evening, I called on Parnell at Morrison's and we set out for the Rotunda. It was a dry, warm August evening and as we crossed the Carlisle Bridge, I saw, to my surprise, great crowds of people converging on Sackville Street from every direction, all walking towards the Rotunda. I had never seen such crowds at a Home Rule meeting in Dublin before. A group of men, stern-faced and purposeful, acting as stewards, ushered us through.

As we entered, I saw to my astonishment that the assembly hall was packed. Every seat was taken and people were standing two and three deep at the back and in the aisles. Even the gallery was overflowing; people were sitting on the balcony steps or standing at the back, craning forward for a better view.

As Butt and Parnell ascended the platform, I stood at the side of the hall, unable to move further, hemmed in by the surge of people pushing behind us, trying to get a glimpse of the speakers.

Butt spoke first. He was as passionate and eloquent as ever; he spoke of the success of the Home Rule Party and how the English would soon realise the earnest desire of the Irish people to obtain Home Rule. The crowd listened attentively and applauded politely.

Parnell then stood to address the crowd and, as he did so, the thousands of people in the hall rose, as one, to give him a huge ovation. The cheering and shouting and clapping and stamping of feet rippled like a wave from the back of the hall up to the platform, surged along the corridors and flowed onto the streets outside, where it washed over the crowds. Those outside took up the cheers and I could hear Parnell's name being chanted repeatedly, whilst inside shouts of 'Long live Parnell' and 'God save Parnell' echoed around the hall. It made the back of my neck tingle.

The applause and cheering must have lasted a full five minutes. Parnell stood, at the front of the platform, as stiff as stone, his hands as usual clenched behind his back, his face impassive and unsmiling. His eyes roved across the audience from one side of the hall to the other and back again. He did not speak and he did not smile. He stood, neither inciting the applause nor seeking to restrain it in any way; he just waited for it to die away. Eventually the crowd roared itself out and fell silent to listen to him. Parnell waited until the silence had taken hold.

'We have been engaged these last few months,' he began, 'in a struggle in Parliament.'

He paused.

'A struggle in Parliament on behalf of the Irish people.'

He paused again, holding the audience to his every word.

'But this English Parliament will not grant us Home Rule. They will not even engage with us on this debate.'

Men and women alike stared at him, scarcely daring to breathe, waiting for his next words. This was not the nervous silence of the speaker I had witnessed at the Rotunda only three years earlier, but the deliberate silence of a speaker controlling his audience. Was it really only three years earlier, in this assembly, that Parnell had stuttered and stammered his way through a few broken sentences about why he wished to represent them? It seemed scarcely believable.

'So we have now become engaged in a more *active* policy,' he said.

As he emphasised the word 'active', the crowd roared their approval and support. Parnell waited again until the cheers died away.

'A policy which tells Disraeli and the English Government that if they will not let us govern ourselves,' – he looked out defiantly at the crowds – 'then we will not let them govern themselves.'

He paused again.

'We will get nothing from England by conciliation,' he continued. 'We will get nothing from England unless we tread upon her toes. And I shall continue to tread upon her toes.'

More huge cheers greeted this declamation and, barely waiting for it to subside, Parnell continued.

'I hate the English and I care nothing for this English Parliament. I care nothing for its forms and traditions. And I care nothing for its outcry at our actions,' – he looked out over the crowds – 'when its very existence is a source of tyranny and destruction for our country.'

At this bold declaration of defiance, the crowds again erupted into further cheers, and everywhere I looked men and women were on their feet, clapping and shouting out their support for Parnell and his new policy of defiance.

On that bright August evening in Dublin, far from the hostility of the House of Commons and out of view of the relentless English press, I watched as the Irish people deserted Isaac Butt and turned to Parnell as their new champion. Whilst Butt looked on, disconsolate and troubled, Parnell looked out at the crowds, stern-faced and unsmiling. He accepted the applause, the support and the challenge. It was an unexpected event and it changed forever Parnell's perception of himself and, indeed, Ireland's perception of Parnell. Isaac Butt was still their leader, but Parnell was now the heir apparent. It was the first dividend of his obstructionist policy.

Part Two

Sixteen

Michael Davitt

BACK IN ENGLAND, Parnell's prediction that Disraeli would release Fenian prisoners proved correct. In early December, when Parliament was in recess and nobody was paying any attention, Disraeli released Michael Davitt from Dartmoor Prison and Biggar arranged for him to come to the House of Commons to meet Parnell.

Like Parnell, Davitt had been born in Ireland but, unlike Parnell, Davitt had been born into poverty, the son of a farm labourer in the West of Ireland. Like Parnell, Davitt had spent his formative years in England but, unlike Parnell, whose education took place in the private schools of Oxfordshire, Davitt received his education in the oppressive manufactories of the sooty, northern town of Lancaster. As a child of ten, Davitt had lost his right arm to a fearsome industrial machine, severed above the elbow. Unable to earn a living by manual labour, he had, thanks to the kindness of a postal clerk, learned to read and write and thus obtained the rudiments of a clerical education.

When they met in the House of Commons for the first time, Davitt was thirty-one years old, coincidentally the same age as Parnell. They both stood about six feet tall – or at least Davitt did once, but he had now a pronounced stoop. His suit – which may have fitted him when he entered prison – was now too large for his emaciated frame and his shirt collar hung loosely around his neck like that of an old man. His hair, originally black, was unkempt, thinning and streaked through with grey; his teeth were discoloured after seven years of malnutrition and his dark complexion had an unhealthy, waxen pallor. His whole physique seemed shrunken, like that of a man in his seventies, not in his thirties. The right arm of his jacket fell limply by his side and he extended his left arm to shake hands with Parnell.

'I wanted to thank you, Mr Parnell, for your efforts to release me,' he greeted Parnell solemnly, his accent a strange mixture of Mayo Irish and northern English.

'I'm glad you have survived your ordeal, Mr Davitt,' said Parnell. 'You must rest and recover your strength.'

'Aye. I will do that,' said Davitt, 'but I must go to Ireland soon.'

'What will you do?' enquired Parnell.

Davitt looked around at all of us. 'I want to journey around. I haven't seen Mayo since I was a boy and there are parts of Ireland I have never seen. So many places that are just names to me. Names and ideas in my head. And I've spent too long in prison for places I've never seen. I want to see the fields in the West of Ireland, the stone walls, the waves of the Atlantic.'

Despite his wretched physical condition, his demeanour seemed reflective, even pensive.

'Just don't do anything that will land you back in gaol, Davitt,' warned Biggar.

Davitt smiled wanly.

'I'm not sure I would survive it,' he said and, turning to all of us, he asked, 'Do you know the most difficult part of prison?'

'I wouldn't know where to start,' murmured Parnell.

'It was not knowing whether a single rifle I had sent back had ever been used against the English or whether they were all rusting in some bog,' said Davitt. 'I swore if I ever got out, my future efforts would not be so futile.'

'You have made your sacrifice, Davitt,' said Biggar portentously. 'You have earned your rest. No one expects any more of you.'

⁓⊷⊶⁓

Davitt's release goaded Parnell into action at the start of the parliamentary sessions in February. Disraeli may have released the prisoners, but that was now insufficient. Parnell interrupted the debate on the Queen's speech on numerous occasions, to serve notice to Disraeli that he would not be bought off so cheaply. Over the following weeks, having asked me to obtain statements from Davitt and any other Fenian prisoners I could find about their time spent in English gaols, Parnell read their testimonies into the record of the House of Commons. Disraeli and his Tories were forced to listen, silent and sullen, as the appalling conditions of the English prison system were exposed by Parnell. Any attempt to interrupt him was met by such a barely suppressed fury that most interlocutors thought better of it and let him finish. Disraeli could not afford to lose another parliamentary session, and within a month the Government set up a Royal Commission to investigate the prisons.

But if Parnell did not obstruct Parliament every evening, there was no doubt in any member's mind that he could, and would, if he deemed it necessary. These sessions were more cat and mouse than the tooth and claw of the previous year. But Parnell sensed that Disraeli was wearying of the constant battles, and matters came to a head again in June. When the Government set down its educational estimates, with no money for education in Ireland, Parnell signalled an all-out obstruction. Disraeli's response was immediate: he would bring in an Education Act for Ireland, establish an Irish Education Board and grant £1 million annually to Catholic schools in Ireland – the first ever measure of education for Catholic children in Ireland, and with significant monies to establish it.

To our astonishment, Isaac Butt tried to claim the credit. He had missed most of the term because of ill-health but he had been, he said, in active correspondence with the Government about the education bill. Perhaps he was; but he missed the point entirely. It was only when Parnell had signalled a resumption of war that Disraeli conceded. The rules of engagement between Disraeli and Parnell were never discussed between them, but were understood by both. When the education bill for Ireland had been announced, Parnell stood aside and allowed Disraeli to complete his legislative programme for the rest of the session.

One evening that session, when I arrived in the Commons, Biggar hailed me in the lobby and introduced me to Tim Healy – whom he, apparently, already knew quite well.

'Harrison, I want you to show Healy the ropes. He's taking up residence here as a reporter for *The Nation*.' Biggar boomed it out as if announcing Healy's arrival to the entire House of Commons, rather than effecting a simple introduction. He seemed oblivious to the staring passers-by – as, indeed, did Healy.

'Harrison here is an old hand already,' said Biggar, 'what's this, your third session?'

I nodded.

'I've read many of your articles, Harrison,' said Healy, shaking my hand. 'They're finely written.'

Healy was younger than I, then in his early twenties. He was of medium height but frail in build, with short cropped hair, a sharp nose, a beard and eye-glasses. He had a serious demeanour, with the intensity and fervour of a revolutionary. *The Nation* was a fine newspaper owned by his uncle, Alexander Sullivan and, from that day on, Healy became a member of our inner circle.

As we stood talking, Parnell came over to us and Biggar introduced Healy to him. Parnell welcomed him to the House and Healy shook his hand vigorously up and down, as if it were a water pump.

'Are you free to join us for dinner later on?' asked Parnell graciously.

'I certainly am. I certainly am,' beamed Healy. 'Thank you very much indeed, Mr Parnell. I'd be honoured to join you.'

Parnell nodded to us and disappeared, and Healy and I went up to the Strangers' Gallery which, as usual, was almost deserted.

'So how long have you been working for Mr Parnell?' said Healy. He had a musical, singsong Cork accent, which in England sounded like the voice of an old friend. Beleaguered as we were, every Irish accent was welcome.

I told him, briefly, of the events of the last few years.

'I am sorry I missed the last session,' he said. 'I read as much as I could about it. By God, Parnell had them on the run; by God, he did.'

He had a jerkiness in his speech and a constant twitching in his movements, which betokened a nervous and excitable temperament.

As we waited for the debate to start, his legs kept moving in a
nervous jiggle and he fidgeted constantly with his paper and pen. But
when the debate started he quietened down and became absorbed
in taking his notes. We watched as Parnell took the floor for hours
on end to delay some measure or other. Healy put aside his pen and,
leaning forward on the rail, listened raptly to Parnell's words. When
he had finished, Healy turned to me.

'Will you look at Parnell?' he said. 'He has no fear of them at
all. He is like a spike. We must hammer him into the British, so we
must.'

Healy may have been a novice, but he was a natural polemicist,
and over the coming months his articles for *The Nation* were vivid
and partisan. He recounted all the obstructionist episodes of that
session, with such relish for Parnell and such disdain for Isaac
Butt that he did much to increase Parnell's popular acclaim and
to reduce Butt's standing throughout Ireland at that time. Indeed,
Healy became utterly captivated by Parnell, by the strange enigma
of Parnell's aloof personality and by the extraordinary resolution
with which he confronted a hostile House of Commons.

During these months, I continued to write occasional articles for
Justin McCarthy and the *Daily News*. Fortuitously, at this time, I
was also asked to cover the Law Courts for the newspaper and, as
I watched the trials, I became increasingly fascinated by the arcane
processes and dignified rituals of the law, and I began to consider
whether I might read for the Bar myself. When I mentioned it to
McCarthy, his response was emphatic.

'You must do it tomorrow,' he said excitedly. 'Join an Inn of
Court immediately. Don't think about it for one moment. You are
young. You have the energy and you have the time. It is my greatest
regret that I never did it.'

His encouragement and enthusiasm were irresistible, and within
weeks I was accepted into the Middle Temple as a student. I had
written to my adoptive father to tell him what I proposed and he
had replied by return expressing his full support, insisting that he
would discharge all my fees, that he had saved for them for many

years in the hope and expectation that I might do medicine as he had, but that he was almost as delighted that I had decided upon the law. In truth, the course of studies was not demanding, and the following summer I was called to the English Bar.

As the year ended, Parnell seemed to be biding his time. What his next step might be was unclear to me, and, I believe, to him. But if there was no decision to be made, he never sought to make one. He bided his time until the situation evolved.

But, as it happened, the laws of nature intervened, and the fateful year of 1879 became the hinge on which the door to land agitation and land reform suddenly opened.

Seventeen

The Spectre of the Famine

A S THE YEAR turned, a rainy autumn drifted into a mild and rainy winter and then into a warm but rainy spring. As the rains continued to fall, tenant farmers looked anxiously to the skies for relief, rather than to Westminster. The poor harvest of 1877 had been followed by a dreadful harvest in 1878, and now there would be a disastrous harvest in 1879. The arable crops, so vital for paying the rent, rotted in the waterlogged fields; the potato crop, so vital for sustenance, which was grown higher on the hillsides where the water ran off but where the soil was poorer, was hardier, but even it could not survive the wet, warm, humid weather, and late in spring the blight appeared again in the West of Ireland – for the first time in three decades.

The memories of the Great Famine flooded back to labourers and tenant farmers all over Ireland. Every man and woman over the age of thirty-five could remember the horrors and privations of that time, and those of us younger than them had heard the stories so often that we scarcely believed such things could have been allowed to happen in Ireland so recently. We all assumed it could not happen again.

But why not? Thirty years later, nothing had changed. The Irish peasant was still as dependent on the potato as he had been; the Irish people were still manacled to the rack of the land and the landlords still stretched them year upon year; the English Government still looked away, more consumed by what was happening in Constantinople and Delhi than in Clare and Donegal.

This combination of bad harvests and the potato blight led quickly to a state of dire distress in many counties in Ireland, but particularly in the West, where conditions were worst. Month by month, as the harvests failed, the tenants struggled to pay the rents and keep their homes. As each gale day passed and rents were not paid, families were evicted and scattered like chaff all over the country.

With each eviction, it became increasingly difficult for a man to keep his family together; if he were lucky, his daughters might be taken in by relatives and his wife might return to her family, whilst he and his sons roamed the countryside searching for work, begging for food, sleeping under hedges and rocks to shelter them against the cold of the night. Dispossessed and vengeful, many engaged in puny acts of violence against their landlords, burning barns and maiming cattle. This, in turn, led English landlords – many of whom had seats in the Commons and Lords – to demand new coercion measures for Ireland, suffocating political life even more. The baleful, relentless mill-wheel of Irish history was about to turn once again.

In Ireland, the sense of anger and fear was increasing week by week and required only a spark to ignite it.

Canon Geoffrey Burke, the unlikely spark, was a Catholic parish priest in Irishtown, a small village in County Mayo. On his brother's death, the Canon inherited his estate and, when he came into his inheritance, the Canon found all his tenants in arrears, due to the poor harvest and the high rents. He could have reduced the rents in a Christian manner, but he chose not to do so and instead served eviction notices on all his tenants. It was an act of incredible avarice – even by clerical standards – but the Church looked away, more interested in the sanctity of contracts than the injustice of evictions.

News of the plight of Canon Burke's tenants came to Davitt's attention within days and Davitt's response was to call a public meeting in Irishtown to protest at these evictions. Davitt wrote to Parnell for his support, and Parnell asked me to attend and to report back to him.

I took an early morning train to Westport and then took a horse to ride out to Irishtown. As I rode out into the countryside,

I passed a procession of people walking towards Westport, seeking sanctuary and food in the town. They all looked wretchedly thin, almost emaciated; dressed – covered would be a more appropriate word – in rags, falling to pieces on their backs; their hair unkempt; bedraggled and drenched by the rain. Some of the women tried to cover their heads and those of their huddled children with sodden woollen shawls. It was like a journey through a far-off biblical land, a land smitten by God.

As I passed through the villages, I could see that no one had escaped the ravages brought on by the failure of the harvests. There was no laughter here. There were no cries of young children at play, no chatter of women as they went about their chores or men's banter as they worked in the fields. There were no greetings for a stranger. I slowed my horse to a walking pace but the people looked at me sullenly and suspiciously. I must have looked like an overlord to them. I was most powerfully struck by the strange and disquieting silence; it seemed to pervade the landscape like a fog. The people were bereft of energy, almost of spirit. Conditions here were so much worse than on the east coast that they might as well have been two different countries. There was no starvation at Avondale, but here starvation was imminent. Another bad harvest, with no food and no means to pay the rent, and thousands more families would be evicted. And after eviction, death would be a certain end as surely as night follows day. I was truly shocked to see our people in such conditions.

Then, suddenly and inexplicably, as I gazed upon these people I became aware of a presence. At first it was just a sense. A sense that someone was looking at me. I looked around, but the procession which passed alongside all had their heads down, trudging along the muddy roads. I dismounted my horse and watched for a time.

Then I realised what my presentiment was. It was my own mother. She too had made this terrible journey many years ago. She too had walked for miles looking for food, carrying me, her new-born baby, with her. But it was all in vain. I was told – years later – that she had collapsed and died in a ditch on the outskirts of Westport in May or June in the fourth year of the Great Famine. I was found beside her on the side of the road by a local Church of Ireland clergyman. My cries had alerted him, but by the time he came to our aid my mother had already died of starvation and exhaustion. It was, I was told, a miracle that I had survived at all, but the weather had been dry and warm; had it been winter I would have perished beside her. My mother had died far from her home, her family and her parish and no one in the town knew of her or anything about her. No one even knew her name. Given the times, she was taken away in a cart and buried in a pauper's grave. I had tried many times but I had never been able to find her. Until now.

I felt her spirit within me and I looked directly at every face that passed by as if somehow I might stumble across some person who might be a relative, who might recognise my mother's likeness in me. But there was no such recognition.

I knew then why I had been spared. I had been spared to remember; I had been spared, if not to avenge her death, then to ensure, if at all within my power, that such things could never happen again. This, I vowed, would now be my purpose.

With tears in my eyes, I rode on towards Irishtown.

Irishtown was set at a crossroads, on low ground surrounded by hills. The small hovels of the village huddled together for company and, on the outskirts of the village, but set apart from it, was the church, made from solid, grey cut stone. Across from the church was the parish priest's house, the only two-storey house in the village, also made from the same grey cut stone. Further thatched cottages could be glimpsed in all directions outside the village, clumped together in twos and threes. I doubt if the population of the village was more than a hundred souls. But on this Sunday in April, as I rode towards it, it seemed as if upwards of 3,000 people were congregating at the crossroads.

I had never seen such a gathering. Every tenant farmer in Mayo and all his sons must have been there. There even appeared to be what I could only describe as a cavalry squadron of about 100 men on horseback; and for every man on horseback, there were another four men on the ground, keeping order. There was an organising and directing hand, but it was not apparent whose it was. As I approached the church gate, I greeted John O'Connor Power, the Member of Parliament for Mayo, whom I knew from our evenings in Westminster.

The crowd had converged on Irishtown, as arranged, just after midday, and waited quietly outside the church as Canon Burke celebrated twelve o'clock mass inside. I could hear the tinkle of the altar boys' bells at the consecration, the communion and again at the Final Procession. The massgoers emerged from the church, saw the crowds, dipped their fingers in the holy water font, blessed themselves and slipped away. They had known of this gathering for days.

Moments later, Canon Burke, having divested himself of his vestments, emerged from the sacristy door at the side of the church. He was a thin, wiry man, small in stature, with wisps of grey hair. His astonishment was evident as he looked around at the thousands of people who now surrounded his church. He walked slowly to the church gate, where his path was blocked.

'Good morning, Canon.' O'Connor Power boomed out his greeting.

'What's the meaning of all this?' asked the Canon. 'Who are you?'

'I am John O'Connor Power, the Member of Parliament for Mayo.'

'Who are all these people, Mr Power?' said the Canon nervously.

'All will be revealed, Canon,' said O'Connor Power. 'In the fullness of time. For the moment you might just listen to my few words.'

As the Canon was effectively imprisoned in his own churchyard, he had little choice. O'Connor Power clambered clumsily onto a stone wall nearby and addressed the crowd. A large, ungainly man with a pockmarked face, O'Connor Power was nevertheless a fine speaker, and he gave a fiery speech. It started with a fiery denunciation of Disraeli and Lowther, his Irish Secretary; it moved onto a fiery denunciation of landlords, especially rackrent landlords; and it settled on a fiery denunciation of clerical landlords, especially rackrent clerical landlords, of whom Canon Burke was the leading exemplar. The crowd listened to the speech in silence, but when Burke's name was mentioned they broke into such a loud chorus of boos that it must have been heard in the adjoining parishes. The miserable Canon stood with his head bowed, but I felt no sympathy for him. He deserved his comeuppance.

'So, Canon,' O'Connor Power turned to him, 'you have been exposed as a rackrenter, not only before your own parishioners but before all these people. Your name will be infamous tomorrow and forever afterwards, not just all over the county, but all over the country.'

'What do you want me to do?' the Canon asked, mortified by the exposure.

'So, to atone for your sins, I have a document here, which I would like you to sign,' said O'Connor Power.

The Canon looked up, fearfully.

'It's a legal document, Canon,' said O'Connor Power. 'Drafted by the finest legal minds in Connaught. It will pass muster in any courtroom.'

'What does ...?' – the Canon's voice cracked under the strain – 'What does it say?'

'It says,' boomed O'Connor Power, 'that you hereby agree to reduce the rent of all your tenants by thirty per cent and that you hereby agree to waive all the arrears of rent which have accumulated to date.'

'Have I any choice?' asked the Canon.

'None whatsoever, Father,' beamed O'Connor Power. 'Just sign here.' He thrust the document towards the priest.

The prelate stepped forward to take it from his hands and, leaning on a gravestone in the churchyard, he signed his name to the document with a trembling hand.

'Thank you, Father,' said O'Connor Power, taking the document back. 'Now, Father, you see, not only do you have the power to remit sins, you also have the power to remit arrears of rent – for both of which you will be well rewarded in the afterlife.'

O'Connor Power turned to the crowd and, with a flourish, waved the signed document above his head.

There was a great cheer and then the organisers moved in. The crowd disappeared back along the four roads, as quickly and as noiselessly as they had appeared. The only sign of their presence was the churned-up grassy verges of the roadside, where the horses' hooves had sunk into the soft earth.

Later that evening I returned to Avondale and reported on these events and conditions to Parnell.

'I saw scenes today that I thought I would never see,' I said, 'of people beyond despair, on the verge of starvation. The wretched of this earth.'

I must have spoken with more feverish passion than was my wont, because Parnell looked at me in a curious manner. He stood up and poured me a large brandy. I downed it in one gulp and he poured one for himself.

'I shall have to see for myself,' he said.

Eighteen

The Death of Isaac Butt

S EVERAL DAYS LATER, back in London for the next session of Parliament, we dined with Davitt and Biggar at Mario's restaurant in Covent Garden. Mario, despite having arrived from Naples over ten years earlier, still spoke little English. But Italian, Biggar assured us, was the universal language of food, and communication was never a problem. Biggar had been one of Mario's regulars for the last five years and there had grown up between both men an easy familiarity. They were both of similar height and girth, and greeted each other with much handshaking and back-slapping and laughing and utter incomprehension.

Davitt, however, was intense and fidgety over dinner. He had asked to meet with Parnell, and he had no time for niceties or helping Biggar with his choice of dish. He wanted to tell Parnell about what was happening in the West.

'Another failed harvest and there will be famine,' he said. 'I cannot believe it could happen again.'

The table fell quiet and we all listened intensely to him.

'I remember it when I was a boy – the constant hunger, prowling around fields looking for a loose turnip or the root of a carrot which might have been missed – anything to fill my stomach. I never thought I would see it again in my lifetime.'

He leaned forward. 'We need you to get involved with us, Parnell. The people need your leadership, your resolve. They will follow you. I can organise them but I cannot lead them.'

Parnell was uncommitted. 'I can't do everything, Davitt,' he said calmly. 'I can't be in Westminster and also in the West.'

'The Fenians will organise it.' Davitt was forceful. 'Like they organised Irishtown – a military operation. Tell him, Harrison.'

I nodded my assent.

'A cavalry squadron. Yes, I heard.' Parnell smiled.

Davitt gave a rueful look.

'Farmers on plough horses, no more,' he said, 'but it gives them back their pride.'

'How many Fenians are involved?' asked Parnell.

'A couple of hundred, maybe,' said Davitt. 'If anything has to be done, they are the first to volunteer. They want to get involved in this ... this agitation, this land war ...'

Parnell considered the phrase, which he had not heard before.

'We cannot, we will not, stand by and let the English evict us from our homes again,' said Davitt. 'The people are fearful. Very fearful. But your speeches in the Commons have transformed the country. People see you poking Disraeli in the eye. It's giving them courage.'

'I don't want to lead a Fenian movement,' said Parnell firmly, 'they will take it over and turn it into a rebellion.'

'They won't,' said Davitt solemnly. 'I promise you that. We will not use arms. We will urge the people not to use arms. We will not advocate rebellion.'

'What about Butt?' asked Parnell. 'Have you asked him?'

Biggar sighed. 'I saw him last week and he looked very unwell. He doesn't have the energy to lead the Party now. But even if he had, we wouldn't ask him.'

There was a silence.

'Listen, Parnell,' said Biggar. 'You can't remember the Famine. You were barely even born. I tell you, if I didn't see it with my own eyes I would never have thought it possible. People dying everywhere – on the side of the road, in their homes, in ditches, in towns. Carts piled high with bodies, buried in paupers' graves. A million dead. You couldn't believe it was happening. And what did the English do? Nothing.'

I dropped my head in anguish.

Biggar shook his head. 'You know, Parnell, there are many people who remember that as though it were yesterday, and we have sworn it will never, ever happen again.' He banged a fist down on the table, causing the plates to rattle. A number of diners at the nearby tables looked over, but Biggar was oblivious.

'Now here we are again,' continued Biggar, 'on the brink of another famine. People won't go quietly this time. They will die in their homes rather than die in a ditch.'

He leaned back in his chair, but a moment later he lurched forward again, hitting the table and almost overturning the red candle in the bottle. 'I'm telling you, Parnell, it's a powder keg in that part of the country. Go and see for yourself.'

∽∾

Parnell did exactly that. Over the following weeks he and I travelled throughout the West of Ireland. Like me, he was scarcely able to believe what he witnessed: the squalor, the starvation, the poverty and distress; families thrown out of their homes, living on the roadside, or on beaches under currachs, or within the walls of long-deserted castles; the haunted looks of men who had lost everything and had nowhere to turn; the distress of women and children with not enough to eat, roaming the streets of towns, scavenging on scraps.

I could sense the anger building inside him. He wanted to know how such things could happen; how could they be allowed to happen? How could landlords treat their tenants in such a manner? How could the Government look on and do nothing? But his anger found no outward expression: there were no rages, no fulminations. He now began to think how such a state of affairs could be undone. How must it be remedied?

For weeks, Parnell pondered the issue with a ferocious intensity. During conversation, he would often drift off, lost in his thoughts; at dinner, he would remain quiet throughout, moving food around his plate, barely eating anything at all. It reminded me of the time several years earlier when he had studied the House of Commons. From his occasional comments, I could follow his train of thought. Obstructionism – although successful – could not be carried on forever. But a land agitation organised by Fenians would be captured by Fenians and dragged in a direction he did not want to go – a path of violence and armed rebellion. Yet it could be the great popular movement which the Party sorely needed; and, if he could control the Fenians, if he could force their energies down parliamentary channels, who knew what benefits might accrue to the country?

Some weeks later, in mid-May, Isaac Butt died from a heart failure. He had been unwell for a long time and he had been absent from the House of Commons all year. He died a peaceful death at his home, his wife and family beside him to the end. I was saddened by his death; I was fond of him and he always treated me with great kindness. Parnell, too, despite their differences, remembered Butt as a family friend and as a mentor who had helped him in his early days. Unhappily, the rift between them was never healed, but I am not sure it could ever have been – even if Butt had lived another five years. Butt believed we only had to make a reasonable case, which English Members of Parliament, as reasonable men, would understand, and we would gain Home Rule; Parnell grasped the truth of the matter: that the House of Commons did not consist of reasonable men but of men of privilege and wealth. Arguments had to be won not by reason but by power.

In truth, Butt died when his role was complete. The future belonged to Parnell, whether Butt lived or died. But he was a good man and, were it not for his debts and overwork, he might have achieved more. Butt's death did raise the question of the leadership of the Party, but Parnell did not contest it and William Shaw was elected leader for the following year.

Nineteen

Westport

BY THE TIME of Isaac Butt's death, Parnell had made up his mind: he would lead the land agitation. He wrote to Davitt that he would speak at Westport on Sunday 8th June at a meeting which Davitt was already organising.

But the day before the Westport meeting, whilst still in Dublin, I read with dismay an article in the *Freeman's Journal* in which Archbishop McHale warned the people against attending the meeting. I went in search of Parnell immediately. I found him in the reading-room of Morrison's, engrossed in a scientific journal. Sometimes I think he only stayed in Morrison's because of its subscriptions to so many scientific periodicals. He always read one in preference to a newspaper.

When I got his attention, I read out those parts of the article by the Archbishop warning people against attending the Westport meeting, organised as it was by 'a few designing men' acting together in 'unhallowed combinations', seeking to bring about 'impiety and disorder in Church and Society'.

Parnell shrugged it off. 'It doesn't refer to me,' he said.

'It's not finished.' I continued to read. 'Certain Members of Parliament have unwittingly consented to attend to lend their support to this group and they should be warned that this will not do.'

'I have said I will go,' said Parnell, and went back to reading his journal.

'You are not going to ignore the Archbishop?' I asked in surprise.

Parnell did not even deign to reply.

An hour or so later, Michael Davitt unexpectedly appeared at the hotel in a state of some agitation, and soaked through. It was another downpour of a day.

'Parnell!' said Davitt. 'I came as quickly as I could.'

'What's happened?' Parnell was alarmed at Davitt's obvious agitation.

'The Archbishop has denounced the meeting in the papers. And I heard he also denounced it from the pulpit at mass this morning,' said Davitt.

'Oh, yes.' Parnell was unconcerned. 'Harrison read it out to me earlier.'

'It's always the same with the Church,' said Davitt angrily. 'Their spies tell them Fenians are involved. So they condemn our meetings. But, Charles, we have told everyone that you are going to come. If you withdraw now ...'

'I'm not going to withdraw,' said Parnell sharply.

Davitt was taken aback. 'But Archbishop McHale ...?'

'I told you I would speak at Westport tomorrow and that is exactly what I shall do,' Parnell said haughtily.

Davitt let out a huge sigh of relief.

'You are a brave man,' he said.

Parnell ignored the comment. 'More important than the Archbishop,' he continued, 'we must agree that whatever we do now must solve this land question once and for all. The time for half measures is over.'

'What do you mean – half measures?' Davitt was mystified.

'Butt's demand, the Party's demand, for a fair rent, free sale, etcetera, etcetera,' said Parnell.

'But Disraeli has refused all of these,' I said.

'Precisely,' said Parnell, 'so the time has come to increase the demand.'

Davitt and I looked at Parnell as if he had failed to grasp the realities of the situation.

'If you can't get these demands through, what on earth makes you think Disraeli will give in to the larger demand?' I asked.

'If obstructing Disraeli has taught me one lesson,' said Parnell, 'it is that to achieve anything, we have to create such a problem that he cannot ignore us. If we hurt those around him, they will force his hand.'

'So what do you suggest?' I asked.

'The root of the problem is that the peasants who till the land don't own their land. The landlord does,' said Parnell.

He got up and paced the room, head down, hands clasped behind his back.

'And if that is the problem, then we have to rid ourselves of landlords once and for all,' he said. 'And to rid ourselves of landlords, we need to transfer the land from the landlords to the people.'

He spoke as if he were setting out the proofs of a mathematical theorem.

'And just how do you propose to do that?' I asked.

'Well, there are two options,' he said. 'Either we have a full revolution as they did in France, behead all the landlords – God knows it is long overdue – and confiscate their lands, or we force them to sell the land to the tenants at a fair price.'

After a moment, perhaps sensing our incredulity, he stopped his pacing and glanced over at us.

'And, as we are unlikely to succeed with a revolution, then we must force them to sell. There is no other option.'

'There is no other option' – the same words he had used before setting out on the obstructionist path. He had come to the conclusion of the theorem and he accepted its logic.

'They make too much money from their tenants,' he continued, 'so we must ensure that that stops. We have to ensure that life is made so uncomfortable for the landlords that they want to sell.'

'Parnell, that is just not practical!' I said. 'Where would a tenant get money to buy his land when he can't even get the money to pay his rent?'

'No, that is not the issue,' said Parnell. 'The Government could lend them the money to buy out the land and they could repay it over twenty or thirty years. That part is simple. The greater problem is to destroy the enemy's will. To destroy the landlords' will, to bring them to a point where they want to sell. That is the battle.'

We listened in silence as Parnell set out his plan, pacing backwards and forwards in the room.

'On this, we have been fighting the wrong enemy on the wrong battlefield. We will fight this battle in Ireland – not in the House of Commons – but in every home, in every village, in every town throughout the country. The tenants' homes will be their battlefields and the landlords will be the enemy. Not Disraeli. We must stand up to these landlords, like the bullies that they are. We must break their spirit so that they will want to leave.'

He stopped and looked directly at Davitt.

'So, Davitt, if you really want to start a land war, then we fire the first shots tomorrow.'

The following day, as the train pulled in to Westport station, we heard – long before we saw – a large brass band playing on the platform. Parnell was greeted by Davitt, his organising committee and a huge crowd. We walked the short distance from the station to the town square, where a wooden platform with a wooden rail had been erected. As the street opened onto the square, I stared in disbelief at the size of the crowds; there must have been at least 30,000 people there, in a sea of green banners and green flags; just as at Irishtown, a contingent of 'cavalry' and stewards lined the square and the main street, keeping order. This was by far the largest gathering Parnell had ever addressed. If he was nervous – which he always was – it was contained within him, hidden from view, only evident in his hands, clutched tightly behind his back.

Davitt spoke first, a lengthy disquisition on the pernicious evils of landlordism, the urgency of a peasant proprietary and the need for collective action. Davitt was never a great speaker; he never sought to communicate with his crowds but to lecture to them. His speech was full of worthy phrases such as 'inalienable' and 'hereditary', which went completely over their heads.

Then it was Parnell's turn to speak. He moved to the front of the platform and gripped the rail tightly with both hands.

'I am glad to be here today.' His voice rang out clearly across the square. 'I only heard yesterday that the Archbishop wanted me to stay away. But I had given my word to you that I would be here and I am sure that the Archbishop would not wish me to dishonour myself by breaking my word to this meeting.'

There were huge roars of support for this declaration of defiance towards the Church. Parnell then resumed.

'For years, we have asked the English to reform the land laws,' he said, 'and for years they have refused. We have asked them for a fair rent and they have refused. We have asked for the right of free sale and they have refused. We have asked for fixity of tenure. They refused that too.'

Parnell paused and gripped the rail even more firmly, until his knuckles showed white. There was no sound in the square save for the wheezing of horses, the comforting metallic sounds of bridles and the fluttering of banners and flags.

'Very well,' he continued. 'The English have had their chance. They have had many, many years to give us what we asked for. Well, we are not asking anymore. We are now demanding.'

He looked out on the huge crowd.

'We demand our land back. We demand the land of Ireland for the people of Ireland. We shall not settle for anything less.'

The crowd erupted into roars and cheers of support.

'I would be deceiving you today,' Parnell continued, 'if I told you that you should rely on the exertions of the Irish Members of Parliament, because if your Members of Parliament were determined and resolute, they would help you. But they are not. And they will not help you. You must rely on yourselves alone. You must act together. And if you stay together I will not desert you.'

I looked out at the thousands of people staring up at Parnell, their attention riveted on him, their hopes etched on their strained faces.

'We live in bad times,' he continued. 'You live in bad times. The harvest has failed for each of the last two years, and it looks as if it will now fail for a third year. And yet the landlords demand the same rent as in better times.'

Parnell looked down, as if considering his next words.

'So what must you do?' Parnell paused, allowing the question to fill the square.

'You must go to your landlord and offer to pay a fair rent,' he said. 'Now you ask: what is a fair rent? It is a rent that you can reasonably pay according to the times. And if the landlord

refuses to accept this, then ask him to appoint a mediator, to see
if the rent can be agreed between you. And if he will not do this,
then you must withhold the rent altogether, until he comes to a
reasonable view.'

Huge cheers greeted this proposal also.

'But,' continued Parnell, his voice beginning to rise in anger, 'this
much is clear. If the existing rents are insisted upon by the landlords,
then there will – eventually – be a repetition of the terrible scenes of
1847 and 1848.'

He looked around the square.

'And you must not allow yourselves to be dispossessed as you
were dispossessed in '47.' He stopped again, to allow the full
horror of this memory to flood back to those old enough to have
experienced it.

His voice rang out around the square.

'You must show your landlord that you intend to keep a firm grip
on your homesteads.'

On hearing this last phrase, the crowd erupted into a frenzy of
sustained cheering and shouting. I could see it in their faces: he had
lit the bonfire. A firm grip on their homesteads! That was a phrase
they could understand. All that talk about a peasant proprietary
– let the politicians fight over that – but until that was done, they
would keep a firm grip on their homesteads. Parnell was now their
leader and if their leader told them to keep a firm grip on their
homesteads then, by God, that is precisely what they would do.
Parnell had told them to do this and he was no Fenian demagogue;
he was a landlord. *And* he had stood up to Disraeli in the great
House of Commons and poked him in the eye; and if Parnell could
do that, there in the great House of Commons, then, by God, they
could do the same to their landlords here in Westport. And if not to
the landlord, then to his agent. And if a poke in the eye wouldn't do
it, then a pike in the eye might get the message across. 'But whatever
you do, keep a firm grip on your homesteads', the phrase resonated
with them: practical and defiant.

But even more than the message itself, it was the tone of Parnell's
speech, his tone of angry defiance, of controlled rage, which spoke to
them. He said what he intended to say with no rhetorical flourishes.
He told them what had to be done – pay less rent and keep a firm

grip on your homesteads. He *demanded* that it be done. It was this angry, defiant, revolutionary message which ignited the land war in that extraordinary summer of 1879.

When the speech was over, Parnell was cheered back to the railway station by the brass band and the steaming crowds. We got back to Dublin that evening, picked up our belongings and went straight out to Kingstown, to catch the night sailing to Wales and the early morning train to London. That evening, Parnell was back on his feet in the House of Commons, speaking in a debate about flogging in the navy. I marvelled at his energy – but I couldn't emulate it, and I caught up on my sleep in an old, cracked leather armchair in front of the fire in the Commons library.

Parnell's message at Westport spread like a forest fire throughout the towns and villages of Mayo; from Mayo it spread to Sligo, Leitrim, Roscommon, north to Donegal, and south to Galway, Clare, Limerick, Kerry and Cork. Davitt and his Fenian organisers travelled rapidly from town to town, directing the fire, feeding the flames. They set up a series of rolling meetings in towns throughout the country. These meetings were drumbeats sounding the martial message up and down the west coast: reduce your rents; pay what you can; pay no rent if you cannot agree terms; keep a firm grip on your homesteads; trust to yourselves. In every town and in every village, tenants were organised, and they followed Parnell's lead; they acted together, they offered a reduced rent and, if it was not accepted, they gave the rent to the Land League to hold for the landlord until a mediator was appointed and the rent was agreed. All along the west coast of Ireland, groups of volunteers sprang up. Until then, the people had seemed paralysed by the fear of another famine. Now another famine was upon them. It was as if they suddenly awoke to discover their house was on fire and their families about to perish. There was a demonic energy unleashed that long and difficult summer, which would not be quieted.

When Parnell returned to Avondale in mid-August, at the end of the parliamentary session, there was no time to rest. Throughout that summer and autumn, Parnell spoke at huge Land League rallies all over the country. The message never varied: simple, direct, effective. People came in their thousands because they wanted to hear Parnell, they wanted to see him, but, more than that, they wanted to be part of the great national movement which was now sweeping through the country.

But how Parnell could translate its energy into change was entirely unclear to me.

Twenty

An Eviction

SOME WEEKS LATER, in early November, Parnell was in Avondale when a telegram arrived after breakfast. He read it quickly, then crumpled it up and threw it in the fire.

'Davitt's been arrested,' he said.

I was horrified. 'Where?' I asked.

'Gurteen, in Sligo,' said Parnell. 'He was addressing a Land League meeting last night.'

Later that morning, another heavy bundle of post arrived for Parnell. It seemed everyone in Ireland was writing to him to ask for his help, or simply to say they were praying for him.

Parnell never read any of his correspondence; he left it to me to read and reply accordingly. But that morning there was one letter which caught my attention, from the Mayo Land League. It read:

Dear Mr Parnell.

This is to inform you that Mr and Mrs Dempsey and their five children is to be evicted on Thursday 4th November. I was told to write to you about it. We will be there to help them with whatever we can but the eviction papers have been served. Mr Dempsey is poorly but they have said he will be turned out anyway.

Signed: Joseph McNamara
Secretary
Mayo Land League.

I am not sure why I showed the letter to Parnell – it was not the first letter we had received about an eviction but, for some reason, it spurred Parnell to react.

He immediately dictated a telegram, calling a meeting of the Land League at the Imperial Hotel in Dublin the following evening at eight. I sent it to the members of the Land League Committee, with instructions to send it on to their men.

The following evening, we set out for Dublin and made our way to the Imperial Hotel on Sackville Street. From a distance, I saw what looked like a huge bonfire at the base of Nelson's Pillar but, as we got closer, I saw it was a crowd of 1,000 men with burning torches, the flickers of light showing unsmiling and determined faces. Parnell walked towards them, nodding in acknowledgement, and they parted silently to let him through. We walked on to the Imperial, where we met Biggar and Dillon, along with Thomas Brennan and Tom Kettle, men who were beginning to emerge as leaders in the land movement.

'We brought your crowd, Parnell,' said Biggar.

'More than I would have thought,' said Parnell, with a wry smile.

'We didn't force anyone,' said Biggar, 'they all wanted to come.'

Parnell turned and walked quickly through the foyer of the Imperial and up the stairs, taking them two at a time. He crossed the drawing-room, and within a moment he had flung open a window and stepped out onto the balcony.

'There's Parnell.' I heard the shout going quickly through the crowds below, and they surged forward to hear him speak.

Parnell stood on the balcony, his bearded face and slim form silhouetted by the drawing-room lights behind him. The torches flared and flickered in the darkness below, casting their glow on the upturned faces, expectant, determined.

'Michael Davitt has been arrested and tonight he is in gaol in Sligo, awaiting trial,' Parnell said, his voice booming out in the night air.

'And yesterday I heard that Mr and Mrs Dempsey and their five children will be evicted from their home in Balla tomorrow. So we face our first test. Our first opportunity to show we mean what we say.'

He banged his fist on the wrought-iron rail of the balcony, to hammer out the beat of his last few words.

'When we said we would keep a firm grip on our homesteads, we meant precisely that. And when we say we will rely on ourselves alone, we mean what we say.'

Parnell looked at the crowd below.

'Tonight,' he shouted, 'I am taking the night train to Mayo and tomorrow morning I am going to Balla to stop this eviction. Who will come with me?'

There was such a throat-splitting roar of acclamation that it raised the hair on the back of my neck. It brought people rushing out to the front of the hotel to see what the commotion was about, but when they saw what must have seemed to them like a bunch of thugs congregated outside, they quickly went back inside.

Within minutes, Parnell had walked quickly down the stairs, through the foyer and back onto the street. There was about him a grim resolve which seemed to match the grim faces on the streets below.

'Walk with me, gentlemen,' he said to Biggar and me, and he plunged through the crowds of men, who parted once more to let him through. He took his place at the head of the crowd and started walking back up Sackville Street. Within minutes, the men had fallen in behind him, like an army regiment, torches held aloft. We marched up Sackville Street to the Liffey and then west along the Quays, past the Four Courts and on to Kingsbridge station. People stood back and gawped at us as we passed. We must have looked like a lawless band of brigands. At the station, a stone water-basin with a lion's head was used to douse the torches, and within the hour the train pulled out of Kingsbridge, with our men standing in the aisles and the doorways or squashed three to a seat. Someone stayed to send a telegram to the Land League organisers in Mayo saying that we were on our way.

'When did you concoct this plan, Biggar?' I said to him, when we were all seated.

'What plan?' Biggar asked, expansively. 'I have no idea what the plan is. I thought the locals would face down the first evictions. I didn't think Parnell would actually do it himself.'

We dozed on and off throughout the night and arrived in Mayo before dawn. Balla was some miles away and, as we had no carriages, we walked. The dawn appeared imperceptibly as we walked, a grey, cloudy half-light. Parnell set quite a pace – he was always a vigorous, energetic walker.

When we arrived at Balla, we were met by another huge crowd. There must have been another thousand men gathered there, with banners and flags, and accompanied by a small contingent of cavalry. The Mayo Land League had organised their men well and Parnell now found himself at the head of a small army. We were directed to the Dempseys' house just beyond the village, and we arrived there shortly after eight o'clock.

Just beyond the village, on the left side of the road, stood four or five pitiful-looking hovels. Each had a low door to let in people and light and air. There were no windows. The roof was primitive: just sheaves of rushes, bound together with rope, placed criss-cross on the roof and fastened to the front of the house by wooden pegs hammered into the mudden wall. It looked as it could hardly keep out a summer drizzle, let alone winter downpours.

Outside the second house, slumped on a wooden chair, was Mr Dempsey. He was incongruously dressed: he had on a ragged worsted overcoat and a crumpled hat, but his feet were bare and his trousers held up by string. He was coughing constantly, a racking cough which convulsed his whole body, and his wife stood anxiously beside him, staring now at the huge crowd walking towards the cottage. There were five children of various ages hovering outside; the two youngest, girls no more than four or five years of age, were standing close to their father, their childish hands grasping and twisting at his trouser legs for comfort. The families in the adjoining houses also appeared as we arrived, and looked on in amazement at the oncoming crowds.

Parnell approached Mr Dempsey and shook his hand.

'Good morning,' he said. 'Are you Mr Dempsey?'

'I am,' the man said, trying to get up.

'Stay where you are, Mr Dempsey. I'm Charles Parnell.'

Mrs Dempsey put her hand to her mouth, the shock and surprise evident in her face.

Parnell turned towards her. 'Good morning, Mrs Dempsey,' he said gently. 'What time are you expecting the bailiffs?'

'About ten o'clock,' said Mr Dempsey. He struggled to stand up.

'My poor husband has been sick for weeks now,' said Mrs Dempsey. 'We've tried to put them off but they wouldn't listen. They said we had more than enough time to put matters to rights. But what can we do?' She started to wring her hands in her apron. 'What can we do? Please God, help us.'

One of her neighbours moved to comfort her.

'What do we do now?' asked Biggar.

'We wait,' said Parnell, and he promptly sat down on a large stone marking the edge of the road.

'Right, lads,' Biggar shouted. 'Take a rest.'

The column of infantry moved, almost as one, to sit down on the road where they had been standing or on the stone walls beside the road. The line stretched right back beyond the village.

Biggar and Brennan continued to chat to the Dempseys about their rent and their arrears, about their children and their health, but Parnell sat where he was, looking around at the village and the houses. He held aloof from any further intimacy with the Dempseys, not out of scorn, but more out of a strange sort of shyness. He did not have Biggar's ability to talk to everyone.

There was a chill to the air, and people got up occasionally to stamp their feet and keep them warm. Even at nine o'clock, the frost on the fields was still visible; the November sun would not melt it. Dillon, as usual, had his head in a book and was lost to the world.

Just after ten o'clock, we heard a commotion and a large group of constables, some on horseback, and some bailiffs in a cart could be seen making their way towards us. Our men got up from the road, moved to the side to let them pass through and then closed in behind them.

Parnell stood up and a group of men gathered around him to protect him, as though they had been drilled to act as his bodyguards. A further group of men lined up two deep, barring the way to the cottage. It was, I thought, a practised manoeuvre.

The bailiffs brought the cart slowly to a halt near the cottages, and one of the policemen on horseback drew alongside the cart and shouted aloud towards the Dempseys, 'We don't want no trouble here, d'ye hear me?'

No one replied.

'We're here to evict the Dempseys because they've not paid their rent,' said one of the bailiffs defiantly. 'They've had plenty of opportunity.'

'Who are you?' said Parnell.

'Who are you, more like?' replied the bailiff.

'I am Charles Stewart Parnell,' said Parnell sternly. 'I am a Member of Parliament for Meath and I am President of the National Land League. Now, who are you?'

'I am Finbarr McGrath,' said the bailiff. 'The bailiff in Castlebar.'

'Do you have that, Mr Harrison?' Parnell shouted loudly to me, so that every member of our infantry could hear it too. 'Write down this gentleman's name: Finbarr McGrath, Bailiff, Castlebar.' I scrambled about for a pen and paper and made a note of his name.

'What do you want taking my name for?' The bailiff was now a worried man.

Parnell ignored him.

'What is your name?' he said to the second bailiff.

There was no reply.

'What is your name?' roared Biggar suddenly.

'Jack, Jack O'Brien,' mumbled the second bailiff.

'From where?' roared Biggar.

'Castlebar,' he replied, looking nervously around him at the menacing crowd.

'Jack O'Brien, Bailiff, Castlebar,' said Parnell clearly. 'Have you that name also, Mr Harrison?'

I nodded.

Parnell nodded to the third bailiff. 'And you, what's your name?'

But before he could answer, the officer in charge intervened.

'What's all this for?' he said.

'One moment, sir, if you will,' said Parnell, imperiously gesturing at the policeman to wait.

'Your name, sir,' Parnell repeated to the third bailiff.

'Jimmy Murphy,' he said.

'From where?'

'Castlebar.'

'Jimmy Murphy, Bailiff, Castlebar,' Parnell said loudly. 'Do you have that name, Mr Harrison?'

I nodded again, but had no idea what Parnell was doing.

'Gentlemen,' said Parnell to the bailiffs. 'Now we have your names, you are known to us.'

The officer looked uneasy.

'Look, Mr Parnell,' he said. 'We don't want no trouble here. We're just here to make sure this all goes off peaceful.'

'That's why we're all here too,' said Parnell coolly. He turned back to the cart.

'So, gentlemen, what is your business here?' he said loudly.

'We're here to evict the Dempseys,' stammered the head bailiff.

'At whose request?' Parnell asked.

'The landlord's.'

'And who is the landlord?' asked Parnell.

'Lord Mountmorres,' the bailiff replied.

'Lord Mountmorres,' repeated Parnell, looking over at me. I took that name down too.

'Let them pass,' said the constable, trying to regain the initiative, 'they are here to carry out a lawful duty. The Dempseys are well in arrears. They haven't paid their rent in months.'

'Mr Dempsey has been ill,' said Parnell. 'He's still ill. As you can see.' He gestured towards the hunched form of Dempsey on the chair. 'When he recovers, as he will, he will work again and pay whatever reasonable rent he should pay.'

'Oh, the rent is reasonable, Mr Parnell,' said the head bailiff in an ingratiating manner, 'you may rely on that.'

'How do you know?' said Parnell coldly. 'Are you the land agent?'

'No, no.' The bailiff retreated into silence.

'Who is the land agent?' said Parnell.

There was a silence.

'Who is the land agent, McGrath?' roared Biggar again.

'Captain Boycott,' said the bailiff.

'Christian name,' said Biggar.

'Charles Boycott.'

'From where?'

'Lough Mask.'

'Do you have that, Mr Harrison?' said Biggar.

'I do indeed, Mr Biggar,' I said, in stentorian tones to match those of Biggar.

'Now, look here, Mr Parnell,' said the constable angrily. 'We are here to carry out this eviction, so let these men do their lawful duty.'

'Do they have the eviction papers?' asked Parnell.

'Yes, yes,' said the bailiff. 'I have them right here.' He put his hand into his inside jacket pocket and pulled out a sheaf of papers, which he handed to Parnell.

'All the papers are there. Everything is in order, Mr Parnell,' he said. 'We have our Court Order from Judge Harvey.'

'Now,' said the constable roughly, 'let these men do their job.' He stood up in the stirrups. 'Dempsey,' he shouted, 'get your bags and baggage out of the house right now.'

Mrs Dempsey began to cry.

'Stay where you are, Mr Dempsey,' Parnell called out.

'Now look, Mr Parnell, we don't want no trouble,' said the constable, 'but we're here to do our duty. You've seen the papers.'

There was a tense silence as Parnell and the constable faced each other.

Then, raising the eviction papers high in the air, Parnell proceeded, slowly and with great deliberation, to tear up every one of them and throw them on the ground.

'There will be no eviction here,' he said.

Within a moment, the policeman whipped out a rifle and waved it threateningly at Parnell. I held my breath. There was a commotion, as the infantry looked as if they would fall upon the policeman if given the opportunity.

'I will ask you for the last time, sir, get out of our way and let us do our job,' the policeman shouted.

Parnell looked at him.

'Do you want to die here, today?' Parnell said calmly to the policeman. 'Because, sir, look around you. If you shoot me, you will be clubbed to death by a thousand men.'

The policeman looked around uneasily, the rifle still levelled at Parnell.

'I am the only person standing between you and your death,' continued Parnell, 'so I advise you to think long and hard about your position.'

After some time, the policeman lowered his rifle, slowly.

'We have every right to evict these people,' he said.

Parnell stood there, with his arms folded.

'You have no right, sir, no right at all, and I would suggest,' he said, 'that you take your men and your bailiffs back to Castlebar. There is a large crowd here and we don't want any trouble.'

The policeman looked around at the thousands of men who had encircled them and who looked menacingly at them.

'You've not heard the last of this, I tell you,' he shouted and then, turning his horse, he led his men and the bailiffs back to the village.

There were loud jeers among the infantry as the constables walked their horses back through them, and wild cheering as they disappeared at the bend of the road.

Mrs Dempsey came towards Parnell, her eyes streaming with tears. 'God bless you, Mr Parnell, God bless you,' she said.

Parnell shook her hand and then moved across the road and jumped up on the stone wall to speak to his troops.

'I said we would keep a firm grip on our homesteads and that is exactly what we shall do,' he said, to great cheers. 'But they will be back again and the next time I will not be here. The next time you must block their way again.' He paused for a moment. 'Meanwhile, Michael Davitt is sitting in a prison in Sligo Town on trial. For speaking to a Land League meeting like this one. I am going to Sligo Town. Who will come with me?'

Again, there were huge roars of acclamation, and Parnell jumped down from the wall, and began striding back towards the town, with Biggar and I on either side, the infantry falling in behind.

'Now that was a great morning's work,' said Biggar. 'I haven't felt like that since … since …'

'Since you threw the Prince of Wales out of the House of Commons,' I suggested, to their great amusement.

∝෴∝

In the following days, I read in the newspapers of new ways of preventing evictions. If the Court directed that the eviction notice had to be served on the tenant or nailed to the front door, then hundreds of men barred the way to the tenant or his front door; day and night the house was surrounded by Land Leaguers; and on many occasions bailiffs who sought to serve eviction summonses were stripped of their clothes and forced to walk back into town in the suits God gave them. After a time no one could be found to serve the summonses any more.

We quickly realised, as Parnell had foreseen, that the battleground in the war against England had now decisively changed. It was no longer the House of Commons; it was a man's home, and Parnell understood well that a man would always fight to defend his family and his home. It was no longer a small force of rebels working underground; it was now a large force of peasant farmers working in full view.

Twenty-One

The Uncrowned King of Ireland

BUT THE NEED for money to fund the League was now paramount and several weeks later it was agreed that Parnell should travel to America to raise funds.

The day before we set sail, Parnell received a telegram from Davitt which he read quickly, and crumpled up in fury.

'They are not going to go quietly,' he said angrily.

I looked at him quizzically.

'They came back for the Dempseys yesterday,' he said, 'and evicted them before dawn.'

Early in the morning of 21st December, we went on board the Cunard ship *Scythia*, a grand ocean liner – unlike the steam packet which chugged between Kingstown and Holyhead – and sailed out of Cork to make the twelve-day voyage across the Atlantic to New York.

We were a party of four: Parnell, myself, John Dillon, who had become increasingly involved with our campaign, and, to my delight, Fanny, who decided to join us to visit her mother, who had been in New York for several months now.

Dillon was an amusing and sociable travelling companion and regaled us with many stories of his travels, which Fanny in particular found highly entertaining. Unfortunately, for Dillon at least, the first storm hit us on the third day out and he had to take to his cabin for days with seasickness. Although Fanny ministered to him like a nurse during the day, it did mean that Parnell and I had Fanny to ourselves at dinner and we fell back into our familiar, easy camaraderie, teasing her about her hairstyle, which she assured us was the very latest fashion.

In contrast to Dillon, Parnell revelled in the wildness of the weather. He found storms exhilarating and he walked the decks when the winds were up and the mountainous waves lashed against the ship.

On Christmas Day we had dinner in the state dining-room. Poor Dillon barely lasted the first course, which left Parnell, Fanny and me to enjoy the evening. Parnell was in festive form and had more than his usual single glass of wine.

I did ask him – after we both had consumed several glasses – why he was usually so abstemious.

'Tell him, Charlie,' said Fanny. 'But this is a family secret, James, so you'll have to promise not to tell.'

'I had an unfortunate experience at Cambridge,' Parnell said ruefully. 'As undergraduates do, I went out one evening, had far too much to drink and got into a brawl.'

I started to laugh at the image of Parnell in a drunken brawl.

'That's not the end of it,' said Fanny, beginning to laugh also.

'No, unfortunately. I wish it were,' said Parnell. 'I had just knocked the other fellow down when a constable came upon us. He started to admonish us and he would have left it at that but I was grateful to him for his common sense and I thought – God knows why – I would offer him a tip. For his kindness. So I took a sovereign out of my pocket and gave it to him. Unfortunately it wasn't a sovereign; it was only a shilling and he thought it was a bribe.' Parnell began to laugh at the memory. 'To this day, I don't know whether he was offended because I tried to bribe him or because he was insulted by the amount!'

This set us all off laughing again.

'But it ended tragically for me,' continued Parnell. 'I was taken before the Court and fined. My college rusticated me for two terms and by then I didn't have any desire to go back to Cambridge. Since then I have been careful what I drink and with whom.' He looked around the dining-room. 'But I think in the middle of the Atlantic I am safe from the long arm of the law.'

We arrived in New York on 2nd January 1880, the second day of a new decade, a new age. It was a cold, bracing morning and I shivered on deck as we entered the harbour. As the ship edged its way to its moorings I saw, to my surprise, a welcoming committee on the quays below: a brass band, an enthusiastic crowd of New York Irish and a horde of journalists, all eager to meet and interview 'Young Ironsides' or 'The Young Agitator', as the American papers were calling Parnell.

As we stood on deck, Fanny saw her mother and sister and waved excitedly to them. Mrs Parnell and Theodosia Parnell waved back from the quays. When the gangways were lowered, but before anyone could disembark, the journalists clambered up the gangway to get an interview with Parnell, so he beckoned them inside and sat in the dining-room for an hour, talking to them about the terrible conditions in Ireland, the approaching famine, the evictions, the Dempseys and his great American heritage. Eventually we disembarked and Parnell greeted his mother and sister with his usual formality. As we drove into Manhattan, Fanny recounted the recent stories of the Land League, Parnell's speeches and the incidents at Balla and Sligo.

We were staying at the Plaza Hotel at Central Park, and over lunch Mrs Parnell cautioned us to be vigilant.

'There are spies everywhere in this city,' she said in hushed tones. 'Everywhere. I told Theodosia that I have a strong feeling we are being followed.'

'Mother,' cried Fanny, 'you are just imagining it.'

'I certainly am not,' said Mrs Parnell with some hauteur. 'I have retained a private detective.'

'To spy on the people who are spying on you,' laughed Fanny.

Mrs Parnell stuck to her theories, despite the playful remonstrances of her daughter. Theodosia was full of news about her imminent marriage to an Englishman named Paget and this, needless to say, obliterated all further conversation about Ireland.

I shall not dwell in too much detail on the American tour – save to say that it was an overwhelming success. We were constantly on the move. Each day brought a different city – sometimes more than one. From New York to Jersey City, Philadelphia,

Boston, Indianapolis, Cleveland, Buffalo, Washington, Baltimore, Pittsburgh, Ohio, Minneapolis, St Louis, and Springfield, Illinois. Parnell spoke at breakfast meetings, lunch groups and after-dinner clubs and to great crowds in theatres and assembly halls. Everywhere he went, he was greeted by crowds of cheering supporters, feted by the local politicians and surrounded by reporters from all over the country. Hundreds of thousands of dollars were raised for the relief of distress and for the Land League.

Parnell was even invited to address the House of Representatives – a rare honour. His speech was, I am afraid, a turgid disquisition on the land problem in Ireland, but no matter: he was now recognised in America as the leader of the Irish people.

There was an organising group behind all this and it was clearly Clann na Gael, the Fenians in America. They organised venues and publicity, brought the crowds, and paid the bills. Parnell met frequently with William O'Carroll, John Devoy and many of the other Irish-American Fenians. I did ask him whether he was at all concerned about his association with these men.

'Not in the slightest,' was his brisk reply. 'Who else would have organised all these speeches, these crowds, if they didn't?'

'Provided you say what they want to hear,' I said.

'They hear what they want to hear,' was his sardonic reply.

But help was required. The burdens of the tour were immense and, although Dillon and I did our best, we needed help. Parnell wired Egan in Ireland to send someone else to assist us. Egan wired Tim Healy and said Parnell wanted him in America. It was a harmless lie, of course, but it did give Healy an exaggerated sense of his own importance from the start.

Healy arrived in New York at the end of February and stayed with Parnell's family for a few days before he joined us in Davenport, Iowa, where I collected him at the station.

'What a family,' said Healy, clutching his bag, when I met him. 'Mrs Parnell is completely off her nut. She kept talking about being followed, that there are spies everywhere. And Theodosia Parnell never stops talking about her wedding.'

'And Fanny?' I asked. 'How is she?'

'A beautiful woman,' said Healy. 'I'd have stayed in New York for her alone.'

It sounded as if he had fallen under Fanny's spell and I looked at him askance but passed no other comment.

Shortly after Healy's arrival, we headed north to Canada, to Montreal. The city was buried in two or three feet of snow after a late winter snowstorm, and we were met at the railway station by an enthusiastic crowd and given greatcoats, mufflers, fur hats and gloves, and carried by sleighs to our hotel. Despite the mufflers, the cold pierced me to the marrow, and I was glad to thaw out by the hotel fire with some Canadian whiskey.

Although Healy had not spoken on the tour, Parnell asked him to do the introduction at Montreal, at a small city hall crowded with the emigrant Irish. I had never heard him speak before, but he was a fine speaker and he gave a stirring speech that evening, calling Parnell 'the indispensable man' and 'the great parliamentary obstructor'. But it was his final words which have resounded through the decades:

'You have heard, ladies and gentleman, that Mr Parnell has crossed and re-crossed the length and breadth of America as the representative of the Land League; he has spoken to the United States Congress as the leader of the Irish people and he appears before you tonight as the uncrowned King of Ireland.'

It was a stirring introduction and the crowds cheered Parnell to the rafters. Curiously, however, Parnell never even acknowledged the soubriquet, either to Healy or to anyone else. It was as if he accepted it as his due.

After Montreal, we had intended to resume our tour in America, but our plans changed abruptly when we got back to the hotel that evening, and a bellboy appeared with an urgent telegram for Parnell. Parnell took it and read it aloud.

'Parliament dissolved. Return at once. Biggar.'

Early the following morning, Parnell, Healy and I left Montreal for New York.

'At least I'll be able to see Miss Parnell again,' said Healy on the train to New York, referring to Fanny. 'She's a fine woman.'

It was an awkward comment, expressing a sense of admiration for Parnell's sister in a tone which was perhaps inappropriate.

'She's not for you, Healy,' said Parnell brusquely. It was a cold, biting comment and Healy was cut as surely as if struck on the face by a riding crop. I could see the colour drain from his countenance as he turned away to look out of the window at the snow-covered countryside. Whether the remark was occasioned by Healy's social inferiority or by something in his character which Parnell disliked, I do not know, but it sowed seeds of rancour between them which, as I was to find out, would flower years later, in the sullen heat of Committee Room 15.

We left New York the next day, taking a carriage to the port, and boarded our ship, *The Baltic*, to the accompaniment of a brass band, playing heroically in the midst of a snowstorm. Parnell stood on deck, bare-headed, to take the full salute from the gallant 69th Irish Regiment, which had turned out in force to see him off.

'Would you look at him?' Healy said to me, with a sneer. 'I think he actually believes he is the uncrowned King of Ireland.'

It had not taken Healy long to withdraw the crown.

In the early days of the voyage, we rested after the rigours of the tour. But after some days, Parnell began to plan for the forthcoming election with Healy and me, discussing candidates and constituencies. In the midst of our discussions, Parnell said, 'I want you to stand for Parliament, Harrison.'

I was taken aback at the suggestion.

'It would be a great honour,' I said, 'but I couldn't afford the expenses.'

'The League will pay your expenses,' said Parnell. 'If they don't, I will. We need to put up good candidates and we need to win as many seats as we can. I don't know what happened to you at Irishtown, but it seems to have changed you. I thought the same at Westport and at Balla. I want you to stand for Wicklow. You should win there.'

'That's very generous, Parnell,' I replied. 'But would you not stand there?'

'No, I want you to take that seat,' he replied. 'I shall stand again for Meath but I also intend to stand for Mayo.'

He turned to Healy. 'And, Healy, I want you to organise the whole election for us and then take the first seat in a by-election and join us afterwards.'

Healy was flattered at the faith Parnell so obviously had in his abilities and it helped him recover his equanimity during the voyage. He accepted the task at once.

'Excellent,' said Parnell, smiling that rare, wonderful smile of his. 'So, gentlemen, a toast to all our future Members of Parliament!'

Twenty-Two

The Leadership

W E ARRIVED BACK in Ireland a few days later, on a damp, cold Sunday morning in March. It was just after dawn as the ship skirted the coastline, the fields of West Cork barely visible in the morning mists and fog. We stood at the ship's rail, looking out for any sign of a welcoming party, but there was none and the biting wind soon chilled us to the bone.

'I would have thought our work in America might have got them out of their beds,' said Parnell, clearly put out.

'He's not so regal now, is he?' said Healy to me, behind his hand. The wound had not yet healed.

Just as we were approaching the harbour, we saw, through the mist, a small tender coming towards us.

'Ahoy there,' a disembodied voice boomed out. Even on a Sunday morning, in the mists off West Cork, the foghorn had the unmistakable northern accent of Biggar.

'You *do* recognise that voice?' I said.

'Anywhere, Harrison,' said Parnell dryly. 'Anywhere.'

The tender soon drew up alongside us and we saw Biggar and Egan on board, Biggar at the bow of the vessel, his left foot on the gunwale.

'I said, ahoy there,' he repeated.

'Ahoy there, Biggar,' I shouted.

'I recognise the voice of young Masser Harrison,' shouted Biggar, his northern accent twisted into an attempted American southern drawl. He made a mock bow. 'And I'm after making 'umble enquiries as to whether there might be an uncrowned King of Ireland on board' – this delivered in an exaggerated Irish peasant accent. News of Parnell's coronation had reached Irish shores.

'He's here, all right,' shouted Healy.

'And if he steps right this way,' shouted Biggar, 'we'll make sure he's well and truly crowned' – to the laughter of us all.

Within a short time, the ship and tender had docked, we were back on Irish soil and we greeted our friends with great affection.

As we took the train from Queenstown to Cork, Biggar brought us up to date with the news during our absence. It was encouraging. Many landlords had agreed to reduce rents by at least twenty per cent – some by as much as forty per cent – until the crisis passed. The relief funds set up had ensured that no one had died of starvation. The weather had been clement and fears of another bad harvest had receded. The worst was over.

We spent the afternoon in Cork, preparing our plans for the election – which was now only three weeks away. The following day, we scattered to the four corners of Ireland to campaign for Parnell, obstructionism, the Land League and Home Rule – in roughly that order.

∽⊖∼

I was also busy with my own campaign and I travelled throughout the constituency of Wicklow, urging the electors to vote for me. I knew every detail of Parnell's views – having listened to them often enough – and so I did a creditable enough job of presenting them to the voters. It was a straight fight between me, the Liberal and the Tory and, to my great joy, in April 1880 I was elected as a Member of Parliament for the County of Wicklow.

The vote throughout England was a thumping defeat for Disraeli and an extraordinary victory for Gladstone – who had supposedly retired five years earlier, but who had apparently been so exercised by the Eastern question that he had returned to the fray. The Home Rule Party won sixty-one seats, hardly a great increase on the fifty-nine seats under Isaac Butt, but of much greater significance was the fact that thirty of these were members personally championed by Parnell and loyal to him. The seven had become thirty.

But this was not without its cost. The last twelve months – of late-night sittings obstructing the House, of travelling all over Ireland for the Land League, of touring America, of an arduous election campaign, of the nervous effort of so many speeches – had left Parnell quite exhausted and, after the results were announced, he limped back to Avondale, in a state of near collapse. He had a persistent pallor and he looked ill, but he refused even to call for a doctor. He rested for a few weeks at Avondale before the demands of Parliament summoned him forth once again.

Some weeks later, the Home Rule Party met in Dublin to elect a leader and Parnell decided to stand. For the first time, I could now attend as a member of the Party in my own right, but I maintained my practice of acting as secretary. Just over fifty Members of Parliament turned up; what the others had to do that was more important I do not know, but it showed that indolence was still a characteristic of the Party.

Biggar, Tim Healy and I met Frank O'Donnell before the leadership vote. We had heard he was not going to vote for Parnell, and we wanted to know why.

'I have my reasons,' said O'Donnell huffily. 'I am an independent Member of Parliament and I shall make my decision in an independent manner.'

'Oh, for God's sake, O'Donnell,' said Biggar, 'get off your high horse. Didn't Parnell and myself pay off your debts to allow you to get back into Parliament?'

I looked at Biggar in surprise. I hadn't heard that piece of gossip before.

O'Donnell had at least the good grace to look embarrassed.

'And I believe I have paid you both back since then,' he said.

'That's hardly the point,' said Biggar. 'Parnell supported you when you needed it.'

'Well, I cannot support any person who has treated Isaac Butt as shamefully as Parnell has done.'

'Butt's dead,' said Healy harshly, 'and that was a long time ago now.'

'Or anyone who has destroyed the Party as Parnell has done.'

'Destroyed the Party?' said Healy. 'He has thirty Members of Parliament now.'

'Who will all do his bidding.' O'Donnell was becoming more sullen.

'Who will force Gladstone to take us seriously!' shouted Healy.

'But look at the men we have lost,' O'Donnell replied. 'Lord Conyngham, Lord Montagu, the O'Conor Don, Colonel King-Harman …'

'Lords and landlords,' said Healy fiercely, 'the Party is better off without them.'

'*Au contraire*, Healy,' said O'Donnell.

'You are an imperialist crank, O'Donnell,' said Healy, with some venom. 'Go and join the Tories. You have no place in our party.'

'Keep calm, Healy,' said Biggar, unusually the diplomat. 'What has this got to do with not voting for Parnell?'

'He is an outsider,' said O'Donnell, suddenly and with some anger. 'He is a foreigner to Ireland. He knows nothing about us. Nothing about our history, our people, our language, our culture. His family is from England; he was schooled in England. He went to university in Cambridge, where he didn't even take a degree, for heaven's sake! He has no degree and no profession. He is scarcely able to speak in public.'

We were all suddenly quiet. Everything O'Donnell had said was true, but somehow he had missed the very essence of the man: his resolve, his natural ability to lead, his absolute self-belief and his ability to impose his will on the English.

As we continued our argument, James J. O'Kelly, having returned from America to be elected, came over to join us. O'Kelly was not one to take the temperature before plunging in.

'What's this, O'Donnell, I hear you want to stand for the leadership yourself?' he said.

'If the Party wants me to consider it, I shall certainly do so,' said O'Donnell haughtily.

'Well, it doesn't,' said O'Kelly brusquely. 'We are a nation of Catholics and we want a Protestant. We are a nation of peasants and we want a landlord. You are neither. Parnell is both. So get out of the way.'

With that crushing rebuff, O'Kelly pushed his way through the doors into the next room and left O'Donnell to his isolation.

That election brought in a great tide of young, ambitious and energetic Irish Members of Parliament, many of whom were to make their names and their reputations over the next ten years; men like Thomas Sexton, T.P. O'Connor, John Dillon and Tim Healy. But, like many great tides, it also brought in much unwelcome flotsam and jetsam. And it quickly became apparent that the most egregious piece of flotsam which the tide had brought in that year was Willie O'Shea, who had stood for Ennis, with the O'Gorman Mahon as his mentor. I met him first at this meeting of Home Rule Members of Parliament, slouched in a chair in a louche fashion, stroking his fingers through his moustache, dressed in a foppish, sapphire blue waistcoat, with a lemon silk cravat and a black velvet frock coat. I daresay such an outfit would not have looked out of place in the smoking-rooms of a gentleman's club in London, but among the well-worn black and grey worsted suits of the earnest members of our party, he stood out like a peacock.

As we waited for the meeting to begin, the O'Gorman Mahon was regaling his listeners with stories of his campaign.

'Of course, one of the advantages of my great age,' he said, 'is that if I see a beautiful young woman I can go up to her directly and kiss her – for Ireland, as I tell her.'

'And as the junior member for Ennis I had to follow him, of course,' said O'Shea, with a forced, too-loud laugh, 'so we spent the whole election drinking pints of porter and trying to kiss the young women of Ennis.' He seemed to be back in his officers' mess.

'And if we had worn our uniforms,' said the O'Gorman Mahon, 'there'd have been no stopping us.'

His stories would have continued but Shaw, as chairman, called the meeting to order.

The election of party leader was a most civilised affair. Everyone who wished to speak could speak and all spoke without rancour or animosity. The speeches went on throughout the afternoon – some for Shaw, some for Parnell. I was quite worn out trying to record all the contributions. But eventually the speeches were over and the votes were cast. Twenty-three votes for Parnell; eighteen for Shaw.

Parnell was, at only thirty-one years of age, the leader of the Home Rule Party, the President of the Land League, and the leader of the Irish in Britain. Truly, he was now the uncrowned King of Ireland.

Twenty-Three

Internal Dissent

IMMEDIATELY AFTERWARDS, SHAW offered Parnell a perfunctory congratulation, which Parnell acknowledged with a
curt nod.

'So, Parnell,' asked Shaw, 'will you sit with the Liberals or the
Tories?'

But before Parnell could even reply, Shaw continued.

'Because I shall sit with the Liberals on the Government benches.
Gladstone has always been a friend to Ireland and I have no intention
of sitting with the Tories after their behaviour over the last five years.'

'We shall sit in Opposition,' said Parnell firmly. 'We have no
agreement with Gladstone and, until we do, we will oppose him.'

'Even if that means sitting with the Tories,' sneered Shaw, 'whom
you have excoriated over the last five years?'

'They are irrelevant now,' said Parnell, 'and, until we know
Gladstone's plans for Ireland, we will oppose him.'

'Well, *you* might,' said Shaw, 'but I intend to exercise my vote as
an independent Member of Parliament, and I – and, I presume, my
supporters – will sit with the Liberals.'

'Oh, for God's sake, man,' said Biggar, with some irritation. 'we
can't have half the Party sitting with the Government and the other
half sitting with the Opposition. We will become a laughing stock.'

'You and Parnell have been making us a laughing stock for the last
five years, Biggar,' retorted Shaw, 'with your nonsensical tactics.'

Biggar was about to remonstrate further, but Parnell silenced him
with a raised palm.

'Very well, Shaw, as you wish,' he said, and called the meeting to
a close.

'Parnell, we can't have this,' said Biggar, coming up to him as everyone was leaving the room. 'A party split already!'

Parnell did not bother to reply.

The new session of Parliament started some days later. Now, as Member of Parliament for the County of Wicklow, I could enter the House of Lords for the ceremony, instead of watching it from outside the gates, as in former years. It was an impressive scene of imperial grandeur. There is undoubtedly a greatness in the English character which had created a free parliament such as this, and had won for them an empire. Perhaps in different times I could have admired the pageantry, but the scenes of the previous winter and the spirit of my mother intruded upon my mind.

After the Queen's speech, along with all other Members of Parliament, I walked across to the House of Commons to take my seat. Even though I had been an acute and fervid observer for the last five years, the House seemed a wholly unfamiliar place to me as I walked into the Chamber for the first time, accompanied by Parnell and Biggar. I gazed up at the gallery where I had spent so many nights; I walked to the despatch box as if in a dream, to take my oath; and then, to cheers from the other members of my party, I took my seat in the House of Commons for the first time, on the bench below the gangway, alongside Biggar and Parnell.

The following day, Gladstone gave a speech outlining all his priorities for the remainder of the year – the Eastern question, Turkey, Afghanistan, South Africa – but, as with the great speeches of Disraeli on such occasions, there was absolutely no mention of Ireland. None. The famine in the West was completely ignored. It was as if the Land League campaign had never happened. It was quite extraordinary.

There was fury that evening in our rooms in King Street, the dilapidated rooms used at that time by the Party to transact its business. Parnell listened to all the members, but he addressed only one, and one who had not spoken – Shaw, who sat brooding throughout the meeting.

'So, Shaw,' he said, 'will you still sit with Gladstone, knowing he will do nothing for Ireland?'

'I will,' Shaw said, unperturbed. 'Gladstone has been a good friend to Ireland and he will continue to be. He will do something for us this session; I'm sure of it.'

Before anyone could voice any further opposition to Shaw, Parnell said, 'Very well then,' and concluded the meeting in his familiar way by seizing his papers and leaving the room.

Later that evening, we went back into the House. I was surprised to see that not only did Shaw and his supporters sit with the Liberals, William O'Shea did also. Some hours later, when Gladstone finished his speech, Shaw stood to speak.

'Mr Speaker,' he said, 'I would like to assure the Prime Minister that he can rely on my support and that of my colleagues from the Home Rule Party on this side of the House. The Prime Minister has been a good friend to Ireland in the past and I am confident he will be again.'

Gladstone stood at the despatch box and bowed graciously to Shaw in acknowledgement. 'I am grateful to my Honourable Friend for his support,' he said.

Parnell rose to his feet. The House was instantly quiet, eager to hear his first speech as leader of the Irish party.

'Mr Speaker.' He began quietly. 'I have listened to the Honourable Member, the Prime Minister, with increasing dismay and, frankly, with incredulity. I have listened to his ambitious plans for the Balkans, India, South Africa and other colonies. And yet, about Ireland there is not a word.' He stopped and looked around the House. 'Not one single word. And yet in Ireland, not a hundred miles away from the Prime Minister's home in Wales, there has been famine this winter, and scenes of eviction and hardship that I would scarcely have believed could exist in this country, in this age, had I not witnessed it with my own eyes.' He paused and looked around the assembly. 'So I propose an amendment to the Queen's speech: that this Government should bring forward immediate proposals to reform the land laws in Ireland.'

I looked over at Shaw, who had been reclining on the Government benches, with one arm resting on the bench behind him. As he listened to Parnell's words, he sat forward to pay closer attention, a frown replacing the self-satisfied smile.

Gladstone stood up to reject Parnell's proposals and Parnell immediately demanded a vote.

Only then did Shaw realise the trap Parnell had set. If Shaw voted with Gladstone, he was voting against land reform in Ireland and would be excoriated in the Irish newspapers and in his native Cork; if he voted with Parnell, Gladstone would know he was wholly unreliable. Faced with such a choice, he simply left the Chamber, to avoid a vote at all, to the jeers of the members of the Home Rule Party on our side. This incident brought about the immediate destruction of his reputation and brought all the other rebels in the Party to heel – apart from O'Shea, who continued, obstinately, to sit with the Government.

As the vote took place, I could see Gladstone staring intently at Parnell, trying to get the measure of this young man, less than half his age, who had destroyed Disraeli's last three years in Parliament and who could certainly do the same to him. An opponent who could so ruthlessly crush a rebellion within his own party could prove quite troublesome.

Later, in the lobby, Parnell chided the O'Gorman Mahon about O'Shea.

'Can't you control your protégé, O'Gorman?' he said. 'Why is he sitting with the Government?'

The O'Gorman Mahon took Parnell's arm as he answered, in a gesture of conspiratorial friendliness.

'I warned him myself, Parnell,' he said sniffily, 'not to sit there under any circumstances. The people of Clare won't tolerate it. Or him.'

'Would he not listen to you?' Parnell was surprised.

'Not in the slightest,' said the O'Gorman Mahon, emphasising every word. 'He told me he intends to be his own man … Just as you were.'

Parnell grimaced.

'He's ambitious, Parnell. Very ambitious. Mark him,' said the O'Gorman Mahon. 'He wants public office and he reckons Gladstone is the man to give it to him.'

Twenty-Four

A Parliamentary Ambush

THE NEXT PARLIAMENTARY strike was not long in coming. Several days later, in the middle of the night – or to be more precise at about one o'clock in the morning – as Gladstone sat on the front bench, writing his daily epistle to the Queen, half listening to a Liberal colleague finishing a debate on some matter or other, O'Connor Power rose to his feet.

'Mr Speaker,' he said gruffly, in that coarse accent of his. 'I wish to move the second reading of the Suspension of Evictions bill.'

I, Parnell, Biggar and over forty other members of our party had been congregating together in the lobbies outside the Chamber, according to a pre-arranged plan. I watched with a mounting sense of excitement as the Speaker called O'Connor Power to speak. He had the floor. Parnell immediately nodded to us to follow him in and we all swiftly walked into the Chamber in twos and threes and took our seats. I counted the rest of the Members of Parliament in the House. There were only about thirty. We had a majority.

Gladstone glanced up from his notes, looked down, and then looked up again in astonishment at seeing so many members of the Irish party in the House at such an hour. It took him only a moment to register the ambush. Parnell had the floor and had introduced his bill; the high ground was his, the timing of the battle was his and he had the numbers. He was about to inflict a humiliating parliamentary defeat on Gladstone.

Gladstone put his royal epistle aside and stood at the despatch box.

'Mr Speaker,' he said, 'we have had no notice whatsoever of this bill.'

'No notice is required, Prime Minister,' intoned the Speaker. 'It is a private members' bill.'

'Mr Speaker.' Gladstone looked crestfallen. 'I would implore my Honourable Friends to have regard to the lateness of the hour; if it could be considered tomorrow, I will give my assurance to the House that adequate time will be set aside for a full debate on the measure.'

Gladstone looked over at Parnell. The Speaker looked enquiringly at Parnell. Parnell shook his head. He had not waited five years for such an advantage to be bought off with a plea of more parliamentary time.

'Perhaps a short adjournment, Mr Speaker,' said Gladstone, 'would be beneficial, whilst we consider the position.'

The Speaker nodded his assent and rose. We followed his example and walked out of the Chamber and into the lobby. There was an eerie silence in the lobby at that hour of the morning.

Moments later, an emissary approached Parnell and enquired whether he could have a word. Parnell detached himself from our group. Head bowed and hands behind his back, he walked down one of the corridors, side by side with Gladstone's emissary, who was talking and gesticulating. I was too far away to hear what they were saying, but suddenly I saw them stop. Parnell nodded and then strode back to our group.

'What happened?' we all asked together.

'I will tell you in a few moments,' he replied, 'after the House rises.'

We trooped back into the House and took our seats.

Gladstone rose – wearily, I thought.

'Mr Speaker,' he said, 'I would like to thank you for the courtesy of the adjournment. The time has been well used and I can tell the House that the Government will consider the measure which has been raised.'

Parnell rose.

'Mr Speaker, I wish to withdraw the measure from further consideration by the House,' he said.

The Speaker rose. 'Thank you, gentlemen. As there are no more measures before the House, we shall rise. Good night, gentlemen.'

Gladstone looked over and nodded at Parnell, before disappearing behind the Speaker's chair.

'What was all that about, Parnell?' said Biggar. 'You had better tell us here and now.'

Parnell waited until all the others had left and we were the only members in the Chamber.

'The lunatics have taken over the asylum,' grunted Biggar, as he looked around the empty Chamber. 'Right, Parnell, out with it.'

'Gladstone promised that if we withdrew our bill, the Government would introduce one in similar terms within a few weeks,' he said.

'And do you trust him?' asked Biggar.

'We have saved Gladstone an embarrassment and we have an agreement,' said Parnell simply. 'He will honour it.'

Parnell was right, of course. Two weeks later, Forster, the new Chief Secretary for Ireland, introduced his Compensation for Disturbance bill. I was asked by Parnell to compare the two bills and I saw no difference of any kind.

We now saw our measure put forward and defended by the Liberals against fierce Tory opposition. Night after night, leading Liberal Ministers spoke out in favour of the bill and, in so doing, had to speak out against the rapacious behaviour of landlords and the unjust treatment of their tenants. Gladstone even declared during the debate that it was 'no exaggeration to say that in a country where the agricultural pursuit is the only pursuit, and where the means of payment of rent are destroyed by a visitation of Providence, that the poor occupier may regard a sentence of eviction as very close to a sentence of death'.

Biggar leaned over to me.

'I must be dreaming,' he breathed. 'The Liberals are doing our work for us.'

I made my maiden speech during these debates, so I knew the provisions of the bill back to front. I spent several mornings in the Commons library, writing out drafts and several evenings in my garret, walking backwards and forwards trying to memorise it. Then, on the evening of 14th June, with my heart thumping, I found myself standing up – with several others – trying to catch the eye of the Speaker of the House.

'The new member for Wicklow.' The Speaker gestured in my direction.

Suddenly, I found I was the only person left standing in the House of Commons. The faces around me blurred into a kaleidoscope of colours and shapes and yet all my senses felt alert.

'Mr Speaker.' I became conscious of the silence which now enveloped the House, as it afforded me the centuries-old privilege accorded to a maiden speaker.

'Mr Speaker,' I began again. For a fleeting instant, my mind flashed back to Parnell's first speech at the Rotunda. But Biggar had cautioned me well: 'When you first stand up in the House, your mind goes blank, so you must have your first few sentences off pat.' His words came gushing back to me.

'This bill must be passed for many reasons,' I heard myself say. 'Firstly, because its principle is correct; if a tenant has made improvements to the land, he should be compensated for those improvements.' My breathing was caught and was becoming irregular. 'Secondly, because the landlords have used the recent famine to evict tenants and this has deprived them of any right to compensation.'

There was a third point, but it had disappeared into the confusion of my mind. I reached into my jacket pocket for my notes and tried, as surreptitiously as I could, to glance down at them. Yes. I had it.

'Thirdly, because the House must now address the terrible imbalance between landlords' rights and those of the tenants, and this bill is a small step in that direction.'

I was up and running. This was, of course, not my first public speech, but the privilege of speaking in the House of Commons was of a different order. Suddenly, just as I began to enjoy it, it was over, and my colleagues were shouting 'Hear, hear' and Parnell and Biggar were clapping me on the back and shaking my hand. I was now a fully-fledged Member of Parliament.

Later that evening, as I was leaving the Chamber, Mr Gladstone came over to me.

'Mr Harrison,' he said, 'congratulations on a fine speech. Well crafted and well delivered. I have no doubt we will hear from you again many times.'

I stammered out my profuse thanks for the compliment and he smiled and passed on by. It was the beginning of a cordiality between us which has lasted to this day.

The newspapers next day made a brief mention of my speech and I read them all avidly. The *Freeman's Journal* referred to me as 'Parnell's protégé'; *The Times* as 'a supporter of Mr Parnell's'. Still, there was nothing nasty written. I began to have more appreciation for the significant and unusual courage which it required for Parnell, Biggar and indeed the others to stand up again and again in the House and to endure national opprobrium in the newspapers.

We awaited the vote on the bill with some anxiety, but it was comfortably passed. The Home Rule Party had won its first victory.

Or so we thought.

Twenty-Five

An Unexpected Visitor

IN THE HOT summer days of late June and early July, the House became unbearably stuffy. On one such afternoon, as Parnell looked pale and unwell and as the heat was stifling, I suggested we go out for some air and take a stroll around Parliament Square, a suggestion to which he readily assented.

As we walked through the lobby, Henry, the senior porter in the House, came limping towards us.

'Mr Parnell,' he said. 'I've been looking for you. There is a lady in the Palace Yard, in the carriage; see over there.' He drew Parnell forward to point to the carriage through the window. 'She asked me to hand you this letter.'

Parnell thanked Henry and tipped him a shilling. He tore open the envelope, read it and put it in his pocket.

'The last thing I need at this moment,' he said.

'Who is it?' I asked.

'O'Shea's wife,' he replied. 'A note to ask if I might meet her and her sister in Palace Yard. You had better come over with me and we'll continue with our walk afterwards.'

We walked over to the carriage, covering our eyes against the glare of the hot sun. As we approached, Mrs O'Shea opened the carriage door to greet us, but remained inside. She seemed delighted to see Parnell and smiled immediately on meeting him – as if he were already a friend of long standing. She was a petite woman with short, dark hair and clear, grey eyes.

'Mr Parnell, I am sorry to call you away from parliamentary business at this hour,' she said. 'Please allow me to introduce myself. I am Mrs O'Shea and this is my sister, Mrs Steele. My husband is Captain O'Shea, one of your members.'

Parnell bowed. 'I am pleased to meet you, Mrs O'Shea, Mrs Steele. May I introduce a colleague of mine – Mr James Harrison?'

I bowed to both.

'Mr Parnell, you haven't replied to any of my letters – and I have written to you several times,' said Mrs O'Shea, in a gentle voice of mock injured dignity, looking at Parnell directly.

'I am afraid, Mrs O'Shea, that I haven't had an opportunity to attend to my correspondence for several days now – the pressure of parliamentary business,' said Parnell.

Parnell, in fact, never opened any of his letters. He relied on me to gather them all and reply to them. I gave him all his social invitations, but he usually never even read them, let alone replied to them.

'That may well be, Mr Parnell,' resumed Mrs O'Shea gaily. 'But I have tried to invite you to dinner on at least three occasions and I have had no reply.' She had a vivacity of spirit, captivating and refreshing, and her clear eyes sparkled with interest.

'Please accept my humblest apologies,' said Parnell, smiling at her gaiety.

'I will forgive you, Mr Parnell,' Mrs O'Shea said, laughing, 'but only on one condition.' Confident and self-assured, her voice had a serene and musical quality.

Parnell laughed in reply, something I had not heard him do for some time.

'And what is that?'

'That you – and Mr Harrison of course – join us for dinner next Wednesday.'

'Unfortunately, Mrs O'Shea, I must go to Paris next weekend for my sister's wedding, but I shall be back the following week,' he replied.

'Well, then,' said Mrs O'Shea. 'We shall arrange it that week and I shall leave it to you to name the evening, so that you can have no excuses. I am staying at Thomas' Hotel, so you can write to me there.'

Parnell bowed and closed the door of the carriage. We watched as the carriage turned and drove away, and we resumed our walk around Westminster Square. Parnell made no comment about the interview, but breathed in the warm summer air and seemed revived by the walk. After some time, we plunged back into the Stygian gloom of the Commons Chamber.

⁕

The following week, Parnell and I travelled over to Paris for his sister Theodosia's wedding and I had the pleasure of spending several days in the company of Fanny. Fanny had written me a charming letter when I had been elected, saying she knew that I would distinguish myself in the House of Commons, that Parnell was constantly praising me to her, that she knew he could not do without my loyalty and friendship; she had written me another to wish me good luck with my maiden speech; and again to congratulate me on it. We had kept up a regular correspondence since I had last seen her in New York. But whether her affection for me was that of a close family friend or more, I did not know; for my part, I did not dare press the matter, as I was too bound up with the family. I thought it would have been inappropriate. Although she had many male admirers, she was still not engaged and, to my delight, she sought me out often and I spent days in her company in a state of delirium, riding in the Bois de Boulogne, walking around Paris, or going for dinner and to the Opera.

Parnell, however, spent much of his time in Paris resting in his room. He seemed greatly debilitated and only ventured out on the wedding day itself.

'Charlie, you must look after yourself,' pleaded Fanny. She sat on the floor beside the sofa on which he was sitting and took his hand in hers. 'You mustn't let anything happen to you.'

Parnell smiled. 'I will be fine.' he said. 'I'm tired, that's all.'

'I am so worried about Charles,' Fanny said to me afterwards. 'I was shocked when I saw him. He looks quite unwell.'

'He's doing too much,' I agreed.

'I've never seen him look so pale, so thin,' continued Fanny. 'Has he seen a doctor?'

'No,' I replied. 'He refuses to. He says it's just tiredness. But it's more than that. He's overwrought. His speeches in the House are so exhausting. He is quite enervated after them. I hear him sighing for hours afterwards, trying to get his breath back, as if he were constricted.'

'Please look after him,' she said. 'I couldn't bear it if anything happened to him.'

❧

When we returned to London the following week, Parnell, Justin McCarthy and I took a cab to Thomas' Hotel on Berkeley Square, for Mrs O'Shea's dinner party. Willie O'Shea was there also, and in amusing form, his anecdotes chosen more for the dining-room than the officers' mess. Mrs O'Shea was charmingly interested in everyone and uninterested in talking about herself. Given her husband's egotism, perhaps this was the attraction of opposites.

After dinner, we went to the theatre, where the O'Sheas had reserved a box; I sat at the front with McCarthy, Mrs Steele and O'Shea, whilst Mrs O'Shea and Parnell sat behind us, and chatted to one another in low tones throughout the entire play. I doubt they watched a single scene and we chided them several times, asking them to hush; this would stop them for a moment, but then after a while they would start up again.

❧

Then, several weeks later, in early August, disaster struck.

The House of Lords threw out our Compensation for Disturbance bill by a staggering vote of 278 to 51. It caused a furore in London as Gladstone sought to reassert his authority over the Liberal Lords, to no avail. But it was particularly calamitous for our party, for Irish tenants, and for the Land League. If the Lords threw out such a modest bill to protect tenants, how could we possibly obtain major land reform? After the initial euphoria, it was a bitter blow. We were back where we started.

Days later, I noticed Mrs O'Shea in the gallery in the House of Commons and went up to her. She was as charming as ever.

'Mr Harrison,' she said. 'How pleased I am to see you. I am here to watch my husband speak – he told me he was to deliver his maiden speech today.'

She answered my question before it was asked and, as I looked down, I could see O'Shea lounging on the Government benches.

'I don't think Mr Parnell approves of my husband sitting with the Government,' she said to me conspiratorially.

'That's true,' I replied. I wanted to add that the whole party disapproved, but I bit my tongue.

'Mr Parnell believes all Home Rule Members of Parliament should sit in opposition. If they don't, he calls them 'West Britons', does he not?' she asked, smiling.

Before I could explain further, Parnell himself appeared.

'Mrs O'Shea,' he said. 'I saw you from the Chamber. What brings you here?'

She repeated her explanation and her comment about West Britons.

'The House can be a place of some robust exchanges,' said Parnell demurely.

'But are you not a West Briton yourself?' said Mrs O'Shea, smiling. 'I thought all the Anglo-Irish were regarded as West Britons.'

Parnell laughed and held up his hands.

We watched the debate for a short time before Parnell suggested we go for tea. We went into the lobby to find Captain O'Shea, but when he came out of the Chamber he had business to attend to in the City, and could not join us. He had, apparently, decided to defer his maiden speech. We managed without him, however, and whiled away the afternoon taking tea at a nearby hotel, gossiping about political events.

'I heard that the very idea of your bill provoked outrage in the Lords, Mr Parnell,' said Mrs O'Shea. 'I have it on good authority that Lord Waterford actually came back from a pilgrimage at Lourdes specifically to vote against it, and he hasn't appeared in the Lords for the last ten years.'

'Did he really?' Parnell laughed. 'Then perhaps we need to go to Lourdes to pray for a miracle ourselves.'

'Is that what is needed?' said Mrs O'Shea. 'A miracle?'

'I don't know,' said Parnell 'But there will be a rage in Ireland about this rejection.'

Soon the conversation moved to other matters and it was time to leave. Parnell offered to see Mrs O'Shea to the railway station and I took my leave.

Twenty-Six

The Speech at Ennis

IT WAS NOT until early September that Parnell had a chance to return to Ireland to rest. But he could not rest for long. He had agreed to speak at Ennis and, although it was now over a year since his speech at Westport, and almost a year since the Land League had been founded, nothing tangible had been achieved to improve the lot of tenant farmers. Worse, the rejection of the bill by the House of Lords brought a surge in new evictions. Landlords now believed that the worst – for them – was over. The harvest had been plentiful that summer; the threat of famine had receded and the Lords had rejected any measure of further protection for tenants. For landlords, the *status quo ante* now prevailed. Rents were due, reductions were refused and families were evicted again in their hundreds.

Parnell and I took the night train from Dublin to Ennis. It meant another sleepless night as the train jerked and rolled noisily at every station throughout the night. We arrived in Ennis at four o'clock in the morning, expecting a quiet walk to the hotel. Instead, the station platform was lit up by hundreds of burning torches, held by a welcoming crowd of thousands. Parnell was cheered all the way to his hotel. He was by now the master of the short, impromptu speech and he thanked them all for getting out of their beds at this hour of the morning to welcome him and exhorted them to get some rest as, on the morrow – no, later in the day – there was serious work to be accomplished.

I slept for a few hours until ten, and after a quick breakfast wandered out to the square at the top of the street. Even at this early hour, a constant stream of people was flowing into town.

The signs of organisation were unmistakable: Davitt stood beside
the platform, speaking to men and pointing to certain streets;
others came up to him looking for instructions; decisions were
made, orders shouted out. A young man made his way back to
his horse, jumped on, bareback, and shouted for ten of his fellow
cavalrymen to follow him. I watched as they went towards one
of the streets leading to the main square; they lined up across the
street, guarding the entrance to the square, and then, on a signal
from their leader, practised a manoeuvre – walking up the street,
five on each side, and then back again to where they started.
Hundreds of stewards with distinctive green armbands moved
in and out of the main square, giving directions and taking up
positions. Over the next few hours, thousands more people
flowed into the town, filling up the square and overflowing into
all the approach roads; banners of all colours flapped in the late
morning breeze, with their messages of 'God Save Ireland', 'God
Save Parnell', 'To Hell With Forster'.

I saw the O'Gorman Mahon nearby and went over to him. I had
expected to see both him and William O'Shea there, as Ennis was
in their constituency. There was, however, no sign of O'Shea.

'Why is O'Shea not here?' I asked. 'He should be here.'

'Well, he should be and he shouldn't be,' said the O'Gorman
Mahon in a delphic manner, nodding his head from side to side to
keep time with his words.

'What do you mean by that?' I asked sharply.

'You're right, Harrison,' he said, 'of course he should be here.
But I have it on reliable authority ...' – he looked at me directly,
as if he were about to impart a great pearl of gossip – 'that our
countrymen in this part of the world have not taken kindly to
O'Shea sitting on the Government benches.'

'I'm not surprised,' I said.

'I know, I know,' said the old warrior. 'I have told him so
repeatedly. But he wants to be his own man.'

'Can Mrs O'Shea not persuade him?' I asked.

'Bah.' He raised his hands in the air. 'Not at all. She has tried. I
have tried. We've all tried. But he doesn't listen to her at all.'

'She seems sensible enough,' I remarked.

'You've met her, then?' said the O'Gorman Mahon, surprised.

'Several times,' I said. 'She and her husband invited Parnell to dinner.'

'Good, good, I'm glad that happened,' the O'Gorman said in a reflective tone.

'Did you know about it?' I asked, surprised by the remark.

'No, no, not at all.' The O'Gorman Mahon was suddenly on guard. 'It was just that I knew O'Shea wanted to invite Parnell to dinner and I encouraged him to do so, so that ...' He paused for a few moments.

'Mrs O'Shea can be so ... charming,' he said, looking at me with what I could only interpret as a leer.

I chose to ignore it.

'Indeed she is,' I said. 'Quite charming.'

The conversation left me vaguely unsettled, as if there were unseen forces at work behind Parnell's back, inveigling him into a trap of which he was unaware.

I went back into the hotel, to find Parnell calmly drinking tea and looking into the distance. He looked quite alone. Suddenly I felt – and I do not know why it happened then – an overwhelming sadness for him. He had chosen this path – it is true – but what demons had driven him to it? Was it his mother's constant admonitions to prove himself worthy of her father's memory? Or the contempt of his American fiancée, who had broken off their engagement because of his lack of distinction? Who knows? But the path he had chosen had put him through the ordeal of a thousand public speeches and a thousand times his will had controlled his nervous energy, like reins on a thoroughbred. I now had some insight, if only from my own speech in the House of Commons, into the singular strain of speaking to a gathering such as the one now assembling outside. They looked to him for leadership, and he could not disappoint.

'Are you ready?' I asked.

He looked at me, seriously, his brown eyes clear.

'What is the crowd?' he asked.

'One of your biggest,' I said. 'Perhaps the biggest. Hard to say how many. Thirty, maybe forty thousand.'

'Davitt does not disappoint,' he mused.

He got up from the table and went over to the window to look out, pulling the curtains aside.

'It doesn't get any easier,' he continued, half to himself, half to me. 'I thought it would but it doesn't. The same overwhelming tension.'

Minutes later, Davitt arrived at the hotel.

'We have a huge crowd here for you, Parnell,' he said. 'They have travelled from all over, from Clare, Limerick, Tipperary, Kerry and even further, to hear you today.'

'Good,' said Parnell briskly, 'let's not keep them waiting any longer' – and, putting on the mask of the public man, he walked quickly out of the hotel.

As Davitt, Parnell and Finnegan – the speakers of the day – ascended the platform, there was a huge roar of cheering and clapping for Parnell. Parnell was, however, the last to speak and, after the fierce denunciations of the previous speakers, his speech at the start seemed rather mild. As he stood at the foot of O'Connell's statue, which dominates the curious oblong square of Ennis, it seemed as if I were watching an apostolic succession, as if O'Connell were anointing Parnell as his successor and the people approved his choice. As his speech gathered momentum, his voice reverberated around the four corners of the square and down through the streets beyond.

'We have tried,' he said, 'to pass a reasonable measure through the House of Lords to help our tenants ... But they killed it off as soon as they could ...'

He gripped the rails in that familiar gesture of tension.

'And so they ... the landlords ... believe that nothing has changed, that nothing will change ...'

He looked out defiantly at the crowds.

'But *everything* has changed. *We* have decided that it will change and so it will change.' He emphasised the last words syllable by syllable. 'They think that they control the situation but they do not. We do. They simply have not realised that yet.' He gestured to the crowd. 'And so, if that is how the English wish to respond, then we shall respond in kind.'

A mood of concentration gripped the crowds.

'They have started their evictions again – I know that – and I know that you have tried to keep a firm grip on your homes. And you should continue with that. But despite your efforts, hundreds have been put out of their homes. And land-grabbers have taken advantage and moved into those same homes. With little thought for the misery done to the previous inhabitants. So, now, what are you going to do with a tenant who bids for the farm from which his neighbour has been evicted?'

The question hung in the air.

'Shoot him,' said a loud voice, to great cheers.

Parnell turned towards the speaker.

'I heard someone say "shoot him",' he said loudly, 'but I wish to point out to you a much better way, a more Christian, a more charitable way, which will give the lost sinner an opportunity of repenting.'

The black humour was not lost on the crowd.

'When a man takes a farm from which another has been evicted, you must show him on the roadside – when you meet him – you must show him in the streets of the town, you must show him at the shop counter, you must show him in the fair and at the marketplace – and even in the house of worship – by putting him into a sort of moral Coventry, by isolating him from the rest of his kind as if he were a leper of old; you must show him your detestation of the crime he has committed.' Parnell's voice blazed out across the silent square.

'You must punish these land-grabbers even more, from now on, so that they will be forced to stop bidding for these farms.'

Great cheers of support came forth from the crowd at this proposal.

'I tell you now,' Parnell continued with greater warmth, 'we shall not rest until this millstone of landlordism is removed from this country. It is a millstone around your necks, throttling you all, throttling your industry and your future and your children's future.'

He paused for breath.

'And if the House of Lords – this House of Landlords – continue this fight with us, they will regret it, because they will lose.'

There were huge roars again at this declaration of defiance.

'Because if five hundred thousand tenant farmers of Ireland strike against ten thousand landlords, I would like to see how they would get enough police to force their payments. So we are not without our weapons,' he said, 'but remember this: Parliament will resume next February and we will get a land bill, but the measure of the land bill we get in the next session will be the measure of your activity and energy this winter. If it requires an earthquake to solve the land question in Ireland, then an earthquake there will have to be.'

The roars and cheers as he ended his magnificent speech of defiance must have been heard as far away as Limerick, and he was mobbed by well-wishers and supporters as he made his way back to the station when his speech had ended.

The extraordinary effects of his speech at Ennis were evident within weeks. It was not that Parnell invented social ostracism as a weapon; it had been spoken of for months throughout that summer, by many different members of the League in many different speeches. But somehow it seemed different when Parnell spoke about it. It was as if he said, 'I will this to be done and it will be done.' People now knew that he meant what he said. He had said he would obstruct the House of Commons and he had done so; he had told the people to keep a firm grip on their homesteads and he had stood beside them when they did. Now he was sanctioning a new weapon: land-grabbers were to be cast out of their communities. Landlords, agents and their summons servers were now not the only enemy; land-grabbers, their accomplices and all those who propped up the whole rotten system of landlordism were now targets for the organised wrath of the Land League. This was Parnell's response to the House of Lords: he intended to make the west of Ireland ungovernable, to force Gladstone and the House of Lords to understand that if they would not pass reasonable measures then they too would suffer. He had obstructed the Government in the House of Commons; now he intended to obstruct the administration of English rule throughout Ireland. The House of Lords had refused to pass a minor measure; they had thrown down the gauntlet. Very well then. Parnell picked up the gauntlet and threw it back in their faces. If they want a fight, we will fight them so hard they will wish they had never started it. That was the aggressive, pugilistic message he sent out from Ennis on that day in September. And it fell on eager ears.

∾◦◦◦∾

After Ennis, Parnell returned to Avondale to attend to estate business, but in the ensuing days he appeared restless and distracted.

On Wednesday, he told me he had some business in London to which he had to attend. He was no more specific than that, and it was clear he wanted to travel alone. He left that evening.

He must have only arrived in London before he turned back again, because he was back in Avondale on Saturday, more agitated and restless than ever.

He was back just in time to catch the afternoon train to New Ross, where he was to speak to another huge gathering. He made another impassioned speech, declaring that landlords were the English 'garrison' in Ireland, and that if we destroyed the landlords, we would destroy that garrison and take a major step towards Home Rule.

The following week he spoke to another 'monster meeting' – as they were now being called, echoing the monster rallies of Daniel O'Connell forty years earlier. Everywhere, the Land League cavalry and stewards organised and controlled these events, ensuring there were no scenes of rowdyism, no drunkenness or breaches of the peace. It was, indeed, a curious feature of such meetings that the constabulary seemed nowhere to be seen. Perhaps it was wiser for them to be out of sight.

But it was the procession at Cork in early October which I remember most vividly in this autumn campaign. Parnell had travelled by train to Blarney, and then by open carriage to the centre of the city. As the carriage approached Patrick Street, tens of thousands of people lined the streets, cheering him on, and bouquets of flowers rained down on him like hailstones; people craned out of windows on upper floors and stood on rooftops to catch a glimpse of him. This was now his city, and he was now their Member of Parliament and the national leader. As the full extent of the salute of the people of Cork became evident, Parnell stood up in the carriage to wave back in acknowledgement, encouraging them all the more. Yet there was never a smile; the same grim, serious face presented itself to them, accepting their fealty.

He looked like a king, and the epithet 'the uncrowned King of Ireland' never seemed more apposite. I remembered the crowds in London who had gathered in their thousands to watch their Queen at the state opening of Parliament; this moment in Cork was as close as a subject nation could get to a coronation of Parnell, an almost regal procession by Ireland's new leader, at the start of a campaign of national liberation. A leader as regal as Queen Victoria and as tough as Gladstone.

But, unlike Victoria and Gladstone, Parnell would be in gaol within a year.

Twenty-Seven

A Mystery

THE FOLLOWING DAY, Parnell travelled back to Dublin and then on to Avondale. He had the rest of the week to relax, but he seemed unable to do so. He was perpetually agitated and restless and he prowled around his study as if it were a cage.

'I must go to London,' he said suddenly. 'That business of mine has not yet been resolved.'

I still did not know what business he was referring to, but from his tone, I knew he would not welcome any questions.

'Tell Davitt I shall be back on Sunday for Roscommon,' he said and, grabbing his bag, which was always at the ready, he called one of his groomsmen to take him to Rathdrum station immediately.

There was no word from him all week and by Saturday, to my surprise, he still had not returned. I sent a telegram to him at Keppel Street and another to the hotel in Cannon Street, to enquire after him, but they were both returned unanswered.

On Sunday morning, I went directly to Kingstown to meet the ferry and to travel on with him to the Roscommon meeting. I waited, restlessly, until the last passenger had disembarked, but still he did not appear.

Eventually, I could wait no longer. I took the train to Westland Row and walked over to Amiens Street to catch the train to Roscommon. I got there by three o'clock – two hours before the meeting – to tell O'Kelly that Parnell must have been delayed in London. O'Kelly, however, was unperturbed.

The meeting went off well, despite Parnell's absence and O'Kelly delivered his usual barnstorming speech, a tirade of anti-landlord abuse and a thinly veiled call to arms. I returned to Dublin by the evening train, when the meeting was over. I walked to Morrison's to see if Parnell was there, but there was no sign of him. Puzzled now, and worried lest something had befallen him in London, I read all the newspapers from cover to cover, but there was no mention of anything untoward. I also sent daily telegrams to the Cannon Street Hotel. But they had no news of him.

Eventually, on Thursday, a telegram arrived for me. 'Will return Saturday. Meet Morrison's 11 a.m. CSP.'

At least he was alive! I travelled to Dublin on Saturday morning and arrived at Morrison's just before eleven o'clock. I walked through the foyer, but there was no sign of Parnell. I looked into the drawing-room: it too was empty. I glanced into the library. There was a gentleman sitting on the sofa, staring into the fire, but it was not Parnell. I went back into the drawing-room to wait but, at 11.15, as there was still no sign of Parnell, I went out to the clerk.

'I was to meet Mr Parnell here at eleven o'clock,' I said to the clerk. 'Have you seen him?'

'Mr Parnell arrived about an hour ago,' the clerk said. 'He said if anyone asked for him he would be in the library.'

I immediately walked into the library. There was, however, no sign of Parnell, only the same gentleman, sitting on the sofa, staring into the fire. He looked up as he heard my approach.

'Harrison,' he said, 'good to see you.'

'Parnell,' I said astonished, 'is that you?'

He was, quite literally, unrecognisable as the Parnell who had left ten days earlier. He had shaved his beard off almost completely, leaving just a narrow sliver along the jawline and under his chin. His hair, too, had been cut in a strange and unfashionable manner.

'Are you all right?' I asked. 'What happened to you?'

'I shaved my beard off,' he said. 'Why do you ask?'

I was so taken aback by his question that it took me some moments to stammer out my answer.

'Well, it's just that … I wasn't sure if something had happened to you … You missed the Roscommon meeting.'

'Yes,' he said absently. 'Yes, I know. Did you go?'

'Yes, I did.'

'Good,' he replied, perfectly satisfied with that answer. 'I knew you would. So you explained I was delayed in London by business?'

'Well, to be honest,' I said hesitantly, 'I didn't know what to say.'
'So what did you say?'
'I said I thought that you had got delayed by business in London.'
Parnell smiled.
'But what did happen?' I asked.
'I got delayed by business,' he said simply.

The meetings of the Land League were now not simply occasions for revolutionary speeches, but assemblies where the alternative writ of the League took hold. We set up tables in each town and village; we took details of complaints against landlords or their agents; we took details of tenants who were in arrears, tenants who feared eviction, and tenants who had received eviction notices. Parish by parish, village by village, and town by town, the League drew up a detailed inventory of the rents paid by each tenant on each estate, the habits and patterns of landlords and their agents, the days on which tenants offered a reduced rent and the response of the landlord. From week to week we targeted landlords and, once targeted, the landlord usually backed down, fearful of how far the League might go. Landlords called it intimidation; the League called it 'negotiating'. If a family were due to receive an eviction notice, local men guarded the house day after day; when the process server came to serve the eviction papers, he was set upon and received a serious thrashing and his papers were destroyed. Forced by his superiors – the landlord or his agent – to return, he would come back several days later with a police escort, but they too would be attacked and beaten back. The police dared not use a firearm – after Balla, they knew they could be murdered in reprisal.

In this way, Parnell's exhortation to tenant farmers to 'keep a firm grip on their homesteads' was translated into a detailed series of actions by the infantry of the Land League. Whether these men were Fenians or merely desperate mattered not. Their actions were justified to themselves and to their communities because Parnell had told them to keep a firm grip on their homesteads. These were men desperate to avoid the destruction of their families, and desperate men will always use desperate measures. These tactics were immediately successful. The great surge of evictions which had occurred in August and September – after the House of Lords had thrown out Gladstone's bill – was now spent. Indeed, after Ennis, the number of evictions fell week by week throughout October, November and December. By Christmas, it was clear that Parnell and the League had been successful in defending countless families threatened with eviction.

Journalists from English newspapers were now reporting Parnell's every speech and his inflammatory comments to crowds and demonstrations throughout the country. Stories of violence and intimidation multiplied throughout the autumn, but Parnell was unmoved. He hated bullies and he saw the English landlords in Ireland as the worst sort of cowardly bullies. 'You have to stand up to bullies,' was a regular refrain of his, and if these bullies, whether landlords or agents, bailiffs or police officers, got a bloody nose – or more – for trying to evict a poor family, then they got exactly what they deserved. He intended to show England that he would make Ireland ungovernable.

Twenty-Eight

The Boycott Affair

I N THE MEANTIME, only days after Parnell's speech at Ennis, a
Father O'Malley, the parish priest of Ballinrobe, and a staunch
supporter of the Land League, rounded up all the men of his
parish and led them over to Captain Boycott's house at Lough
Mask. Boycott was a land agent for Lord Erne, a powerful local
landlord who was seeking to evict dozens of families who were in
arrears. We didn't realise it at the time, but Captain Boycott was
soon to donate his name to the English language.

I heard later that Father O'Malley and his troops walked over
to the stable yard and he spoke – forcefully, I understand – to all
Boycott's farm labourers and groomsmen, and directed them
to stop working for Boycott immediately. He then sent for the
domestic servants and delivered the same message to them. On the
instructions of the Land League, he said, they were to stop working
for Captain Boycott immediately and to walk back with him to
Ballinrobe. Within minutes, all Boycott's workers stopped what
they were doing and walked back to town.

Once back in town, Father O'Malley and his rapidly growing
contingent walked from shop to shop and tradesman to tradesman
in the town, to 'suggest' they did no further work for Captain
Boycott. They all agreed. The blacksmith would not shoe his horse,
the grocery store refused to sell him provisions; the local hotel
refused to sell him food or drink. The post boy would not deliver
his post.

I heard much of this from James Redpath, an American journalist who had come to Ireland that summer to report on the Irish situation for the *New York Herald*, and whom I had befriended. Redpath was an amusing chronicler of the Irish rebellion and had a great instinct for an unfolding story. He wanted to meet Parnell, and I had arranged a lunch for the three of us at the Imperial Hotel in Sackville Street, in the early days of November.

Over lunch, Redpath amused us with stories of Father O'Malley.

'I've never met a man who can drink like him,' he said. 'When I met him first, it was a very cold afternoon, so he poured me a large whiskey and said, "That's a cold one. Have a glass to warm you up." And the next day, the sun was splitting the stones and he said, "That's a warm one" and poured me another glass, saying "This will cool you down."'

'It's probably why he's so popular with his flock,' laughed Parnell.

I asked him who had come up with the word 'Boycott', as the newspapers had been using the term for some weeks now.

'Father O'Malley and I had a few whiskeys late one evening,' said Redpath. 'I was telling him that I needed to go to write my weekly article and that I couldn't keep using words like "ostracism" and "excommunication"; did he know any better word?' Redpath tapped his forehead with his finger. 'And Father O'Malley took another swig of whiskey, thought for a moment and said, "Why not call it a boycott?", so I said "Why not?". I tried it in my next article. Either my editor didn't read it or else he knew what I meant, so I've used it ever since.'

'Have you seen Boycott's letter to *The Times*,' I asked, 'complaining about what's going on?'

'I certainly have,' said Redpath excitedly. 'I have it here, actually. I sent a copy of it to the *Herald* so they could reprint it. There's an editorial to go with it.'

He lifted his overflowing briefcase from the floor onto his lap and began sifting through the piles of torn newspaper articles, writing pads and maps, looking for the article. Eventually, he pulled one of the newspapers out and read out the leader.

'A more frightful picture of triumphant anarchy has never been presented in any community pretending to be civilised and subject to law ...'

'That's a phrase with a ring to it,' said Parnell, 'triumphant anarchy.'

'Where's the bit about … ?' said Redpath, searching the close print of the newspaper. '… Yes, here it is.' He continued to read. 'If such monstrous oppression and spoliation cannot be put down by the constitutional powers about to be set in motion against the leaders of the League …'

He put the paper cutting down on the table. 'They are going to come after you. It's there, Mr Parnell, in black and white,' he said. 'They couldn't spell it out more clearly.'

'But for what?' said Parnell imperturbably. 'I haven't shot anyone. I haven't assaulted anyone. I haven't intimidated anyone. All I have done is to encourage people to send land-grabbers to Coventry, and that's not a crime.'

'That's why Father O'Malley is so keen on the Land League,' said Redpath, 'because it is not violent. But will it always be so?' He looked at Parnell expectantly.

'I will never advocate a rebellion,' said Parnell. 'We would be crushed by the English within days and thousands of people would die. I would never lead our people into such a war. I will not hurl them onto the points of British bayonets. That's what the Fenians still have not realised – we would never win that war. But this …' He leaned forward to emphasise his point. 'This is a war we can win. Gladstone now knows we can make the country ungovernable. English weapons are useless against it.'

'Have you seen what's in today's *Belfast Newsletter*?' asked Redpath.

Parnell shook his head.

'They are calling for a relief force from Ulster to help poor old Boycott,' said Redpath.

'Good,' said Parnell. 'The more trouble, the better. It might frighten Gladstone and the House of Lords into giving us a proper Land Act next year.'

'Can I ask you about your recent speech in Tipperary, Mr Parnell?' asked Redpath. 'It attracted a lot of attention.'

Parnell smiled and I began to laugh.

'Perhaps I am better able to do this story justice, Parnell,' I said. I turned to Redpath. 'Parnell was in Mayo some days ago, and we saw that extra constables had been drafted in to deal with the disturbances there. Parnell enquired where these men had come from and was told they had come from Tipperary, because that county was relatively quiet. So, last week Parnell was invited to a Land League dinner in Tipperary and he stood up at this dinner and upbraided the men of Tipperary. He told them it was a disgrace to all of them that their county was so quiet, that if they didn't have the constables back to Tipperary within the month, their cowardice would endure for generations, but that he knew the men of Tipperary were no cowards, that they had a fighting spirit to equal any county in Ireland.'

Redpath started laughing also.

'And how did they respond?' he asked.

'Oh, with a standing ovation,' I said. 'And the police were back in Tipperary within the week!'

As we continued our conversation during lunch, a waiter approached our table. He coughed into his hand deferentially, before saying, 'I am sorry to disturb you, Mr Parnell, but there is a gentleman to see you.'

'Send him in,' said Parnell.

The waiter nodded at two men who were standing at the entrance to the dining-room. Within moments, one of them, a young man, smartly dressed in a suit and with his coat neatly folded over his arm, came to the table.

'Mr Charles Stewart Parnell?' he said officiously, making a drumbeat of every syllable.

Parnell half turned to look at him, putting his elbow on the back of the chair.

'Yes.'

'Mr Parnell, I am a detective with G Division in the Dublin Metropolitan Police,' the young man said. 'I have come to serve this on you,' and he handed a document to Parnell

'What is it?' asked Parnell.

'It is an indictment to answer criminal charges, sir,' said the detective and, turning on his heel, he walked quickly out of the restaurant with his colleague.

Parnell picked up the document impassively and began to read it aloud.

'The Queen versus Charles Stewart Parnell, Joseph Biggar, John Dillon, Thomas Egan, Thomas Brennan and others.'

He looked at us and smiled.

'I am glad Biggar is included,' he said. 'He would have been very annoyed if he wasn't.'

'No mention of Davitt,' I said, surprised.

'No, strangely,' said Parnell. 'Perhaps, after Sligo, they will leave Davitt alone.'

'You don't mind some questions, Mr Parnell, do you?' Redpath asked, taking out his notepad and pen, no doubt scarcely believing his good fortune that he was present at such a moment.

Parnell shook his head. 'Not at all.'

'Why do you think the Government is moving against you now?' Redpath asked.

Parnell resumed his lunch calmly.

'Gladstone and Forster had to do something,' he said. 'But it's too late now.'

'Why is that?' Redpath asked, scribbling down Parnell's answer at the same time.

'The Land League is well organised now – we don't need the help that such prosecutions would usually give us.'

'What are the charges?' asked Redpath.

Parnell picked up the document and read out the indictment.

'Conspiracy to prevent payment of rent, conspiracy to prevent evictions, conspiracy to create ill-will among Her Majesty's subjects,' he read. 'Guilty on all counts,' he smiled, ' – but you needn't quote me on that.'

Redpath laughed.

'Are you not concerned you will be put in prison?' asked Redpath.

'I doubt any jury in Dublin would convict me,' replied Parnell. 'It's just another of Forster's miscalculations. But if I have to go to prison, so be it. I won't be the first Irish leader to be sent to prison. Nor the last, I expect.'

∽∾

Some days later, Parnell told me that he would not speak at any more Land League meetings for a number of weeks, and asked me to cancel any invitations he had accepted. He had received an invitation from Captain and Mrs O'Shea to stay with them in England and he had accepted.

'I thought you didn't like O'Shea,' I said, surprised.

'I don't,' he said bluntly, 'but I need him back on our side of the House when Parliament resumes in January.'

I was surprised, as Parnell rarely tried to persuade anyone to his point of view.

'What about preparations for your trial?' I asked.

'I shall leave that to you,' he smiled, 'as my learned counsel.'

'Your counsel!' I said, surprised.

'Yes,' said Parnell. 'I want you to act for me.'

'But I have no experience at all,' I said.

'You have to start somewhere,' said Parnell. 'Anyway, I am sure my solicitor will also brief a silk, if not two. You were at all the meetings so you are already fully briefed. How else are you going to learn?'

Twenty-Nine

Another Eviction

AS PARLIAMENT WAS in recess and as the trial was still
some weeks off, I decided to travel to Mayo with Redpath,
to follow the Boycott story. I telegraphed Justin McCarthy
and *The Star* agreed to appoint me as a special correspondent for
the duration. The following day, Parnell sailed to England to spend
a few weeks with the O'Sheas, whilst Redpath and I caught the
morning train to Galway and then to Claremorris, and finally took
a pony and trap to Ballinrobe, a small town just a few miles from
Boycott's home at Lough Mask House. I stayed at the Valkenberg
Hotel on Main Street, an elegant three-storey hotel distinguished by
its gaunt, grey Galway stone.

The boycott of Boycott and the fear of 1,000 armed Ulstermen
marching into town were the only topics of conversation in
Ballinrobe. No one knew when they might come, or how many
there might be, or whether they would be armed, and, in this
uncertainty, rumours thrived like mould in damp: Ulster was about
to invade Mayo; the Land League would respond; civil war could
erupt; the English would have to intervene – and all 'because of
Boycott's bloody turnips', as one local put it. No one in England
seemed at all perturbed by stories of evictions of hundreds of Irish
peasant farmers and their families, but now that a single land agent
was the target, it was suddenly an English crisis!

The following morning, Redpath and I rode out the four or five
miles to Lough Mask House to find the high iron gates closed and
guarded by two constables, who refused to admit us. We waited
for a few moments, looking through the gates at the long avenue,
at the immaculately rolled front lawn and the solid stone house

beyond the trees, almost hidden from view. Redpath suggested we ride around the estate walls until we found a farm entrance but, as we rounded the first bend, our way was blocked by a flock of sheep, herded along by a stocky middle-aged man in tweeds and two constables armed with rifles. We reined in our horses and waited, as these armed shepherds drove the sheep through a gate into a sloping field on our left. Redpath recognised the civilian as Captain Boycott and saluted him.

Boycott came over to us at once, greeting us in a bluff, no-nonsense manner. He was a man in his mid-fifties, of medium height, but he held himself quite erect, perhaps a legacy of his years as a captain in the British Army. He was almost bald, but with thick grey hair at the sides of his head and a full long grey beard.

'Good morning gentlemen.' He spoke with a Norfolk accent and, for a man in the eye of a storm, he seemed calm enough.

Redpath introduced me as another journalist. We had agreed, earlier, that my connection with Parnell was unlikely to endear me to Boycott or, indeed, to any of the constables. I explained to him that I was doing a piece for *The Star*.

'Your letter to *The Times* has caused quite a stir, Captain Boycott,' I said.

'So I see.' He leaned against the wall, his sheep dog worrying around him. The two constables kept a short distance away, leaning on the gate, sharing a cigarette.

I couldn't resist the urge to lead him on.

'What do you think has caused all this?' I asked.

Boycott looked at me, hard and unblinking.

'What has caused it?' he repeated, his voice rising in anger. 'I would have thought it was obvious, isn't it?' he said. 'That damned speech in Ennis! We'd been managing fine up here. Nothing we couldn't handle. A bit more time and we'd have solved it.'

'How would you have solved it?' I asked innocently.

'The tenants hereabouts have been well treated,' he said. 'I've been here for years. I've had no problems with them. Not even last year, when things got a bit ropey with the bad harvest. We offered to reduce the rent. But once the Land League started their meddling, it all went wrong.'

'And what about your eviction notices?' I asked.

'They couldn't pay the rent,' said Boycott directly. 'I'm not running a charity. I'm trying to run an estate. And if the tenants can't pay the rent, I need to find tenants who can.'

It was evident that Boycott thought no more of serving a family with eviction papers than placing traps for rabbits.

'So how are you managing,' I asked, 'without your workers?'

'I can't manage, can I?' said Boycott, but without any trace of self-pity. 'We won't starve, but if I don't get in the crops soon I've lost another harvest.'

He looked up at me. 'I've written to Forster about it. I told him I need soldiers down here.'

I was incredulous.

'Soldiers?' I said. 'To take in your crops? Why should Forster give you that?'

'Because,' said Boycott, 'it's not just about me any longer, is it? It's about law and order in this province. If Forster can't do that ...' He shrugged and left the sentence unfinished. 'But what I don't need,' he said, 'is 500 Ulstermen from Belfast looking for a fight.'

∽ৡৡৡ∼

Days later, I was awakened in my hotel in Ballinrobe, at the first bleak light of a November dawn, by the clatter of marching hobnailed boots and the loud, indecipherable monotone of a Drill Sergeant, barking out orders which only his soldiers could understand. I dressed quickly and went outside. It was a cold, wet morning and I watched, shivering, as hundreds of thoroughly drenched and miserable-looking soldiers passed by the hotel door, marching into Ballinrobe. Forster had granted Boycott his wish.

Over the following days, the town grew tense and increasingly anxious about the arrival of the Unionist force. With an army already in the town, everyone was now certain that a huge force of Ulstermen must be marching on Lough Mask, and would arrive within days. This had all the makings of a serious battle, and I sent Parnell daily telegrams apprising him of the situation. To my surprise, I received no reply. His presence would have been reassuring to the Land League and Ballinrobe. But he never came.

The next day, we learned that only fifty Ulstermen were allowed and that they were on the march from Belfast. Telegrams to the town announced their progress: by midday they were in Athlone; by one o'clock they were at Ballyhaunis. Redpath and I decided to ride over to Claremorris to witness their arrival for ourselves.

The Ulstermen arrived at Claremorris in mid-afternoon and, with their knapsacks on their shoulders, sauntered out of the station, to be confronted by large crowds shouting abuse at them; a cordon of cavalry and infantry, with bayonets drawn, prevented the crowds from rushing at them to provide them with a more physical welcome. Within minutes, a bugle sounded, and the cavalry began an orderly march out of Claremorris to Ballinrobe; the cavalry were followed by a group of infantry, then the fifty Ulstermen in double line, and behind them a further platoon of infantry and a cohort of dragoons. Following on were an ambulance wagon, some provisions wagons and, finally, those crowds who chose to follow the procession out of town, hissing, shouting and jeering.

The light fades early in mid-November in the west of Ireland, and by half-past four it was almost dark. Soon it started raining again. The infantry trudged along, heads down, their rifles cradled in their hands and leaning against their shoulders; the officers on horseback walked their horses beside them, the collars of their greatcoats pulled up for protection against the rain.

The weary, wet, miserable column arrived in Ballinrobe at about half-past nine that evening, after five hours marching in the rain. They were greeted by a jeering crowd, booing and shouting at them as they squelched into town, but lines of infantrymen on both sides of the main street prevented any closer contact. They marched down to the infantry barracks and slept there overnight.

The following morning it was still misting rain, and after breakfast the troops and volunteers headed out of Ballinrobe for the last few miles to Lough Mask House. Redpath and I followed them over.

As the column filed its way through the narrow gates of the Boycott estate, I saw rows of tents pitched on Boycott's once perfect front lawn and camp fires smoking everywhere. The army had moved in the previous day and, having been refused food by all the local shops, the soldiers had had to slaughter and butcher scores of

Boycott's cattle and sheep to feed the men the previous night. The detritus of the evening meal was scattered all around the lawn.

As the column of soldiers and volunteers marched up to the front of the great house, Boycott and one of his nephews were there to greet them, Boycott holding a double-barrelled shotgun in the crook of his elbow, whilst his nephew had a Winchester repeater held loosely down by his side.

The leader of the Ulster expedition, Captain Somerset Maxwell, brought his men to a halt and casually saluted Boycott.

Neither made any attempt to shake hands with the other. There was no friendship here – simply a desire on both sides to stake out positions. For the Ulstermen, it must have been a disappointing and anticlimactic moment at the end of such a long march.

The army had erected tents for the volunteers, and later that evening they bedded down for their second night on Mayo soil.

Redpath and I returned to Ballinrobe that evening, thankful for our warm beds in the Valkenburgh Hotel. I was even more thankful at two o'clock in the morning, when I was awakened by claps of thunder and, looking out of the window, saw torrential downpours of rain driven by gale-force winds. I found it hard not to smile, as I tried to imagine just how miserable the inhabitants of the lawns of Lough Mask House must now be. The weather gods were certainly in alliance with the Land League that November.

Shortly after breakfast, Redpath and I rode over to Lough Mask House again. The storm had cleared and army discipline had been imposed. The men were already hard at work – picking potatoes, turnips and mangolds and threshing corn. Work proceeded briskly enough, and Redpath and I spent an indolent day watching other men work hard – always an agreeable practice. In the afternoon, we heard a rumour that an attack on the house was planned for that evening and, in response, another battalion of infantry from the Ballinrobe barracks were marched out to Lough Mask House, to pitch their tents and add to the mayhem on the front lawn.

I do not know what gave rise to such rumours, but they were groundless nonsense. The Land League had no intention of attacking anything. The Fenian elements in the League ordered everyone to keep their firearms out of sight and out of use. The whole place was a tinderbox: a damp and squelchy tinderbox, admittedly, but one which might explode nevertheless. If this expedition had arrived in the long, hot, angry days of August, who knows what might have happened, but the discipline of the Land League held firm.

The press's interest in this story grew ever more intense, and over the following days journalists began to arrive into Ballinrobe from England, France, Germany, America, Italy and beyond.

Our days now took on a rhythm and routine. Each morning after breakfast, Redpath and I and the other journalists rode over to Lough Mask House to watch the harvesting of Boycott's crops. The Ulstermen worked purposefully, and acre by acre the harvest was gathered. With each passing day, thousands of Boycott's worthless potatoes and turnips were saved, but hundreds of his valuable cattle and sheep were lost, slaughtered to feed the men bivouacked on his front lawn; his chickens, ducks and geese had their necks wrung and were plunged into army cook pots, and his timber was felled to make army camp fires. For the hundreds of soldiers gathered around, their days were spent idly enough, waiting lest anything should happen. But it never did.

Then, one morning, something unusual was afoot. We saw Boycott rushing out of his house, accompanied by a Captain of the Hussars. Within minutes, Boycott was on horseback, galloping down the drive, followed by six cavalrymen in full uniform. There must have been news of an attack somewhere and so we followed them down the avenue and out the front gates. I imagined that one of the estate walls might have been breached and the natives were pouring in.

I expected Boycott and the cavalry to follow the estate wall around the road, but instead they struck off left, heading away from the estate and away from Ballinrobe. We rode hard after them until, four or five miles along the road, we saw the cause of all the alarm: a herd of cattle sauntering along the road, stopping occasionally to munch the lush roadside grasses before lumbering forwards. It would have been a perfectly normal sight on an Irish country road – save that no herdsmen accompanied the cattle. They had been deliberately let out of the field and driven away from Boycott's farm. As Boycott and his armed cavalry rode towards them, the dumb animals, frightened by their pursuers, ran on further, until Boycott caught up with them and barred the way.

Then, under the armed protection of the Hussars, the herd was driven back to Lough Mask House and through the main gates. By early evening, the telegraph office in Ballinrobe was humming the story to the great newspapers of London, Paris and New York: Her Majesty's finest Hussars were rounding up stray cattle in the byways of County Mayo.

As the days went on, it was clear that the gathering of the harvest would soon be completed and, indeed, two weeks after they had arrived the Ulster relief expedition had picked their last turnip and were ready to leave. The weather throughout had been grim. Winter seemed to come early that year and there were so many thunderstorms, with sleet and snow, that the men must have been frozen solid in their tents on Boycott's lawn. The final night, before the expedition's departure, the weather gods obliged for one last time and delivered another torrential downpour for the entire night. As we rode over to Lough Mask House on the final morning, the scene on the lawn was one of unremitting, bedraggled wretchedness. Boycott's once beautiful lawn was now a churned-up mud field.

We watched as the soldiers and the labourers packed up their rucksacks, dismantled their tents and loaded up the wagons. Then they all assembled before the front steps of the house, where Boycott was standing, legs apart, arms folded.

Captain Maxwell walked over to shake Boycott's hand and Boycott handed him a letter and asked him to read it to his men. Maxwell, with great deliberation, unfolded the letter and, turning to his men, shouted to them to listen.

'Gentlemen.' Maxwell's rasping northern accent boomed out. 'I cannot allow you to depart from Lough Mask without expressing to you brave men ... my deep and heartfelt gratitude to you for the generous aid you have rendered to me by saving my crops and for the many sacrifices you have endured on my behalf ... But I am compelled, for reasons now well known, to quit, with my wife, a happy home where we had hoped with God's help to have spent the remainder of our days. Yours faithfully, C.C. Boycott.'

Captain Maxwell folded the letter ceremoniously and handed it back to Boycott and shook his hand. Then, turning round to his men, he shouted, 'Three cheers for Captain Boycott.'

A huge cheer greeted this, followed by three loud, full cheers for Boycott. When they were done, a soldier's voice cried out, 'And three cheers for Captain Maxwell.'

A further three throaty cheers were given for Maxwell and, as the cheers died away, Boycott came down the steps and shook hands with every one of the fifty Ulster volunteers, thanking them all.

Within minutes, we watched the Hussars leading the soldiers and the labourers down the front avenue, singing 'For They Are Jolly Good Fellows'. Captain Boycott helped his wife into the covered wagon, on which their trunks were already placed and then, jumping up himself, signalled to the driver to leave. The wagon jolted down the lane, carrying Captain Boycott away from Lough Mask House for the last time.

We turned our horses and followed them to Ballinrobe.

As the cavalcade marched through Ballinrobe, I saw, to my astonishment, that the whole town was deserted. The shops had all been closed up and shuttered. The houses all had their curtains drawn. It was as if the whole town had turned its back on Captain Boycott and the English army. As the procession moved through the town, I saw, at a distance, the solitary figure of Father O'Malley, standing sombrely beside his church, his Bible in his hand, dressed in his black cassock and white collar. He nodded at me and watched the procession as it filtered through the town. Suddenly, I saw him look beyond me and start walking towards me, in some agitation. As I followed his look, I saw an elderly, frail woman, dressed in a black shawl, standing outside her house, glaring at the cavalry procession as it passed her front door.

Father O'Malley walked up to her.

'Mrs Riney,' he said loudly. 'I warned you to let the British Army alone. How dare you come out and intimidate Her Majesty's troops? Shame on you. Go on, get back inside, do you hear me?'

The old woman gave him a sullen look, stepped back inside her door and slammed it shut. Redpath suddenly started laughing.

'If Mrs Riney is intimidating the British Army, then you really have won,' he said.

Having stayed in Ballinrobe for almost three weeks, I, too, was ready to leave. Redpath and I caught the train back to Dublin, sharing a carriage with Boycott and his wife; but Boycott was not in a communicative mood and it was an uneventful journey.

I read later that Boycott stayed at the Hamman Hotel in Upper Sackville Street, guarded by four or five detectives. He had intended to stay in Dublin for some weeks, but he was followed everywhere by a jeering mob and, when the proprietor of the hotel was threatened with a 'boycott', he asked the Boycotts to leave. Days later, on 1st December 1880, Boycott left Ireland on the early mail boat to Holyhead. Now, I thought, he knew the full desolation of being evicted from his own home.

Part Three

Thirty

The State Trials

IN EARLY DECEMBER, shortly after Boycott's departure, Parnell returned to Avondale but, despite several weeks of rest at the O'Sheas, he seemed in poor health and quite exhausted. We talked about the Land League and the forthcoming State trials, but his mind seemed to be elsewhere and there was about him a lassitude which I had not seen before.

Then, within a week, he was gone again. He had received an invitation to spend Christmas with the O'Sheas and had accepted, even though his trial on the conspiracy charges had been fixed for 28th December. He said he wanted to rest with the O'Sheas before it started. I sought to remonstrate with him that he was needed here in Ireland to prepare for his trial but he was dismissive of these concerns.

Throughout December I was busy with preparations for his trial. As there were fourteen defendants, the Land League had retained four QCs and four junior counsel, of whom I was one. My work was to compile the statements of our witnesses as best I could.

On the first morning of the trial, at an early hour, I met with Parnell, Biggar and all the other defendants and their friends and supporters in the foyer of Morrison's Hotel. There was an air of almost festive jollity about the group, as if they were meeting for a Christmas lunch rather than for a State trial. Healy was there also, twitching with excitement.

At about ten o'clock, Parnell's solicitor, the venerable Mr V.B. Dillon, suggested that it really was time to go and so, on that cold, crisp December morning, with Parnell, Justin McCarthy and John Dillon at the front, we all trooped out of Morrison's and walked down to College Green, left along Dame Street and down Parliament Street to the quays. I walked alongside Biggar, who seemed delighted at the prospect of standing trial.

'You're not a true Irishman, Harrison,' he said, beaming at me, 'unless you've actually been put on trial by the British.'

'Are you not afraid you'll be found guilty?' I asked.

'I am guilty,' he said, looking almost offended, as if I were suggesting he might be unpatriotically innocent, 'but there isn't a jury in the country who will convict Parnell or any of us at the moment.'

As I looked ahead, I could see Parnell engaged in conversation with McCarthy. He too seemed gloriously unconcerned, as if he were taking a stroll in the city, or a tour of the Four Courts, instead of standing trial. I think I was more nervous defending them than they were about facing trial.

Given the hour and the Christmas holiday, the streets from Morrison's to the quays were almost deserted, but as we approached the Four Courts, I saw a huge crowd gathered along Inns Quay and stretching across Essex Bridge.

As we approached, Edmund Dwyer Gray, the Lord Mayor of Dublin, walked towards us, leading the crowds. I was surprised to see him there. As proprietor of the *Freeman's Journal*, he had taken a jaundiced view of the Land League at the start, but his recent editorials were more friendly and now he seemed an enthusiastic supporter. I mentioned my surprise to Biggar.

'You haven't heard what happened, then?' asked Biggar.

I shook my head.

'Dwyer Gray told me that Davitt – Davitt, of all people – had called into his office with a copy of an offending editorial and told him that if the *Journal* continued to oppose the League, Davitt would have a hundred copies burned at a hundred Land League meetings and start another newspaper with American money.'

'Pure intimidation,' I said.

'No other word for it, Harrison,' said Biggar, starting to laugh. 'But it's *effective* intimidation. That's the point. Gray told me he couldn't afford to ruin his family so he switched sides.'

Ahead of us, I saw Gray shaking hands with Parnell.

'Your welcoming committee, Mr Parnell' – he gestured back at the crowds behind, who gave a great cheer. 'We're here to send a message to Gladstone.'

'And the jury,' said Parnell.

Gray put his arm through Parnell's – perhaps an overly familiar gesture, but one which Parnell did not resist – and the two men marched arm-in-arm to the Four Courts, the crowds falling in behind, cheering and singing snatches of Irish songs. As we approached, women began throwing flowers at Parnell, all the way to the front door of the Courts. Parnell stopped at the entrance and, flanked by the granite pillars, turned to the crowds, bowed graciously and thanked them for all their support. Then, turning quickly, he walked through the double doors.

Biggar and I pushed our way through the closing crowds and followed him in.

The great Round Hall of the Four Courts was packed with litigants and their lawyers, witnesses and bystanders. Queen's Counsel and Junior Counsel, all wigged and gowned, stood around holding their briefs in the crooks of their elbows, their attorneys officiously thumbing through sheets of official documents to pluck out something now urgently required at the last moment. It was time for me to join them. I walked quickly along the corridors, past the Court of Appeal and through the doors of the Law Library. I went downstairs to the robing-room, dressed quickly for court and rejoined the melée in the Round Hall.

' … possibly our last Christmas as free men.' I could hear Biggar's voice and guffaw booming out above all others.

Before I could catch more, a tipstaff walking ahead of his judge cried out for a path to be cleared and we all moved back to allow His Lordship to pass through on his way to Court 2, a court just off the Round Hall. It was time for me to take my seat and organise my papers.

The State trials were not the only cases listed for hearing on this first morning of the Hilary term, but they were certainly the most sensational. Just before eleven o'clock, Parnell and his co-accused filed into court and took their places on the benches below the registrar. Their supporters packed the public benches and the gallery and soon the small courtroom was overflowing with people.

Over the next few days, the Attorney General presented the case for the Crown. Everything he said was true, but it was not illegal, and the pathetic fragility of their case became evident when the Attorney General began to read aloud one of Fanny Parnell's long poems as an example of illegal, seditious literature. The whole crowd in the courtroom – with the exception of the judges and prosecution counsel – began to laugh at such a ludicrous accusation and then, spontaneously, began to applaud. I could not resist a smile, and was sorry that Fanny was not here in person to witness this great public appreciation of her verse.

Throughout the following days, Parnell sat in court, apparently indifferent to the speeches made or indeed to the evidence adduced. He had with him a number of scientific journals borrowed from the hotel library at Morrison's and he pored over these for hours on end, apparently oblivious to what was going on around him. I doubt he would even have heard his own name if he had been called upon to give evidence. His behaviour seemed to set the example. Even the jurors seemed indifferent to the evidence and spent most of their time talking quietly among themselves. The crowds of visitors who attended court each day were only there to see Parnell. And to comment on his unusual appearance! Parnell had taken to wearing a tight-fitting skull cap when he was indoors. He had become concerned that his hair was thinning and, conscious of his appearance, he had been advised to wear a skull cap to keep the follicles warm. It was a curious concession to vanity which, up until then, I did not know he possessed. But this was not the time to question him about it.

The evidence continued for several days but, early the following week, Parnell decided he wished to travel back to London for the State opening of Parliament in early January, despite his counsel's advice that as a defendant he should be present in court each day.

'What can they do?' he asked us outside court. 'Arrest me? Forster has timed this trial to ensure I will not be in London when Parliament resumes. I do not intend to let him have that victory.'

If Parnell went, Biggar went.

I also obtained a release to allow me to return to Westminster with them for a few days.

The next day, when Parnell appeared in the House, he was greeted with huge cheers from all the Irish Members of Parliament. Forster looked on in dismay as he saw his adversary striding into the House of Commons for the afternoon debate. He must have wondered how a member on trial for undermining Her Majesty's rule in Ireland could also be free to partake in debates in Her Majesty's Parliament. Parnell, for his part, took his seat calmly, kept his eyes on the Minister at the despatch box and made no attempt to speak.

But the Queen's speech, that day, showed just how much the political landscape of England had changed. The years when Ireland was never mentioned were now gone. Indeed, her speech was dominated by Ireland: Parliament had been recalled early because of Ireland; law and order had broken down in Ireland and so there would be a new coercion bill; serious grievances existed among the tenants and so there would be a new land bill for Ireland.

The House of Commons was in a ferment for days, as it vented its considerable anger over the lawlessness in Ireland. This anger was directed particularly against Parnell, but it embraced all Irish Members of Parliament. Biggar was in his element: he revelled in all this criticism and abuse and seemed to enjoy the attention it brought upon him. Indeed, he spent much time goading his opponents and the angrier they seemed, the more he laughed at them, thereby increasing their fury all the more.

'There's no greater sport in a bullring,' he said loudly to me, one evening in the Chamber.

'Provided you're not the bull,' I said.

He looked at me with a broad smile.

'The bull is on that side of the House, Harrison,' he said, jabbing his finger over at the Government benches. 'The great Liberal bull and behind him John Bull, being goaded into a blind fury with no idea what to do. And there's our matador.' He pointed at Parnell, who was on his feet, apparently oblivious to the outrage as he made some comment on a point of order.

I also noticed around this time that Willie O'Shea had dropped his insistence on sitting with the Liberals and now sat with the Irish members on the opposition benches. Parnell had obviously been successful in persuading him to rejoin us, or else he felt the winds were turning!

Forster insisted on bringing in the coercion bill before the land bill and our opposition was furious. We argued repeatedly that if the land bill were passed first, this would take the poison out of the situation and reduce the need for coercion. Forster, however, was determined to push coercion through and Gladstone, seemingly in an agony of indecision, committed himself to it on the advice of Forster.

But we were now very concerned: the power of arrest without trial in the coercion bill would, we knew, result in the immediate arrest of all Land League leaders – including Parnell – and the arrest of the League's leaders would almost certainly destroy the organisation. So Parnell now led us on another all-out war of obstruction. We proposed amendment after amendment to the Queen's speech; instead of passing the Commons in a day, it took over three weeks. Having made Ireland ungovernable, Parnell seemed intent on doing the same to the House of Commons. This was an obstruction in which I was now, for the first time, an active participant and so, along with Parnell, Biggar, McCarthy, Healy and many others, I too rose day after day in the Commons with minor amendments, major amendments, motions to adjourn, motions to report progress, motions to reconsider, motions to do whatever the exigencies of the situation required. With over thirty Members of Parliament dedicated to our obstructionist course, we would keep the House up all night for months on end.

In late January, Parnell, Biggar and I returned to Ireland for the final days of the trial. Throughout the Four Courts, everywhere Parnell went, he was surrounded by people wanting to shake his hand, clap him on the back, wish him well. When he left the courtroom for lunch, a crowd followed him; when he returned to court, he received thunderous applause from the crowds packed inside. He received it all with a reserved graciousness and then settled in for the afternoon's evidence and his scientific journals.

Eventually, on the final day, the closing speeches were given, the jury retired to consider their verdicts and we all waited, loitering in the Round Hall, the late-afternoon sunshine streaming through the windows of the cupola above.

Within an hour we were called back into court.

'Have you reached your verdict, Mr Foreman?' asked the judge.

'We have, Your Honour,' replied the foreman, a stout, suited man in middle age.

'Well, Mr Foreman,' said the judge severely, 'what is your verdict?'

'We find all of the defendants,' said the foreman, 'not guilty.'

A great cheer went up from the public galleries.

The judges considered trying to restore order but, realising the better part of valour, they rose, bowed quickly and left the courtroom. They had scarcely left the court when one of the jurymen shouted out: 'Long live Parnell.'

This brought another great cheer as Parnell, Biggar, Healy, Sexton and all the others shook the hands of their wellwishers, their counsel and their attorneys.

'No time to lose,' cried Parnell, 'the last mail boat is at half-past six' – and, to the cheers of the crowds, we all set off to catch the night sailing to England and the next day's debate in the House of Commons.

Thirty-One

The Guillotine

THE FOLLOWING DAY, just after the Speaker began the afternoon proceedings, Parnell, Biggar, Dillon, Sexton and the other acquitted defendants strolled into the House, like actors on a cue, to the great cheers of the Irish Members of Parliament. As I walked in behind them, I could see Forster scowling with discontent.

Within minutes, Parnell was on his feet, denouncing Forster for the political show trials with which he had tried to discredit him and the other leaders of the Land League.

As I looked at Gladstone across the floor of the House, I thought he looked tense and overwrought; he listened to the passionate, angry denunciations of Parnell and he nodded in agreement so many times that I doubted that he was in favour of coercion at all. Parnell's icy contempt for Forster's abilities and for Gladstone's capitulation seemed to disturb Gladstone even more. It was as if Parnell were his baleful, relentless conscience and the coercion bill a stain on his reputation.

For eleven days and eleven nights, we kept the House of Commons strapped to the wheel, obstructing it as best we could. Most nights we stayed at it until dawn. With seven Members of Parliament, Parnell had wrecked Disraeli's Government; with thirty Members of Parliament, Parnell was in complete control of the House, deploying his troops to block whichever measure he thought fit.

Each evening Parnell rose in his place, a brooding presence, waiting for silence before he began his speeches: pouring scorn on Forster or Gladstone for their craven ineptitude. It seemed that many of the Liberals became increasingly troubled by their own consciences, as Parnell articulated the Irish cause in a manner which commanded their attention; this was not a piteous plea for justice – that was never his way; nor was it an appeal to their reason, as Isaac Butt had sought to make; this was the cold, savage fury of a revolutionary, who forced members to look to the consequences of their folly and who demanded that an account be taken.

In early February, as Monday evening drifted into Tuesday and Tuesday evening drifted into Wednesday, the House of Commons marked its third day and forty-one hours continuous sitting, with the ever-present Irish member on his feet, objecting to every comma in the coercion bill. We heard rumours that Gladstone would not tolerate this much further, but what he would do was not apparent.

Then, one afternoon, Gladstone and Forster took their seats on the front bench and I saw Gladstone nod almost imperceptibly to the Speaker.

The Speaker rose to interrupt John Dillon, who was speaking at the time.

'I thank the Honourable Member for his contribution,' said the Speaker, 'but it is now clear that the House has been completely frustrated in its debates due the efforts of the Irish members.'

I watched with the other Home Rule Members of Parliament as the Speaker paused. He looked around the House to seek the attention of all.

'And, having consulted with the Prime Minister – and the Leader of the Opposition – I now declare a State of Emergency. Therefore,' the Speaker resumed haltingly, 'I propose to introduce closure on this debate and call for a vote accordingly.'

There was a huge cheer from both sides of the House.

The House of Commons, for the first time in its hundreds of years of history, had ended the tradition that Members of Parliament could speak as long as they wished. It was, for many members, a shocking and bitter loss of privilege, and one for which they held Parnell accountable. For his part, he was long past caring – if he ever did – about the arcane, ancient privileges and prerogatives of members of the House of Commons. What he did care about was that his main weapon for bludgeoning the House of Commons had now been knocked out of his hands. We were now powerless to delay legislation going through the

House. As the Irish members objected to the motion for closure, Parnell remained silent, his face quite without emotion, but I could see him looking at Gladstone as if to take a new measure of the ruthlessness of his opponent.

Forster's coercion bill was immediately reintroduced, immediately voted on and immediately passed. It took only one hour.

But matters worsened the following day, when Sir William Harcourt, the Home Secretary, rose to announce that Michael Davitt had been arrested in Dublin that morning, and was now being taken back to Portland prison for violation of his ticket-of-leave conditions.

The House of Commons resounded with the huge cheers of the Tories and the Liberals alike at this news. It sent a chill down my back. These people really were our enemies.

Like many in our party, I was outraged by this act of barbarism and ignorance by Forster and Gladstone. If there was one person who had constantly urged people not to engage in violence, it was Davitt. In this febrile atmosphere, we all began to wonder who would be next. Parnell? Biggar? Dillon? Might I be arrested as an associate of Parnell?

Parnell stood up to confront Harcourt.

'I would ask the Home Secretary to explain to the House which of the conditions of Mr Davitt's ticket of leave he is supposed to have broken,' he said to a jeering House.

But Harcourt just sat there on the front bench, his arms folded tightly around his bulging midriff, grinning inanely, and refusing to answer the question.

Dillon jumped to his feet and demanded that Harcourt give his reasons to the House for the arbitrary arrest of a citizen. The Speaker ruled him out of order but Dillon refused to sit down. He demanded to be heard.

'I only wish,' Dillon shouted furiously, 'that Ireland had the means of waging a civil war, because I can say in plain view of this House that if I were a farmer about to be evicted from my home, I would open fire and shoot as many people of the evicting party as I could.'

There was a shocked silence at these wild, violent words, and then the predictable roars of abuse from all sides.

'You have no right to the floor,' said the Speaker severely to Dillon. 'I have not called on you to speak.'

'I am not waiting on you to call on me to speak,' shouted Dillon angrily. 'You have lost the respect of this House with your partisan rulings and I will not be silenced by you. I will be heard.'

There was uproar in the House at this exchange. The Speaker immediately – to the cheers of the members – told Dillon to sit down.

'I shall not sit down, sir,' said Dillon. 'I shall stay standing to protest this disgraceful imprisonment of my friend Michael Davitt.'

'You shall sit down, sir, or you shall be suspended,' roared the Speaker, his face reddening with rage.

'I shall not sit down,' Dillon roared back, 'until I have been heard.'

'Then you are suspended, sir,' the Speaker shouted.

'I shall not be suspended either,' shouted Dillon defiantly. 'until I have said what I wish to say. You, sir, have lost your authority in this House.'

Above the uproar, the Speaker called for the Sergeants-at-Arms, who approached hurriedly and listened to his instructions. They then approached Dillon, one on either side and grabbed his elbows.

'I shall surrender, sir, to the use of force,' said Dillon loudly and, shaking his hands free of his captors, he allowed them to walk him out of the Chamber.

The Speaker sought to resume the debate and restore his authority. After some moments, when calm had been restored, Gladstone rose to speak.

'I wish to inform this House about the reasons we had to arrest Mr Davitt,' he said.

Parnell rose in his place, silent and malevolent.

'On a point of order, Mr Speaker,' he said.

The Speaker nodded.

'I move that the Prime Minister be no longer heard,' Parnell said loudly, a request akin to demanding that the Prime Minister should sit down and be quiet.

There was uproar – again – as members shouted Parnell down for suggesting for the first time in the history of the House that Her Majesty's First Minister be silent.

Above the din, the Speaker shouted, 'Mr Parnell, that is not a point of order,' and, looking at Gladstone, 'Mr Gladstone, you may resume.'

Gladstone stood at the despatch box but Parnell refused to resume his seat.

'Mr Speaker,' Parnell repeated. 'I said, I move that the Prime Minister be no longer heard.'

'I have heard you, Mr Parnell,' said the Speaker, 'and I have ruled against your motion.'

'I do not accept your ruling,' said Parnell.

'It is a ruling of the Speaker,' said the Speaker, 'and it must be accepted by every member in this House.'

'I, for one, have no intention of accepting it,' said Parnell coldly.

'Then I shall suspend you, Mr Parnell,' said Speaker, 'and I must ask you to leave the Chamber.'

'I shall not leave this Chamber,' said Parnell. 'I have a right to represent the Irish people and I shall not be silenced by you.'

'Then you leave me no choice, Mr Parnell,' said the Speaker in a resigned voice. He called over the Sergeants-at-Arms again.

Parnell remained standing at his place until they approached and then – using Dillon's words, 'I shall surrender to force' – he was walked out of the Chamber by the Sergeants-at-Arms.

Even before he had left the Chamber, Biggar rose to his feet, roaring like a cattle dealer at fair day that this was an outrageous assault on the leader of the Irish nation and demanding that Gladstone be no longer heard. The Speaker demanded that he sit down. Biggar refused and, when the Sergeants-at-Arms returned, the Speaker directed them to lay hands on Biggar and escort him out.

Healy was next to his feet to make the same point, and within minutes he joined Dillon, Parnell and Biggar in the lobbies outside the Chamber.

My anger was as overpowering as theirs and, as Healy was led out, I stood up in my place to demand that Gladstone no longer be heard. I heard the cries of 'Shame on you' from the Liberal benches, but I ignored them and continued to shout over them. Gladstone looked at me, sternly, as if I were too young a member to have earned the right to behave in such a fashion, and soon I too was named by the Speaker, suspended and ejected by the Sergeants-at-Arms.

The next up was Thomas Sexton. His short speech, parts of which I could hear, even as I was being ejected from the Chamber, has stuck in my mind to this day.

'When you have destroyed all our rights, gentlemen,' he said solemnly to the House, 'you will be left with precious few of your own.'

By now it was clear that every single member of the Irish parliamentary party would stand and denounce Gladstone and Forster, and we watched from the gallery for several hours as each of them stood to object, was suspended, refused to obey the Speaker and was ejected from the House. Thirty-six Irish Members of Parliament were expelled that afternoon over three-and-a-half hours, and the Commons was in uproar for the whole day.

The Party meeting that evening was feverish with anger. Coercion was now inevitable and it would come quickly. Now that Davitt had been arrested, we expected Parnell and all the other leaders of the League would also be arrested. It was only a matter of time. There was a view among many that this was now the time to walk out of the House of Commons en masse, to return to Ireland and to set up our own assembly. But Parnell was decisive.

'We stay in Westminster,' he said calmly. 'The fulcrum of power is in the House of Commons, and the closer we are to its centre the more power we can wield.'

It was for him, essentially, a question of physics.

'There is nothing for us to do if we return to Ireland,' he continued, brooking no dissent. 'We will see the land bill through. I don't believe Gladstone will arrest any of us until it is through – he needs our votes. But he may move against the League before that.'

Turning to Dillon, he said, 'Dillon, I want you, Healy, O'Kelly, Biggar and Harrison to go to Paris tomorrow. I want you to move the League's funds there immediately to avoid them being confiscated. I shall join you in Paris in a few days. We will decide then what other steps need to be taken.'

Thirty-Two

Paris

EARLY THE FOLLOWING morning – on Tuesday – we left for Paris. I say, left, but fled would be a more accurate expression. We did not know whether we might be arrested at any stage along the journey and it was with considerable relief that we boarded the ship at Dover for the afternoon sailing to Calais and arrived in Paris that evening, at the Hotel Brighton on the Rue de Rivoli.

Over the next few days, we divided up the work and set about opening bank accounts, instructing lawyers and such matters. We expected to see Parnell on Thursday, but by Friday he still had not arrived. I enquired at the porter's desk whether any telegrams had been sent for us but there were none. There were, however, some telegrams and letters for Parnell, but I left these at the desk as they were marked 'Personal'.

The following morning – Saturday – Parnell had still not arrived.

'Where the devil is he?' Healy was growing impatient. 'He told us he would be here on Thursday.'

'He did say "a couple of days later",' I said.

'That's two days, Harrison,' said Biggar, 'but it's not like him to be late.'

'He left you high and dry at Longford in October, or have you forgotten that?' growled Healy.

'He was unwell at the time,' I said.

'Maybe he is unwell now,' said Healy, 'but why the devil hasn't he sent us a telegram?'

'Perhaps he's too unwell to venture out,' I said.

'Well, you should send one to him,' said Healy impatiently, 'see where he is.'

I left immediately and sent a telegram to Keppel Street and to his hotel rooms at Cannon Street. I even sent one to Avondale, although I had no reason to think he might be there. I enquired again of the hotel clerk whether there were any messages for me. Once again, the clerk shook his head. There were, however, further telegrams and letters for Parnell. I took these from the clerk and returned to the meeting-room we had commandeered just off the hotel foyer.

'No message from Parnell,' I said, 'but there are messages being sent to him here.'

'Who from?' snapped Healy.

'I have no idea,' I said, taking them from my pocket. 'There are about five of them, all from England.'

I put them on the table. Healy leaned forward, swiftly gathered them up and flicked through them.

'A woman's handwriting,' he remarked.

No one bothered to reply.

Biggar got up and started pacing around the room.

'If he's sick, then he needs a doctor. If he is in Keppel Street, we need someone to call on him,' he said. 'If he's been arrested, we need to find out immediately.'

'Justin McCarthy lives beside Keppel Street,' I said.

'Send McCarthy a telegram immediately,' said Biggar. 'Ask him to see if Parnell is there and to check the Cannon Street Hotel.'

'I sent a telegram to Avondale as well – just in case,' I said.

'Why on earth would he go to Avondale,' said Healy, 'when he is supposed to come to Paris?'

Healy picked up the letters from the table, took off his spectacles and peered closely at the handwriting again.

'I'm sure that's a woman's handwriting,' he mused.

'He might have been arrested,' said Biggar, ignoring Healy.

'If he was arrested we would have heard about it,' said Dillon. 'It's not as if they kept Davitt's arrest a secret.'

'We should look at his letters,' said Healy. 'They might give us some clue about where he might be.' He picked one up and waved it in the air. 'We're not the only ones he told he was going to Paris.'

'We will not open those letters,' I said indignantly. 'They are his private letters.'

Biggar agreed. 'Aye, leave them alone,' he said. 'They are none of our business.'

I took the letters from Healy and returned them to the hotel clerk for safekeeping. There were still no messages from Parnell, and I sent off further telegrams to McCarthy and again to Avondale.

◦~∞~◦

On one of the evenings, whilst we waited for Parnell to arrive, James O'Kelly and I stayed up until the early hours, drinking cognac and exchanging confidences. O'Kelly, short, barrel-chested and then in his early thirties, was one of our more colourful Members of Parliament. Lively and intelligent, with a sardonic wit and a ready smile, he had already led an extraordinary life. He had joined the Irish Republican Brotherhood when he was only fifteen but, bored by its inaction, he had joined the French Foreign Legion and fought in Algeria and Mexico; but, after a time, he bored of the rigours of the Legion and deserted it to rejoin the Irish Republican Brotherhood. All this I had pieced together in my earlier conversations with him. But I had noticed that in Paris he had disappeared for hours on end each day, without explanation, and, perhaps emboldened by the cognac, I asked him where he went. I wasn't prepared for the direct answer I received.

'I went to see my first wife,' he said, looking at me sheepishly, 'and my son.'

'Your wife!' I said, surprised. 'I didn't know you were married.' Then, as my befuddled brain went through his words, 'Your first wife. You mean, you have a second?'

O'Kelly nodded and gulped back another brandy.

'It's a long story,' he said.

I looked at him.

'I'm not in any hurry,' I said.

His stories of his romantic adventures were all of a piece with his stories of his war adventures: scarcely believable but absolutely true, as I found out much later.

'We got married for all the wrong reasons,' he said, 'she was expecting our child. But the marriage couldn't work, so she came over to Paris where she lives with my brother Aloysius, who is a painter here.'

I raised a quizzical eyebrow.

'With your brother?'

'Oh no, not in that way,' said O'Kelly, laughing easily. 'No, no, they just share a house. There is no attachment between them. But it seems to work. And if I am in Europe I try to see my son – and my brother – whenever I can.'

'And what about your second wife?' I asked, becoming more curious by the moment. 'Where does she live?'

O'Kelly looked sheepishly into his empty glass and then poured himself another brandy,

'I'm not sure,' he replied.

'Not sure!' I exclaimed. 'How can you not be sure where your wife lives?'

'She left me last year,' he said. 'I think she's still in New York, where we lived, but she doesn't want to see me.'

'Why ever not?' I said, mystified.

'It may have been because I hadn't told her I was already married,' said O'Kelly, with a straight face.

The answer was so unexpected and so bizarre that I began to laugh out loud. O'Kelly, however, assured me it was true and, for some reason, that set us both off laughing uproariously and forged a friendship between us which lasted throughout the difficult years that followed.

෧෧෧

Sunday and Monday brought no further news of Parnell's whereabouts. Justin McCarthy wired us that he had no idea where Parnell was; he was not in Keppel Street or at his hotel or in the Commons. No one had seen him for days. We waited around the hotel in a state of increasing anxiety. It was now over a week since Parnell had said he would join us and there was still no sign of him. We began to believe that something quite serious must have happened to prevent him from joining us. As there was still no news that he had been arrested, it became increasingly possible that someone might have attacked him or injured him in some way.

We passed the time as best we could, but everyone became increasingly fractious as the days wore on – partly out of anxiety, partly out of helplessness, but also because there was urgent parliamentary business to attend to in the House of Commons, and yet we were idling in Paris for days on end.

We met again after breakfast on Saturday. It was now over ten days since Parnell had said he would join us, and Healy was becoming angrier by the day.

'This is intolerable,' he said. 'We shouldn't be wasting our time here. We should be in London.'

He got up swiftly and left the room. Within a moment he was back, waving the bundles of letters for Parnell, which had been kept at the hotel desk. He threw them down on the table.

'Look at them, will you?' he said. 'Count them.'

I looked at him, puzzled.

'Same number as yesterday and the day before,' said Healy. 'Four letters for Parnell from the same hand. All last week. All posted from England on Monday, Tuesday and Wednesday.'

'Well?' I said.

Healy sat down impatiently.

'He was supposed to be here on Wednesday,' he said, 'and he hasn't shown up for the last ten days. So why hasn't this woman sent letters on Thursday, Friday, Saturday, every day this week … ?'

He looked around fiercely, his fingers drumming on the table.

'I tell you, there's a woman involved,' he said.

'Well, if there is,' said Biggar, 'it's no business of ours.'

'It is, by God,' said Healy. 'If it's no business of ours, then what are we doing here for days on end, waiting for Parnell to turn up?'

He glared around the table at us.

'I say we open one of the letters and then send a telegram to Parnell at her address,' he said.

'No, Healy,' Biggar said loudly. 'You won't do anything of the sort. That's his private correspondence and you have no right to open it.'

Biggar walked to the door. 'I'm going to see if anything has arrived yet.'

'I'll join you, Biggar,' I said, and we went back to the hotel clerk to ask for the umpteenth time whether any messages had come for us.

He shook his head, with a polite and rueful smile. '*Ah, non, Messieurs, pas encore.*'

'Mercy bocoop,' said Biggar.

It was hard not to smile as I listened to Biggar murdering the
French language, but this was not the time to joke him about it. We
stood in the foyer, watching the bustle of people coming in and out
of the hotel.

'I will go back to London,' he said, 'and see if I can find him.'

'I'll go with you,' I said.

'No, Harrison,' he said, 'you'd better stay here. I'll telegraph you
if I find him and if he comes here, you send for me.'

We went back into the room. As we came in, I became aware that the
conversation died suddenly and there was a strange, conspiratorial
glance between Healy and Dillon. My attention was drawn to the
pile of letters scattered on the table, and I saw that one of the letters
had been opened. Its two cream sheets, creased in the middle, lay on
top of its envelope.

Biggar saw it at the same time.

'You opened the letters, Healy!' exclaimed Biggar angrily.

'I did,' retorted Healy heatedly, 'and I was right. There is a
woman involved.'

'I don't care if there is or not,' said Biggar, 'it's none of our
business.'

'And it's O'Shea's wife,' said Healy, pushing his glasses back on
his nose, triumphant at his knowledge of the great secret. 'He's
carrying on with O'Shea's wife. The letters are all lovey dovey.
Darling Charles, my own love ... that sort of thing. Read it yourself.'

I was dumbstruck by the revelation, as was Biggar, who slumped
back on to his chair. I cast my mind back to the times when I had
been in their company and I had not noticed even a look which was
out of place. But there were signs, if I had looked hard enough. His
unexplained disappearance for a week in October, when he should
have been at Roscommon and the lengthy stays with the O'Sheas
in November, when the Boycott affair was at its height, were now
explicable. It was an intrigue which I had missed completely, due
perhaps to my naiveté in such matters. I made no judgment on
Parnell though. He had been a loyal friend to me and I would repay
his loyalty. I never liked O'Shea and if the marriage had broken

down, then it had broken down. The story now was the scandal. The secret had to be buried. It was evident even then that an adultery scandal would certainly destroy Parnell.

I reached over the table and quietly gathered up the ravished letters. I folded them, put them carefully back into their envelopes and put them all securely into my inside pocket until I could return them to Parnell.

'You had no right, Healy,' I said, 'it was absolutely none of your business.'

Healy glared at me defiantly.

Biggar sighed. 'This stays between ourselves. Is that clear?'

He looked around at all of us. 'Is that clear, Healy?' he snapped. 'The consequences are unthinkable.'

Healy nodded.

'Dillon?' asked Biggar.

Dillon nodded also.

'Right, then,' said Biggar. 'Now I am going back to London to find Parnell, and I will telegraph you when we find him. Until then, you stay here for another few days.'

'I'm coming with you, Biggar,' I said.

Biggar and I left the room, packed our bags, and within an hour were in a carriage heading for the Gare du Nord. We had hardly left our hotel when our subdued silence was suddenly broken, as Biggar looked out of the carriage and exclaimed, 'My God Almighty. There's Parnell.'

A carriage had sped by, but I had not seen who was in it.

'Missewer, Missewer, turnez vous,' Biggar shouted at the driver.

'*Comment?*' The cab driver shrugged his shoulders uncomprehendingly.

I told the driver we needed to go back to the hotel and minutes later the carriage turned and we were back outside the Hotel Brighton. It was indeed Parnell. He had descended from his carriage and was paying the driver when we caught up with him.

'Parnell, Parnell, how good to see you.' Biggar embraced him. 'We were getting quite anxious.'

Parnell greeted us with a warm smile and shook our hands. Biggar glanced at me as Parnell was attending to his luggage.

'No questions, Harrison,' he said. 'Leave him be.'

We went back into the hotel, but the others were not there. They must have gone out for a walk. We took our rooms again and, minutes later, joined Parnell in his rooms for coffee.

'How was your journey?' Biggar asked Parnell earnestly.

'Fine. Fine,' said Parnell. He sipped his coffee.

I picked up the book which he had been reading – a rare event in itself.

'*Alice in Wonderland*, Charles?' I said quizzically.

'Yes, I've been reading it all week,' he said. 'Curious little book, isn't it?'

Biggar snorted.

'Christ, Parnell, the whole country is seething, we've fled to Paris, we're all wondering whether we'll be arrested, and you're reading *Alice in Wonderland*.'

Parnell smiled.

'It took my mind off things,' he said.

'Good,' said Biggar. 'Well, there's something I need to tell you. Something's happened.' He looked over at me, anxiously clenching his hands together.

Parnell looked at him, putting down his coffee cup on the table.

'We were concerned when you didn't turn up on Wednesday or Thursday,' said Biggar. 'We thought something might have happened to you.'

Parnell stayed silent, his gaze fixed on Biggar.

'We sent telegrams to you everyday, but there was no reply,' continued Biggar, perhaps waiting for Parnell to proffer an explanation.

Parnell, however, offered no explanation for his absence.

'Anyway, Parnell, matters came to a head,' continued Biggar briskly. 'Some letters had arrived for you at the hotel and Healy insisted on opening your correspondence.'

Parnell became quite still.

'We objected strongly, Harrison and I,' said Biggar. 'We told Healy it was out of the question, but this morning, when our backs were turned, when we were out of the room, in fact, Healy opened one of your letters.'

Parnell went pale but said nothing.

'I have them here, Charles,' I said and, taking them out of my jacket pocket, I handed them to him.

Parnell took the letters and, seeing the one which had been opened, took it out of its envelope and read it quickly.

'Who else has read this?' he said, closing it.

'I don't know,' I said. 'Biggar and I were out of the room. Perhaps only Healy.'

'You may rest assured that Harrison and I have not read it,' said Biggar. 'I don't know about Dillon and O'Kelly.'

There was a knock on the door.

'Come in,' said Parnell.

The door opened and Healy, of all people, at all times, walked in.

'How are you, Parnell?' he said nonchalantly. 'I heard you had turned up.'

'Get out of my sight, Healy,' Parnell said angrily, in a low tone. 'And don't come into this room until you are invited.'

Healy, red with humiliation or anger, I am not sure which, turned and, like a cur, slunk out of the room.

There was a long and pained silence, broken only by the loud ticking of the clock on the grey marble mantelpiece. Eventually, Parnell got up and walked over to the long louvered window. He opened it and stepped out onto the balcony looking over the Luxembourg Gardens. Biggar and I looked at each other, unsure of what to do next.

'Thank you, gentlemen,' said Parnell, coming back into the room after a few moments. 'Now we have business to attend to.'

We went downstairs and joined the others in the meeting-room. There was a strained silence, and no one even rose to greet Parnell or to ask him where he had been for the last week.

Extraordinarily, Parnell never offered any apology for his delay in coming to Paris, or any explanation about what had delayed him. There was no hint of any turmoil. The meeting was, as usual with Parnell, brisk and efficient. The items of business were introduced, considered and decided upon. Parnell had, he informed us, reflected on matters during the week: in future, the Land League would be run from Paris by Egan and O'Kelly; he wanted Dillon to go to America to raise more money for the League; and the League's activities in Ireland would continue as before. Healy remained noticeably quiet throughout and Parnell never addressed any remarks to him.

When the meeting ended, Biggar pulled me aside.

'This matter must never get out,' he said. 'We must never discuss it again.'

I nodded in agreement.

'I am travelling back to London with Healy,' said Biggar. 'I will impress that upon him again.'

He paused. 'How we deal with O'Shea if he ever finds out, I do not know.'

'I gather they live separately anyway,' I said.

Biggar looked at me, with a raised eyebrow.

'You're very well informed,' he said. 'How do you know that?'

'The O'Gorman Mahon told me,' I said.

'How the devil does he know?' exclaimed Biggar, and then corrected himself. 'Of course, he would know. O'Shea tells him everything! What else did O'Gorman tell you?'

'That O'Shea and his wife have been estranged for years; that he lives in London and she lives in Kent; and that he has mistresses in London and in Madrid.'

Biggar contemplated this information with some amusement.

'I am not surprised,' he said, 'but we still have to make sure this never comes out. If it does, I shudder to think what might happen.'

Later that evening, Healy and Biggar returned to London. With Healy gone, Parnell seemed to breathe more easily. There was something about Healy that made people uneasy. He had a sharp intelligence, but he had an even sharper tongue and there was about him a certain viciousness. His poisonous barbs had, so far, been reserved for our opponents, but I wondered what would happen if they were ever aimed in our direction. He was also a ferocious Catholic and an unbending moralist – in short, a prig; and now he had information in his power which could destroy Parnell. Healy's look of gloating superiority, of smugness, almost of triumph, when he told us of the secret in the letter remain with me still. His earlier hero worship of Parnell had now wholly curdled.

I did suggest to Parnell that if he had written to me to let me know where he was, I could have made his apologies to the group. But he looked at me directly.

'You must learn the ethics of kingship, Harrison,' he answered. 'Never explain, and never apologise. I could never keep my rabble together if I were not above the human weakness of apology.'

It was a troubling statement, but I kept it to myself.

Thirty-Three

A Duel

I RETURNED TO London with Parnell some days later and shortly afterwards Gladstone introduced his Land Act. Parnell, Biggar and I sat down to read it through in an alcove in the House of Commons, the April sunlight streaming in, illuminating each particle of dust.

The more we studied the bill, the more we realised that Gladstone had really struggled to come to grips with the enormity of the problem. It seemed that Gladstone, like Parnell, was determined to break the power of the landlords in Ireland. The Act would bring about a revolution in land ownership in Ireland as decisive as anything which had occurred during the French revolution, but it would be done in an English manner, slowly and methodically and in accordance with the rule of law.

Ironically, the true star of the debates over the land bill was Tim Healy. He had mastered its provisions so thoroughly that at times the House was reduced to a drawing-room conversation between Healy and Gladstone, as Healy probed and picked and analysed and argued over the minutiae of the new bill. Eventually, Gladstone came to appreciate Healy's command of the issues and his understanding of the bill and over the months he accepted many of Healy's amendments.

Indeed, the respect and cordiality which developed between Gladstone and Healy throughout these debates was noticeable. As Gladstone complimented Healy's mastery of the bill, Healy seemed to beam with pleasure. As Parnell grew colder towards him, Healy turned like a sunflower to the greater warmth of Gladstone and a curious friendship grew up between them. Thereafter, it was hard to get Healy ever to say a bad word about Gladstone and his admiration of him grew in direct proportion to his dislike of Parnell.

Parnell intervened on many occasions and attended the House every night of the debate. But as the session progressed, he appeared to be increasingly unwell. He was pale and, even in the cold of the evening, appeared to be feverish, almost clammy. As I sat beside him, I could hear him sighing deeply, as if constantly trying to get his breath back. But whenever he stood to make his interventions, he seemed to banish those symptoms at will, only to relapse into weakness once his contribution had been made. I became increasingly concerned about him and I told him he should rest, that he wasn't needed every night of the debate.

'I have been invited down to Brighton,' he said. 'I think perhaps I will go.'

'The sea air will help you,' I said, trying to reassure him. I assumed Mrs O'Shea had invited him but he made no reference to her.

I wondered whether the strain of the intrigue was beginning to tell.

 ❧

Some weeks later, in mid-July, on another hot and humid London afternoon, Parnell and I were standing idly in the lobby of the House of Commons, just before the House resumed, when I saw O'Shea striding over to us. I saluted him but he ignored me entirely and, walking swiftly up to Parnell, thrust a letter into his hand.

'Read that, sir, and give me your immediate reply,' he said rudely, and strode off.

Parnell tore open the envelope and read the note quickly. I could see his jaw clenching. He read it again a second time, before handing it to me.

'I may need you in France,' he said.

I took the note. It was difficult to read as the handwriting was so poor. Perhaps it had been written at great speed – or perhaps under great agitation.

13th July 1881

Sir,

Will you be so kind as to be in Lille or in any other town in the north of France which may suit you or your convenience on Saturday next the 16th inst. Please let me know by 1pm today where to expect you on that date so that I may be able to inform you of the sign of the inn at which I shall be staying. I await your answer in order to lose no time in arranging with a friend to accompany me.

I am your obedient servant,
W.H. O'Shea.

'Lille. With seconds! A duel!' I said in disbelief. 'He's challenged you to a duel.'

'So it would appear,' said Parnell calmly. He stood, as he often did, when in a difficult situation, rigid and immobile.

'You might consent to be my second,' he murmured.

'Of course, Charles,' I said, 'but you cannot let this happen.'

'I shall not decline the challenge,' said Parnell firmly.

'Perhaps not, but you must get him at least to delay it, until he has time to calm down.' I was appalled that the intrigue between Parnell and Katharine had taken such an unexpected turn.

Parnell said nothing, but stood stock still, staring at some unknown object in the distance.

'How on earth,' I said, 'has he found out?'

Although Parnell knew that Biggar and I were aware of the liaison he never acknowledged it to us and we, of course, never mentioned it to him. He was not a man given to intimate conversations, even with his friends.

'I don't know,' said Parnell.

The bell sounded to call us in and we walked back into the Chamber. Over the next few hours, Parnell spoke on the land bill debates on a number of occasions. I marvelled at his composure. I, by contrast, was in turmoil. At about seven o'clock, he whispered over to me that he was going to leave. I knew he was going to visit Mrs O'Shea. I did not tell anyone about the duel – not even Biggar. It was best kept secret for the moment.

I spent the evening walking around London in a state of nervous dread. What if Parnell were killed in the duel? What if he were injured? If the scandal leaked out, it would destroy the Land League. It could even destroy the land bill, just as it was about to pass through the Commons.

The following morning, I called around to Keppel Street, but Parnell was not there. I took a cab to the Westminster Palace Hotel and found him in the hotel library, in an armchair beside the fire, reading his scientific journals and drinking some tea. He seemed utterly at ease.

'Have you spoken with O'Shea?' I asked anxiously.

'No,' said Parnell, 'but I have written to him, accepting his challenge. We leave for France in the morning.'

I sat down on the armchair opposite him. 'Charles, are you mad? You can't go ahead with this duel.'

'It's not in my hands,' said Parnell simply. 'The matter is with O'Shea. He has challenged me and I have accepted.'

He picked up his journal, but then put it down again.

'You didn't expect me to refuse the challenge, did you, Harrison?' he said.

I shook my head.

There was a further silence.

'And what if you are killed?' I asked.

He shrugged his shoulders, apparently untroubled by such a possibility.

'O'Shea has to make the same calculation,' said Parnell. 'He won't want to be killed in a duel in France.'

'That may be,' I said, 'but he was a captain in the army. He's better used to these situations than you are.'

Parnell raised an eyebrow.

'A commission purchased for him by his father,' he said contemptuously, 'and sold by him before he had seen any combat.'

'Does he know you're a terrible shot?' I asked.

Parnell smiled.

'No,' he said, 'and I shall not tell him. But believe me, Harrison, O'Shea will back down. In my experience, bullies are always cowards and O'Shea is nothing more than a farmyard bully.'

As we sat in the library, a hotel porter came in.

'Ah, Mr Parnell, sir,' he said, 'there you are. I have a message for you.'

Parnell took the letter handed to him and read it.

'It's another letter from O'Shea,' he said glancing up at me. He read it out:

Sir,
I have called frequently at the Salisbury Club today and I find that you are not going abroad. Your luggage is at Charing Cross Station.

Your obedient servant,
W.H. O'Shea.

Parnell looked over at me. 'As I told you,' he said. 'The man is a coward.'

I was taken aback. 'Why do you say that?' I asked. 'He is keeping you to the duel.'

'I doubt that,' said Parnell calmly. 'Why would he go to the Salisbury Club at all? Let alone frequently. Why would he doubt me? Unless he is nervous. He has challenged me and I have accepted.'

'He doesn't appear to have got your letter,' I said.

'That may be,' said Parnell. 'No matter. He will get it later today. He's now worried I will accept the challenge and that he will be killed or maimed. That's why he is stalking the Salisbury.'

'What does he mean: "Your luggage is at Charing Cross Station"?' I asked.

'I left a portmanteau with Mrs O'Shea at Eltham,' said Parnell dryly. 'I presume he has had it removed.'

He went over to the escritoire and pulled out some notepaper. He wrote a few lines and read them aloud, half to himself.

Sir,
I have replied in the affirmative to your previous letter and you will find from the contents of the letter referred to, that your surmise that I refuse to go abroad is not a correct one.

Yours faithfully,
CSP.

He put the letter in an envelope and went out to the foyer, to give it to a messenger to deliver it to O'Shea immediately.

'Who is O'Shea's second?' I asked.

'I have no idea,' said Parnell, 'and as no one has contacted me about it, I think we can assume O'Shea has no intention of going through with his challenge.'

We stayed to have lunch, and just after lunch Katharine's sister, Mrs Steele, came into the hotel. She saw us in the drawing-room and came over to us directly.

'Mr Parnell, Mr Harrison,' she said. She seemed agitated and unsmiling.

We rose to greet her and to ask her to join us.

'I am glad to have found you.' She took her seat beside us.

'I wonder, Mr Parnell,' she said, 'if I might have a short talk with you.'

I immediately excused myself and went outside for a walk. It was a beautiful summer's afternoon, and I walked around Westminster, wondering whether it was really possible that Parnell's intrigue could cost him his life.

I returned to the hotel after about an hour. Mrs Steele had left.

'Mrs Steele is trying to negotiate a dignified withdrawal by O'Shea,' said Parnell.

'How does she know about it?' I said, amazed. 'Did Mrs O'Shea tell her?'

'Apparently not,' said Parnell. 'O'Shea told her himself! According to O'Shea, he went to Eltham unexpectedly and saw my portmanteau there. There was a scene with Mrs O'Shea; O'Shea left and went straight to Mrs Steele's house, late at night. He must have told her of his suspicions.'

Later that afternoon, we returned to the House of Commons. The debates on the land bill were continuing and Healy was jousting with Gladstone and the Speaker, but I found it impossible to concentrate on the debates. Biggar was oblivious to the drama which was unfolding. His wise counsel might have been invaluable, but Parnell was adamant he was not to be told.

Sometime after supper, at about nine o'clock, during the recess, I saw O'Shea approaching us in the lobby.

'Parnell, come over here,' he said insolently.

Parnell, grim-faced, followed him across the lobby to an alcove on the far side. I watched as O'Shea spoke heatedly to Parnell and jabbed his finger into his chest on a number of occasions. After some moments, Parnell returned to me.

'You can unpack your suitcase, Harrison,' he said, with a wry smile. 'We won't be travelling to France.'

'Thank God for that.' I exhaled deeply. 'What did he say?'

'He muttered something about a misunderstanding between Mrs O'Shea and himself,' said Parnell, 'and that it has now all been resolved.'

Delicacy demanded that I not enquire any further. The crisis had been averted – for the moment.

Thirty-Four

Kilmainham Gaol

PERHAPS BECAUSE THE near calamity made him realise that time was not on his side, Parnell was active in the final few weeks of the debate on the land bill. There were agitations from the more extreme sections of the Land League that the bill did not go far enough, but Parnell ignored them. Five years of dealing with Disraeli made Parnell appreciate how unusual it was for any English Prime Minister to have an interest in Irish affairs – particularly one as powerful as Gladstone. Parnell knew that any gains for Ireland would have to be won step by step. The fight for Home Rule was never going to be a war of independence, as with the American colonies; it could only be a gradual progression, year by year, victory by victory.

The bill passed through the Commons with a considerable majority. Although fiercely resisted in the Lords, it was passed there also, partly because scores of landlords with estates in the west of Ireland and seats in the House of Lords came to London especially for the debate and begged their colleagues to vote in favour of the bill, believing that their own lives would be at risk if the bill did not pass. The power of the landlords was now decisively broken.

Exactly one year earlier, I had watched as the House of Lords had thrown out a minor bill to compensate tenants, giving a signal to landlords all over Ireland that they could evict their tenants with impunity. But Parnell alone had blocked their way. He had not only stopped the advancing enemy, he had rallied his troops, and he had launched such a devastating counter-attack that the landlords were now on the defensive. Without armies, without fleets, and even without arms, he had organised regiments of tenant farmers, drilled and disciplined by the Land League, behind his leadership. In his speech in Ennis he had declared war on landlords; he had waged that war with weapons of his own choosing and on battlefields of his own choosing in the west of Ireland. Within a bewilderingly short period of time, Parnell had made the country ungovernable.

But now that the Act was passed, we knew that Gladstone no longer needed Parnell or his votes. The fear of arrest was now uppermost in all our minds.

∽∾

Weeks later, Parnell travelled to Dublin for a great National Convention of the Land League, to celebrate the passing of the Land Act. It was almost dark when we arrived, but we managed to find a hansom outside the station to take us to the Rotunda.

As we emerged at the end of Harcourt Street, our carriage was surrounded by an enormous crowd of supporters, carrying torches and shouting out Parnell's name. A group of men stopped the horses, unshackled them and, picking up the shafts, pulled the carriage along by themselves, urged on by the enthusiastic crowd. Parnell, the least sociable of men, stood, waving to the crowds and shouting for Ireland. It was a scene of unceasing pandemonium, as we headed down Grafton Street and along College Green towards Trinity and the House of Lords. As we passed the old parliament, Parnell shouted to his men to stop a while and, as the crowds swelled around us, Parnell stood up to address them, one hand pointing to the parliament building – like a statue, I thought, that one day would be erected in his honour.

'There,' he said, 'is our old parliament.' His voice carried in the still night air, as his supporters quieted themselves to listen to him. 'There is a place of memories which no Irish man could ever forget … Those who are not yet born will thank you who are alive today for taking part in the great work of the Land League … The spirit shown in the gaols and in every corner of Ireland will never die until it destroys the alien rule which has kept our country in chains and sweeps away that detestable rule – with its buckshot and its bayonets – far over the channel whence it can never return.'

This fiery rhetoric was greeted with loud cheers and with the now familiar cries, 'Long live Parnell' and 'God save Ireland'.

He gestured to them to quieten and the crowd fell silent, their faces held upwards, looking at him. In the darkening hours of that mild September night, it seemed that Parnell's hold over the Irish people was now hypnotic and total. As he looked around, his voice rang out over their heads.

'We say to England: you have endeavoured to rule us for 700 years and your failure is more disastrous now than it has been at any time during those long years ... And we say to England ... you have been tried and you have been found wanting. You had better give it up and if you don't give it up soon the united voice of the civilised world will bear it no longer.'

A huge roar went out, and torches were waved up and down in enthusiastic support for his words. He sat down again in his carriage and we were carried all the way down Sackville Street.

'You know the police are taking down every word you say?' I said to him.

'I would be disappointed if they were not,' said Parnell, smiling.

'You are giving Gladstone the perfect cause to arrest you.'

'I am quite sure Gladstone has already decided to have me arrested,' said Parnell. 'I must make sure that I have stirred up enough trouble to keep them going during my imprisonment.'

When we arrived at the Rotunda, the great crowds inside rose as one to give Parnell another great ovation. As I looked on, I thought that this was not just another political meeting; this was a great national convention of delegates from every Land League organisation throughout the country. This was the first representative assembly held in Ireland for over 100 years and it had sprung up, as if from the soil itself, as a response to the land agitation. And I realised then that Parnell had achieved what we had never thought possible: he had brought us our own representative assembly and yet he had also kept our parliamentary forces at Westminster. Our country was no longer on its knees: it had risen to its feet. Never again would we fall back to where we were.

Never again.

⁘

In October, Parnell told me of his intention to go to London for a few days to visit Mrs O'Shea. On the day before he was due to go, I joined him for breakfast at Morrison's to go over some Land League business. As we were talking, there was a knock on the door and Larkin, one of the hotel porters, stuck his head in.

'Mr Parnell,' he said, in a whisper, 'there's two gentleman here to see you. I think they're from the Castle.'

'What do they want?' asked Parnell.

'I don't rightly know,' said Larkin.

'Ask them their names, Larkin, will you?' said Parnell kindly. 'And their business.'

Larkin nodded and closed the door. Within minutes he was back.

'A Mr John Mallon, sir.' said Larkin. 'Says he is Superintendent of Police. The other wouldn't give me his name. He's a constable. They wouldn't tell me their business.'

He began to get a little agitated.

'Mr Parnell,' he whispered, coming into the room and closing the door behind him, 'I think they're here to arrest you.'

Parnell looked over at me.

'But, Mr Parnell, sir,' Larkin said excitedly, 'you can escape. There is a door on the landing,' – he gestured with his hand – 'leads to the back of the house and out on the back street. You'd be out in a minute. I could tell them that you had left.'

'No, Larkin. Thank you,' said Parnell, standing up to shake his hand. 'Tell them I'll be down in a few moments. I have some letters to write.'

Larkin looked disconsolate, but went downstairs to tell them. I stood guard at the open door in case the policemen might rush up the stairs to arrest Parnell, but they did not. Parnell sat calmly at his desk, writing a number of letters and when he had finished he straightened his necktie, put on his waistcoat and coat and went downstairs.

In the foyer, Superintendent Mallon was sitting in an armchair, his overcoat still on, twirling his hat in his hands. His sidekick was planted in front of the door, as if somehow Parnell might make a break for it.

'Good morning, Mr Parnell,' said Mallon.

Parnell nodded at him.

'I have a warrant for your arrest,' said Mallon grimly.

Although I had been expecting this for months, the cold formula of the words sent a chill through me.

'On what charge?' said Parnell calmly.

'There is no charge,' said Mallon stiffly.

'And where am I to be taken?' he said.

'Kilmainham Gaol,' said Mallon tersely.

'I would like Mr Harrison to accompany me, Mr Mallon,' said Parnell. 'I have some last-minute instructions I wish to give him.'

Mallon nodded and gestured to Parnell to lead the way. The other constable moved aside and Parnell stepped into Dawson Street. There was a carriage directly outside the hotel. A third constable held open the door.

It was about nine o'clock on a cold, windy October morning and such passers-by as there were took no notice of the scene. Within minutes, we were in the carriage heading towards College Green, and as we passed the old parliament building, two more police carriages joined us there, one in front and one behind. The three carriages then passed up Dame Street, turned into Parliament Street and then along the south quays, past the Four Courts. At the quays, a troop of mounted police took the lead in escorting the carriage the rest of the way, out past Kingsbridge Station and on to Kilmainham Gaol.

'Contact Biggar, Dillon and McCarthy,' said Parnell, in a low voice. 'Also Fanny and my mother. And could you see Mrs O'Shea gets this letter?'

He pressed a note into my hand. I assured him that I would deliver it to her personally. Parnell nodded his thanks.

'What will happen now?' I asked.

Parnell shrugged his shoulders.

'I expect Captain Moonlight will take my place,' he said grimly.

He leaned back in the carriage and sighed. 'Perhaps it's just as well,' he said. 'I shall have some time to consider our next step.'

Within moments, the carriage had arrived at Kilmainham Gaol. With its thick squat walls and castellated turrets, it looked more like a fortress than a gaol, an Irish Bastille.

Parnell and I descended; we shook hands and, following the soldiers and Mallon, he walked the few short steps to the prison door, without a backwards glance and with his head held high. I watched as the heavy gates of the gaol banged noisily behind him, and I was left alone, staring up at the stone sculpture above the gate of the gaol, a figure of three ghoulish serpents writhing around one another, their fangs bared, their eyes staring venomously at anyone who dared to enter that terrible place.

Thirty-Five

Prison Life

I WALKED BACK towards the city with a sense of increasing anger. How could this have happened? How could Gladstone, who had seen Parnell in the House of Commons, day after day, night after night, debating his cause, give an order to imprison him without charge? I tried to imagine the outcry in England if Gladstone had arrested Disraeli without charge and cast him into prison.

I walked along in a daze. All around me, Dubliners were going about their daily business, oblivious to the shocking event which had just taken place in their midst. There had been no army to defend him, no war fought to take him: just constables arresting him quietly in a city hotel after breakfast.

I hailed a passing hansom to take me to the General Post Office on Sackville Street and sent off telegrams to Biggar and Healy in London and to Fanny and Mrs Parnell in New York. I also sent one to Mrs O'Shea. Then, without even packing, I dashed out to Kingstown to catch the next sailing to Holyhead.

I arrived in Euston later that evening and caught a cab to Mrs O'Shea's home at Eltham in Kent, only a short journey from London. I had never visited before and I was not sure whether Captain O'Shea would be there. However, as Captain and Mrs O'Shea lived apart, I thought it unlikely. If he was, I would simply say that Parnell had asked me to tell Captain and Mrs O'Shea in person that he had been arrested. I would have to find an opportunity to give the letter to Mrs O'Shea surreptitiously. These stratagems and deceptions occupied my mind until the carriage drew up outside Wonersh Lodge in Eltham.

It was a large house, set behind high pillars and high gates and surrounded by a stone wall. The carriage brought me to the front door and I asked the driver to wait.

I rang the doorbell and Mrs O'Shea's maid answered the door. She ushered me into a drawing-room, where Mrs O'Shea was waiting.

'Mr Harrison, Mr Harrison,' she said. 'How is he? I got your telegram.' She was visibly agitated, almost in tears.

'Mr Parnell gave me a letter for you,' I said, and handed it to her. She opened it and read it through immediately and, as she did, she began to weep silently. She placed her handkerchief to her face to compose herself.

I described the morning's scene to her. She asked after every detail and made me repeat each element of the story at least three times.

'Oh, my poor Charles,' she said.

I was moved by her obvious distress and her concern for him.

'He had been expecting this for some time,' I said, trying to comfort her. 'He had prepared himself.'

'I know, Mr Harrison, I know,' she said, 'but what are his conditions like?'

I told her I did not know, that I had not been allowed further than the prison doors that morning, but that I would be visiting him the next day.

'Will you take a letter to him?' she asked.

Even in her distress, she was charmingly polite and solicitous and insisted on getting her maid to serve supper for me, whilst she went into another room to write her letter. After a short while, she returned and handed me her note.

I took my leave and returned to London, where I went directly to the Westminster Hotel. I had telegraphed Biggar that I would meet him there at two o'clock in the morning.

When I arrived, I found Healy there also. They were both in gloomy humour. I did not mention my visit to Eltham, as I did not wish Healy to know about my meeting with Mrs O'Shea.

'If Parnell is taken, then none of us are safe,' said Healy. 'I still can't believe Gladstone did it.'

'He's a ruthless old man,' said Biggar venomously, gulping down a brandy. 'I heard Willie O'Shea was "joyful" to hear of Parnell's arrest.'

'That's because he can have his wife back now,' interjected Healy tartly.

We cut our conversation short, as Biggar and Healy decided they would not return to Ireland with me and, later that morning I caught the first train to Holyhead alone. I picked up the newspapers at Euston: Parnell's arrest was on the front page and the editorials all gushed support for Gladstone, who had received the news of Parnell's arrest at the Guild Hall banquet, where he was being honoured by the City of London. The irony that Gladstone had received the freedom of London on the same day that he had deprived Parnell of his freedom in Dublin went unremarked on in all the papers.

But when I arrived into Dublin in late afternoon, it was clear that the news of Parnell's arrest had been greeted in a quite different manner; there were stories of disturbances and riots throughout the city. Later that day, I heard that John Dillon, James O'Kelly, William O'Brien and others had all been arrested and thrown into Kilmainham to join Parnell.

The following day, I went over to Kilmainham to see Parnell. I had envisaged dismal conditions, but to my surprise Parnell's cell was large and bright, with two windows looking out over an exercise yard below. It even had a fireplace. It was, I realised later, the biggest cell in the prison, built at a time when nobles could pay for a more comfortable stay. Parnell greeted me cheerily and he seemed in good spirits.

I told him of my meeting with Mrs O'Shea and of her distress and gave him her letter. I also told him the day's news, the Guild Hall reception in London and the riots in Dublin, but he had read the newspapers.

'I'm allowed any amount of reading material,' he said, 'so perhaps you could purloin some engineering journals in the Morrison for me.'

I left after an hour, heartened to see him in such good form, and I wrote a note to Mrs O'Shea, reassuring her about his prison conditions.

Over the following days, the police continued their arrest of the League leaders and each day I visited Parnell in prison there was a new arrival: Sexton, then Brennan, then Kettle. There was a certain gallows humour about their combined plight and as the prisoners were allowed to mix freely in the landings and halls, they could now have interminable discussions about what they should do next.

Over the next few months, I visited Parnell in prison on most days. The prisoners were all placed in cells on the West Wing, a large open space with cells on three levels and a glass roof. During the day, their cell doors were open and they could walk in and out of each other's cells at will. The prison regime was mild, almost comfortable, in a Spartan manner. The prisoners were allowed as many visitors as they liked; they had plenty of exercise and fresh air in the exercise yard. They were allowed newspapers and books. Visitors could even bring food. But I had never been in a place which was so perishingly cold. The gaol was built on a hill, to allow the winds to blow through the prison and disperse the fetid air, but as the corridors and cells were exposed to the elements, the bitterly cold winds blew through the place all day and all night, and the walls themselves radiated damp.

As the weeks of his imprisonment turned to months and as the autumn turned to winter, the chilling dampness of the prison began to affect Parnell. He grew increasingly prone to colds and chest infections and he regularly had to be removed to the infirmary for observation and treatment.

I also spent much time with Dillon, who was ill for most of his imprisonment and was confined to his bed much of the time. Each time I visited, he seemed to have received a new box of books. I picked up some of the titles: Berkeley's *Principles of Human Knowledge, Essays by Francis Bacon*, a volume of Shelley's poetry and, opened by his bedside, a medical treatise on diseases of the digestive tract.

'No one can say you don't have a catholic taste in reading matter,' I remarked, holding up the last-named book.

Dillon groaned. 'This prison diet is causing me agonies. But if I don't eat, I just get weak.'

The poor fellow was not in good health and I did indeed wonder whether he would survive the imprisonment. But Dillon himself was truly unconcerned.

'If I died for Ireland, I would die content,' he said mournfully, before clasping his stomach as another spasm of pain hit him.

'We don't want you to die for Ireland, Dillon,' I said to him cheerfully. 'We want you to live for Ireland.'

But I was worried about him and insisted that the doctor move him to the infirmary for treatment.

~∽∾~

Towards Christmas, Parnell asked me to travel to Eltham to see Mrs O'Shea. In her correspondence, she was fretting about him and his continued imprisonment, but Parnell was adamant she was not to visit him in prison. I travelled over to England in mid-December and went to Eltham the following day. I was shown into the drawing-room, where Mrs O'Shea rose to greet me. To my great surprise – and discomfiture – I saw that she was expecting a child.

She greeted me with her usual charm and warmth, but the tears were welling up.

'Tell me how he is, Mr Harrison, truthfully,' she said. 'I keep getting letters from him in which he tells me not to worry, that he only has a cold or a fever or that the doctor only has a slight concern.'

Her concern and love for him were so palpable that I was deeply moved. I assured her that I had left Parnell in good health and in good spirits, that he was eating well and resting and getting much exercise.

'He has even started playing handball again,' I said.

'Yes,' – she laughed through her tears – 'he told me that in one of his letters. But he seems to be getting so many colds and fevers.'

'The prison is damp,' I said, 'but he lights the fire in his cell every day.'

'I have a gift for him,' she said, 'for Christmas. Will you give it to him for me?'

She went over to a table on which there were two small boxes, wrapped in red Christmas paper with a red ribbon.

She began to weep again as she handed one to me, but after some time she composed herself.

I assured her I would give it to him.

'I also have a small gift for you, Mr Harrison,' she said, handing me the second gift. 'But it's not to be opened until Christmas Day,' she admonished me, trying to be cheerful.

Some time later I took my leave, taking with me her gifts and letters for Parnell.

The following evening, when I was alone with Parnell in his cell, I told him of my meeting with her and of her distress. I did not mention her condition – it did not seem appropriate; I assumed he knew of it from her correspondence.

I visited Parnell on Christmas Day, with Katharine's gift and gifts from many of his family. It was a memorable day in the gaol, as all the prisoners' families and friends were permitted to visit and to bring food. The makeshift tables we assembled in the West Wing of the prison were laden down with turkeys, hams, puddings, mince pies and Christmas cakes. James O'Kelly, who had a fine voice, sang Christmas carols, in which we all joined and Dillon, who had recovered, read some poetry. Parnell sat at the middle of the table, enjoying the camaraderie and banter of his prison friends and it was early morning before we were ushered out of the prison.

During Parnell's stay at Her Majesty's pleasure, Biggar, who, to his chagrin, had not been arrested, had decided that a spell in Paris could not do him any harm. Unfortunately for him, whilst he was there, he succumbed to the mature charms of an Irish lady who resided in Paris, a Miss Highland. She was referred to ever afterwards as Biggar's 'Highland fling'! I heard about it first when Biggar approached me, somewhat crestfallen, one afternoon, to see if I could join him for lunch to discuss a 'confidential and delicate personal matter'.

Over lunch in a quiet restaurant in Covent Garden, he poured out the whole story to me: how he had met Miss Highland, how an infatuation on both sides had developed, how in a moment of ardour he had proposed marriage to her and how she had accepted.

I congratulated him on his good fortune.

'The story doesn't end there,' he said gloomily.

'I had reasons – good reasons – to reconsider my rash, my impulsive gesture.' He looked at me as if he were in agony. 'For heaven's sake, man, I don't want to be married. Not at my age.'

'So you have told her,' I said sympathetically.

'I have indeed,' he said miserably.

'Well, then, that's the end of it,' I said.

'That's what I thought, too,' said Biggar, 'but just this morning I received a writ in the post. She has sued me for breach of promise.'

He fumbled about his coat pockets and drew out an envelope.

'I was hoping you might act for me,' he said.

I read the writ through carefully. The woman scorned had decided to come to London to vent her fury, presumably to cause Biggar the maximum embarrassment.

'You will need a silk as well,' I said.

'I know,' said Biggar, even more miserably. 'I'm going to ask Charles Russell.'

Charles Russell QC was a member of our party; but, even more importantly for Biggar's purposes, he was one of the leading silks at the English Bar.

'I'm too old to be sowing my wild oats,' he groaned. 'I'm too old to even get married, for heaven's sake.'

'I thought becoming a Catholic would have stopped you carrying on like that,' I said, unable to resist the target. Biggar's conversion some years earlier to the faith of his countrymen had been an occasion for some ribaldry among us all.

'Not now, Harrison,' groaned Biggar. 'How could you?'

Poor Biggar was so unnerved by his upcoming case that I hadn't the heart to tease him any further.

I never mentioned it to anyone, but Healy got hold of the story from his journalistic contacts and his wicked stories about 'Biggar the Boulevardier' were soon doing the rounds. Unfortunately for Biggar, the case did indeed go to trial and he had to pay the dear lady £400 compensation for breach of promise. It was an expensive affair, but, as he said afterwards, recovering his *joie de vivre* over a bottle of Haut Brion, not as expensive as it might have been had he married her!

Thirty-Six

A Daughter

IN EARLY FEBRUARY, I, Biggar, Healy, Frank O'Donnell and other Members of Parliament who had not been imprisoned attended the House of Commons for the new session, but in Parnell's absence, we floundered. His certainty about strategy and his calm assurance at times of crisis were attributes that none of his lieutenants had. We tabled numerous resolutions of protest at his ongoing imprisonment and spoke out many times for his release, but we did not wish to antagonise Gladstone, as he was the only person who could decide to set Parnell free.

Some days after Parliament had commenced, I received a telegram from Mrs O'Shea, asking me to come to Eltham as soon as I could. I went that very afternoon, and when I arrived I was shown into the drawing-room, where Mrs O'Shea was cradling her new baby. She welcomed me effusively.

'I wanted you to see my little girl,' she said.

'When was she born?' I asked, offering her my congratulations.

'Yesterday,' she said, smiling. 'I wanted Charles to know as soon as possible.'

I tried to remain as calm as I could, but I think the shock must have been evident in my face.

'I was hoping you might take him this letter directly,' she said. 'I won't trust it to the postal service, not after what happened in Paris.'

I stayed a short time longer and then took my leave. I travelled back to Ireland the next morning and went straight from Kingstown to Kilmainham Gaol. Even in the walk from the front gate of the prison down the dark, dank passageways to Parnell's cell, I was frozen solid. The bitter February wind blew right through the prison and I found Parnell shivering on a chair close to the fire, with a greatcoat on and a rug on his knees. He got up when he saw me.

'How good to see you, Harrison,' he said, shaking my hand. 'Have you news?'

I handed him his letter.

He tore it open and moved over to the lamp, to read it under the light. It was a short letter, written on two sheets and he read it through quickly.

'A girl!' he cried excitedly. 'I have a daughter, Harrison. Have you seen her? What is she like? How is Katharine?'

I congratulated him heartily and he embraced me. I answered all his questions as well as I could and repeated my answers in response to his repeated queries.

But, as our conversation went on, Parnell's mood became more gloomy.

'Thanks to Gladstone, I am in prison for the birth of my daughter,' he said. 'What is he waiting for?'

I shook my head. I had no news for him about his release.

'He has done his worst. He has smashed the League to pieces. What more does he want?' Parnell was getting more agitated.

I told him about the last few weeks in Parliament and our efforts to complain about his continued imprisonment. He nodded in acknowledgement.

'Mrs O'Shea said she would wait until you were released before she christened the baby,' I said.

'Then I will need to get out as soon as I can.' He moved the lamp over to his desk and sat down to write a letter.

'Sophie,' he said to me, as he wrote. 'I think we should call her Sophie – after my sister.'

I waited some time longer before taking my leave but, even during my short stay, the cold of the prison had gone right through me and I was chilled to the bone. I was shivering until I got home into my bed and piled it high with blankets.

I returned to London the next day and met Mrs O'Shea again that evening to pass on the messages and the letter.

The following evening, I had dinner with Biggar and I told him of my meeting with Mrs O'Shea and her new baby.

'I know of it already,' he said.

I was astonished.

'You didn't see the announcement in *The Times* today, then?' he said.

He pushed a crumpled, thumbed copy of the newspaper across the table to me, opened on the page of Court & Social announcements.

'No,' I said. 'I never even thought to look.'

'I kept it out for you,' he said. 'I thought you might miss it with all your travelling.'

I read the announcement aloud. 'On 15th February, at Eltham, to the wife of W.H. O'Shea Esq MP, a daughter.'

'O'Shea thinks she's his,' said Biggar gruffly. 'Why else put it in the paper?'

'And Parnell thinks she's his,' I said, 'and I am sure she is. I saw her this morning. She looks exactly like him.'

'Bah, all children look the same,' Biggar exclaimed. 'Ugly and unrecognisable for years. But how can they both think it is their child?'

The delicacy of the situation was excruciating.

'I don't think we should enquire any further,' I said. 'I would say O'Shea knows very well the child is not his. He is putting the notice in the paper to save a scandal.' I still had not told Biggar about the duel.

'Maybe,' agreed Biggar, 'or maybe she put it in herself.'

'Perhaps,' I said. 'It is somewhat curiously worded.'

'Yes,' mused Biggar. 'I noticed that myself.'

⟊

Even in April, there was still no sign that Gladstone intended to release Parnell and the others from prison. Moreover, the letters from Mrs O'Shea began to cause Parnell increasing concern. His baby, Sophie, was unwell and did not seem to be getting better.

As the weeks dragged on, I could see that Parnell's frustration at his imprisonment grew more intense and his nervous sensibility became more strained.

'I should be with Katharine and Sophie, not locked up in this wretched prison,' he said angrily one evening. 'What is Gladstone waiting for?'

He walked over to the window of his cell to gaze out on to the exercise yard below.

'I tell you, Harrison,' said Parnell quietly, almost pensively, 'I am sick of the whole wretched business. The gut-wrenching speeches, the incessant travelling, the tension, the all-night sessions. I'm sick of it all. I shall not do it anymore. When I leave prison I may retire and live in Avondale, or go to France with Katharine and our daughter. I want to lead a simpler life, far from all this.' He gestured at the dank, grey prison walls.

He looked back at me.

'And when I ask the Irish people from my prison cell to stop paying rent so we can make our last stand together, what happens? They go and make their own little huckster deals with their landlords and ignore me entirely. And months later, I am still mouldering in prison. For them!'

A sense of bitterness and disillusionment with the Irish people was beginning to take hold. They had relied on him, and he had led them in their land campaigns. Now that he needed to rely on them, they had dissolved like the morning mist in a summer sun.

Parnell's woes were intensified some days later, when he received a letter from his sister Delia, in Paris, to tell him that her son had died suddenly of typhoid.

'I must get out of here,' he said to me impetuously, on my next visit. 'Harrison, I want you to send a telegram – urgently – to Forster. Tell him of the death of my nephew and say I want permission to attend his funeral.'

I sent the telegram that very afternoon and Parnell was granted permission immediately. It appeared that the Government was now in as much of a quandary about what to do with Parnell as he was about how to get out of gaol. That, however, was a consideration for another day. The following morning, I went to Kilmainham to collect him and we went directly to Kingstown to catch the morning sailing for London, stopping only to allow Parnell to retrieve his luggage from Morrison's. The hotel had kept it safely since his arrest in October.

When we arrived in London, Parnell took a carriage to Eltham.

The following day, I met him in the Cannon Street Hotel. I asked immediately about his daughter.

'She is quite ill,' said Parnell gloomily. 'The doctors are not sure if she will survive.'

I was shocked. I did not think until that moment that there was any fear for her life.

To make matters worse, Willie O'Shea insisted on seeing Parnell that very day – before he left for Paris. Parnell asked me to join them for lunch – I don't think he wanted to meet O'Shea on his own. There was no warmth between them; they were barely even civil to each other. But as I saw O'Shea's ruddy complexion, I realised with a jolt how unwell Parnell looked, after so many months in prison.

'I have written to Gladstone about you,' said O'Shea to Parnell, when we had taken our seats.

Katharine had already warned Parnell of this, so that Parnell would not be taken by surprise.

'Why did you do that?' he asked.

'I think it is a good time to start discussions again between you and Gladstone,' O'Shea said, 'and I have written to him to offer myself as an intermediary. An honest broker. I believe I am the best possible person to conduct these negotiations.'

He did not elaborate on why he thought he was the best person to do so. But then, he did not need to. Ever the opportunist, he now saw an opportunity to play a role upon the stage as the great peacemaker between Gladstone and Parnell.

'Has Gladstone replied?' asked Parnell.

'He has,' said O'Shea portentously. 'Immediately.'

'To say what, exactly?' said Parnell.

'To ask whether I had your authority to write to him. Whether the initiative had come from you.'

'And you said … ?'

'Absolutely not,' said O'Shea severely. 'I told him it was my initiative entirely.'

'Continue the communications if you wish,' said Parnell, 'but be clear on one thing.'

'What?' asked O'Shea.

'Do not offer him anything without my authority,' said Parnell brusquely. 'Is that understood, O'Shea?'

'We will see how the negotiations progress,' said O'Shea.

Parnell stood up from the table abruptly.

'I must catch the train to Dover.'

'Oh, yes,' said O'Shea. 'I've heard about your nephew.' It was a perfunctory acknowledgement.

Parnell nodded curtly and left the restaurant, without even shaking hands. Extraordinarily, neither Parnell nor O'Shea ever mentioned Katharine's new child. I wondered throughout lunch how it might come up, but she was never even mentioned.

⟡

Parnell stayed in Paris for almost a week, as the funeral of his nephew was delayed; a detailed post-mortem was required before the body could be released. However, when he returned to London, he went to Eltham immediately and I received a telegram asking me to come down to Eltham the following day.

When I arrived, I found the house in a state of unusual and foreboding quietness. I was shown into the study, where Parnell and Katharine were sitting in front of the fire. Beside Katharine, there was a cradle, with their little daughter, Sophie, sleeping inside.

'How is she?' I asked.

'Not well,' said Parnell quietly. 'The doctors say they cannot do anything more.'

Katharine looked pale and overwrought. She seemed close to tears and kept looking at the cradle, standing up every now and then to make sure her baby was comfortable. After some moments, she took Sophie out of the cradle to hold her in her arms, and then handed her to Parnell.

'Poor little Sophie,' he said, over and over again, as he rocked her back and forth.

That evening, O'Shea arrived at Eltham and we all had dinner together – except for Katharine, who excused herself to nurse Sophie.

O'Shea was in ebullient form, full of his own self-importance and of the role he now hoped to play. He never referred to Sophie once, all evening. He never enquired after her; he never sought to see her. His only focus was on his own self-appointed mission.

'I have had two letters from Gladstone,' he said. 'I think he now realises that I am the best person to conduct these negotiations.'

Parnell listened absently, moving his food untasted around his plate.

'I have told him,' continued O'Shea, 'that it is in the interests of all parties that some ... disinterested party ... assumes the role of mediator.'

'What does he want?' asked Parnell sharply.

'He wants you to condemn all the outrages and agitations carried out by the Land League since you've been in prison,' said O'Shea.

'I have already condemned them,' said Parnell.

'I know,' said O'Shea, 'but he wants you to do it again.'

'I shall not,' said Parnell. 'Once is enough. He should know that. What else?'

'He wants you to withdraw the "No Rent" manifesto and to call on tenants to support the Land Act.'

Parnell looked at O'Shea intently.

'I shall not withdraw it, but you can tell Gladstone it is a dead letter,' he said. 'You can tell Gladstone that these are *my* terms. First, I want all arrears of rent to be forgiven. Second, I want the land purchase provisions in the Act extended. If Gladstone can do both of these then, as far as the Land League is concerned, there would be a full settlement of the land question for all practical purposes.'

'I shall communicate these terms to Gladstone and Chamberlain immediately,' said O'Shea.

'Chamberlain!' exclaimed Parnell. 'What has Chamberlain to do with this?'

I was surprised also. We had had no further discussions with Chamberlain ever since he had saved Parnell from suspension several years earlier.

'I believe,' said O'Shea, puffing himself up, 'that Chamberlain is the coming man. He will be the next Irish Secretary. Perhaps the next Prime Minister. Mark my words. He is especially interested in this matter and I have spoken to him on numerous occasions to let him know of my involvement and to keep him informed.'

'This is no business of Chamberlain's,' said Parnell angrily.

It was an awkward evening. I could see it was painful for Parnell to concentrate and he repeatedly sought to end the exchange as quickly as possible. Eventually, I stood up to go and prevailed upon O'Shea to take a cab with me back to London. He spoke for the entire journey about the importance of his role, his relationship with Chamberlain and how, if he managed to broker this agreement with Gladstone, he expected to be rewarded with a place in the Government. He never referred – not even once – to the unusual circumstance of Parnell remaining behind in his wife's home, or to the declining health of his wife's child.

I returned to Eltham early the next morning and was shown into the study. After a few moments Parnell appeared, pale and tired.

'My poor little Sophie passed away this morning,' he said.

'Charles, I am so sorry,' I said. I stood, awkwardly, not sure whether to embrace him, but he moved to the window and the moment was lost.

'Katharine and I nursed her through the night.' His voice was hushed, almost to a whisper. 'But her fever was too high. She died just as the dawn came.'

Parnell sighed heavily, as if he could not get his breath.

After some time, Katharine came quietly into the study, carrying little Sophie in her arms. She was pale and tearful.

'Our poor darling,' she said to me.

'I am so terribly sorry,' I said, trying to find some words of comfort.

'My only comfort is that Charles was here,' said Katharine, after a moment, 'and that Sophie was christened before she died.'

The following day, a melancholy procession took place to the nearby church and cemetery, with Katharine and Charles, their baby Sophie in a tiny coffin, Katharine's three other children and me. I prayed with them as they buried their daughter and watched as Parnell comforted Katharine, as tenderly as any husband.

Immediately after the funeral, Parnell had to travel back to Dublin, to return to Kilmainham Gaol that very evening. His permission for leave had not been extended. He was more downcast and melancholy on that journey than I had ever seen him before. It was a terrible, terrible day.

Thirty-Seven

The Kilmainham Treaty

IN THE DAYS that followed Parnell's return to gaol, I heard from O'Shea, and other voices around the lobbies in the Commons, that Gladstone wanted to find a way out. He wanted Parnell released. Forster, however, was completely opposed. So, if Parnell was released, Forster would have to resign; and the gossip was that Gladstone would nominate Chamberlain to replace him.

O'Shea, in exuberant form, buttonholed me one afternoon and asked me to join him on the terrace of the House. He introduced me to Joseph Chamberlain, with whom he was clearly on terms of intimacy, and to Charles Dilke, an intimate of Chamberlain's. I had observed Chamberlain from a distance for a long time before I made his acquaintance. Slim, clean-shaven and youthful, he cut an intriguing figure in the House of Commons in the way that the coming man always does. Moreover, he was charming: quiet and reserved yet utterly engaging. Dilke, by contrast, was effusive and amusing but with sly, hooded eyes, constantly seeking out a weakness.

'How is Mr Parnell's health?' Chamberlain asked solicitously. 'I heard he has suffered a lot in Kilmainham.'

'He has indeed,' I said. 'I've never known a place so cold. He might as well have been sleeping outside on the Wicklow Mountains.'

'Let us hope, then, that Mr O'Shea's efforts on his behalf will soon bear fruit.' Chamberlain smiled.

'Mr Gladstone has as good as assured me that Parnell shall be released very soon,' said O'Shea, beaming with satisfaction.

'Mr Parnell is lucky to have such a devoted friend as you, Mr O'Shea,' said Chamberlain.

I think O'Shea may have actually simpered with delight at the praise.

'Forster's goose is cooked, Harrison,' said O'Shea gleefully. 'There will be a vacancy in Ireland. Which I hope will go to you, Mr Chamberlain.' O'Shea looked over at Chamberlain. It was clear that Parnell's release was a matter of profound indifference to O'Shea: it was merely a means to an end, a stepping stone to fulfilling his ambition. If Chamberlain were appointed Chief Secretary, O'Shea believed he would be appointed Under Secretary.

'We must hope Mr Parnell's health remains strong until he is released,' said Chamberlain.

O'Shea disappeared for a moment to gladhandle someone else. Dilke looked at him as he left and, when he disappeared from view, leaned forward and beckoned conspiratorially to me to do likewise.

'You should know, Harrison,' he said, 'that the Home Secretary has told the entire cabinet that Mrs O'Shea is Parnell's mistress.'

I recoiled involuntarily at such an indelicate disclosure.

Dilke smiled at the effect his revelation had had on me.

'Don't be so shocked,' he said. 'We are all men of the world.'

I glanced at Chamberlain, who looked at me with a bemused expression, as if challenging me to deny it.

'It appears the Home Office spies told Harcourt,' continued Dilke suavely, 'and he, as Home Secretary, felt duty bound to tell the cabinet. Not, mind you, that it came as a complete shock to many of us.' Dilke picked up his cup of tea and sipped it delicately.

I said nothing, unsure how to respond to this sudden, unexpected confidence.

'Is O'Shea aware of this?' I asked, eventually.

'Aware of what?' asked Dilke. 'If you mean the business between his wife and Parnell, of course he is. Harcourt's spies tell us that he knows all about it and is entirely complicit. If you mean, is O'Shea aware that the cabinet knows, that Gladstone knows, no, not at all. Why should he be?'

'Shh, he's coming back,' said Chamberlain quickly, as O'Shea returned to join us.

Moments later I took my leave, my head full of the intrigues taking place, the circles within circles which were now enveloping Parnell.

෧ᲪᲘᲮ

Events moved rapidly over the next few days. The cabinet met on Monday and, despite Forster's opposition, agreed to Parnell's release. On Tuesday, Parnell, Dillon and O'Kelly were set free, having been imprisoned for almost seven months.

Parnell emerged from Kilmainham Gaol a changed man. The terrible conditions of the prison had destroyed his health and his constitution never really recovered. But it was not only that. He had lost his faith in the Irish people. He had given the people everything he had, but they had betrayed him. He never trusted them again.

But if he no longer trusted the people, he preserved his real hatred for Gladstone. It was Gladstone who had imprisoned him; it was because of Gladstone that his health was broken; because of Gladstone that he had not been there for the birth of his baby daughter; because of Gladstone that he had missed his baby's life on earth; because of Gladstone that he had to return to his prison cell on the day he had buried his daughter. He never forgave him. After Kilmainham, Parnell turned inward upon himself, upon Katharine and upon his own family. He would never again be the same public man.

෧ᲪᲘᲮ

The next day, we travelled back to London and on Thursday, early in the evening, just as Forster was getting to his feet to give his resignation speech, Parnell re-entered a crowded House of Commons to reclaim his seat, cheered to the rafters by all the Irish Members of Parliament. He looked coldly at Forster, before resuming his seat below the gangway.

As Forster tried to speak, Biggar could not resist a parting kick to the Irish Secretary.

'Good riddance, Buckshot!' roared Biggar across the floor at Forster. 'You knew nothing about Ireland when you started and you still know nothing.'

The House of Commons was not a place for sensitive souls.

That same day, much to O'Shea's chagrin, Gladstone appointed his nephew, Lord Frederick Cavendish, as Chief Secretary for Ireland.

I knew Cavendish slightly and he was popular with Irish Members of Parliament. Hesitant and bookish, he had never urged coercion on Ireland; he believed the grievances of the Irish people needed to be addressed and he promised to be a more enlightened appointment than Forster. O'Shea was crestfallen. His great scheme to become Under Secretary for Ireland had come to naught.

On Saturday, Parnell, O'Kelly, Biggar and I went to Portland Prison to meet Davitt, who was also to be released that day. Davitt had been in Portland for over a year and, although he had not had to endure hard labour, he did not have the privileges of his fellow prisoners in Kilmainham. However, despite his privations, he seemed in good health. He had had little access to newspapers and so, in the carriage travelling back to London, we brought him up to date with recent events.

'And I believe after Gladstone has passed the next land bill he will go on to consider Home Rule,' said Parnell.

'In which case we could be looking at the first cabinet of the new Irish parliament,' said Biggar. 'All in this carriage.'

'And what role would you take, Biggar?' said O'Kelly, smiling.

'I would be Speaker,' said Biggar. 'You can't have people speaking all night, wasting valuable parliamentary time – it's a disgrace!'

'And Davitt, what would you be?' Biggar continued.

'Director of Prisons,' said Davitt dourly, to our great amusement.

It did seem, on that bright May afternoon, that we might soon take a huge step forward, but within hours all these bright hopes lay in ruins.

Thirty-Eight

Murder in the Park

THE FOLLOWING MORNING, we arranged to meet in the Westminster Palace Hotel for breakfast at eleven o'clock, but when I got to the hotel I found Biggar already there – ashen-faced.

'You look as if you've seen a ghost,' I said.

'You haven't heard?' said Biggar incredulously.

'Heard what?' I asked.

'Cavendish has been assassinated,' said Biggar.

'Lord Cavendish!' I was shocked. 'Assassinated? Where?'

'In Dublin,' said Biggar. 'In the Phoenix Park. In broad daylight. Stabbed in the heart.'

I sat down on the sofa.

'And he wasn't the only one,' said Biggar. 'They also killed Burke, the Under Secretary.'

'Burke? Who killed them?'

'A group calling themselves "The Invincibles".'

He handed me his *Observer*.

'Read it for yourself.'

The details of the murders were appalling and chilled me to the core. Cavendish and Burke had been walking in the Phoenix Park when they were attacked by a gang of four or five masked men, all of whom had escaped.

I was still reading about it when Parnell came through the hotel foyer, looking gaunt. It was evident he too had heard the news.

He sat down wearily on one of the sofas. 'Just when we were beginning to make progress ...' he said. 'These ... stupid imbeciles, these fanatics, destroy it all with their mindless violence.' He was in despair. 'What did they think they were doing?'

No one said anything in response.

'Who are these Invincibles, Biggar?' said Parnell. 'Have you heard of them before?'

Biggar shook his head.

'Are they Fenians?' asked Parnell.

'I don't know,' said Biggar.

'I went to see O'Shea on my way here,' said Parnell. 'I told him to take a message to Gladstone that I would resign immediately – if he thought it necessary for me to do so.'

'Why would you resign, Charles?' I asked. 'This has nothing to do with you.'

'Aye,' said Biggar. 'Why would you leave your fate in Gladstone's hands, for God's sake?'

'Gladstone has to know that I had no knowledge of this assassination whatsoever,' said Parnell. 'It's his own nephew. His own nephew, for heaven's sake! What did those idiots think they were doing?' His fury was raging.

'And if Gladstone accepts your resignation?' said Healy. 'What happens then?'

Parnell shrugged his shoulders. I think he was past caring.

We waited with some anxiety for O'Shea's message from Gladstone. Over the coming hours we were joined by John Dillon, Justin McCarthy and Frank O'Donnell.

'The Tories will say Gladstone has gone soft,' said Biggar.

'There will be another coercion bill,' said Parnell.

'Then that's the end of Home Rule for another generation,' said Healy gloomily.

Later in the afternoon, O'Shea strolled into the hotel. We all went over to him immediately.

'I passed your message on to Gladstone,' he said, slowly and deliberately, as if English were not our first language. 'His secretary asked me to wait.'

He paused for dramatic effect.

'Eventually, Gladstone himself came down to see me.'

'Oh, for God's sake, get on with it, man,' said Biggar, his impatience and dislike of O'Shea evident in equal measures.

'Gladstone said,' continued O'Shea haughtily, 'that his duty did not permit him to entertain Mr Parnell's proposal, but that he was deeply sensible of the honourable motives by which it had been prompted.'

'Is that verbatim?' said Healy.

'Of course it is,' said Biggar. 'Who else but Gladstone speaks like that?'

Parnell looked neither relieved nor disappointed. He had made the appropriate gesture and Gladstone had made the appropriate response.

'It does mean, of course, that Gladstone will have to appoint a new Chief Secretary,' said O'Shea.

His great plans for self-advancement had been reborn!

On Monday, the House of Commons met to condemn the assassinations. Gladstone found it hard to hold back his tears as he delivered his tribute to his slain nephew and the House fell silent as it listened to his tribute.

Some time later, Parnell stood to speak. He, too, was listened to in silence.

'I can assure this House,' he said, 'that I have nothing but unqualified detestation of this horrible crime …'

This condemnation should have been unremarkable, except that I had never heard him condemn any outrage before – ever. He had shrugged his shoulders at the murder of Lord Mountmorres and at similar killings. Davitt may have condemned them, but Parnell never did. I learned later that even the Fenians were taken aback by the vehemence of Parnell's denunciations, but he was in earnest. It was not just the violence he objected to: it was the sheer idiocy of it, the fact that the people who engaged in such acts seemed to have no sense of the futility of their actions.

After the Phoenix Park murders, Parnell no longer trusted the Fenians. From now on, he would work alone.

Within days Gladstone asked Dilke to be Chief Secretary, but he refused and so Gladstone nominated George Trevelyan. He obviously had no intention of appointing Chamberlain to Ireland. O'Shea's hopes were dashed again.

Several days later, Parnell asked me to go down to Eltham to see him. As the carriage drove through the gates of Wonersh Lodge, a number of shots rang out. The horses reared up, and the cabbie managed to restrain them with some difficulty. When I had alighted, he disappeared swiftly back down the front avenue, barely waiting to collect his fare. I could hear repeated shots coming from the far side of the house. I approached the house and craned my neck carefully around the wall, lest the gunman was aiming in my direction.

About twenty yards away, Parnell, his back to me, was carefully aiming a revolver at an archery board and firing repeated shots at it.

'Parnell,' I shouted. 'Don't shoot, it's me.'

He turned around, smiled and beckoned me over.

'A spot of target practice,' he said. 'The police were here yesterday to warn me to take care for my own protection. They had information that people might want to kill me.'

'Yes, I know,' I said. 'They were at Keppel Street also.'

'So they said,' said Parnell. 'What's your shooting like?'

'It's been a long time since I have done any shooting,' I said.

'Well,' said Parnell, 'now is your opportunity. Best of ten shots. Closest to the bull's eye for a shilling.'

I agreed, remembering his brother's jibes about Parnell's marksmanship.

'I should warn you,' said Parnell, 'my shooting is improving.'

Fifteen minutes later I pocketed a shilling.

'You should buy a revolver,' said Parnell, 'and keep it about you at all times.'

I was alarmed to hear of these precautions, but Parnell seemed utterly unconcerned. We went inside for dinner. Even though it was only a short time since Sophie had died, Katharine seemed more composed.

After dinner, and after Katharine had left us to our cigars, Parnell said, 'I have asked Katharine to meet Gladstone.'

I was taken aback.

'What will Gladstone think when he sees a letter from Mrs O'Shea?' I asked.

'Katharine will tell him that she is acting on my behalf alone, and she will ask Gladstone not to mention it to anyone,' said Parnell.

'Not even to Mr O'Shea?' I asked. Parnell nodded.

'That will raise further questions,' I said, and immediately regretted it. I coloured with embarrassment.

Parnell was not to be dissuaded.

O'Shea had forced himself on Parnell as his intermediary, but Parnell was never going to tolerate for long a situation not of his own making. To choose Katharine as intermediary, though, would send a clear signal to Gladstone that Katharine was Parnell's mistress. What else could he think? To receive secret messages from William O'Shea and Katharine O'Shea, both ostensibly on behalf of Parnell, could admit of only one interpretation. I thought about telling Parnell that the whole cabinet was aware of his relationship with Katharine, but I decided against it.

Thus began an intrigue within an intrigue. I became embroiled in it only peripherally, as I occasionally delivered letters from Parnell to Edward Hamilton, Gladstone's private secretary at Downing Street.

Edward Hamilton had guessed at the truth of the matter at once.

'Nothing surprises me anymore about your Mr Parnell,' he said to me, on one of my visits, 'not even that he would use his mistress to communicate with Mr Gladstone.'

I was embarrassed, but there was nothing I could say to respond to the charge.

Sensing my discomfort, Hamilton pressed home his advantage.

'Mr Gladstone has a peculiar fascination with fallen women,' he said.

'Mrs O'Shea is not a fallen woman,' I said indignantly, but Hamilton smirked and indicated that he would forward the letter to the Prime Minister.

Thirty-Nine

A Sea of Troubles

SOME MONTHS LATER, Katharine summoned me to Eltham, and I could see from her face that something had happened.

'There has been some very bad news,' she said.

'Is Charles all right?' I was worried that he might have had an accident.

'It's his sister Fanny,' said Katharine.

I could feel my heart beating faster. 'What's wrong?' I asked.

'The very worst news,' said Katharine. 'We have just heard that Fanny died yesterday.'

'Died?' I tried hard to conceal my emotion, my bewilderment at this shocking, unexpected news. 'I wasn't even aware she was ill. What happened?'

'It was a complete accident,' said Katharine. 'She appears to have taken some medicine by mistake.'

I could not say anything for several moments, but bowed my head, too overwhelmed to restrain my tears.

She came towards me and sought to comfort me.

'How is Charles?' I asked.

'Absolutely distraught,' said Katharine. 'I have never seen him so upset – not even for Sophie.'

I went into the study, where Parnell was sitting in front of the fire. He got up as I entered, his eyes red from weeping, and we embraced.

'Charles, I am so sorry,' I said.

'I know you loved her too, James,' said Parnell, looking directly at me.

'What happened to her?' I asked.

'I know very little,' said Parnell. He reached up to the mantelpiece to retrieve the telegram and handed it to me. It read:

Dear Charles. Dreadful news. Poor Fanny found dead this morning. Accidental overdose of sleeping draught. Mother.

'I can't even get to her funeral,' said Parnell, 'I wouldn't get there in time.'

He put his head in his hands. Katharine came in and sat on the side of his chair to comfort him.

'I know you loved her too,' repeated Parnell. 'I used to tease her about you. I think she felt the same about you.'

'She was so beautiful,' I said, 'and, yes, I did love her. But I didn't dare say anything.'

'Why ever not?' asked Katharine.

I could feel my hands trembling.

'I just couldn't,' I said.

Forty

The Kingmaker

THROUGHOUT THE NEXT few years, I spent much time in London, attending the House of Commons, but Parnell rarely attended. There was little to do and the years passed off quietly. After Kilmainham he retreated into his life with Katherine and two daughters, Clare and Katie, were born during this time. He waited. And waiting was, for Parnell, always a weapon to be considered. Waiting for others to make their move, to make a mistake, to create an opening; waiting for the climate to change, for events to unfold. He was content to leave parliamentary matters in the hands of Biggar, Justin McCarthy, Tim Healy, Thomas Sexton, John Redmond and others, all competent, conscientious men. But there was never a doubt in anyone's mind that Parnell was 'the Chief'.

I was invited to Eltham at least once a week for dinner, to bring all the Westminster gossip, which Katharine particularly enjoyed. It was, by now, a curious household: Parnell lived there with Katharine and his two children. But Katharine's three children by O'Shea also lived with her there and O'Shea came to Eltham every weekend to see them. Remarkably, it all seemed to pass off in a civilised manner. It was never addressed by any of them, in any way whatsoever. It simply existed as a state of affairs.

Throughout that year, O'Shea seemed to be scheming incessantly with Chamberlain. Chamberlain himself was also scheming for Gladstone's throne, and his attitude to Ireland was typical of many Liberals at the time: he wanted to throw us a bone to keep us quiet. His great plan was to create a Central Board, a glorified national county council. Parnell warned O'Shea that it would never satisfy the demand for Home Rule, but, as it turned out, O'Shea was not listening.

A new election was coming and, under recent reforms, the number of voters and seats would increase, particularly in Ireland. Parnell was now a man to parlay with. As the election drew closer, Parnell sent me and his other emissaries deep into the enemy camps to discuss terms. He began the extraordinary process of playing the Tories off against the Liberals and vice versa. It was high-wire politics, and I doubt any other Irish Member of Parliament could have engaged in it with such success. It was inconceivable that Biggar or Healy, Dillon or McCarthy, could have done it. But Parnell, with his extraordinary self-belief, knew precisely what he wanted to accomplish.

In early May, Parnell began to reappear in the House of Commons, a sign of a quickening interest on his part and a sign to us that he had sensed an opening.

O'Shea had told Parnell that Chamberlain and Dilke had offered their resignations to Gladstone, but that these had not yet been accepted. There was disaffection in the cabinet. This was the opening Parnell had been waiting for, and in early June he struck.

The Tories had tabled a vote on some arcane matter in the budget; Chamberlain and his supporters had absented themselves from the Commons in high dudgeon and Parnell had arranged for a significant number of Irish Members of Parliament to attend. We voted with the Tories and defeated the Government. Gladstone and his Government had to resign immediately. They could not stay in office if they lost a budget vote. There was some disquiet among many of our members that Parnell had put Gladstone out of office, but he was unrepentant.

The Tories, under Lord Salisbury, took power and Lord Carnarvon was named as Chief Secretary for Ireland. Parnell immediately sent Justin McCarthy as an emissary to Carnarvon to negotiate a deal for Irish support; in return for a lapse of coercion, more funds for land purchase and more funds for Catholic education, the Irish would continue to support the Tories. These requests were immediately granted and the ongoing revolution of land ownership continued.

∽✆∾

Sometime later, Parnell approached me in the Commons.

'I have a task – a delicate task – which I need you to undertake,' he said. 'I need you to go to Clare. I need to find out what the mood is for O'Shea. Will they return him again?'

'I doubt it,' I said.

'I doubt it, too,' Parnell said gloomily, 'but I need to be sure.'

The following week, I journeyed back to Ireland and travelled throughout the County of Clare, meeting men connected with the Home Rule Party and the Land League to sound them out on O'Shea's nomination.

'If O'Shea sets foot inside this constituency again, we will shoot him,' was one of the milder responses I received. It was clear O'Shea was despised throughout the county. The people had long memories of how he had sided with the Government whilst Parnell and the Party sat with the opposition. I reported all this to Parnell.

'I thought as much,' he said. 'But I must find O'Shea a safe seat. He wants to be back in the Commons.'

'Do you want him back?' I asked.

'I'd like it if he drowned in a bog,' said Parnell curtly. 'He's causing me no end of problems.'

'Where does he want to stand?' I asked.

'I'm not sure he even wants to stand for the Party,' said Parnell. 'He's talked about standing for the Liberals.'

'Good riddance,' I said with feeling.

'Indeed,' said Parnell, 'but not yet.'

'What about the divorce?' I asked.

'Not while Katharine's Aunt Ben is still alive,' said Parnell.

'And how is she?' I asked.

'Still very much alive,' he said wryly.

Throughout that summer, Parnell and Gladstone corresponded with one another through Katharine. As ever, Parnell's judgment of Gladstone proved to be accurate. Now in advanced years, Gladstone concentrated on what his final priority should be if he were re-elected in November. The words first uttered almost twenty years earlier came back to haunt him. 'My mission is to pacify Ireland,' he had said then and it was now clear that if he wanted to pacify Ireland, he had to pacify Parnell and to pacify Parnell he had to offer Home Rule.

In early November, I joined Parnell in Dublin and we went to meet Willie O'Shea in the Shelbourne Hotel. O'Shea was out of sorts that day. He had been confined to the hotel for days, complaining of a bad cold and he was feeling sorry for himself. He looked pale and venomous as he sat on the sofa in the Lord Mayor's lounge, awaiting our arrival. It was now only weeks away from the election and Parnell still had not found a seat for him to contest, a fact which clearly rankled with O'Shea. He could barely contain himself when we sat down.

'I hope, Parnell, you're here to tell me you've found me a seat,' he said.

'You can't blame me, O'Shea, if the people of Clare don't want you to return,' Parnell said coldly.

'Don't play games with me, Parnell,' said O'Shea viciously. His agitation caused a sudden coughing fit. 'You know damned well if you went to Clare and campaigned for me I would be elected.'

'I don't know that,' said Parnell, 'and, in fact, Harrison told me that nothing I did would make any difference for you in Clare.'

'What would Harrison know,' said O'Shea dismissively, 'about the voters in Clare?'

'I travelled down there last month, O'Shea,' I said, trying to hide my increasing dislike of him. 'They don't want you to show your face there ever again. They threatened to shoot you if you did.'

This news made him apoplectic with anger, but before he could retort he was wracked by another coughing fit.

'You'd better find me another seat,' he said to Parnell, when he recovered.

'I've written to Gladstone to see if you could stand for the Liberals in Antrim,' Parnell replied.

'Antrim!' exclaimed O'Shea. 'Bloody Antrim. I wouldn't stand a chance.'

'Well, the election is only weeks away,' said Parnell. 'We may have to wait until afterwards. There may be opportunities for you then.'

'There'd better be,' said O'Shea, 'but I don't want to stand for the Liberals. I want to stand for the Home Rule Party.'

'Then will you sit with the Party,' asked Parnell 'and vote with us on all matters?'

'And take your precious party pledge!' said O'Shea peevishly. 'I certainly shall not. I have no intention of being your poodle, responding to your beck and call.'

'We're all taking the pledge, O'Shea,' I said. 'You can't be the only one in the Party not to do so.'

'I can and I will,' said O'Shea belligerently.

'We might get an English seat for you,' said Parnell.

'I don't care where the seat is,' said O'Shea, 'but I must have a seat. Chamberlain has as good as promised me …'

'Promised you what?' said Parnell sharply.

O'Shea looked at us slyly, as he realised he had blurted something out unintentionally. He tried to bamboozle his way out of it.

'Nothing,' he said. He took refuge in another minor bout of coughing. 'That's if I even live past this election.'

Parnell repeated his question, his voice cold with anger. 'What has Chamberlain promised you?'

'Look, Parnell,' said O'Shea defensively. 'Gladstone will not last for ever and when he is gone Chamberlain will be Prime Minister. If that happens, he has as good as promised me that I will become Chief Secretary for Ireland.'

'Chief Secretary.' I was incredulous. 'You!'

'I have been working with Chamberlain for years – ever since I got you out of prison, Parnell, for which, by the way, I received no thanks. We're trying to put forward proposals to the cabinet on Ireland.'

'Who's "we"?' said Parnell curtly.

'Chamberlain and I,' said O'Shea.

'You actually believe you are negotiating with Chamberlain for Home Rule?' Parnell was incredulous now.

'I do, yes.' O'Shea was defiant.

'You have no authority from me to do anything of the sort,' said Parnell.

'Yes, that reminds me,' said O'Shea, ignoring Parnell's remarks. 'You misled me, Parnell, over that central board matter. It caused me no end of trouble with Chamberlain, so I suggest you find me a safe seat.'

He leaned forward and jabbed a fleshy finger at Parnell.

'Because I tell you, now, I have no intention of lying in a ditch and lying low. I have been treated like a blackguard by you and I mean to hit you back with a stunner. Everything is ready. I have packed my shell with dynamite and it will smash you and your reputation with your deluded countrymen to smithereens.'

Parnell grew pale at the brutality of the attack.

'I have letters, Parnell,' O'Shea said threateningly, 'letters which will destroy you. So, listen carefully to me. I don't want any more beating about the bush. No man has ever behaved more shamefully to another than you have to me. I don't want to see you or talk to you again until you have found me a safe seat.'

It was blackmail, plain and simple.

O'Shea was raising his voice, causing some of the genteel ladies in the Lord Mayor's lounge to look reprovingly at him.

Parnell rose to his feet and left the salon, in a cold fury.

When the election was eventually called in November, Parnell spent days campaigning all over Ireland. The mood of the country was with him and it was clear that he would carry the whole country for Home Rule.

But it was the election in England on which Parnell focussed his determined concentration. Before any votes were cast, he demanded that I get reports on every constituency in England, with the likely Irish vote in each constituency. If the Irish voted for Gladstone and the Liberals – as they would do naturally – then the Liberals would win the election by a considerable margin. But if the Irish in England voted for the Tories – an unpalatable choice for many of them – it would be a much more close-run affair. The more Parnell considered the situation, the clearer it became that he should urge the Irish in England to vote for the Tories.

'Gladstone will not thank you for it,' I warned him.

'I didn't thank him for putting me in prison,' said Parnell sharply.

A few days later Parnell issued his election manifesto to the Irish people in Britain, urging them to vote for the Tories. It was a brave and extraordinary decision, but such was his ascendancy over the Party that it was never questioned or challenged.

But there was a darker side to this tactic, to which I was party. He persuaded Grosvenor, the Liberal Chief Whip, to let Parnell himself stand for Liverpool. In return, Parnell traded the support of some Irish voters in difficult Liberal seats. Then, days before the election, Parnell withdrew his own nomination and substituted that of O'Shea. It was a tortuous and devious strategy and it almost worked, but O'Shea failed to get elected by only fifty votes.

The result of the election, however, was a great vindication of Parnell's strategy. The Liberals won 335 seats, the Tories 249 seats – a difference of eighty-six seats. The Home Rule Party won eighty-six seats in Ireland – the exact number required to hold the balance of power. It was an extraordinary, an historical coincidence.

Moreover, this was not the rag-bag party of office seekers, time-servers and whiners of Isaac Butt's time, but eighty-six disciplined and committed Home Rulers, all of whom were made in Parnell's image, who followed his leadership to the letter, and who had taken the party pledge to vote with the Party in all matters.

The two had become seven at the time of obstruction; the seven had become thirty at the time of the Land League; the thirty had now become eighty-six; and these eighty-six Members of Parliament now controlled the House of Commons and the Government of the Empire. In less than ten years, Parnell had gone from being the sole voice of obstructionism to becoming the Kingmaker of British Governments.

Forty-One

The Galway Mutiny

BUT ALL WAS not well. If only twenty-five voters had switched allegiance in Liverpool, then history might have been so different. O'Shea would have been elected and Parnell would not have had to continue his increasingly desperate search to find him a seat. O'Shea did not take his defeat well and he turned on Parnell in Eltham the following weekend.

'I don't intend to wait forever, Parnell,' he snapped. 'You'd better find me another seat – quickly.'

As it happened, there was to be a fresh election for Galway and O'Shea demanded the nomination from Parnell.

'If you are prepared to sign the party pledge, you can stand,' said Parnell.

'I will not take your pledge, Parnell,' said O'Shea. 'I have no intention of becoming your lackey.'

'If you don't take the pledge, you will not stand for the Party,' said Parnell firmly.

But Katharine must have persuaded Parnell otherwise. I knew she was fearful that O'Shea would expose them both.

I heard about Parnell's change of mind days later, not from Parnell, but from T.P. O'Connor, whom I met in the lobby of the House of Commons.

'Parnell seems almost to be losing his mind,' O'Connor said to me.

'What do you mean?' I said, puzzled.

He lowered his voice.

'I heard it only yesterday from Parnell himself – outside in the Palace yard – that he intends to run O'Shea for Galway without the pledge. Is he mad?'

It was difficult not to sympathise with O'Connor's agitation.

'O'Shea is a duplicitous double-dealing fool,' he said. 'It's because of his wife. It's the only explanation.'

Parnell's secret was leaking out. O'Connor had not been in Paris when the intrigue had been first exposed, but in the intervening years most of the members of the Party had heard the rumours. It was hardly surprising. People wanted to know where Parnell lived, what were his circumstances, was he married, what did he do when he was not in the House. O'Connor was not seeking confirmation from me about the affair. It was now a given fact. He wanted to know whether Parnell was really prepared to impose O'Shea on the Party to cover up his secret.

'I got all the reasons from Parnell,' continued O'Connor, 'as to why O'Shea should stand, Kilmainham and all that. Chamberlain. Everything except the truth. Which is to shut O'Shea up, I suppose?'

I looked down at the patterned tiles on the lobby floor. I didn't know what to say.

'Tell him he is stirring up a hornet's nest, Harrison,' said O'Connor.

Within hours, Biggar and Healy also confronted me.

'We've heard,' said Healy, with menace. 'O'Connor's told us that Parnell's going to run O'Shea for Galway. Tell us this is not true, Harrison.'

'I can't,' I said. I shrugged my shoulders.

'And is O'Shea going to take the pledge?' said Biggar angrily. 'Because he's been telling everyone he has no intention of taking the pledge.'

'I don't know,' I said. 'I haven't spoken to Parnell.'

'This has got to stop!' Biggar shouted. 'It has gone far enough.'

I had never seen Biggar opposed to Parnell before and I was shocked.

'Parnell cannot decide where his mistress's husband is going to stand,' said Healy, his voice rising with furious indignation. 'Why doesn't she just divorce him?'

I explained about Aunt Ben.

'Oh, Christ,' said Healy, then immediately blessed himself for taking the Lord's name in vain. 'As if it wasn't tawdry enough.'

'What can Parnell be thinking?' said Biggar. 'We have a good Home Rule candidate in Galway already. Young Lynch has been ready to fight this re-run.'

'We can't just throw over Lynch,' said Healy irascibly. 'We're not here merely to do Parnell's bidding.'

'Listen, Harrison,' said Biggar, taking my elbow and moving me out of Healy's earshot, 'you have to tell Parnell about this. He's out of touch here, you know. He's hardly been to the House of Commons in months. Things have changed.'

There was, I knew, truth in that charge. Parnell now seemed to have little interest in attending the arid debates in the House of Commons. He left everything to his colleagues. He rarely even bothered to have regular meetings with the Party. But I could see that, away from the great tension of the House of Commons and cocooned among his family, his health was beginning to improve.

The truth was that after Kilmainham, Parnell had retreated from public life. He spent all his time with Katharine and his daughters. Missing the birth of his first daughter and missing most of her life on this earth had caused him agony and regret. Parnell was not a religious man and he did not believe in an afterlife, so there was no comfort there. Katharine had often said that Parnell's absence from her had caused her to suffer so much that it had killed her little girl – a dramatic, if over-fanciful, view, but one which had an effect on Parnell.

But I was, by now, becoming deeply concerned. T.P. O'Connor, Biggar and Healy were senior officers and behind their voices, presumably, lay the voices of many other members of the Party.

I travelled to Eltham that evening and, over dinner, I tried to explain to Parnell the increasing anger of our colleagues.

'It has to be done this way,' he said firmly. 'I have O'Shea threatening all manner of things if he isn't elected at Galway.' He went over to his desk in the study and wrote out a lengthy memorandum.

'I want you to take this to O'Brien tomorrow,' he said. 'Tell him I want it published in the *United Irishman* as soon as possible.'

'Can I read it?' I asked.

'Of course,' said Parnell, 'the whole country will be reading it tomorrow.'

I read through the sheaves of paper quickly. Parnell had written that it was imperative that O'Shea be elected in Galway, that O'Shea had an important alliance with Chamberlain and that he had provided valuable services to the Party during the Kilmainham treaty negotiations; but the final fury was in the last sentence, which stated that if O'Shea was not elected, Parnell would resign immediately.

I paled as I read it.

'Parnell,' I pleaded, 'this is not wise.'

Parnell looked at me, coldly.

'I have made my decision, Harrison,' he said. 'Please take it to O'Brien.'

I remonstrated further, but Parnell was adamant. I returned to London immediately and travelled to Ireland the next day, to make my way to the newspaper offices in Sackville Street. O'Brien read the note with mounting fury.

'How could Parnell leave himself so open to this?' said O'Brien. 'He's had five years to persuade Mrs O'Shea to get her divorce. Now he runs the risk of exposure or blackmail every day.'

It was evident O'Brien also knew about Parnell's relationship with Katharine O'Shea.

'Will you print the letter?' I asked anxiously.

'Of course I will,' said O'Brien. 'I was for Lynch and I can't stand O'Shea, but we cannot afford to lose Parnell.'

꙳

Days later, I went directly to Galway to canvass for O'Shea, a sour assignment. I arranged to meet Biggar and Healy on the train down. It was a difficult journey. Their anger against Parnell was palpable and it was clear that Parnell had a major mutiny on his hands. Biggar and Healy were going to Galway to canvass for the other Home Rule candidate. Parnell's threat to resign had just been published in that morning's newspapers and I found it difficult to believe that Biggar, of all people, was turning against Parnell.

'I have followed Parnell every step of the way, Harrison,' said Biggar, 'but I will not support this, this outrage.' He was twitching with anger.

I muttered something about O'Shea's importance because of his friendship with Chamberlain.

'That's poppycock and you know it,' said Biggar fiercely. 'The candidate's wife is Parnell's mistress. There is nothing more to be said. It's all about hushing up O'Shea.'

Healy flung down the morning paper on the table between us, in disgust.

'O'Shea's election address is in there already,' he said.

Biggar snatched it up and read it through quickly.

'He's going ahead with it,' he said. 'O'Shea has absolutely no scruples.'

'Nor has Parnell, evidently,' said Healy.

It was difficult to hear Parnell's name now being traduced by both of them. We talked of nothing else all the way to Galway and I tried to persuade them, but by the end of the journey they were still unmoved. We parted at the station but agreed to meet later in the day.

I sent a telegram to Parnell immediately to warn him of what had happened, and the following day Parnell himself arrived in Galway with James O'Kelly and Thomas Sexton, T.P. O'Connor and William O'Brien. He had come to crush the mutiny.

It was now a question of Parnell – not O'Shea – and, faced with the new reality, Healy withdrew his opposition. Biggar, however, would not, but he was outvoted and Lynch's name was withdrawn as the Home Rule candidate for Galway.

Days later O'Shea was elected a Member of Parliament for Galway.

Throughout the following months, further intrigues continued. Chamberlain corresponded with Parnell through O'Shea and Parnell responded through O'Shea, but this was really an elaborate feint. The real correspondence continued between Parnell and Gladstone through Katharine. It was a bizarre and complex situation and required the skill and self-assurance of a confident ringmaster. But eventually, through these secret channels of correspondence, Parnell was assured that Gladstone, if restored to office, would introduce a Home Rule bill.

The die was cast and, in a concerted and prearranged vote, we sided with the Liberals to vote the Tories out of office. Gladstone became Prime Minister again at the age of seventy-six.

But over the next few months, small difficulties between Parnell and Chamberlain – of themselves insignificant – assumed a later devastating importance. Parnell thought Chamberlain a parvenu who was not to be trusted and who, like all English Members of Parliament, was best kept at a distance. After Kilmainham, Chamberlain – now aware of Parnell's involvement with Katharine – expected a more compliant and ingratiating Parnell but, again, misjudged him completely. Chamberlain sought to construct a compromise between our demands for Home Rule and the refusal of the English to grant us Home Rule, but Parnell rejected his scheme outright, as a glorified system of county councils. When Chamberlain sought to undertake a tour of Ireland to drum up support for his scheme, Parnell instructed William O'Brien to make it so hot for him that Chamberlain had to abandon his trip entirely.

But the true extent of Chamberlain's resentment of his treatment at Parnell's hands soon became apparent to us all.

Forty-Two

The Home Rule Bill

WE HAD HEARD that Gladstone would bring in a Home Rule bill shortly and we were on tenterhooks for weeks.

Eventually, on the appointed day in early April, I went to the House of Commons and sat with Parnell, Biggar, Healy, Dillon and all the other Irish Members of Parliament on the opposition benches. I had never seen the House so crowded. Every member wanted to take his seat that afternoon. The Sergeants-at-Arms had even placed chairs on the central floor separating the benches and the public galleries were crowded even before lunch. I looked up to the gallery and thought, with sadness, how Fanny should have been there to witness her brother's great triumph.

At about six o'clock in the evening, Gladstone entered the House from behind the Speaker's chair, carrying a sheaf of papers and, eventually, when he was ready, the Speaker called on him.

Gladstone put his papers on the despatch box and took a moment to look around the House, at the Liberal benches, the Tories, the Irish, the Visitors' Gallery.

'Mr Speaker.' His voice rang out around the House, clear and strong. 'I wish to introduce to this House a bill for the establishment of an Irish parliament ...'

I could feel the hair rise on the back of my neck. This was it. This was the moment of our independence. This was the time when the English would at last grant Ireland her freedom, after 700 years. The House hushed as we listened to the details. It appeared that Gladstone was truly determined to solve the Irish question once and for all, before he left Parliament.

When Gladstone had finished, Parnell rose in the Chamber, to our great cheers, to say that he believed the bill would provide for the final settlement of the Irish question and he believed that the Irish people would accept it as such.

Over the following days, scores of members debated the bill back and forth. Each speech on each side seemed to be effective in persuading some member one way or the other. The Tories were clearly against it to a man. But the Liberals had a majority when we voted with them, so it was now a question of how many Liberals would vote against Gladstone.

Just like the Members of Parliament, the newspapers of the day were divided, as was much of London society. It soon became known that the Queen was resolutely opposed to Home Rule, but the Prince of Wales was in favour. The issue of Home Rule was now undoubtedly the central political question of the day.

But the debate in the Commons was not all Parnell had to be concerned about. Days before the final vote on the Home Rule bill, Biggar slapped a copy of the *Pall Mall Gazette* into my hand.

'Read that,' he said gruffly, pointing to a small, insignificant article with the headline 'Parnell's Suburban Retreat'. It described a small accident Parnell had had at the weekend when his brougham had knocked into a florist's cart. In itself this was hardly newsworthy, as no one had been injured, but it was a curiously worded piece, saying that whilst Parliament was in session Mr Parnell usually took up residence at Eltham. In itself it was nothing; it made no reference to Willie O'Shea or to Katharine. But to those who knew the secret, it was clear the paper knew of the liaison. How else could one explain the story, or the wording, or the timing? And if that paper knew, how many others knew?

'I think we can safely say the *Gazette* is on to it,' said Biggar.

As we talked, Healy joined us, and peered over my shoulder at the article.

'They're on to him at last,' he said. Almost with satisfaction, I thought.

Just then Healy spotted O'Shea walking through the lobby.

'O'Shea,' he called out to him loudly and beckoned to him to come over.

O'Shea walked over to us briskly, unaware of the article until that moment.

'Healy,' he said. 'What's the matter?'

'I was hoping you could tell me,' Healy replied and, snatching the newspaper out of my hand, he thrust it at O'Shea. 'Read that and tell me what's the matter.'

O'Shea, puzzled, took the paper and read the article quickly.

'Your grubby little secret is out now,' Healy said, with a malicious sneer.

'What are you talking about, Healy?' O'Shea said, his face reddening.

'Leave it alone, Healy,' warned Biggar.

But Healy would not be restrained.

'You sold your wife to Parnell for a seat in Galway,' said Healy, with biting viciousness. 'I hope you got full value.'

O'Shea looked as if he had been struck in the face. He paled. But before he could reply, Healy continued.

'You thought no one knew. You thought we didn't know. But we've known for years. You're a cuckold, O'Shea, and Parnell has played you for the fool you are, for years.'

'That's enough, Healy,' said Biggar and I simultaneously.

O'Shea put his hand to his face and rubbed it nervously for a few moments.

'Known what?' he said, trying for another moment to hide his embarrassment. 'There is nothing going on between Parnell and my wife.'

Healy laughed derisively.

'Nothing going on! You're a bigger fool than I thought, O'Shea. We know damned well there is, and so do you. You thought you'd trade your wife for political favours with Parnell and that we wouldn't know about it. What did you think, O'Shea, when Parnell imposed you on Galway? Did you think we didn't know your wife was Parnell's mistress? Did you think we didn't know you were a cuckold? The whole Party knew. The whole county knew. Did you really think we were so stupid as to believe that claptrap of Parnell's – that he actually needed you? Don't make the mistake of thinking we are as stupid as you are.'

O'Shea went purple with rage and looked as if he might hit Healy, but instead he glared at him and, without another word, turned away and walked out of the Commons.

Parnell spoke on the Home Rule bill on the day of the final vote. It was a moderate speech and he appealed to the House to pass the bill. But his previous firebrand speeches, his obstructionism and his revolutionary conduct made many Members of Parliament unsure of his true intentions. I became aware from furtive whispers in the lobby that many MPs did not believe he would accept this bill as the final settlement of the Irish question, but only as a point of departure for further agitation.

Gladstone's final speech was an extraordinary, eloquent and impassioned plea for justice for Ireland. It was the finest oration I ever heard in the House. As he stood at the despatch box, with his back almost to the Speaker, he spoke to the dissenters on his own back benches.

'Go into the length and breadth of the world,' he said. 'Ransack the literature of all the countries. Find, if you can, a single voice, a single book, a single newspaper article … in which the conduct of England towards Ireland is anywhere treated except with profound and bitter condemnation. Are these the traditions by which we are exhorted to stand? No. They are a sad exception to the glory of our country. They are a broad blot upon the pages of its history.'

Never, I thought, had an English Member of Parliament – let alone an English Prime Minister – spoken with so much passion about the Irish cause. As I watched him make his final speech, it was hard not to admire his integrity, his generosity and his courage. He truly was the Grand Old Man of the House of Commons and this was the issue on which he had staked his entire reputation and that of his Government.

For days, we worried frenetically about whether we had the votes. The lobbies and the tea-rooms, the smoking-rooms and the bars were inundated with rumour and counter-rumour. We tried to keep a tally but the names and numbers changed by the day, and – as the vote came closer – by the hour.

When the debate was over and it was time to vote, I saw O'Shea rise with great deliberation and, leaving his seat, he walked out of the Chamber and out of the Party. He was not going to vote in favour of Home Rule, lest it grant Parnell a victory.

As we watched him go, Biggar leaned over to me. 'If O'Shea costs us the vote,' he said, 'I'll kill him myself, with my bare hands.'

'He sold his wife,' said Healy, with asperity. 'Why should we be surprised that he has sold his country?'

As we went into the division lobbies for the final vote, we were all tense with anxiety. We knew the numbers were close. Every Liberal lost to us was a matter of great concern, but we still did not know, as we trooped through, how many we would lose. The tellers counted and recounted, and counted again. They conferred and eventually agreed. They approached the despatch box and announced the results. Everyone in the House and in the galleries held their breaths. I could not remember a vote as tense as this, ever before.

'Those in favour, 311.'

'Those against, 341.'

We had lost. By thirty votes. Fifteen Members of Parliament. If only fifteen Members of Parliament had changed their minds, Ireland would have obtained Home Rule. It was agonisingly close, but it had been lost.

The result was greeted with total silence. All the members knew we were not going away. We would haunt them as long as was necessary.

I put my head in my hands in disbelief. Parnell and Biggar also looked stunned. Parnell sat quite still, staring ahead at the Liberal benches.

Fifteen Members of Parliament. If O'Shea had voted, then only fourteen. Chamberlain and his coterie had all voted against. We had marked them carefully in the division lobbies. It was Chamberlain all along. He was in high dudgeon because his own lesser scheme had been rejected by Parnell and by Gladstone; he was offended that Parnell had set the Irish newspapers on him, when he had sought to go to Ireland to drum up support for his scheme; his vanity was ruffled because Parnell did not extend to him the same attention as he did to Gladstone.

As we stood around, disconsolately, in the lobbies, we saw Chamberlain passing out of the Chamber. Parnell stood, with his arms folded and as Chamberlain walked past, said in a voice loud enough for all around to hear, 'There goes the man who killed Home Rule.'

Chamberlain looked at him sourly and passed on by.

As the evenings shortened and the summer light disappeared, Parnell seemed to fall into a melancholic torpor. I continued to visit him at Eltham every week, but a series of undiagnosed maladies affected him – colds and chills, loss of appetite, loss of weight, loss of energy. It was terrible to watch. Katharine nursed him carefully day and night. She ensured he saw the best doctors in London, but his illness remained undiagnosed. Severe strain and nervous exhaustion were the closest opinions any doctor was prepared to consider.

What he needed, after the terrible strain of the intrigues with O'Shea and the battle for Home Rule, was a protracted period of peace and rest to recover his health. But that he was not allowed; instead, his enemies moved to destroy him before he could regain the initiative.

Part Four

Forty-Three

The Times Intervenes

IN THE EARLY months of the following year, a series of events began which, even now, I scarcely believe could have happened. *The Times* began a series of articles, trumpeted as an exposé of Parnell's links to crimes committed by the Land League. Parnell and the Home Rule Party, it wrote, were the visible head of an invisible serpentine body that was, beneath the surface, secretly engaged in assassinations and assaults, outrages and intimidation throughout Ireland. It alleged that all these secret criminal acts were, if not directed by Parnell, then connived at by him.

It demanded a robust response but, instead, Parnell ignored it completely.

Emboldened, *The Times* ran a second article a week later, adding, for good measure, that if anything it said was untrue, then Mr Parnell could of course sue the newspaper for libel and it would defend itself fully. The self-satisfied grin of the editor was practically visible through the newsprint.

It demanded a full response and, again, Parnell did nothing.

In the third week, *The Times* ran another article, as biting and as savage as the previous two. These articles now began to work their poison in the House of Commons, as Balfour introduced yet another Tory coercion bill and carried all before him. The cup of Home Rule which had been raised to our lips had now been dashed to the ground. We were going backwards.

Still Parnell did nothing.

Tempers were running high in the House. For many Tories, these articles confirmed what they had always suspected. One of their number, Colonel Saunderson, spoke out against us with great anger, shaking his fist across the floor of the House and calling us all criminal conspirators and murderers.

Healy was beside himself with rage.

'You're a liar, Saunderson, a damnable liar,' he shouted angrily across the floor.

Sexton shouted out that Saunderson was not only a liar but a coward, and that if he repeated those charges outside the House, he would thrash him to within an inch of his life. This brought another violent response from the Tories, and the session was adjourned in uproar.

'Where is Parnell?' fumed Healy. 'Where the hell is he?'

Parnell had been absent from the House almost continuously since the previous June, when the Home Rule bill was lost.

'He should be here,' said Biggar, grabbing my sleeve and pulling me out of Healy's earshot. 'Harrison, you must urge him to come. He can't stay away from the House forever.'

I promised I would urge him to come.

But before I could meet him, *The Times* published a further article, which caused consternation among Members of Parliament of every party.

It was a letter, supposedly written and signed by Parnell only days after the Phoenix Park murders, which read:

15th May 1882

Dear Sir,

I am not surprised at your friend's anger but he and you should know that to denounce the murders was the only course open to us. To do that promptly was plainly our best policy.

But you can tell him and all others concerned that though I regret the accident of Lord F. Cavendish's death I cannot refuse to admit that Burke got no more than his deserts.

You are at liberty to show him this and others whom you can trust also, but let not my address be known. He can write to the House of Commons.

Yours very truly.
Chas. S Parnell.

A chill ran through me as I read the letter. It looked convincing. To see Parnell's signature on such a letter was particularly damning. It was as if the letter revealed the truth of Parnell's innermost thoughts, and the phrase 'that Burke got no more than his deserts' could only mean that Parnell approved of the murders. The sentence 'let not my address be known' begged a series of other questions. Was knowledge of Parnell's liaison with Katharine beginning to leak out?

I immediately sought out Biggar and found him with Justin McCarthy.

'It damned well isn't true,' Biggar fumed. 'He was furious about the murders. He wouldn't write a letter like that so soon afterwards.'

McCarthy was gloomy.

'You really must meet him, Harrison,' he said. 'He must reply to this.'

As we spoke, a Liberal Member of Parliament, whose name I did not know, came up to us.

'Where did they get that letter?' he said. 'I took up *The Times* this morning. It quite spoiled my breakfast.'

'It's a forgery,' said Biggar emphatically.

The member grimaced. 'I doubt that,' he said. '*The Times*! The best newspaper in the world! Taken in! I don't think there's an Englishman in the world who would believe that.' He shook his head. 'I am staggered by it. It's done for Parnell. And Home Rule.'

Later that afternoon, I took a cab to Eltham to meet Parnell. I was shown in to see Katharine.

'I've seen it,' she said quickly. 'I read it to him at breakfast.'

'And what did he say?' I asked, wondering about his reaction.

'And ... he said nothing. Not a word.' She shrugged her shoulders. 'He read it himself and then continued buttering his toast and read the rest of the paper – as if it didn't concern him in the slightest.'

I went into the study, where Parnell was weighing some pieces of rock on a scales.

'Harrison. Welcome. Come over and look at this.' He waved me over to inspect his work. 'I have just purchased a new scales. It's much more sensitive. It can weigh even miniscule amounts of gold.'

He continued to talk in some detail about his new scales and his constant experiments in extracting gold from rock in Avondale and the Wicklow Mountains. After a moment, sensing perhaps that I didn't quite share his enthusiasm, he said, 'But you didn't come to find out how my experiments are progressing.'

'They must have forged your signature,' I blurted out.

'Well, I wouldn't have thought you had much doubt about that,' he said calmly, 'but I would have thought *The Times* would have checked their facts before printing a story like that.'

'What about all the other articles?' I asked.

Parnell shrugged his shoulders.

'What can I do? They've been taunting me for weeks to sue them for libel. But I've spoken with Russell and he has advised against it.'

'As would I,' I said. 'There is no jury in England which would give you a verdict.'

'His sentiments precisely.' Parnell smiled. 'Just as there is no jury in Ireland which would convict me.'

He paused for a moment.

'O'Shea is behind this,' he said.

'O'Shea?' I was startled by the suggestion.

'Of course. If it's not my signature, then who forged it? It's O'Shea,' said Parnell. 'It must be. And he threatened me with letters, remember.'

I had forgotten O'Shea's threat in the Shelbourne Hotel until then.

'Ask Biggar and O'Kelly to find out who is the forger,' said Parnell. 'They have the contacts.'

I told him that I had met Biggar and McCarthy earlier that day.

'They believe you must come to the House of Commons at once and explain your position,' I said. 'And I agree with them.'

Parnell thought about it for a moment and then, with that alacrity so characteristic of him when action was required, he changed and put on his overcoat, and within the hour we were on our way back to Westminster.

Parnell had now become such a famous figure in the House that all eyes turned towards him as he entered and took his seat. He didn't even appear to notice.

It was much later in the evening before Parnell had a chance to speak, but the House was still full, as many members awaited his explanation.

When he got to his feet, there was a murmur of voices, all commenting on how wretched he looked. Indeed, it was hard to ignore. He had lost a considerable amount of weight. His frame, once slim and vigorous, now appeared attenuated and weary; his sallow skin was now spectrally pale; his eyes seemed glassy, without the shine they once had; and the slightest exertion – even standing in the House – seemed to bring him out in a clammy sweat.

McCarthy leaned over to me, in some shock.

'My God, Harrison,' he said. 'I had no idea Parnell was so ill. He looks wretched.'

'Mr Speaker, sir.' Parnell's voice was weak and thin, but he had the rapt attention of the whole House. 'When I first heard of this villainous forgery – I heard of it before I read it – because I do not take *The Times* …'

Biggar snorted with laughter at Parnell's offhand, casual contempt for the newspaper of the English establishment.

'When I heard that a letter of this description, bearing my signature, had been published in *The Times*, I supposed that some autograph of mine had fallen into the hands of some person for whom it had not been intended and that it had been made use of in this way. But when I saw what purported to be my signature, I saw plainly that it was an audacious and unblushing fabrication … There are only two letters in my whole name which bear any resemblance to letters as I write them. I cannot understand how the managers of a responsible journal could have been so hoodwinked, so hoaxed, so bamboozled – and that is the most charitable interpretation I can place on it – as to publish such a production as that, as my signature … This is not the time to enter into full details as to comparisons of handwriting but if the House could see my signature and the forged fabricated signature, they would see it bears no resemblance to mine.'

As so often with Parnell, his performance had a leaden quality to it. Perhaps he believed that all he had to do was to deny that the signature was his and that would be the end of the matter; that, in an assembly of gentleman, his word would be believed. But the House had longed ceased to be an assembly of gentlemen – if it ever was – and he was not convincing. I looked over at Salisbury, and I could see he was not convinced. If Salisbury believed *The*

Times, then there were no circumstances under which he would do business with Parnell.

Later that evening, Tim Harrington, another Home Rule Member of Parliament, joined us for a brandy in the members' library. He put down his copy of *The Times*, opened on the page of the facsimile letter, in front of us.

'How are you going to answer that, Parnell?' he asked, tapping the article with his forefinger.

Parnell smoothed the paper on the table and leaned over it closely.

'I haven't made an "S" like that since 1878,' he said calmly.

Harrington looked at Biggar and me, as if he hadn't quite heard correctly.

'I hope that's not how you intend to respond,' he said. 'Because if it is, I'm telling you, there is not an Englishman who will believe you.'

Forty-Four

Fuel to the Fire

DESPITE PARNELL'S INEFFECTUAL response, matters might have been allowed to rest, if it were not for Frank Hugh O'Donnell, who sought me out in the Commons one afternoon, several weeks later. I hadn't seen much of O'Donnell over the previous few years. After his rebuff by the Party he had left London, years earlier, to work in the capitals of Europe as a 'gentleman of letters', as he put it himself. He had not achieved the fame which he had sought, and he had watched with envy as lesser men – particularly Parnell, in his view – had grown in fame and stature over the years. He had grown tired of Parnell's star eclipsing his own.

'Tell me, Harrison,' he said, 'is Parnell going to sue *The Times* over these articles?'

'No,' I said. 'Russell advised him against it, and if anyone should know, it's Russell.'

'Well, I intend to sue,' said O'Donnell severely. '*The Times* has named me also in those wretched articles. It was scurrilous. I won't stand for it. I intend to protect my reputation, even if he doesn't.'

He still had his monocle, I noticed, and took it out to glare at me fiercely.

'I can't tell you how many letters I have received from ambassadors and envoys from numerous embassies, enquiring if I had been previously involved in such matters. Everyone reads *The Times*, you know, all over Europe. My reputation has been destroyed. *The Times* has said I was a Land Leaguer! Me! Who opposed the Land League from the start. It's insupportable. After all I've done for them. Written for them. They now lump me in with Parnell, the crookback, Healy and all the others.'

O'Donnell's distaste for his former colleagues was evident.

'I wouldn't advise it, O'Donnell,' I said. 'It could ruin you if you lose.'

'I have already consulted with a leading barrister,' he replied huffily, 'and he has advised me that I have a strong case.'

'Perhaps you do,' I said, 'but it may not be enough to convince an English jury.'

'And how many English jury trials have you done, Harrison?' he asked contemptuously.

'None, I accept, but ...' I started to respond.

'Perhaps when you have, I will seek your advice.' O'Donnell was as haughtily rude as ever.

I shrugged my shoulders. I had tried to warn him.

'And I will not let this stain on my reputation go unpunished,' said O'Donnell. 'It has not only soiled my reputation with all the embassies of Europe, it has also soiled the reputation of the Home Rule Party. And if I do not take this action, the stain will remain. What I do, I do not only on my own behalf but on behalf of the entire nation.'

O'Donnell was as much in love with himself as ever.

'And the libel damages if you win?' I asked. 'Will you donate those to the nation?'

He was an irresistible target.

O'Donnell coughed.

'Well, Harrison,' he said. 'I will consider the disbursement of funds at a later time. But you can rest assured that I will make a substantial contribution to the Irish nation.'

Over the following months, events followed a predictable course. O'Donnell took his libel action against *The Times*, and the matter came up for hearing the following July, in the High Court in London. I slipped into court to watch. O'Donnell had retained a Mr Ruegg – a worthy but junior member of the Bar. *The Times*, by contrast, had retained Sir Richard Webster QC, the Attorney General and a leading silk, an inequality of arms which was bound to make its presence felt over the course of a long trial.

But it wasn't a long trial.

To my surprise, Ruegg decided not to call O'Donnell as a witness. O'Donnell would have been a poor witness: conceited, arrogant and lofty – I doubt any English jury would have had any sympathy for him. But in a libel action, particularly one such as this, the plaintiff had to be called to give evidence of how the articles had damaged him.

When Ruegg indicated he had no further witnesses, Lord Chief Justice Coleridge intervened.

'Are you not putting the plaintiff in the box?' he asked Ruegg. 'You had given me to understand you would do so.'

'So I shall, My Lord,' replied Ruegg, 'in reply to the defendants, when they answer my client's complaints.'

'But *The Times* may elect not to call any witnesses,' said Coleridge, 'and you will be incapable of putting Mr O'Donnell in the box if that is so.'

O'Donnell leaned over to remonstrate with his counsel. He seemed to be asking if this was possible, but his counsel waved him away.

'That is our evidence, My Lord,' said Ruegg.

'Don't say you weren't warned,' said Coleridge.

Webster's case was simple: *The Times* stood over every word it had written; all the articles referred to Parnell and the Parnellites; there was no reference to O'Donnell in any of the articles, and therefore he could not have been identified and defamed; insofar as O'Donnell had ever been mentioned, it was only in the most tangential and innocuous asides. Moreover, the worthlessness of his case was proven by the fact that he had refused even to give evidence and, as the plaintiff's case was non-existent, *The Times* would not call any evidence to answer it.

The judge turned to O'Donnell's counsel.

'Have you anything to say, Mr Ruegg?'

Ruegg protested that Webster had not gone into evidence, but Coleridge silenced him immediately.

'I warned you this might happen,' he said, 'but you insisted, nevertheless. It is not for me to advise counsel on their proofs. I have heard enough.'

O'Donnell's counsel resumed his seat and the judge gave his direction to the jury. They retired to consider their verdict, and returned within five minutes with a verdict for *The Times*.

But the real problem in the case was not that O'Donnell had lost; that had been a certainty from the start. It was that Webster and *The Times* had unearthed an entirely new batch of letters, which Webster read out in open court. Many seemed innocuous, but several were incendiary. The most damning was a letter dated 9th January 1882 – several months after Parnell had been imprisoned – which read:

9th January 1882

Dear E,
What are these people waiting for? This inaction is inexcuseable. Our best men are in prison and nothing is being done.

Let there be an end to this hesitency. Prompt action is called for. You undertook to make it hot for old Forster and Co. Let us have some evidence of your power to do so.

My health is good, thanks.

Yours very truly.
Chas S. Parnell.

This letter was, as Webster characterised it, an incitement to murder by Parnell. What else could it be?

Webster told the court, in ringing tones, that *The Times* would never disclose its source for these letters – 'Nay, not even if it lost us the verdict in this trial,' he said – because the person who obtained the letters would undoubtedly be murdered. Webster was so persuasive that even I began to wonder whether Parnell had engaged in secret correspondence, without my knowledge.

The letters which had been read out in court were published in *The Times*, the day after the verdict, and when I read them any doubts which I might have entertained evaporated. The fact that two of the words – 'hesitancy' and 'inexcusable' – were spelled incorrectly leaped off the page. Parnell was punctilious about his spelling and it proved – if proof were needed – that the letter was not his.

But the publication of these further letters did enormous damage to Parnell. They seeped into the consciousness of the House of Commons and middle England, and made many people wonder whether Parnell really was complicit in the terrible assassinations of Cavendish and Burke in the Phoenix Park, all those years ago. The fact that he had not taken a libel action convinced many people that the articles were indeed true.

Forty-Five

Chamberlain Unmasked

THE ARTICLES CAUSED such a furore in the House that various Members of Parliament were determined to set up an investigation – but for entirely conflicting reasons. Gladstone demanded one, because he did not wish to be associated with Parnell anymore if the allegations were true; Parnell wanted one, to clear his name; Salisbury wanted one, because he was convinced the allegations were true and he intended to put not only Parnell but also the Home Rule Party – and, indeed, the entire Irish nation – on trial.

It was during this debate that the long-gathering animosity between Chamberlain and Parnell now erupted into open view.

'Mr Speaker, sir,' Chamberlain said. 'I have formed a judgment on the Honourable Member for Cork, of his character, his honesty, his sincerity and his patriotism, that will not allow me easily to accept the charges that have been made against him … I took an active part, as I am not at all ashamed to confess, in securing the release of the Honourable Member from Kilmainham Gaol. But the thing which has shaken my confidence in the Honourable Member's ability to disprove these charges, which are now made against him … is his apparent reluctance to face a full enquiry.'

I was astonished at the insolence of this attack on Parnell's character. Chamberlain had actually waited until Parnell was in the Chamber to charge him, to his very face, with complicity and cowardice. Perhaps, in the wave of assaults on Parnell by *The Times*, Parnell's enemies had become inured to his failure to respond. But an attack on Parnell in the newspapers by an unknown opponent was one matter; an attack on his personal honour to his face, in the House of Commons, was quite another.

Parnell stood to reply, his face pale with fury, his tone sulphurous.

'Mr Speaker, sir,' he said. 'I would like to take this opportunity of thanking the Right Honourable Gentleman, the member for West Birmingham, for his kind reference to me and for the unsolicited character which he was kind enough to give me when he addressed the House. He spoke of a time not long ago when, he said, he entertained a better opinion of me than he does today.'

Parnell paused for a moment.

'However, I care very little for the opinion of the Right Honourable Gentleman.'

There were cries of 'ooh, ooh'.

'*I* have never put men forward,' continued Parnell, 'to do dangerous things which I shrank from doing myself. Nor have I betrayed the secrets of my colleagues in Council. My principal recollection of the member for West Birmingham, before he became a Minister, is that he was always most anxious to put men forward to do work which he was afraid to do himself.'

The House fell silent.

'And *after* he became a Minister,' continued Parnell, 'my principal recollection of him is that he was always most anxious to betray to us the secrets and counsels of his colleagues in the cabinet and, while in consultation with them, to undermine their counsels and plans in our favour.'

The House erupted – not against Parnell, but against Chamberlain.

'Judas!' and 'Judas Chamberlain!' – the shouts echoed and re-echoed across the Chamber, from Liberals and Home Rule members alike. Parnell's arrow had hit its mark. Chamberlain's colleagues had long suspected him of being a dishonourable opportunist, in league with the Irish party, scheming against Gladstone and then scheming against the Irish party. As I looked over at Gladstone, I could see him nodding his head in agreement at Parnell's words.

Chamberlain went pale.

But Parnell had not finished.

'If this Special Commission is extended into these matters – and I see no reason why it should not be – I shall be able to make good my words by documentary evidence – which is not forged. It is not the first time that fair play has been denied to Irishmen and I do not suppose it will be the last. It is not the first time that you have poisoned the bowl and used the dagger against your political opponents in that country where you could not overcome them in a fair fight.'

Chamberlain rose to reply.

'Whenever I communicated to you, Mr Parnell,' he said, 'whether about Kilmainham or about the Central Board, I did so with the full knowledge of Mr Gladstone.'

The House, however, was not with him.

'Moreover, I have a document in your handwriting, Mr Parnell,' said Chamberlain angrily, 'which said that you would accept my scheme for local government.'

'I did write such a document,' said Parnell, 'but it was with an express stipulation that it would not satisfy our demand for Home Rule.'

'That is untrue,' said Chamberlain, 'and I have proof.'

'Then produce it,' said Parnell angrily. 'It is another lie.'

'I shall, sir,' said Chamberlain, 'within days.'

But some days later, Dilke approached me in the House. He came as an emissary from Chamberlain.

'Harrison, about those letters,' he said. 'I have just met with Chamberlain and O'Shea.' He spoke quietly – ruefully, almost. 'I think there has been a misunderstanding.'

'You mean, Chamberlain realises he's in the wrong,' I said, smiling at him.

'Well, it's O'Shea – again – who has caused the problem,' said Dilke.

'That should hardly surprise you,' I said.

'No, not now,' said Dilke, 'but this was a few years ago.'

'Is Chamberlain going to publish the letters or not?' I asked.

'No, he's not,' said Dilke. 'O'Shea duped Chamberlain as much as he duped Parnell. Parnell *had* written that he would not accept the local government scheme.'

'Twice,' I said. I had re-read the correspondence also.

'Quite,' said Dilke. 'But these two letters were written to O'Shea.'

'To be passed to Chamberlain,' I said.

'Indeed,' said Dilke, 'but O'Shea didn't pass them on. He suppressed them.'

I was astonished at O'Shea's duplicity.

'And,' continued Dilke, 'at the time O'Shea believed – apparently – that he could negotiate a local government scheme with Chamberlain that would solve the Home Rule problem.'

'For which he would be well rewarded,' I finished.

Dilke nodded.

'So, now Chamberlain has realised the full extent of O'Shea's double-dealing, he can apologise to Parnell,' I said.

'He can't bring himself to do that,' Dilke responded, 'but he will write a letter to *The Times*.'

'Why didn't he just deal with Parnell directly?' I asked, shaking my head in disbelief.

'You know perfectly well why, Harrison. He will have nothing to do with Chamberlain. Or with me. He will have nothing to do with the English. He hates us all,' said Dilke emphatically. 'And we can't get at him as we can with any other man in English public life. He is a foreigner, and dealing with him is like dealing with a foreign power.'

Several days later, Chamberlain wrote his letter to *The Times*. It was full of irrelevant detail and obfuscation, but to everyone who had followed the controversy it was a humiliating retreat. He had accused Parnell of double-dealing and claimed he had documentary evidence. Now, he accepted that that was not the case. Instead, Parnell had exposed Chamberlain as a dishonourable double-dealer and in the very theatre in which Chamberlain sought to build his career. It was an attack from which Chamberlain's career never recovered.

Parnell, at last, was beginning to turn on his enemies.

∽◦⊝◦∾

Days later, Salisbury set up the Special Commission to put Parnell and the Home Rule Party on trial. Every single outrage over the last decade was to be investigated. Over sixty Irish Members of Parliament were charged with Land League crimes, including Biggar, Sexton, William O'Brien, Sullivan, Harrington, Justin McCarthy,

J.J. O'Kelly, John Redmond, T.P. O'Connor and many others. The Home Rule Party chose to brief Sir Charles Russell QC to lead the defence and initially the Party intended that the junior brief should be given to Healy.

Parnell, however, intervened.

'I will not have Healy representing me in this matter,' he said to me. 'I need someone I can trust, not someone who is waiting for the right moment to stab me in the back.' He did not refer to the incident in Paris. 'I want you to take the junior brief.'

I pointed out that my experience was limited to the State trials and Biggar's breach of promise suit and a few other minor cases.

'A case like this will make your reputation,' Parnell said, waving away my objections. 'Make sure it doesn't destroy mine.'

Healy beckoned to me in the lobby one evening.

'I hear Parnell has spiked me getting the Commission brief,' he said, subdued and crestfallen.

I nodded.

'Why did he do that?' he asked.

I shrugged my shoulders. I had no intention of divulging Parnell's confidences to Healy.

'I was told I was going to get that brief,' Healy continued. 'Don't I know everything about those meetings? Didn't I organise most of them?'

His singsong accent seemed accentuated by his rising anger.

'I suppose those blasted Paris letters did it for me.'

I would have thought that much was obvious, but I held my peace.

'There will always be another brief, Healy,' I said, trying to reassure him.

'Not like this one,' said Healy, shaking his head. 'This is a once-in-a-lifetime case. The entire Irish nation on trial! The fate of the Party resting on the outcome. You know, if Salisbury wins he will press criminal charges against us all. He intends to turn us all into common criminals.'

'We had better win, then,' I said.

'I heard you got my brief,' said Healy. 'Well, good luck to you, Harrison.' It was said with evident bad grace, but I understood his disappointment.

I spent many, many weeks that year reading the brief and the more I read, the more dismayed I became. Until then, I had not realised the extent of the enormous network of spies, secret agents and paid informers used by the English throughout Ireland during that time. Detailed notes had obviously been taken at every Land League meeting, throughout all those years. The English had used the weakness of the vulnerable and their crushing poverty to turn them into informers. After days reading their statements, I felt as if I were wading in a pool of stagnant, putrid water. The visible battle over land cloaked another invisible but vital battle, for the national spirit – were we a nation of rebels or informers?

Parnell, however, was utterly uninterested in all the details I sought to discuss with him.

'The letters are all,' he said. 'Concentrate on the letters. If we win on those, the rest is irrelevant.'

I had asked Biggar and Davitt, weeks earlier, to bang the drum. All their contacts in the Fenian world were touched, to ascertain who had forged the letters. Parnell was still convinced it was O'Shea, and we spent much time looking in that direction, but to little avail. The trail had gone cold.

Forty-Six

The Parnell Commission Begins

O N THE FIRST day of the Parnell Commission, in late October, I went early to the Law Courts on the Strand, but even at that hour there were hundreds of Irish men and women crowding around the entrance to the Courts, overflowing onto the street, to the curiosity of passing Londoners. For a moment, I wondered had the Land League sprung up again to organise a meeting in London.

I pressed my way through the throng and made my way to the robing-room, and then to the tea-rooms, papers in hand.

I was in that state of feverish excitement which I had experienced before when great scenes of political drama were about to commence and I had a seat to watch or a part to play. I knew it would be days before I would have to take a witness and so I could enjoy the spectacle without getting too agitated on my own account.

In the tea-rooms, I was joined by Charles Russell and the other Junior for the Party, Henry Asquith. Asquith, at the time, was a rising star at the Bar, with a great reputation and a kindly disposition. We both, however, deferred to Russell who, at the time, was one of the great leaders at the English Bar. Tall and broad, clean-shaven and clear-eyed, he was a man of formidable intelligence and courtroom presence. He had already led me in Biggar's Parisian escapade, but this was a trial of a different order.

'I have spoken to Webster,' Russell told us. 'He's going to be at least two or three days opening the case, so we will get the measure of it then.'

Just after half-past ten, we walked down to Probate Court No. 1, which was so crowded we had to push our way through into the well of the court to take our seats on the benches.

Davitt was already there, sitting on a bench at the side of the court. I nodded at him and he acknowledged me unsmilingly. As I took my seat, I saw many of my friends and colleagues, standing around, conversing. Biggar, of course; Justin McCarthy, J.J. O'Kelly, T.P. O'Connor. Even Healy had come to watch the start of the proceedings. Of Parnell, however, there was no sign.

There was a tension in the court, as counsel spread out their papers and readied themselves, pausing occasionally to share a joke among themselves, QC to QC, Junior to Junior. Sometimes, the hierarchy of the English Bar seemed as impenetrable to me as the ranks of the English aristocracy. The attorneys shuffled endlessly through mounds of papers and clerks stood by, poised to do their attorneys' bidding. Everyone gave the impression of being busy and in so doing, I thought, inadvertently gave an impression of being ill-prepared.

Russell swivelled around, to talk amiably but somewhat distractedly to us and to glance around the court.

'No sign of Prince Hamlet yet,' he said to me.

I looked around again, to see if I could see any sign of Parnell.

'He is coming, isn't he, Harrison?' said Russell.

'He assured me he would be here,' I said.

J.C. McDonald, the manager of *The Times*, came in, a broad smile on his face as he shook hands with Webster and Sir Henry James, the silks retained by the *The Times* to prosecute their case. He took his seat on the solicitors' benches, facing his counsel.

Just after eleven o'clock, I heard the crier call 'Silence in court' and everyone rose.

As we did so, I saw Parnell slip in unobtrusively, nod to Russell and seat himself on the solicitors' bench.

The tipstaffs stood behind the judges' seats, waiting expectantly for their Lordships to enter. In a moment, the three judges entered the court, bowed and took their seats.

The registrar picked up the papers to his left, removed the pink ribbons and, intoning the formal title of the proceedings, read out all the names of Members of Parliament against whom charges were to be proved. These included: 'Joseph Gillis Biggar, Thomas Sexton, William O'Brien, Charles Stewart Parnell, Timothy Sullivan, William Redmond, Justin McCarthy, John Dillon, James

J. O'Kelly, John Redmond, Thomas Patrick O'Connor, Timothy Harrington.'

It seemed to take an age and there was a silence in court when all the names had been read aloud. All Members of Parliament. All members of the Home Rule Party. It suddenly became clear, in stark and unequivocal terms, that this was now a great political trial. England intended to put Ireland on trial for daring to resist her imperial rule.

The registrar then began reading the list of 'particulars' of the offences in which the Members of Parliament had been engaged: the organisation of the Land League in Ireland and in America; seeking the independence of Ireland as a separate nation; the expulsion of English landlords; the promoting and incitement of crime; the payment of persons who assisted in and committed such crimes; holding meetings and making speeches, inciting crimes and boycotts, outrages, murder and intimidation; advocating resistance to law and impeding the detection of crime.

As the list of particulars of the alleged crimes went on and on, my attention began to wander, until I caught Biggar's mischievous eye. With every successive charge being read out, he nodded his head vigorously in agreement, as if to say 'Yes, I remember that'.

The presiding judge, Sir James Hannen, conferred with his colleagues one last time and then called on Webster, the Attorney General, to begin.

Without a note and without referring to any of the books on the table before him, Webster rose and began a four-hour oration, a diatribe against the Land League. He would show, he said, that the Land League was nothing more than a vast, nefarious Irish-American conspiracy to attain independence and to commit any crime, including murder, to achieve its object. Not for the first time, as I listened to his speech, I reflected on the great gulf of misunderstanding between the English and the Irish character: the oppressor, who believes his rule is benevolent and the Irish peasant ungrateful; and the oppressed, who reacts violently to any shackles on his freedom and who regards the oppressor as malevolent and dictatorial. Webster would show, he told us, that the chief obstacle to Irish independence was the English garrison of landlords, that the Irish intended to starve that garrison out and that the Irish peasant had an insatiable 'land hunger', which could only be assuaged by seizing land from its true owners. I wondered whether Webster had any inkling of the irony of his remark but, judging from the jut of his jaw, I doubted it.

His speech lasted all that day and all the following day, and all the day after. It was mild that October, and the crowded courtroom became stuffy and malodorous. The tedium was only broken on one occasion when, on the third day, Webster said to the court: 'Your Lordships will see in the notes of the speeches taken down by constables a recurring phrase – "*An diggin tu*" – which I understand, My Lords, is a phrase in Erse.'

'What is Erse?' asked Mr Justice Day, suddenly coming to life.

'I understand, My Lord, that it is the ancient Irish language,' replied Webster ingratiatingly, 'and the phrase means "nail his ears to the pump".'

The Irish contingent in court burst into sudden laughter. Webster looked around in confusion.

Russell rose to his feet.

'I hate to interrupt my friend in the midst of his opening speech,' he said soothingly, 'but he is quite mistaken in his translation. "*An dtuigeann tu*" is an entirely innocent phrase. It simply means "do you understand?". It doesn't mean "nail his ears to the pump" or "his hands to the cross" or any such thing – much as the Attorney General might wish it so.'

Webster muttered an apology.

'No matter, My Lords,' he said, 'it is of no significance.'

Indeed, I thought, except to show the total lack of comprehension of the Irish by the English.

Throughout the following days, Webster took us on a tour of Ireland, county by county, reciting details of speeches, outrages and crimes, all of which, he said, had been caused by the Land League. He sought to link speeches made months earlier to murders committed months later and even to link a particular speech to a particular murder. But early in the fourth day, I noticed the first yawn from Mr Justice Day and on the fourth afternoon I wondered if Mr Justice Smith had actually nodded off. People began to drift in and out of court, too uncomfortable or too bored to remain sitting throughout Webster's entire speech.

Eventually, Webster called his first witnesses – police witnesses – who gave evidence about notes they had taken at various Land League meetings during that time. Their evidence was uncontentious. We did not deny that such speeches had been made. But early on the sixth day, Webster sprang his first ambush.

'I would like to call my next witness – Mr William O'Shea,' he said.

Russell was on his feet immediately.

'I must protest, My Lords,' he said. 'We were told Mr O'Shea would not be heard for some weeks yet.'

'Yes, My Lords,' said Webster in reply, 'that was the case. But, unfortunately, Mr O'Shea has to travel to Madrid on urgent business and he may be away for some months.'

'That may be,' said Russell, 'but I have not prepared his cross-examination.'

'You have absolutely no right, Sir Charles, to object to the order of witnesses,' said Mr Justice Day, with some asperity. 'We will hear Mr O'Shea now.'

O'Shea took the stand. I glanced over at Parnell, who refused even to look at O'Shea in the witness box, but stared ahead, seemingly lost in his own thoughts.

Webster took O'Shea through his evidence: his early political career and his role in the Kilmainham treaty negotiations, many years earlier.

'Were the terms of the negotiations reduced to writing?' said Webster.

'Yes, indeed,' said O'Shea.

I could see that Parnell was startled by that disclosure.

'Do you have that document with you?' asked Webster.

'Yes, I have it here,' said O'Shea.

He reached into his jacket and pulled out a memorandum, folded in two.

Webster said: 'Did you write this document?'

'No,' said O'Shea. 'It was written by Mr Chamberlain.'

Biggar let out an involuntary snort of derision. I think it was a reflex action, whenever he heard Chamberlain's name.

Webster ignored the intervention.

'Perhaps you could read it out for the court.'

O'Shea opened the memorandum and began to read:

22nd April 1882. If the Government announce a satisfactory plan for dealing with arrears Mr Parnell will advise the tenants to pay rents and will denounce outrage and resistance to law and all processes of intimidation ...

'So,' said Webster. 'Mr Parnell believed he could control the number of outrages by denouncing them?'

'So it would appear,' said O'Shea dryly.

'Now, can I ask you to look at another letter?' Webster gestured to his attorney to hand another letter to O'Shea. 'This is the letter of 15th May 1882 which was published in *The Times*.'

O'Shea took the letter, scanned it briefly and nodded.

'You are familiar with the letter, I take it,' said Webster.

'I read it in *The Times*, like everyone else,' said O'Shea.

'And you are familiar with Mr Parnell's signature?'

'Very,' said O'Shea shortly.

'He wrote to you many times?' asked Webster.

O'Shea nodded curtly.

'Then can I ask you, Mr O'Shea, whose signature is that on the letter?' asked Webster.

'I am not an expert in handwriting, sir,' said O'Shea, with the practised hesitancy of the most accomplished liar.

'I am aware of that,' said Webster sweetly, 'but whose handwriting do you believe it to be?'

'I believe it to be that of Mr Parnell,' said O'Shea clearly.

There was a silence in court, as his evidence linked Parnell to the letters directly, for the first time. Parnell remained impassive, staring straight ahead, glassy-eyed.

'Thank you, Mr O'Shea' said Webster.

It did not matter to Russell now that he was unprepared for O'Shea. He knew that if he left O'Shea's evidence unquestioned for weeks on end, it would remain in the public mind, like an untreated, festering infection. He rose to his feet.

'You acted as an emissary of Mr Parnell's during the Kilmainham negotiations, did you not, Mr O'Shea?' he asked.

'I did,' said O'Shea.

'Did Mr Parnell ever request that his own release should be a condition of the negotiations?'

'Never,' said O'Shea, 'in fact, he forbade me ever to mention it to Chamberlain.'

'And did not Mr Parnell place particular emphasis on the arrears of rent for tenants?'

'It was his cardinal condition,' said O'Shea.

'And did he not say that if the arrears of rent could be settled by Mr Gladstone, that would be a fair settlement of the land question?'

'That is correct,' said O'Shea.

'And does it not follow,' said Russell, 'that if the land question was resolved, the level of outrages would be reduced?'

'Perhaps,' said O'Shea, shrugging his shoulders, unwilling to concede. The judges, however, all took the point.

Russell moved smoothly on to another area of questioning.

'You were with Mr Parnell immediately after the Phoenix Park murders?' asked Russell.

'I was,' said O'Shea.

'How would you describe his demeanour at that time?'

'He was very much affected by them,' said O'Shea. 'They were a cruel blow to his policy.'

'Did you undertake a most confidential commission for Mr Parnell at that time?'

It was an artful question, aimed at O'Shea's vanity.

'I did indeed, sir,' said O'Shea.

'What was that commission?' asked Russell innocently.

'Mr Parnell asked me to tell Mr Gladstone that he would resign his seat, if Mr Gladstone believed it would assist him at that time.'

There were murmurs around the court at this unexpected disclosure.

'And do you remember the Prime Minister's response to you?'

'Naturally,' said O'Shea. 'He said he was deeply sensible of Mr Parnell's honourable motives, but that it was not necessary for him to resign.'

'So, in the light of your knowledge of that matter, in which you played an important role, is it really possible that Mr Parnell could have written such a letter as has been published?'

'I was surprised when I read it, certainly,' said O'Shea, cornered by the question.

'When did you first see it?' asked Russell sharply.

'In *The Times*, like everybody else.' O'Shea's response was measured.

'And did you think it was genuine?' asked Russell.

'I did not think the sentiments were genuine,' said O'Shea uneasily, realising this could be his only answer. 'But I thought his signature was.'

'Indeed,' said Russell sarcastically, 'but his signature could have been affixed to any letter.'

O'Shea nodded – unhappily, I thought.

'I have no further questions for this witness,' said Russell and O'Shea was free to leave.

Russell turned back to Asquith and me on the junior benches.

'O'Shea is telling the truth. He never saw that letter before it was published. Someone else has forged it.'

I nodded in agreement. Parnell had been so fixated on O'Shea's involvement that we had looked hard for evidence to prove he was the forger, but, like Russell, I thought O'Shea had answered that question truthfully. Our forger lay elsewhere.

'Tell Biggar, Davitt and O'Kelly to redouble their efforts,' hissed Russell. 'We must find out who forged those letters.'

Forty-Seven

Webster *v*. Rafferty

THE PARNELL COMMISSION then settled into an endless and tedious succession of informer witnesses. The tedium was relieved, I remember, by one particular witness: an Irish peasant called Rafferty from County Mayo. Rafferty had apparently suffered a beating from Land League members, after taking a house from an evicted family. The Government had served him with a subpoena to give evidence against those members of the Land League who had assaulted him.

But that event had occurred in Mayo – where he still lived. This was the High Court in London – Rafferty's great opportunity for redemption.

Webster began with what he thought would be an uncontroversial question.

'I believe, Mr Rafferty,' he said, 'that you were at a Land League meeting at Westport, County Mayo, on Sunday, 9th September 1879.'

'Indeed an' I wasn't. I was never at a Land League meeting in my life,' said Rafferty, with a large smile on his ruddy face, 'either on a Sunday or any other day.' The word 'league' was pronounced 'layge', almost unrecognisable to an English ear. 'I don't think there were any layge meetings in Mayo, at all at all, at that time.'

Webster looked up from his notes, astonished at such a gigantic untruth.

'I am sorry, Mr Rafferty?' he said, as if he couldn't believe his ears.

Rafferty repeated his answer more loudly, in case Webster hadn't heard it.

'No, I heard you the first time,' said Webster, 'but Constable Irwin said yesterday that you were there.'

'Aye, I heard him say that,' said Rafferty cheerfully, 'but he was wrong.'

'You do know Constable Irwin?' said Webster.

'Very well,' grinned Rafferty, 'we are on speaking terms. I pass an occasional word and he passes an occasional sentence.'

There was supportive laughter from around the courtroom.

'And he says you were there,' said Webster.

'And I say he was wrong,' said Rafferty defiantly.

I sat back on the bench to enjoy his evidence. A trial of wits between an Irish peasant and an English Attorney General had to be relished. Had it been about a contract or a tort, Webster would have undoubtedly bested him, but in discussing peasant business in the West of Ireland, it was an unequal contest.

'Indeed, Mr Rafferty!' said Webster, moving on quickly. 'I believe you were accosted by members of the Land League for taking a neighbour's house after they had been evicted. You were accused of being a land-grabber.'

'Yerra no,' said Rafferty, 'that was all a big misunderstanding.'

The Irish contingent in the courtroom laughed again.

'A misunderstanding!' exclaimed Webster.

'Didn't I think the Kielys had left for Galway where her family was from?' said Rafferty, 'that's all it was.'

'So what did the Land League men say to you?'

'Sure amn't I after telling you. No Land Laygue men said anything to me,' said Rafferty.

'Well, did any men say anything to you?' said Webster.

'Well sure, didn't some good neighbours of mine come to tell me that the Kielys would be coming back in a few days,' said Rafferty, 'and that I would have to leave.'

'And what did you say in response?' asked Webster.

'Be God then, says I, we'd better be off and leave them to it,' said Rafferty.

'I believe that you told Constable Irwin that the Land League men had accosted you.'

Rafferty looked as if he were startled by that statement.

'Who said I said that?' he said, in mock amazement. 'I said nothing of the sort because they did not.'

'We have statements,' insisted Webster, 'wherein Constable Irwin said you told him that men from the Land League had thrown you out of the house – 'bag and baggage' was, I believe, the phrase you used.'

'Not at all,' said Rafferty, emphasising every syllable. 'Those men *helped* me move out of the house, with my furniture and my belongings and that's what I told the constable.'

'That's not what he said,' said Webster, bewildered.

'Yerra, the constable sometimes has difficulty understanding my accent,' said Rafferty, 'and sometimes I spake some words in Irish and the constable has no Irish.'

Webster tried one more time. 'I believe that you told the constable that the Land League men had beaten you from one end of the house to the other,' he said.

'Yerra now, the way it was, we were all in such a rush to get my things out and get the house ready for the Kielys coming back that we kept bashing into one another. That's all it was. It was a small house, like, and there was a lot of us moving around. But no harm was meant, like.'

'But the constable has stated in his notes that you had a black eye and bruises on your face.' Webster was becoming visibly agitated by his recalcitrant witness.

'Sure, in my rush to have the house ready for the Kielys and my rush to remove all my furniture, I kept banging my head into the sill of the door. Sure, wasn't it lower than my own house and I kept banging into it, and that's all that happened.'

The courtroom erupted into laughter once more and Webster cut his losses and released his witness.

Other witnesses, however, were more amenable, and we listened to story after story of intimidation, assault and even murder. Lady Mountmorres gave evidence of the murder of her husband and fainted during Russell's cross-examination; Lord Kenmare's agent gave evidence about the great serenity of tenants in Kerry before the advent of the League, and their gross rebelliousness after the League had swept through the county.

It was all lively, entertaining fare and the pace never slackened, but it never seemed to address the central issue which gave rise to the Commission – the Parnell letters.

Forty-Eight

The Witnesses for
the Prosecution

EVENTUALLY, HOWEVER, IN mid-February, on the fifti-
eth day of the hearings, we heard that *The Times* – at last
– intended to bring on their witnesses to prove the letters.
Shortly before midday, Webster stood up and, in a dramatic voice,
called out: 'Mr Joseph Soames.'

Mr Soames, the solicitor for *The Times*, walked to the witness
box and took the oath. A heavyset man, in middle age, he looked
like the solid embodiment of his profession and he answered the
questions confidently, accustomed to the courtroom.

'Can you tell us, Mr Soames,' said Webster, 'when you were first
consulted about the facsimile letters signed by Mr Parnell?'

'Certainly,' said Soames, leaning forward so that their Lordships
could hear him clearly. 'I first saw them towards the end of the year
in 1886 – some months before they were published.'

'And how did they come to your attention?' asked Webster.

'They were brought to me by Mr McDonald, the manager of *The
Times*,' said Soames.

'And you believed these to be letters written by Mr Parnell?'
asked Webster.

'Well, at first, of course, I had to make certain,' said Soames. 'I
mean, I had no way of knowing whether it was in fact Mr Parnell's
signature or not.'

'So what steps did you take to satisfy yourself that it was Mr
Parnell's signature?' asked Webster, turning sideways to his witness
so that he could address his questions clearly to their Lordships.

'I took steps to obtain copies of Mr Parnell's signature from
other sources,' said Soames. 'I travelled to Ireland to obtain copies

of official summonses which had been signed many years ago by Mr Parnell, when he had been a Justice of the Peace in County Wicklow. I also obtained copies of letters Mr Parnell had written from the House of Commons. I requested one of our journalists to write to Mr Parnell to obtain a letter of admission to the House. There was other correspondence available also, so we compared all these signatures to Mr Parnell's signature on the facsimile letter and we were satisfied it was his.'

There were murmurs of approval in the courtroom at Soames' thoroughness.

'And was that the only precaution you took to ensure the signature was that of Mr Parnell?' asked Webster.

'No, no,' said Soames quickly. 'I am not a handwriting expert. No, sir. We retained an expert – Mr Englis – who came to the offices of *The Times* and reviewed all the letters there. He compared the actual signatures of Mr Parnell which we had obtained and the signature on the facsimile letters.'

'And what was his conclusion?' asked Webster.

'His conclusion was that the signatures were all those of the same person. That they were all those of Mr Parnell.'

Once again, a buzz of voices could be heard in the courtroom.

'Did you ask Mr McDonald where he got the letters?' asked Webster.

'I gather that he got them from Mr Heuston,' said Soames matter-of-factly.

'And who is Mr Heuston?' said Webster.

'He is, I believe, the Secretary of a Unionist Association,' said Soames.

'Thank you, Mr Soames.' Webster sat down.

Russell rose to cross-examine.

'Did you also examine the Kilmainham Gaol Register?' he asked.

'I also looked at the prisoners' book in Kilmainham Gaol, yes,' said Soames. 'Every prisoner has to sign in.'

'And you have that here, I believe,' said Russell.

'I do,' said Soames, and he handed the gaol ledger to Lewis, Parnell's solicitor.

'Perhaps we might have a look at it,' suggested Russell.

The book was passed over to him and he opened it on the table. Parnell rose from his seat to peer at the old register. He ran his finger down the list of the prisoners until he came to his own name, said something about his signature to Russell and resumed his seat.

'This seems a markedly different signature to the signature on the facsimile letter,' said Russell.

'There are differences, certainly,' acknowledged Soames, 'but Mr Parnell has had diverse styles of writing his signature during his career.'

'Indeed,' said Russell and he looked down to his papers to reshuffle them and to retrieve certain notes.

'Turning to another matter,' Russell said. 'Did you enquire of Mr McDonald where Mr Heuston had obtained the letters?'

'I understand he got them from Mr Pigott,' said Soames.

Until recently, I had not seen or heard of Pigott for years. My last meeting with him, before our preparations for trial, had been when I negotiated with him, on Parnell's behalf, to purchase his newspapers for the Home Rule Party. However, I had noticed him in the courtroom during the previous few days. I looked over and, when I saw him still there, standing near the door at the back of the court, I jotted down a note and handed it to Russell.

Russell paused to read the note and nodded.

'My Lords,' he said, 'I understand from my junior that Mr Pigott is in court at the moment. I would ask that he remove himself from the court during Mr Soames' evidence.'

The judges nodded, and a clerk escorted Pigott from the court.

'Did you meet Mr Pigott?' Russell resumed.

'I did,' said Soames.

'And did he tell you where he got the letters?' asked Russell.

'He did not. And I did not ask him. And I will tell you why I did not ask him,' said Soames, anticipating the next question.

Russell nodded at him to continue.

'Because he told me, at the outset, he would never tell me where and from whom he obtained the letters.'

'So you took him at his word?' said Russell.

'Of course,' said Soames. 'Why wouldn't I?'

'Did you know that Mr Pigott had a grievance against Mr Parnell?' asked Russell suddenly.

Soames looked surprised.

'I had not heard that. No.'

'He did not mention to you that his newspaper had been bought out by Mr Parnell?' said Russell.

'No,' said Soames.

'And that he was subsequently aggrieved that Mr Parnell had not paid him what he regarded as a fair price and that he had subsequently closed down his newspaper?'

'No, he never mentioned that to me.'

'Did you offer to pay Pigott for the letters?' asked Russell sharply.

'Absolutely not,' said Soames, apparently indignant at the very suggestion. 'But he did ask for money.'

'How much money?' asked Russell.

'Five thousand pounds,' said Soames.

There was a gasp of amazement from the court at this exorbitant sum.

'But you refused to pay?'

'Absolutely.'

Russell finished his cross-examination of Soames abruptly. Despite Russell's best efforts, *The Times*' story was still intact.

⁘

The Attorney General called his next witness, Mr J.C. McDonald, the manager of *The Times*. His examination in chief by Webster was short.

'Can you tell the court how you received these letters?' Webster asked.

'Certainly,' said McDonald. 'I was contacted by a Mr Edward Houston. He told me he had letters in his possession which were deeply incriminating for Mr Parnell.'

'And did you know Mr Houston before this discussion?'

'I did.'

'How so?' asked Webster.

'He was involved in a Unionist group and he had written a pamphlet hostile to Mr Parnell.'

'Did Houston tell you where he got the letters?'

Parnell – A Novel

'Not at the time, no,' said McDonald. 'But some months later he told me he had received them from Pigott.'

Henry Asquith took the cross-examination of McDonald and I watched as he stood up beside me, his notes meticulously arranged before him.

'Mr McDonald, did you ever ask Houston where Pigott had got the letters?' asked Asquith.

'Of course,' said McDonald, 'but, as you heard from Mr Soames, Pigott said he would never divulge this source. He said his life depended on it.'

'So, what was your reaction when you examined the letters?' asked Asquith.

'Oh, I knew they were Parnell's letters, no doubt about it,' said McDonald.

'On what basis?' asked Asquith.

'I compared all the signatures on all the letters. They were all the same.'

'On all the letters Mr Pigott gave you?' said Asquith.

'Yes,' said McDonald.

'So, you were certain in your own mind that these were all letters signed by Mr Parnell?'

'I was.'

'Even before you saw the letters which Mr Soames obtained, with the real signatures of Mr Parnell on them?'

'They merely confirmed my view,' said McDonald.

'That is not the question I asked you, Mr McDonald,' said Asquith sharply. 'You had formed your view even before you saw Mr Parnell's true signature?'

'Yes,' said McDonald defiantly, 'and I was correct. Because when I saw his other signatures, they were exactly the same ...'

'The same?' said Asquith quizzically, leaning forward on his bench. 'Even an amateur can see there are differences in the signatures.'

McDonald smiled and, taking off his pince-nez, which he twirled around with his fingers, he said: 'Certainly there are differences. He tried to disguise his signature.'

'But the writing on the letters is in a different hand to the signatures on the same letters, is it not?' asked Asquith.

'Indeed it is,' agreed McDonald.

'And the writing on the envelopes is different again,' said Asquith.

'Yes,' agreed McDonald. 'But, as Mr Houston explained to me, it is quite common for Irish leaders to use different types of handwriting: one for the body of their letters, one for their signature and one for their envelopes.'

There was an outburst of laughter in the court at this ludicrous explanation.

'But,' persisted Asquith, 'why would you believe such a thing?'

McDonald looked at Asquith and paused for a moment.

'I am not bound to tell you why that was my opinion.'

'But you are,' insisted Asquith. 'You are under oath.'

'Well, let's simply say it was my opinion,' said McDonald. 'I cannot put it any further than that.'

Asquith began to get exasperated.

'Did you make any enquiries of Mr Pigott as to where he had obtained the letters?' he asked.

'Absolutely none,' said McDonald, with complete serenity.

'And yet these documents were in your hands for many months before you published them.'

'That is so.'

'And why did you choose 18th April 1887 to publish the facsimile letter with Mr Parnell's signature on it?' asked Asquith.

'Because it was the date on which the Government was to debate the coercion bill. It was a most fitting occasion,' said McDonald.

'So,' replied Asquith, 'you thought it would assist in the passing of the coercion bill.'

'Which it did!' confirmed McDonald.

I glanced over at Parnell who was, as ever, gazing absently at the crowded courtroom. Not even the calculated malice of *The Times* appeared to disturb him.

He seemed curiously detached from the drama, as if it had nothing to do with him.

꩜

As each witness took their turn, Webster seemed increasingly reluctant to linger with them. His next witness was Houston, who had obtained the letters from Pigott. His examination in chief was cursory and it seemed only moments later that Russell was beginning his cross-examination.

'Can you tell the court when you first met Mr Pigott?' Russell asked.

'Yes, it was towards the end of 1885,' Houston replied.

'How did you come to meet with him?' asked Russell.

'I had known of him, of course,' said Houston, 'as a journalist. I was writing a pamphlet at the time and I asked Mr Pigott to assist me with it.'

'What was the pamphlet on?' asked Russell.

'Mr Parnell,' said Houston briskly.

'Indeed,' said Russell, 'and is this the pamphlet?' He held up a copy of the pamphlet by a corner, between his thumb and forefinger, as if it were a noisome object.

Houston nodded.

'And this was a pamphlet which was hostile to Mr Parnell?' asked Russell.

'Indeed,' affirmed Houston.

'So, after this was published, what was your relationship with Mr Pigott?'

'I asked him to carry out further research for me,' said Houston.

'Of what nature?' asked Russell.

'I wanted him to investigate any connections Mr Parnell had with criminal activities,' said Houston expansively.

'That was your suggestion,' said Russell.

'It was.'

'And did he agree to take on this ... commission?' asked Russell.

'Enthusiastically,' said Houston.

'And did you pay him for this ... this ... this research?' Russell was becoming increasingly disdainful.

'Of course. One pound per day, plus expenses,' said Houston.

'A generous rate,' said Russell.

'A fair rate,' countered Houston, 'given what he found.'

'How much did you pay him all told?' said Russell.

'One thousand, seven hundred and eighty pounds,' said Houston.

There were loud gasps of surprise in the courtroom.

'And how did you arrange these funds?' asked Russell.

'I paid him some myself. I borrowed the rest,' said Houston.

'So it has cost you almost one thousand, seven hundred and eighty pounds,' said Russell.

'No,' said Houston. '*The Times* has repaid me the whole sum.'

Russell feigned surprise.

'The entire sum?'

'Yes.'

'And did you make a profit on this transaction?' asked Russell.

'Not one penny.' Houston seemed offended at the very suggestion. 'I kept receipts of all expenditures. I showed them to Mr Soames and he ensured that I was paid in full.'

'So the only person to profit was Mr Pigott?' said Russell.

'Well, he was paid his agreed rate of one pound per day, if that's what you mean,' said Houston, unwilling to let Russell put words in his mouth.

'And do you know where Mr Pigott obtained these letters?'

'I know where he got them and when, but I do not know from whom,' said Houston.

'How do you know that?' asked Russell.

'Mr Pigott wrote to me on numerous occasions, to keep me informed of his investigations,' said Houston.

'I see,' said Russell. 'Did you receive many such letters from Mr Pigott?'

'Yes,' said Houston. 'A few dozen, I should think.'

'And do you still have these letters in your possession?'

'No,' said Houston. 'I do not.'

'Oh,' said Russell, surprised, 'what has become of them?'

'I destroyed them,' said Houston.

'Destroyed them!' exclaimed Russell. 'How?'

'I burnt them all,' said Houston defiantly.

'When did you destroy them?' asked Russell.

'Some months ago.'

Russell was astounded.

'When exactly, Mr Houston,' he persisted, 'did you destroy them?'

'In December,' said Houston.

Russell looked at their Lordships before continuing.

'You destroyed these letters only two months ago, after this trial had commenced and after you had received a subpoena to testify at this trial?'

'That is correct.' Houston was unapologetic. 'I wanted to destroy all clues as to the original sources of the letters.'

'Did you consider whether this was fair to Mr Parnell?' asked Russell.

'I do not think Mr Parnell is entitled to any consideration,' said Houston brusquely.

There was another reaction of surprise throughout the court. I glanced over at Parnell, who smiled at Houston's obvious hostility.

'Those letters might have established where Mr Pigott obtained these letters,' said Russell, in evident exasperation, 'and yet you destroyed them all.'

'Correct,' said Houston, 'and I would do exactly the same again.'

'Did you believe these letters to be genuine?' asked Russell.

'Of course they are genuine.'

'You acquired them from Mr Pigott,' insisted Russell, 'and you do not know where he acquired them.'

'No, I do not,' said Houston, 'and I do not want to know.'

'Clearly,' said Russell, 'and you have gone to great lengths to ensure we do not know.'

As it was now just past four o'clock, the judges rose for the day and Russell, Asquith and I walked over to Russell's chambers to discuss the matter further. Despite Russell's and Asquith's best efforts, the case for *The Times* was still intact. The final witness on the letters was Pigott, and if *The Times'* case against Parnell was to be undermined, then Pigott had to be undermined. Asquith and I tried to discuss his cross-examination with Russell, but he was becoming increasingly tetchy and wanted to be left alone, so after a few moments, we left him to his preparations.

Forty-Nine

The Cross-Examination of Pigott

T HALF-PAST TEN on Thursday morning, the Attorney
General called Pigott to the witness box.

The usher echoed the name throughout the court: 'Mr
Pigott.' I saw movement at the back of the court, as someone
attempted to shove past them to press his way to the front. Then,
emerging from the crowd, I saw Pigott, short, stout and bald, with a
large white beard, his cheeks flushed with anxiety over his impending
appearance in the witness box.

In his first questions, the Attorney General took Pigott through his
early life, his work as a journalist, how he had met Parnell and how
he had commenced working for Houston trying to uncover any links
between Parnell and crime.

Webster did his job well and Pigott's answers were assured.

'So, Mr Pigott, I would like to turn now to these letters, which have
been the subject of much discussion in this hearing,' said Webster.

Pigott nodded.

'Can I ask you, Mr Pigott, when did you first come upon these
letters?'

Pigott launched forth upon his well-prepared explanation. He
had, he told the Court, made acquaintance with a gentleman named
Eugene Davis, who had written for his newspaper many years
earlier. He had arranged to meet Davis in Lausanne in early 1886;
he had told Davis about his commission from Houston, and Davis
had told him about a 'remarkable' letter he had heard about, written
by Parnell, in which Parnell had shown no remorse over the Phoenix
Park murders, and had expressed the view that Mr Burke had got no
more than his just deserts.

'This was the first time I had ever heard of this letter,' said Pigott, 'so I immediately resolved that I should find it.'

'And how did you go about that?' asked Webster.

'I returned to Ireland,' said Pigott, 'and then I heard that some Irish Americans whom I knew were in Paris, so I went to Paris to meet them and they gave me the letters.'

Webster continued his cross-examination in this desultory mode and moved swiftly on to how Pigott had obtained the second and third batch of letters. Then, without warning, Webster suddenly finished his examination and sat down.

Russell rose to his feet to begin his cross-examination.

I had expected him to begin with how Pigott had obtained the letters, but instead, to my surprise, he picked up a blank sheet of paper from his bench.

'Mr Pigott,' he said kindly, 'can I ask you to take this?'

The sheet of paper was handed from counsel to attorney to registrar and placed in Pigott's hands.

Pigott looked at the piece of paper on both sides, but said nothing.

'I want you to write down a few words, Mr Pigott,' said Russell, 'at my dictation.'

A quill was provided for Pigott by our attorney.

'Would you like to sit down, Mr Pigott?' asked Russell kindly.

'No, thank you.'

'How would you normally write?' intervened Mr Justice Day.

'Sitting down, Your Honour,' said Pigott.

'Very well then, you should sit down,' said Judge Day, 'and write as you normally would.'

A chair was provided and Pigott took his seat, put the paper on the ledge in front of him and looked up expectantly at Russell.

'Now, Mr Pigott,' said Russell. 'I want you to write down the word "livelihood".'

'Livelihood?' asked Pigott.

'Correct,' said Russell.

There was a silence in court as we heard the sound of Pigott scratching the quill on the paper, as he wrote out his word. When he had finished, he looked up at Russell.

'Now the word "likelihood",' said Russell.

Pigott, laboriously, wrote out that word also.

'Now your own name,' said Russell.

Pigott looked surprised, but said nothing and, hunched over the ledge, wrote out his own name.

'Now I would like you to write out the word "proselytism",' said Russell with emphasis.

'Proselytism?' repeated Pigott.

Russell nodded but did not reply, and Pigott scratched out the word.

'Now, most importantly, Mr Pigott, the name "Patrick Egan",' said Russell.

Pigott nodded and wrote out those words also.

'Now, perhaps I could ask you to hand the sheet to my solicitor,' said Russell.

Pigott was about to do so when Russell exclaimed: 'Oh, Mr Pigott, one final word, I had almost forgotten. Could I ask you to write the word "hesitancy"? With a small "h" please.'

Asquith leaned over to me. 'He has him now,' he whispered.

Pigott, however, did not even appear to notice, but continued at his task, writing out the required word.

When Pigott had finished, Russell said:

'Thank you, Mr Pigott. And now, perhaps you could hand the sheet of paper back to my solicitor?'

Lewis stood up to retrieve the document.

Webster rose to his feet, beside Russell.

'Perhaps we could arrange to have that document photographed?' he said.

But before anyone could reply, Russell roared at him.

'Sit down, sir and do not interrupt me in my cross-examination with such a request.'

The Attorney General resumed his seat immediately, flushed with embarrassment. I doubt he had ever been addressed in such a fashion before in court, but Russell was not going to allow any person – not even the Attorney General – to derail his cross-examination with trivial requests. The judges did not intervene.

Russell turned back to Pigott.

'Now, Mr Pigott,' he said, 'the first publication of these articles on Parnellism and Crime was on 7th March 1887.'

'I did not know that,' said Pigott.

'Well,' said Russell, 'you can take it that that is correct.'

'Very well then,' said Pigott.

'And you were aware of the intended publication of these letters of Mr Parnell, were you not?' asked Russell.

'No, I was not aware of it at all,' said Pigott.

'What?' exclaimed Russell. 'You were not aware that the letters which you had procured were about to be published?'

'No, I was not,' insisted Pigott.

'Were you not aware that grave charges were going to be made against Mr Parnell?'

'No,' insisted Pigott. 'I was not aware of it until they actually commenced.'

'Is that your evidence – under oath – Mr Pigott?' said Russell calmly, looking down at his papers.

'It is,' said Pigott, 'absolutely.'

'Very well then,' said Russell, looking at the judges. 'There can be no mistake about that then.'

Russell then flicked through some papers on his bench and eventually pulled out a letter, which he handed to the witness.

'Is this your letter?' he asked. 'You needn't bother to read it through. Just tell me, is that your letter?'

There was a silence in court as Pigott looked at the two leaves of the letter, holding them up close.

'I think it is,' he said eventually.

'You think?' said Russell. 'Have you any doubt?'

'No,' admitted Pigott hesitantly, 'it is my letter.'

He handed it back to Russell. Russell turned to place his left foot on his bench and, leaning his elbow on his thigh, he began to read out the letter.

'My Lords,' he said, 'this is a letter from Mr Pigott to Archbishop Walsh of Dublin, written on 4th March 1887 – three days before the first article published by *The Times*. The letter is headed "Private & Confidential" and it begins:

My Lord,

The importance of the matter about which I write will doubtless excuse this intrusion on your Grace's attention. Briefly, I wish to say that I have been made aware of certain proceedings that are in preparation with the object of destroying the influence of the Parnellite party in parliament.

I cannot enter more fully into details than to state that the proceedings referred to consist in the publication of certain statements purporting to prove the complicity of Mr Parnell himself and some of his supporters with murders and outrages in Ireland to be followed in all probability by the institution of criminal proceedings against these parties by the Government.

Pigott paled in the witness box.

'You wrote this letter to the Archbishop, Mr Pigott,' said Russell. 'It is your letter.'

'Yes,' stammered Pigott, taken aback, 'but that letter was written under the seal of the confessional.'

There was an outburst of laughter in court.

'Indeed,' said Russell.

Pigott looked at Russell uneasily.

'What were these "certain proceedings", to which you were referring in this letter?' asked Russell.

'I do not recollect,' said Pigott.

'Turn to their Lordships and repeat that answer,' said Russell acidly.

Pigott turned to the three judges.

'I do not recollect,' he repeated.

'You are prepared to swear on oath that you did not know what the certain proceedings referred to in your letter were?'

'Yes,' said Pigott.

'Writing three days before the first letter was published.'

'Yes,' said Pigott.

'Letters which you had procured for *The Times*.'

Pigott nodded.

'Is it not clear, Mr Pigott, that your letter to the Archbishop was warning him about the Parnell letters?'

'No, not at that date,' said Pigott. 'I don't think the letters had been obtained at that time.'

'I do not want to confuse you, Mr Pigott,' Russell said courteously, 'but that cannot be correct. Your letter is 4th March 1887 – just three days before the first Times article was published.'

'Oh, yes,' said Pigott, correcting himself, 'some of the letters had been obtained by that time.'

'So, isn't it clear that the phrase "certain proceedings" in your letter referred to the letters you had procured for *The Times?*'

'No,' stammered Pigott. 'I don't think I was referring to the letters. I think I must have been referring to the forthcoming articles in *The Times.*'

Russell closed his trap.

'But you told us – not one moment ago – that you did not know anything about the forthcoming articles in *The Times,*' he said.

Pigott coloured and began to look confused. The heat in the courtroom was making him perspire heavily, and he took out a crumpled handkerchief to wipe his brow and his cheeks.

'Yes, yes,' he said. 'I said that. I find now that I am mistaken. I must have heard something about them at the time.'

'Try not to make another such mistake, Mr Pigott,' said Russell sharply. 'Now, let us resume with your letter to the Archbishop. You state in the letter that "the proceedings referred to consist in the publication of certain statements". Is this not a clear statement, Mr Pigott, that you knew that the paper was about to publish these letters?'

'I suppose so,' said Pigott.

'So you did know, at the time of this letter, that *The Times* intended to publish these letters – that is what you were saying to the Archbishop?' said Russell.

'I must have known,' said Pigott uneasily.

Russell read out a further paragraph from Pigott's letter to the Archbishop. 'Your Grace may be assured that I speak with full knowledge and am in a position to prove beyond all doubt and question the truth of what I say. And I will further assure your Grace that I am also able to point out how these designs may be successfully combated and finally defeated.'

'Was that true, Mr Pigott?' asked Russell.

'It could hardly be true,' said Pigott, 'as I did not have full knowledge.'

'So, why would you write something to the Archbishop which was false?'

'I suppose, to give strength to what I said.' Pigott shifted uneasily in his chair.

'You added an untrue statement to a true statement, to add strength to what you said?' asked Russell.

'Yes,' said Pigott.

'So, did you believe the letters which you procured for *The Times* to be genuine?' asked Russell.

'I did,' said Pigott.

'And do you still believe them to be genuine?'

'I do.'

'So, why did you write "I will further assure your Grace that I am able to point out how these designs may be successfully combated and finally defeated"?' asked Russell again.

'I do not know,' said Pigott.

'You must know,' said Russell. 'This is what *you* wrote, that you could point to how these letters could be combated and defeated.'

'I cannot really conceive ...' muttered Pigott.

'Try,' said Russell coldly.

'I cannot,' said Pigott helplessly.

'Try,' said Russell again.

'It is no use,' said Pigott, throwing up his hands in a gesture of helplessness.

'May I take it, then, Mr Pigott, that your answer is that you have no explanation?' said Russell.

'None,' said Pigott.

Russell continued reading the letter. 'I assure your Grace that I have no other motive except to suggest that your Grace would communicate the substance to some one or other of the parties concerned to whom I could furnish details and proofs and suggest how the coming blow may be effectually met.'

'You mentioned "proofs" here,' said Russell. 'What proofs, Mr Pigott, did you have as to how the coming blow could be met?'

'None,' said Pigott, shrugging his shoulders. 'I can remember nothing about it.'

'Even now,' said Russell, 'assuming the letters to be genuine, can you remember how they could be dealt with or combated?'

'No,' said Pigott. He looked ashen-faced and kept his head down as he answered the questions.

Russell looked through some more papers, to let everyone draw breath. After some moments, he resumed.

'Now, Mr Pigott,' he said, 'did you believe the charges in the letters to be true or false?'

'How can I say,' said Pigott, 'when I do not know what the charges were?'

Russell appeared to become impatient.

'First of all, Mr Pigott, you procured and paid for a number of letters.'

'Yes.'

'Which, if genuine, would have grave implications for those persons involved.'

'Yes.'

'Did you believe those charges to be true or false?'

'I believed them to be true.'

'And you still do so?'

'Yes.'

'Then I will read another part of your letter to the Archbishop.' Russell turned back to the letter:

'I need hardly add, that did I consider the party really guilty of the things charged against him I should not dream of suggesting that your Grace should take part in an effort to shield them. I only wish to impress on your Grace that the evidence is apparently convincing and would probably be sufficient to secure conviction if submitted to an English jury.

Yours truly,
Richard Pigott.

'What do you say to that, Mr Pigott?' asked Russell quietly.

Pigott looked deathly pale.

'I have nothing to say.'

'Nothing!' exclaimed Russell.

'Except that I could not have had the actual letters in my mind when I wrote that letter,' he said. 'I must have been referring to something else. I must have had something else in my mind.'

'What else had you in your mind?' asked Russell.

'It must have been something far more serious than the letters,' said Pigott.

'What was it, then?' asked Russell.

'I have no idea,' said Pigott.

'But it was something far more serious than the letters?' said Russell, as if he took him at his word.

'Absolutely,' said Pigott.

'Can you give us any clues as to what it might have been?'

'I cannot,' said Pigott.

'Or where you might have heard it?'

'No.'

'Or from whom you might have heard it?'

'No.'

'Or when you heard it?'

'No.'

'So it is still locked up – hermetically sealed, as it were – in your own bosom?' asked Russell sarcastically.

'No,' said Pigott, 'because whatever it was, it has flown out of my bosom.'

There was another burst of laughter in court. Pigott looked around the crowded courtroom and tried half-heartedly to join in the laughter, thinking perhaps that he had said something witty.

Russell looked at the clock, nodded to the judges and ended his cross-examination for the first day, leaving the laughter of the courtroom still ringing in Pigott's ears, as he descended from the witness box.

'He's smashed him,' said Asquith to me, as we picked up our papers, 'and he's only just started.'

We started to walk back with Russell to his chambers, but he wished to be left alone. He would not rest until his cross-examination was complete.

Fifty

Pigott's Evidence Resumes

THE FOLLOWING DAY, Pigott resumed his evidence.

'Mr Pigott,' said Russell, 'I want to take you back to tell us again how you happened upon the letters which you gave to *The Times*.'

Pigott looked at Russell, but said nothing.

'You said,' continued Russell, looking down at his notes, 'that Mr Eugene Davis told you about the existence of these letters.'

'Yes,' said Pigott, 'that was where I heard it first. In Lausanne.'

'And that you went back to Ireland to start your search.'

'Yes,' said Pigott. 'I wrote to some Irish Americans who I thought could help me.'

'And you then discovered that they were coming to Paris?' said Russell.

'Yes,' said Pigott, 'and I went over to Paris to meet them.'

'And who did you meet in Paris?' asked Russell.

'Maurice Murphy,' said Pigott.

'Who was he?' asked Russell.

'He was an emissary of the Clan na Gael Brotherhood,' said Pigott grandiosely.

'And where did you meet him?' asked Russell.

'I happened to be walking around the streets of Paris and I just came across him,' said Pigott.

'Just came across him!' exclaimed Russell in surprise. 'That was fortunate indeed.'

'Extremely fortunate,' agreed Pigott rapidly. 'But I would have arranged to meet him, had I not come across him. I told Murphy about what Davis had said about the Parnell letters and I asked him if he knew anything about them.'

'And did he?' asked Russell.

'No, he didn't,' said Pigott. 'But he told me he would investigate the matter for me.'

'And did he?' asked Russell.

'He did,' said Pigott.

'So when did you meet Mr Murphy again?' asked Russell.

'Only a few days later,' said Pigott.

'Where?'

'I arranged to meet him in a café,' said Pigott, 'and Mr Murphy told me that he had discovered the letters of Mr Parnell which I was looking for – and some letters of Mr Egan – and various other papers, in a black bag.'

'Oh,' said Russell pretending to be astonished, 'that was another stroke of luck.'

'Indeed it was,' said Pigott, 'so I told Murphy I would buy them, provided he showed them to me first.'

'What did he say to that?'

'He agreed to show them to me there and then,' said Pigott, 'so I went to a house he knew and perused them.'

'You perused them,' said Russell, 'and did you purchase them?'

'Not then,' said Pigott. 'I hastened back to London to meet Mr Houston and he instructed me to return and purchase them immediately. But when I got back to Paris, Mr Murphy told me that the letters were the property of the Fenians in America and they would not sell them.'

'So what did you do then?' asked Russell.

'I sailed to America immediately,' said Pigott, 'to get their consent.'

'On one pound a day, plus expenses?' asked Russell sarcastically.

'Yes,' said Pigott, ignoring the sarcasm, 'that was the rate I had agreed with Mr Houston. I didn't delay in America. I met with a Mr Breslin, whom I had been told to meet, and he agreed to the sale of the letters. He gave me a letter of consent for Mr Murphy.'

'So you sailed back to Europe?' said Russell.

'Yes,' said Pigott. 'I went back to Paris to meet Mr Murphy.'

'When was this, Mr Pigott?' asked Russell suddenly.

'About June 1886,' said Pigott.

'Just as the Home Rule bill was going through the House of Commons,' said Russell.

'I think so,' said Pigott. 'I can't be sure of those dates.'

'So you went to meet Mr Murphy in Paris,' said Russell. 'You went to his home, I suppose.'

'No, I didn't,' said Pigott. 'I didn't have his address.'

'Didn't have his address!' echoed Russell. 'So how did you meet him?'

'I bumped into him in the street again,' said Pigott.

'Again!' exclaimed Russell. 'You bumped into him in the street for a second time?'

Pigott began to perspire and and pulled out his handkerchief to blow his nose.

'Yes, I was very fortunate.'

'So, he agreed to sell you the letters?' asked Russell.

'Not immediately,' said Pigott. 'I showed him the letter of authorisation but he told me he needed others to consent also.'

'Who were these others?' asked Russell.

'I never met them before,' said Pigott.

'Who were they?' repeated Russell.

Pigott explained.

'I went to a café in the Rue St Honoré with Murphy. We went downstairs to a private room. There were five men sitting around a table and before they would hand over the letters they made me swear an oath that I would never divulge the source of the letters – not even in a court of law.'

There was another outburst of laughter at Pigott's story and Pigott, looking around the court, started to laugh sheepishly.

Russell took a glass of water and waited for everyone to settle down again.

'These men just happened to be there, even though you had bumped into Mr Murphy by chance?' said Russell.

Pigott nodded, but said nothing.

'What did they make you swear on, Mr Pigott?' he asked. 'Was there a bible to hand in this café on the Rue St Honoré?'

'No,' said Pigott, 'it was a Catholic prayer book.'

'And that was how you got the first batch of letters?' asked Russell.

'It was,' said Pigott, 'and I gave them to Mr Houston.'

'There was a second batch of letters also, I believe,' said Russell, 'which you also procured for Mr Houston and *The Times*.'

'That is correct, Sir Charles.'

'Can you tell us how you got those?'

'I was in Paris again some months later.'

'When exactly?' said Russell.

'Last year,' said Pigott, 'about January 1887. I bumped into a man called Tom Brown in Paris.'

'Just met him in the street!' exclaimed Russell.

'Yes,' said Pigott nervously.

'Just as you did, twice, with Mr Murphy?'

'Yes.'

'That was exceedingly fortunate,' said Russell.

'Exceedingly,' agreed Pigott, 'but it turned out Mr Brown was looking for me. He had heard I was looking for certain letters,and he told me he had discovered some more.'

'How many letters were in this batch, Mr Pigott?' said Russell.

'There were two letters signed by Mr Parnell and one signed by Mr Egan.'

'And did Mr Brown give you these letters there and then?' asked Russell.

'Oh no,' said Pigott, apparently affronted by the suggestion that the transaction could be so casual. 'No, Mr Brown also brought me to the café in the Rue St Honoré.'

'The same café?' exclaimed Russell.

'Yes,' said Pigott, 'and I went to the same room and I was asked to give the same oath again.'

'To the same five men?' finished Russell. 'Who just happened to be there?'

'Yes,' said Pigott, 'the same five men.'

Again there was laughter in the court at the increasingly ludicrous nature of the story.

'And you brought these letters back to Mr Houston.'

'Yes,' said Pigott immediately.

'And how much did you pay for these letters?' asked Russell.

'Five hundred pounds,' said Pigott.

'For three letters?' said Russell. 'And what was your payment?'

'I was paid ten per cent,' said Pigott. 'Fifty pounds.'

'So Mr Houston gave you five hundred and fifty pounds,' said Russell. 'Five hundred pounds for the letters and fifty pounds for yourself.'

'Yes,' agreed Pigott.

'Did you get a receipt for that money?' asked Russell sharply.

Pigott looked surprised.

'No, I didn't ask for one. Men such as these do not give a receipt. It was not a normal transaction.'

'Indeed,' said Russell. 'Did Mr Houston meet these men?'

'No,' said Pigott.

'What, none of them? Not even Mr Murphy or Mr Brown?'

'No,' said Pigott.

'He simply took you at your word that you had met these men and paid them five hundred pounds?'

'Yes,' said Pigott.

I glanced over at Houston and McDonald, who sat grim-faced on the bench as they listened to Pigott's story – evidently for the first time.

'What about the third batch of letters?' said Russell. 'How did you acquire these?'

'I was in Paris again some months later,' said Pigott, 'July 1888, I think, when I met a man I had never met before.'

'In the street?' suggested Russell.

'Yes,' said Pigott, 'and he offered to sell me three more letters. He had heard from Mr Brown that I was a buyer.' Pigott tried helpfully to explain.

'How much did Mr Houston pay you for these letters?' asked Russell.

'Two hundred pounds,' said Pigott.

'No questions asked,' said Russell.

'No questions asked,' agreed Pigott.

Russell took up a copy of the infamous letter in which Parnell had apparently written that Burke had got his just deserts.

'You are familiar with this letter, Mr Pigott?' said Russell.

'I am, now,' said Pigott.

'I want to direct your attention, Mr Pigott,' said Russell, 'to another set of correspondence altogether.'

'What correspondence is that?' Pigott looked apprehensive.

'You engaged in a correspondence with Mr Parnell many years ago — in 1881 — about the purchase of your newspaper by Mr Parnell, did you not?'

Pigott nodded.

'Now, Mr Pigott.' Russell was calm. 'I want to read out to you one of the letters published by *The Times*. It purports to be a letter from Mr Patrick Egan to Mr Parnell.

Dear Sir,
Your two letters of the 12th and 15th inst are duly to hand and I am also in receipt of communications from Mr Parnell informing me that he has acted upon my suggestion and accepted the offer made by B.

Yours very faithfully
P. Egan.

You saw that letter in *The Times*, Mr Pigott?' said Russell.

Pigott nodded, his mouth opening and closing in a nervous manner.

'Now, Mr Pigott, here is a letter which Mr Egan wrote to you in 1881, when he was negotiating the purchase of your newspaper. It reads as follows.'

Russell picked up a letter from his desk and started reading aloud.

Dear Sir,
Your two letters of the 12th and 15th inst are duly to hand and I am also in receipt of communications from Mr Parnell informing me that he has acted upon my suggestion and accepted the offer made in your first letter.

P. Egan.

'Now, Mr Pigott,' said Russell, 'I am sure you would agree that there is great similarity between these two letters.'

Pigott nodded.

'They are, in fact, absolutely identical,' said Russell. 'A remarkable coincidence.'

'Indeed,' nodded Pigott, 'a remarkable coincidence' – and then, as if to show he was intent on being helpful, he added: 'Indeed, so remarkable as to be exceedingly improbable.'

'Indeed,' said Russell, 'exceedingly improbable and so the forger of these letters to *The Times* must be someone who had received this letter from Mr Egan or had access to it. Would you not agree?'

Pigott gulped and nodded, but said nothing.

Throughout the next hour, Russell put other letters in front of Pigott – letters sent by Parnell or Egan to Pigott, which contained phrases or sentences which – extraordinarily – also appeared in the forged letters of *The Times*. Pigott could not account for any of them.

Eventually, Russell paused for a moment, helped himself to a pinch of snuff and blew his nose loudly into a blue handkerchief.

'Now, Mr Pigott,' he said, 'supposing you wanted to forge a man's signature.'

'Why would I want to do that?' Pigott tried to laugh, nervously.

'Please indulge me, Mr Pigott,' said Russell. 'If you were to do so, it would be a great help to have in your possession an actual letter signed by that man, would it not?'

'I suppose it would,' said Pigott. 'I never thought about it before now.'

'Indeed,' said Russell, 'so what would you do?'

'I don't know,' protested Pigott. 'I can't say I have any experience of such a thing.'

'Yes, but let us know how you would set about it,' persisted Russell.

'I don't wish to put myself in that position at all,' said Pigott.

'But, Mr Pigott,' said Russell, 'we are merely speaking theoretically.'

'I don't think discussing a theory is any help,' said Pigott.

'Well, let me suggest a way,' said Russell. 'Would you, for example, put a delicate tissue paper over the letter and trace out the signature and some of the words?'

'Yes, that is the way,' said Pigott, looking at the judges, 'but I don't see what it has to do with me.'

'How do you know it is the way?' asked Russell sharply.

'Well … I suppose that would be the way,' answered Pigott nervously.

'How do you know?' asked Russell. 'Have you tried?'

'No. No. But I suppose it would be the easiest way.' Pigott was looking increasingly hunted.

'Is Mr Parnell's signature a difficult signature to imitate?' asked Russell.

'I do not know,' said Pigott.

'But what do you think?' asked Russell.

'It is a peculiar signature, certainly,' said Pigott.

'Why so?' asked Russell. 'Because it is a strongly marked one?'

'I am not competent to give an opinion,' Pigott said defensively.

'Well, would you say it was a difficult or an easy signature to imitate, Mr Pigott?' said Russell.

'Considering its peculiarities, I would say – difficult,' said Pigott.

'I ask you these questions, Mr Pigott,' said Russell, 'because there is a further peculiarity about these letters printed in *The Times*. They purport to be written in 1882.'

Pigott nodded.

'But Mr Parnell will say that the signature of *The Times* letters is not the one he used in 1882 – that he signed his name like that only until 1881 and thereafter wrote his name in a different manner.'

'I don't understand your point,' said Pigott.

'Well, Mr Pigott,' said Russell, 'you have a letter from Mr Parnell to you from 1881, with his original signature. But the following year – in 1882 – Mr Parnell began to use a different signature and yet the signature in *The Times* letters of 1882 is his signature of one year earlier.'

There was a sharp intake of breath in the courtroom, as the direction of Russell's examination became clear to all.

Pigott replied: 'I don't see what any of this has to do with me. Maybe he did change his signature in 1882. What of it?'

'But you had a copy of his signature in your possession from 1881, when he wrote to you,' said Russell.

'Yes, I did,' said Pigott.

'And that is the form of the signature which appears on the facsimile letter. How do you account for that?'

'I cannot account for it,' said Pigott.

Russell paused for a moment, before starting on a different line of attack.

'I want to go back to yesterday,' said Russell, 'when you wrote out some words for me.'

Pigott nodded.

'One of the words I asked you to spell yesterday, Mr Pigott, was the word "hesitancy".'

'Yes.' Pigott nodded in recollection.

'Is that a word you are accustomed to use, Mr Pigott?' said Russell.

'I have used it often, yes,' said Pigott.

'Because you spelt it incorrectly,' said Russell.

'Oh, did I?' said Pigott casually.

'Yes, Mr Pigott, you did,' said Russell coldly. 'You spelt it h-e-s-i-t-*e*-n-c-y, with an "e", rather than as it should be spelt: h-e-s-i-t-*a*-n-c-y. You spelt it with an "e" rather than an "a".'

'I see,' said Pigott.

'Now, Mr Pigott,' said Russell, 'can I ask you to look again at the facsimile letter published by *The Times* ?' Russell handed up the letter again to the witness.

'Now, look at this letter, Mr Pigott. On the third paragraph, you will see the writer of this letter also spells the word "hesitancy" incorrectly and, indeed, makes the same mistake as you did.'

The silence in court was intense as everyone now concentrated all their attention on Pigott. Even the judges looked at him expectantly.

Pigott took out his handkerchief and mopped his brow.

'Well … Well … All I can say is that the wording in this letter must have got into my brain – with all the attention it's getting. I must have read that letter in *The Times* hundreds of times. But, sure, everybody spells that word wrong.'

Pigott wound himself round and round, trying to come up with as many possible explanations as he could in a few sentences.

'Indeed, Mr Pigott,' said Russell. 'But I want to show you yet another letter.'

He withdrew another letter from the pile of papers on the top of his bench. 'One you wrote to Mr Egan in 1881, during the negotiations for your newspaper.'

Russell handed up this letter to his attorney, who handed it to Pigott.

'You will see, Mr Pigott, that in 1881, in your letter to Mr Egan, you have spelt "hesitancy" incorrectly there also.'

Pigott said nothing, his mouth opening and closing as he sought to gather his thoughts and come up with a new ruse to cover his increasingly uncomfortable position. The noose was drawing tightly around him.

Russell waited for an eternity for a response, but none came.

'What do you have to say about that, Mr Pigott?'

Pigott looked up at him and shrugged his shoulders weakly.

'Spelling was never my strong point,' he said quietly.

The crowd in the court laughed aloud again, as Pigott's ridiculous excuses were exposed, one after the other. Russell took his fobwatch from his waistcoat. It was just after four o'clock and he nodded at the judges. They took the hint, rose, bowed to the court and retired and I watched as Pigott limped down heavily from the witness stand and left the courtroom, friendless and alone.

Fifty-One

The Case Collapses

THE CASE WAS due to resume on Tuesday at eleven, but even by ten o'clock the court was thronged with people. Word of Russell's cross-examination had spread over the weekend and everyone wanted to be present to watch the final act of destruction. At half-past ten the judges came in and took their seats. The registrar called out Pigott's name and we waited for Pigott to shuffle up from the back of the court. Parnell sat at his usual place, staring impassively at everything going on around him.

'Mr Pigott,' the registrar called a second time. Still no appearance.

After a few moments, the registrar called out again.

'Mr Pigott, please. Mr Pigott.'

There was still no response in the courtroom.

Russell looked over at Webster enquiringly, but Webster shrugged his shoulders.

'Sir Richard,' said Judge Hannen, 'where is your witness?'

Webster got to his feet slowly and beckoned over to Soames to come towards him. Soames whispered something to him and Webster went quite pale. He straightened up.

'I am afraid, My Lords, that Mr Pigott has not been seen since eleven o'clock last night.'

There was a gasp in court.

Russell jumped to his feet.

'I would request that Your Lordships issue an immediate warrant for Mr Pigott's arrest,' he said.

There was consternation among *The Times'* legal team, as solicitors and counsel and clients all huddled together to discuss their response.

'Have you any other witnesses, Sir Richard?' asked Mr Justice Hannen.

Webster rose reluctantly to his feet.

'My Lords, the unexpected non-appearance of Mr Pigott has made it necessary for us to consider our position and we would ask the court to rise for a few moments.'

Russell was up immediately and, pointing his finger at Soames, he said: 'We shall search this matter to the bottom, for we say that behind Houston and Pigott, there is a foul conspiracy.'

He brought his fist down onto the bench with a resounding smack.

The judges rose to allow Webster consider his position and the crowds stood up and mingled, buzzing with conversation.

An hour later, Soames, McDonald and Webster reappeared, looking utterly dejected.

When the judges came back into court, they announced that a warrant had been issued for Pigott's arrest.

Russell rose again.

'There is another matter, My Lords, to which I now wish to draw your attention. Last Saturday, Mr Pigott, without notice or invitation, went to the house of a Mr Labouchere and offered to make a full confession.'

Judge Hannen leaned back in his chair in evident surprise.

'And Mr Labouchere decided he would not take Pigott's confession alone, so he sent for a colleague – a Mr George Sala – and when Mr Sala appeared, Mr Pigott confessed that he was the forger of the letters and he has signed a statement to that effect.'

There were loud, triumphant cheers from Parnell's supporters in the court.

'Is this true?' Mr Justice Hannen asked Webster.

The Attorney General nodded miserably.

'Well, then,' said Hannen to Russell, 'you can hardly be surprised that he has not turned up this morning.'

'I certainly am surprised.' Russell was unyielding. 'He was under the guard of two detectives from Scotland Yard at all times and I expected them to guard him carefully.'

Webster rose and handed in a copy of Pigott's confession to the judges. Russell insisted on the confession being read out in court. Mr Justice Hannen obliged and read it out in full.

'I make this confession of my own free will and without any monetary inducements. No one except myself was engaged on these works. I picked out words and phrases from Mr Parnell and I traced his handwriting by placing the letters to the windows and drawing them on a piece of tissue paper.'

Parnell sat calmly beside Soames and McDonald as this confession was read out. His expression never changed. There was not a flicker of emotion, not a smile or a frown. He listened to the confession as if it had nothing whatsoever to do with him.

When the confession had been read out, Judge Hannen looked down over his glasses, at Webster.

The Attorney General rose to his feet, slowly, in response.

'I have communicated with my clients, My Lord,' he said, so quietly that even I, in the bench behind, had to strain to hear. 'We must now admit that no one should place any weight on Mr Pigott's evidence and my clients' instructions are to withdraw the question of the genuineness of the letters from the court, with a full acknowledgement that the evidence does not entitle us to say that they are genuine ...'

Webster looked down for a moment, his hands folding and unfolding a piece of paper.

'And I am instructed to say,' he said, 'that *The Times* expresses its sincere regret for the publication of the letters.'

Russell bounded up.

'I had hoped for a stronger statement of regret from my learned friend, but no matter. It will not alter the course upon which we have set out. We will present our own witnesses to prove our own case.'

'Perhaps you should call your own witnesses now, Sir Charles,' said Mr Justice Hannen, 'and we can consider their evidence at this time.'

Russell nodded. 'I call upon Charles Stewart Parnell.'

Parnell stood up and calmly walked to the witness box. After he had taken the oath, Russell said to him: 'I intend to put some letters to you, Mr Parnell.'

Parnell nodded in acknowledgement.

'These are letters which have been published by *The Times* and I want you to give evidence as to whether you wrote these letters or not.'

The first of the forged letters was passed up to him.

'Did you write this letter?' asked Russell.

'I did not,' said Parnell.

Another letter was handed up.

'Is that your signature, Mr Parnell?' asked Russell.

'That is not my signature,' said Parnell.

All persons in court listened intently, as Parnell gave his evidence in a quiet, dignified manner, his voice appearing even quieter in contrast to the booming voice of Russell. There was about him no hint of triumphalism at the discomfiture of *The Times*. He answered all questions put to him in the same understated manner, with the words 'That is not my letter', 'That is not my writing'. After a short time, he had finished his examination. *The Times*' case against him had collapsed in total ignominy.

Days later, news reached London that the police had traced Pigott from London to Paris to Madrid and had found him at his hotel in Madrid. Pigott, realising he was to be arrested, went back to his room, ostensibly to collect his overcoat and, using a pistol which he had with him, shot himself through the head.

O'Shea, it later transpired, was in Madrid at precisely this time. It was, I thought, an unlikely coincidence.

After the destruction of Pigott, Parnell returned to the House of Commons and, as he appeared to take his seat, all the Irish Members of Parliament rose to their feet to applaud him. As we did so, I saw Gladstone rise also to applaud and, behind him, the entire Liberal Party followed his lead; soon every single member on both sides of the House was standing to applaud Parnell, as he took his usual seat below the gangway, beside Biggar and McCarthy. But Parnell took no notice of the applause. He never so much as looked up or acknowledged it in any way. He had travelled the full journey from being the most hated Member of Parliament to the most acclaimed; and, just as he had ignored the House when it opposed him, so now he ignored it when it praised him. He simply took his seat and turned his attention to the speaker at the despatch box.

The mood of the House had been transformed; men who had been convinced that Parnell had condoned the murders of Cavendish and Burke now realised they had misjudged him. He was, they now realised, an honourable man. More, they were confounded that he had taken the false attacks on his character so stoically and with so little recrimination. His exoneration convinced all the Liberals and, indeed, many Tories that here indeed was an historic figure, the leader of the Irish nation and a man whom they could trust: it redoubled their resolve to pass a Home Rule bill.

At the next recess, Chamberlain came over to shake Parnell's hand, but Parnell, on seeing him approach, turned his back on him and engaged me in conversation. Chamberlain withdrew in embarrassment and anger. Some Tories tried to congratulate him also, as they passed on the way out of the Chamber, but their good wishes went unacknowledged and unthanked.

'They are English and I hate the English.' His words, spoken so many years earlier, echoed in my mind. I could understand his hatred in the darkest days, but it is hard to hate your enemy when he is applauding you and bowing in respect as you make your way to your seat in his parliament. But I think he did retain that hatred for them at all times and I think he hated Gladstone to the very end.

Some months later, in December, Gladstone invited Parnell to his country house at Hawarden, to discuss the final details of a new Home Rule bill. It was now only a matter of time before there would be a new election, a new Home Rule bill and the start of a new parliament in Dublin. This time, there would be no Chamberlain, no O'Shea and no set-backs.

There was further good news later that year, when the other storm cloud over Parnell's home life seemed to disappear with the long-overdue death – if I may be so cruel – of Katharine's Aunt Ben, at the age of ninety-six. She had died an enormously wealthy woman and in her will she had left her entire fortune to Katharine – with explicit instructions that Willie O'Shea was never to have any control of the funds. Now – at last – matters could be finalised between Katharine and O'Shea; a quiet divorce could be arranged and hopefully O'Shea would disappear for a long time, perhaps to India, where the climate might give him a serious tropical infection to detain him there indefinitely.

After Hawarden, Parnell returned to Eltham for Christmas and I returned to Ireland. I remember that Christmas of 1889 in Dublin as a charmed time. An air of great gaiety and festive cheer pervaded the city, an air of expectation that, on the eve of a new decade, it was now only a matter of time before we had our independence. Seven hundred years of conquest, ninety years without our own parliament and now, suddenly, it all seemed within our grasp. There was a sense of exhilaration at the prospect and a sense of great national pride in Parnell. He was like a proud stag surrounded by a pack of hounds, all trying to bring him down: *The Times* had tried to destroy him; Salisbury had tried to destroy him; Chamberlain had tried to destroy him; the Special Commission had tried to destroy him; but he had succeeded in defeating them all. The Tories would soon be ousted, Gladstone would be elected on Home Rule and the Lords would not dare oppose him. One year until an election, another year to pass the Home Rule bill and in two years time we would have our first Irish Prime Minister in Parnell. In my idler and more fanciful moments, I wondered whether even I might have a ministry and a place at the cabinet table.

But all that changed on 28th December 1889.

Part Five

Fifty-Two

O'Shea *v.* O'Shea and Parnell

O N THAT FATEFUL day, I received a telegram from Biggar, early in the evening.

'Harrison. *London Evening News*. Urgent. Biggar.'

I went out immediately to find a copy, but it was not easy. All the shops had sold out, as every passer-by grabbed one on their way home. I had to walk from Fitzwilliam Square to Grafton Street before I found a newsboy, shouting it out at the top of his voice: 'Read all about it. O'Shea sues for divorce. Parnell named in adultery scandal.'

The secret was out. The storm was now upon us. I paid the newspaper boy and went into the Shelbourne to read through the pages and pages of the story, with a terrible sense of foreboding. O'Shea had issued his divorce writ on Christmas Eve. Of all times! The truth of the article was beyond doubt: the newspaper had sent a reporter to O'Shea that very morning to corroborate the story; it had even obtained a copy of the writ – which it reprinted in every detail – alleging that the adultery had taken place from April 1886 until the present date. My first thought was that he was wrong by at least six years! Why had O'Shea chosen that date, when he had known as long ago as the summer of 1881, when he had challenged Parnell to a duel? Then I realised: it was the very month Gladstone had brought in his Home Rule bill! O'Shea wanted people to believe that, at the very time Gladstone was trying to solve the centuries-old dispute between our two nations, Parnell was corrupting his wife. I sat back in an armchair in the Lord Mayor's lounge and ordered a large brandy. I needed to think. What effect would this have on Parnell? On Gladstone?

I looked at my watch. It was too late for the night sailing. I would go to London early the next morning.

I found it difficult to sleep that night and tossed and turned until first light. I was happy to rise early and make my way out to Kingstown and thence to London. I got to Eltham late that evening.

Katharine was distraught.

'How could Willie have done this?' she said, almost in tears. 'He has destroyed everything.'

Parnell, however, seemed quite resolved.

'It is better to have it all out in the open,' he said softly. 'Now the whole world will see what a despicable coward O'Shea has been all these years.'

I was taken aback by his reaction.

'Charles, this is not about O'Shea,' I said. 'It's about you.'

However, he bristled at any suggestions of impropriety on his part. I think he believed from the start that his behaviour was beyond reproach. If the O'Sheas were leading separate lives, then, according to his views, their marriage was at an end and he and Katharine were free to enter into their relationship.

'This is all part of a plot on the part of *The Times* to avenge their defeat over the Pigott letters,' he said, 'and I've told the papers that.'

'But this has nothing to do with *The Times*,' I replied. 'This is O'Shea's doing.'

He looked at me as if I were still too naïve to understand the ways of the world.

'O'Shea wouldn't do this by himself. Someone has put him up to it.'

'My sister!' exclaimed Katharine suddenly.

'Why would your sister want O'Shea to do this?' I asked, in surprise.

'There has been trouble about Aunt Ben's will,' said Parnell.

'My sisters are unhappy that Aunt Ben has left me her entire fortune,' said Katharine, 'but they never nursed her as I did. Why, they hardly even visited her. And now they have decided to challenge the will. It will take years to resolve in the courts.'

'Another Jarndyce and Jarndyce,' I murmured.

'What's that?' asked Parnell.

'Dickens, Charles,' I said. 'It doesn't matter.'

'My sister has told Willie to sue for divorce and to accuse me of adultery. That will blacken my name in the judge's eyes,' said Katharine. 'I might end up with nothing.' She became upset again.

'How are you going to fight this, Charles?' I asked.

'I don't want to contest the divorce and neither does Katharine,' he said.

'But if you don't contest it, what happens with the will?' I asked.

'I don't know,' said Parnell. 'We need to meet our solicitor and discuss these matters with him.'

'What should we do next, James?' asked Katharine.

'There are pleadings to be filed,' I said. 'Particulars of the claim. A defence.'

'We will not put in a defence,' said Parnell.

'A counterclaim,' I continued.

'What could we counterclaim?' asked Katharine.

'Desertion, adultery, connivance, perhaps,' I replied.

I was uncomfortable talking to her about the most intimate details of her marriage in such an open manner, particularly in front of Parnell.

'And how long before it comes to court?' asked Parnell.

'Six months,' I said, 'perhaps a year, at the most. It depends on how quickly it's pushed by all parties.'

Over the next few days and weeks, the newspapers – apart from *The Times* – treated the story with great caution. The Irish papers had no such concerns. They all supported Parnell, unreservedly, confident that he would defeat these allegations also, in time. But these were not mere allegations. This time, O'Shea was speaking the truth.

Biggar, in particular, was very concerned.

'I knew this would do in Parnell,' he said gloomily, over lunch one day in early January. 'Ever since Paris. Is that really nine years ago? How can the secret not have leaked out in the last nine years? It's miraculous.'

'Everyone knew about it,' I said, 'but no one ever wanted to talk about it.'

'Why the hell didn't he sort it out before now?' said Biggar savagely. 'Christ, after Galway he should have left her or forced her to get a divorce.'

'He doesn't want to leave her, Biggar,' I said. 'He loves her. They have two little girls.'

'Why didn't he force her to get a divorce?'

'He tried to, but she knew her aunt would disinherit her.'

'Christ, what a tangled web,' said Biggar, 'and Parnell caught up in the middle of it, and with him Home Rule.'

'Her aunt only died a few months ago,' I said.

'So, the fate of Home Rule now depends on the death of a little old dowager,' said Biggar. He shook his head. 'It's a long way from a Fenian uprising.'

'We have come a long way because of Parnell,' I said, 'and we need to stand by him now.'

'I'm not sure I can anymore,' said Biggar. 'I don't mind his adultery. That's his own business. But sticking us with O'Shea in Galway. That has left a bad taste with everyone, Harrison. You know very well it has.'

I had no reply.

'And then O'Shea refusing to vote for Home Rule, two months later.' Biggar was becoming angrier with every passing minute, as he recollected O'Shea's faults. 'But the one thing I can't quite fathom is: why now?'

I told him of Katharine's view that it was to spoil the settlement of her aunt's estate.

'There's more to it than that,' said Biggar. 'It's done to destroy Parnell, not Mrs O'Shea. O'Shea is so consumed with bitterness against Parnell that he is set on bringing him down entirely.'

⁓

Throughout that year, the inexorable machinery of the Courts of Justice lumbered forward in jerky fits and clanking starts, as *O'Shea v. O'Shea and Parnell* progressed towards trial.

Parnell and Katharine had seen their solicitor and Queen's Counsel had been retained to advise on the divorce case and also on the probate proceedings being taken by Katharine's relatives against her aunt's will. I was again asked by Parnell to take the junior brief.

I was of the view that the best way to resolve the divorce case was to bring about a rapid settlement of the dispute over the will. If that could be done, then O'Shea could be – to put it crudely – bought off to withdraw his divorce petition. Then Katharine herself could issue divorce proceedings and Parnell would not be involved at all. So we set about trying to settle the dispute over the will, but it proved utterly intractable.

I would like to say that preparations for the divorce case took me months, but that was not the case. Although Katharine wanted to contest the case, Parnell did not. He wished to offer no defence and, therefore, few preparations were required. We had, however, filed a counterclaim, in which Katharine claimed that O'Shea had been unfaithful to her on at least seventeen occasions – including, bizarrely, an allegation that O'Shea had a liaison with her sister, Anna Steele. I questioned her closely about this, as I was reluctant to put such a dramatic plea into the counterclaim unless it could be defended but she was adamant it was to be included.

The ship was sailing straight for the rocks. I tried to warn Parnell, but he didn't want to listen. Perhaps he believed he would survive the political damage which would ensue; perhaps he did not care any longer. His sole resolution was to be free to marry Katharine. I was helpless. As his friend, even as his counsel, there was nothing more that I could do.

Members of the Party were also becoming increasingly desperate and Biggar and Healy buttonholed me one day in the Commons and dragged me off to the smoking-room for a chat.

'Tell me it's settled, Harrison; please God, tell me it's settled so I can sleep easily,' Biggar enquired.

I shook my head.

Healy had followed the procedural wrangles and the byzantine processes of the law with a greater interest.

'Well, if it's not settled, is he going to contest it?' he asked me.

I told them I couldn't discuss the case with them, but Healy took this as a no.

'Is he off his nut?' he asked. 'If he doesn't contest it, O'Shea can say whatever he likes about him in open court.'

Biggar nodded in agreement.

'Sure, that'll be the worst of all worlds,' said Healy. 'God knows what O'Shea will say then.'

'O'Shea has no intention of settling it,' I said.

'Bah, every man has his price,' said Biggar, 'particularly a whore like O'Shea.'

'Which O'Shea whore are you talking about?' said Healy viciously.

I stood up and walked away.

&

In February of that year, we received another great shock when Biggar died unexpectedly, in his sleep. It was a terrible blow to us all, at a time when we needed him greatly. I lost a great friend and Parnell lost an honest counsellor, who never shirked telling him the truth, as he saw it. Their falling-out over Galway had been patched up and I believe that in the events which were to follow, Biggar might have been a restraining hand on Healy. But with Biggar's death, one of the pillars of the pier had been lost and the defences were now weakened against the oncoming tides.

&

Many months later, in November, on the eve of the trial, Parnell and Katharine had a consultation in chambers with the QC whom Parnell had retained, Sir Frank Lockwood. His advice was clear: contest the case so that O'Shea would not have the ground to himself.

'But what is the point?' asked Parnell. 'If Mrs O'Shea contests it, then the court may not grant the divorce.'

'That is certainly true,' admitted Sir Frank, 'but if you don't contest it, then all of Mr O'Shea's allegations will be heard in full; he will be called to give evidence; he can say whatever he likes, and you will have no one to cross-examine him.'

'And what about my counterclaim?' asked Katharine.

'Well, if you wish to prosecute that, Mrs O'Shea,' said Lockwood, 'then you will certainly have to contest his application and you will also have to give evidence yourself.'

He paused, to let her consider this element of the matter.

'But I have to say, Mrs O'Shea, that your evidence of adultery between Mr O'Shea and your sister seems – if I may say so – rather scant,' he said.

'I don't have any proof,' said Katharine hesitantly. 'I wasn't spying on them.'

'In my experience, Mrs O'Shea,' said Lockwood, 'that would be unusual. Not unprecedented, but unusual.'

There was a silence in the consultation room as they considered his advice.

'It would also, of course,' Lockwood resumed, 'cause a huge scandal, Mrs O'Shea, if you were to give such evidence against your own sister.'

'Can it not be heard in private?' pleaded Katharine.

'I'm afraid not,' said Lockwood, 'and a case such as this will attract enormous interest. As you are no doubt aware, Mr Parnell.'

Parnell nodded.

'I am not qualified, Mr Parnell, to offer you advice on that side of things,' said Lockwood. 'But from a legal point of view, if you do not contest the case then you will be found guilty as a co-respondent, which is a finding by the court that you engaged in adultery with Mrs O'Shea. The consequences of that are a matter for you to assess. You are a man of politics. I am a man of the law.'

'Can it be adjourned?' asked Katharine.

'Not at this late stage, no,' said Lockwood.

'Can it not be adjourned until after the case of my aunt's will?' said Katharine. 'If that were heard first, then I am sure I could buy Mr O'Shea's silence.'

'Unfortunately, it cannot,' said Lockwood sympathetically. 'We have tried to settle the matter. We offered twenty thousand pounds to Mr O'Shea, as you instructed us, Mrs O'Shea.'

Katharine nodded.

'I even indicated to my opponent, as you may recall, that we might be prepared to go to sixty thousand pounds. Triple our first offer! But he refused that out of hand also. So I am not sure that even waiting until after the will suit has been heard would make any difference.'

Katharine began to sob.

'Why has he done this?' she cried. 'What have I ever done to deserve this humiliation? He left me ...' She left the sentence unfinished and looked up at us, with tears in her eyes. 'He abandoned me years ago to go off with his mistresses – in London, in Madrid, everywhere. He simply abandoned me to my fate. If it wasn't for my aunt, I don't know what I would have done. What could I have done?'

'Well, you could have issued divorce proceedings against him many years ago,' said Lockwood matter-of-factly.

'My aunt would have disinherited me,' said Katharine.

'Would it have made any difference if Mrs O'Shea had issued the writ immediately after her aunt's death?' asked Parnell.

'Very little, Mr Parnell,' said Lockwood. 'Given the timing, Mr O'Shea would have simply counterclaimed, alleging adultery against Mrs O'Shea and naming you as the co-respondent. It would be just the same tomorrow.'

'And if I contest this divorce and tell the truth, then I shall be tied to that man until I die, and if that should be, then I pray that death will not be far off.' Katharine's distress was increasing.

'That resolves it, Sir Frank,' said Parnell after a moment. 'We shall not contest this case. Let O'Shea say what he likes. We know the truth of the matter. Let it be done and we shall be rid of him and free to marry.'

'You might like to reflect on it overnight,' said Sir Frank.

Parnell rose and nodded. 'I shall,' he said, 'and I shall telegraph you by eight o'clock tomorrow morning, but there will be no change.'

'Very well,' said Sir Frank.

Fifty-Three

The Trial

ON SATURDAY MORNING, I arrived early at the Law Courts in the Strand and robed. I met Lockwood in the robing-room, where the Robing Master, obsequious as always, was helping him into his gown. Lockwood, looking into a mirror, straightened his wig, pulled his collar until it was comfortable and fixed his tabs before he turned to me.

'Ah, Harrison,' he said, in a friendly fashion. 'I got a telegram from Parnell this morning. Eight o'clock, just as he promised.'

'What did it say?' I still did not know what Parnell intended to do.

'Instructing us not to contest the application,' said Lockwood.

My surprise must have been visible.

'I know,' he said. 'A grave error, in my opinion. Still, I warned him. O'Shea will have a free rein. We can't even cross-examine him, so he can say whatever he wants.'

'This could be a disaster,' I said.

'No "could" about it,' said Lockwood.

We gathered our briefs and went upstairs to Court 14, on the first floor. Even at a quarter to eleven, the small courtroom was crowded – particularly with journalists, many of whom I recognised from the Special Commission.

Lockwood pushed his way through the crowded court to the empty front benches reserved for silks and I squeezed into the juniors' bench behind him. I looked across and saw O'Shea, talking to his attorney. He saw me, but made no acknowledgement.

At eleven o'clock precisely, the tipstaff opened the door from the judge's chambers and walked into the courtroom.

'Silence in court,' he said. 'All rise.'

Mr Justice Butt, a slight man with large spectacles, came into court. He bowed to the assembled counsel and took his seat.

The registrar picked up a bundle of papers in front of him, untied the pink ribbons and read: 'In the matter of William O'Shea, Plaintiff, and Katharine O'Shea, Defendant, and Charles Stewart Parnell, Respondent. Are there any appearances on behalf of the parties?'

Sir Edward Clarke QC, counsel for Willie O'Shea, stood up and mumbled to the court that he appeared for Mr O'Shea.

Lockwood rose immediately.

'I appear, My Lord, in this matter,' he said, his voice clear and authoritative, 'with my junior, James Harrison, for Mrs O'Shea. I have to tell Your Lordship that my instructions are not to take any further part in these proceedings.'

His Lordship, who had been taking notes of the appearances in the large leather-bound ledger on his desk, looked up sharply.

'I was quite unaware of this, Sir Frank,' he said. 'This court was told that the matter would be fully contested and has set aside six days for that purpose.'

'I, also, was unaware of it,' interjected Clarke.

'I apologise to Your Lordship,' said Sir Frank, 'but my most recent instructions were only received this morning and they are, not to contest the matter in any way.'

'Very well, gentlemen,' said His Lordship dryly. 'Is there any appearance by counsel for Mr Parnell?'

With a sinking heart, I heard Lockwood say: 'No, My Lord, there will be no counsel to represent Mr Parnell.'

'Very well, Sir Frank,' said Butt. 'Now, Sir Edward, we should empanel the jury.'

The twelve men of the jury, who had been sitting in the jury-room next door, filed through and took their places. Normally, Lockwood would have moved on to his next brief, but he swivelled around to me.

'I think I'll watch this out,' he said. 'The brief fee has been earned and it's not often we can watch history unfold and be paid for the privilege.'

Clarke kept his opening speech short and went straight into evidence, calling O'Shea as the first witness. O'Shea took the oath and sat erect, looking like the cavalry officer he had once been.

'You are Captain William O'Shea?' asked Sir Edward. 'Until recently a Member of Parliament for Galway?'

'That is correct,' said O'Shea, in a clear, loud voice.

'And you are married to Mrs Katharine O'Shea?'

'That is correct.'

'And you were married to Mrs O'Shea in 1867, is that so?'

'Yes, it is.'

'So you have been married to Mrs O'Shea for twenty-three years, is that correct?'

'It is.'

'And you have had five children with her, is that correct?'

'Yes.'

I gasped with disbelief. O'Shea had claimed Clare and Katie as his own children. I leaned forward to Lockwood.

'That is a downright lie,' I whispered to him. 'Two of those children are Parnell's.'

Lockwood half-turned and shrugged his shoulders.

'What can we do?' He spoke in a low voice, behind his hand. 'It's out of our hands.'

Clarke continued with O'Shea.

'And you have enjoyed a full and loving relationship with your wife?' he asked.

'Until recently, yes.' O'Shea looked shifty and uneasy as he gave his answers, aware that I was listening to his every word.

His testimony went on for some hours and it was as complete a tissue of lies as I have ever heard. Lockwood would have exposed him as a liar, as certainly as Russell had exposed Pigott. But here, there would be no cross-examination, no exposure. O'Shea had the court to himself. He talked about his close personal friendship with Parnell; the services rendered by him during the Kilmainham treaty negotiations to obtain Parnell's release; the wonderful marriage he enjoyed with Katharine; their family life together; the fact that he kept an apartment in London, but that he went to Eltham every weekend to see his wife and his children. He was, however, forced to admit – because it had already been put in the pleadings – that he had once suspected an irregular association between Parnell and Katharine and had challenged Parnell to a duel.

'And what was the result of that challenge?' enquired Clarke knowingly.

'Oh, Mr Parnell apologised,' said O'Shea gruffly, 'and my wife explained to me that I had misunderstood certain appearances – improprieties, as they seemed to me.'

'And you accepted your wife's assurances?' asked Clarke.

'Of course,' said O'Shea brusquely.

'And did marital relations continue after this incident?' asked Clarke.

'We continued as before,' said O'Shea, without blushing. 'We resumed our full marital relations, as we had always done.'

My face felt hot with embarrassment as I listened to O'Shea, without a trace of emotion or embarrassment, giving evidence in court, to a room full of strangers and journalists, about the most intimate details of his marital relationship. I was glad that Parnell and Katharine were not in court to listen to this terrible invasion of their privacy. I did wonder if Parnell, inured by his experiences at the State trials and the Special Commission, had decided that Katharine's protection was now the most important consideration for him. Perhaps he had decided that if there was any damage to be suffered, it would be to him and to his political reputation, and not to her. The terrible brutality of the trial would have crushed Katharine's fragile sensibilities.

I had no doubt that O'Shea was lying about his ongoing relations with Katharine throughout the last decade. Perhaps I am naïve, a romantic fool, but seeing Katharine and Parnell as I did throughout all those years, I do not believe that she betrayed Parnell or that she was capable of such a sustained betrayal as O'Shea alleged. O'Shea, by contrast, was a ruined character: vain, arrogant, overly sure of his own mediocre abilities and as careless of the truth as he was of his marriage. But his evidence went unchallenged and was listened to with a mixture of disbelief and glee by the journalists in court.

Clarke had served subpoenas on servants from Eltham and Brighton and these were now called to give evidence.

The first of them, a scullery maid called Mary Kavanagh, was a slim, timid girl, with long brown hair tied back off her face. I knew her from my visits to Eltham.

'You are employed by Mrs O'Shea,' began Clarke.

'Yes, sir,' said Mary, looking nervously at him.

'And you are employed as a housemaid at Wonersh Lodge in Eltham, is that correct?'

'Yes, sir,' said Mary. It was evident she did not want to be in court, answering these questions.

'And how long did you work for Mrs O'Shea?'

'About four years,' she said.

'Starting when?' said Clarke kindly.

'In March 1886,' said Mary.

'And was Mrs O'Shea a kind mistress?'

It was an artful question, designed to put Mary completely at ease.

'Oh, she was so kind; she was one of the kindest women I ever met. She never had a cross word to say to me or to any of the girls,' she said to the jury.

'And did you know Captain O'Shea?' asked Clarke.

'Yes, sir,' said Mary. 'Captain O'Shea usually came to Eltham on Sunday to see the children.'

'And did he ever stay the night at the house?' asked Clarke.

'Very rarely,' said Mary.

'And do you know Mr Parnell?' asked Clarke.

'Oh, I certainly do.' Mary's face lit up. 'My mother's Irish, sir; she says prayers for Mr Parnell every night. He is a saint in her eyes.'

There was laughter in the courtroom.

'Quite,' said Clarke sarcastically. 'And did Mr Parnell ever stay at the house?'

'Very often,' said Mary.

'And where did he stay?' asked Clarke.

'How do you mean, sir?' asked Mary warily.

'I think you know what I mean,' said Clarke icily. 'Did he have his own bedroom?'

'Yes, yes, he did, sir,' said Mary.

'And were you responsible for cleaning his bedroom, Miss Kavanagh?' asked Clarke.

'I was, sir,' said Mary, 'and I did so every day.'

'And so, Miss Kavanagh' – Clarke's tone was gentle again – 'and I know this is difficult for you, but you have taken an oath before God to tell the truth.'

'And I am, sir,' said Mary, looking at him earnestly, as if she were terrified that somehow he might not believe her.

'I know you are,' said Clarke sympathetically, 'and so, when you cleaned Mr Parnell's bedroom, was the bed slept in?'

'No, sir,' said Mary, with her head down, 'rarely, sir. Sometimes if he were very tired or unwell, he would sleep there.'

'But not otherwise?' said Clarke.

'No, sir.'

There was a hush in the court as we awaited Clarke's next question.

'So, did he sleep in Mrs O'Shea's bedroom?' asked Clarke.

'He did, sir,' said Mary.

'And you cleaned Mrs O'Shea's bedroom too, I take it?' said Clarke.

'Yes, sir.' Mary's head was bowed, her evidence given neither to the judge nor to the jury but instead entirely to herself. It was forced out of her by the inexorable vicegrips of a court subpoena, an oath before God and the questions of counsel.

'And so, you made Mrs O'Shea's bed every morning?' said Clarke.

'Yes, sir.'

'And it was clear to you that Mr Parnell and Mrs O'Shea slept in the same bed?'

'Yes, sir.'

'Night after night?'

'Yes, sir.'

'After night?'

There was a deep hush in the court, as everyone held their breath during this exchange. The evidence was not challenged. It was the truth. To the outsider, the sordidness of the clandestine affair was now public knowledge.

'And did Captain O'Shea ever stay with Mrs O'Shea at Eltham?'

'Occasionally,' said Mary, lifting her head again, aware that the worst was over.

'And did he ever stay in Mrs O'Shea's bedroom?' asked Clarke.

'Not to my knowledge, sir,' said Mary. 'Captain O'Shea had his own room at Wonersh Lodge and he sometimes stayed in that room.'

'And you cleaned that bedroom too?' said Clarke.

'Yes, sir.'

Clarke paused for a moment, whilst he rummaged through some notes.

'On another matter, Miss Kavanagh,' he said, 'where did Mr Parnell keep his personal belongings, his clothes, that sort of thing?'

'Oh, in his own bedroom,' said Mary eagerly.

'Always?'

'Yes, always.'

'So there was no evidence of him living openly in Mrs O'Shea's bedroom.'

It was a statement, not a question and Mary did not answer it. She just kept her head down.

Clarke then called Caroline Pethers to the witness stand. Mrs Pethers was a stout woman, dressed in unseasonal finery and she walked to the witness box slowly and deliberately, conscious of the attention of the whole court, enjoying every moment of it.

'Can you tell the court your position, Mrs Pethers?' asked Clarke.

'I was the cook to Mrs O'Shea,' she said. 'When she resided at Medina Terrace in Brighton. My husband – God rest him, died last year – was also a manservant there.'

'Thank you, Mrs Pethers,' said Clarke. 'You were the cook, I believe, at Medina Terrace in Brighton from November 1883 to February 1884 – is that correct?'

'It is indeed, sir. Just for those three months,' she replied. 'What happened was that ...' She launched herself on her evidence.

Clarke, however, had no intention of letting his witness roam the paddocks freely in giving her evidence. He reined her in sharply.

'We'll come to that, Mrs Pethers,' he said.

'Sorry, My Lord.' She seemed contrite.

'Who rented the house, Mrs Pethers?' asked Clarke.

'Oh, Captain and Mrs O'Shea,' she said. 'I saw them both at the start and ...'

'And who interviewed you for the position?' interrupted Clarke.

'Mrs O'Shea,' answered Pethers, 'and she ...'

'And whilst you were there, did Mrs O'Shea live at Medina Terrace?'

'She did, My Lord, but not ...'

'And did Captain O'Shea live there with her?' interrupted Clarke.

'No, sir,' said Pethers. 'He came usually at weekends, but apart from that he was rarely there. I believe that he …'

'And whilst he was away,' cut in Clarke, giving the reins a good tug, 'did anyone else stay at the house?'

'Indeed they did, sir,' replied Mrs Pethers. 'A man called to the door, usually, some hours after Captain O'Shea had left. The Captain normally came on a Saturday and left on a Sunday,' she explained helpfully to the jury, 'and …'

'And what was his name?' asked Clarke, looking at the jury.

'Well, he told me his name was Mr Stewart' – she smiled at the jury, following Clarke's gaze – 'and he told me to introduce him to Mrs O'Shea as such. But I knew right away it was Mr Parnell.'

'And how did you know that?' asked Clarke.

'I knew him instantly from his photograph in the papers, didn't I?' she said. 'So of course I recognised him.' She smiled triumphantly at the jury.

'Did Mr Stewart look like this, Mrs Pethers?' asked Clarke and he gestured to his solicitor to hand a photograph of Parnell to the registrar to hand to the witness.

Mrs Pethers took the photograph and held it up to her eyes.

'That's him, all right. That's Mr Parnell,' she said.

'And do you say that he stayed in the house with Mrs O'Shea?' asked Clarke.

'Oh yes. Often,' she said. 'Once I …'

Clarke cut in again, giving the reins another tug.

'I believe you were there one afternoon when Mr Parnell was there and Mr O'Shea came home?' he asked.

'Oh, I do remember that,' she said, smiling. 'I …' – she looked over at Clarke, expecting him to cut her short, but this time Clarke did not interrupt her. The reins were released and the witness was free to roam.

'That was a trifle awkward,' said Mrs Pethers, looking at the jury and the judge, 'because it was a Friday, not a Saturday, raining it was too and Captain O'Shea arrived – unexpected like – at about nine o'clock in the evening. It was dark outside. My husband – God rest him – let him in and then he came up to tell me. He said, "Captain O'Shea has just arrived and Mr Parnell's still here." I said to him "What'll I do, Jimmy?" and he said to me to run upstairs to tell Mrs O'Shea. So, I don't mind telling you, I fairly flew upstairs to tell Mrs O'Shea. I got upstairs to her bedroom and knocked on the door.'

She stopped, uncertain as to why she had not been interrupted in her narrative.

'And what happened then?' coaxed Clarke, unnecessarily, I thought. Nothing would stop this witness now.

'Well, Mrs O'Shea was in there with Mr Parnell,' she said. 'Luckily, Mr Parnell wasn't downstairs. I shudder to think of what might have happened. I could hear them talking – low like – I couldn't hear what they were saying, but some time later Mrs O'Shea comes out – I waited at the door – and she says, "Tell Mr O'Shea I will be down directly." So I went down the stairs to my husband – God rest him – and said to him, "Jimmy, tell Mr O'Shea Mrs O'Shea will be down directly" – which he did, and I went downstairs too.'

'And Mrs O'Shea?' inquired Clarke solicitously.

'Oh, she came down directly,' said Pethers, 'as she said she would …'

'What happened then?' asked Clarke, as if he had no idea in the world.

'Well, there's the surprising thing,' said Mrs Pethers. 'There was a sudden knock on the front door about ten minutes later.'

Mrs Pethers swivelled around to look at the judge and the jury, to ensure she had their full attention.

'And who should appear but Mr Parnell at the front door.'

'Mr Parnell!' exclaimed Clarke, in mock surprise. 'I thought you said Mr Parnell was upstairs.'

'That's just it. He was,' said Mrs Pethers, bringing her story to a triumphant conclusion. 'But after he heard it was Captain O'Shea, he must have climbed down the fire escape at the back of the house and gone along the lane at the back, because he then appeared at the front door – without his winter coat, mind you – I remember that – because that was already in the cloakroom, but my husband let him in, so Captain O'Shea wouldn't have noticed that Mr Parnell didn't have his coat on.'

There had been sniggers of laughter from the journalists, but these now erupted into full-blown guffaws at the scene of domestic farce painted by Mrs Pethers.

'Silence,' the judge murmured. The crowd quietened down at once. No one wanted to be asked to leave.

Lockwood half-turned, and, leaning his elbow on the juniors' bench, whispered back to me.

'This is getting worse. He's being made to look ridiculous.'

Mrs Pethers' evidence – like O'Shea's – was not challenged, and it did indeed make Parnell look ridiculous. I could see the journalists taking down every word she uttered, making notes on every gesture and mannerism.

'And what happened then?' asked Clarke.

'Oh,' said Mrs Pethers, 'the Captain and Mrs O'Shea and Mr Parnell greeted each other as if they hadn't seen each other for some time. It was all perfectly normal and they even asked for some late supper.'

'Had dinner not been served already – I thought you said it was about nine o'clock?' said Clarke.

'Oh, it had,' said Mrs Pethers. 'I had cooked supper for Mrs O'Shea and Mr Parnell earlier like – some lamb chops, done just as Mr Parnell liked them – and he had eaten these, but Captain O'Shea had not eaten, so I was asked to prepare supper for him, which I did in no time.'

She looked at the jury, beaming at her accomplishment.

'And did Mr Parnell have supper again also?' asked Clarke, in mock astonishment, as if he were hearing all this for the first time.

'No, he didn't,' said Mrs Pethers. 'He said he had eaten something earlier in London and it hadn't agreed with him.'

She arched her eyebrows and looked to the jury.

'And him after tucking into the lovely lamb chops I'd cooked for him and downed the lot,' she said, clearly taking umbrage at Parnell's slight on her cooking.

'And what happened then?' asked Clarke.

'Oh, Mrs O'Shea said he must be tired after his journey and asked would he stay the night. Which he did.'

'Mr Parnell or Captain O'Shea?' asked Clarke, mystified by the answer.

'Oh, both,' she said. 'They both stayed.'

Clarke released his witness, to the accompaniment of great guffaws of laughter in the court and called his next witness to the stand.

'You are Mr George Porter?' intoned Clarke.

'That is correct, sir,' said Porter, efficiently and officiously. He spoke as if he had waited all his life to give absolutely precise details in a court of law. Had he another life, I believe he would have chosen to be a constable so he could have done this on a weekly basis, he was enjoying it so much.

'And you are an auctioneer in Deptford in Kent?'

'That is correct, sir.' The same answer, different intonation.

'And can you tell us how you come to give evidence here today?'

'I certainly can, sir,' said Porter. 'I came into my office one day – I have a small office in Deptford, My Lord – I have a larger one in London, sir, but this is more of a country office.' The exact commercial arrangements of Porter's estate agency business were perhaps peripheral to the trial, but he seemed oblivious to that.

Clarke nodded sympathetically.

'And my partner told me that a gentleman had called whilst I was out,' resumed Porter.

'Did he give a name, Mr Porter?' asked Clarke.

'He did, sir. Mr Fox, he said he was,' said Porter. 'I was sorry to miss him. But the message was that he would return the next day, so I made it my business to be there all the following day and, indeed, he came in about eleven o'clock.'

'Mr Fox?' enquired Clarke.

'Well, yes, sir,' replied Porter. 'My colleague pointed him out – as such – and I saw to it from then on.'

'What happened then?'

'He was interested in a particular house in Brockley – on Tressillion Road, so I took him to see it, sir.'

'And did he like it?' asked Clarke, leading the witness by the nose. He could do as he wished, with no counsel to oppose him.

'He did indeed,' said Porter, 'so I told him it belonged to a Mr Preston.'

'And what was his response?' enquired Clarke.

'Well, that's the strange thing, sir,' said Porter, 'because he said he was Mr Preston.'

'I see,' said Clarke, apparently mystified. 'So what did you say to that?'

'Well, I was very surprised, as you can imagine.' Porter, with his eyebrows raised, did indeed sound and look surprised – even now, months after the event. 'So I said to him, 'But I thought your name was Mr Fox?'

'And what he did say to that?' asked Clarke.

'He looked at me directly but said that, no, I was mistaken, his name was Clement Preston, but that he was staying with a friend of his called Fox.'

'And how did you respond?'

'I let it go, sir,' said Porter. 'I put it down as a slight misunderstanding.'

'And do you know now who that gentleman is?' asked Clarke.

'I do indeed, sir,' said Porter triumphantly, 'because I saw his photograph in the paper not two weeks later. It was Mr Parnell.'

'The respondent to these proceedings?' asked Clarke.

'The very same,' said Porter.

'And not Mr Preston?' asked Clarke.

'No, sir, nor Mr Fox,' – Porter anticipated the next question – 'because I showed the photograph to my partner and he said that was Mr Fox, but I knew it was Mr Clement Preston. I mean Mr Parnell, My Lord, if you understand me.'

There was laughter again in court, but it died down as the judge raised his head.

'And the initials of Clement Preston?' enquired Clarke, for the benefit of any juror who might have missed it.

'C.P.,' said Porter, with emphasis. 'Charles Parnell. Oh, it was him all right, no doubt about it.'

'And why do you think he wanted to use a false name?' asked Clarke.

It was a question which demanded a counsel's objection as being speculative, but there was no objection and the judge let the question go.

'Oh, I would have thought it was obvious, sir,' said Porter. 'He came back some weeks later to collect the keys and there was a woman with him. She stayed in the carriage.'

'Did you see her?' asked Clarke.

'No, sir,' said Porter. 'She didn't step down from the carriage so I didn't see her face.'

'So you are not in a position to tell this court whether it was Mrs O'Shea or not?'

'I am afraid I'm not, sir,' said Porter.

'Thank you, Mr Porter,' said Clarke and Porter stepped down from the witness box.

The next witness was Anna Steele – Katharine's sister.

'Your name is Mrs Anna Steele?' said Clarke.

'That is correct.'

'You are related to Mrs Katharine O'Shea?'

'I am her sister,' said Mrs Steele, without any evident warmth at the association.

'Indeed,' said Clarke, 'and clearly you also know Captain O'Shea.'

'Clearly.' Mrs Steele had an evident distaste not only for the question and for the proceedings in general, but also, it appeared, for Captain O'Shea.

'You are familiar, then, with the case being brought by Captain O'Shea against his wife?'

'I am.'

'And I don't need you to comment on it, Mrs Steele, in any way,' reassured Clarke, 'but you are also aware that Mrs O'Shea has brought a counterclaim against her husband?'

'I am,' said Mrs Steele.

'And I know this is difficult for you, Mrs Steele, but I am afraid I have to put this to you. You are aware that in that counterclaim Mrs O'Shea has claimed Captain O'Shea had an adulterous liaison with you, Mrs Steele?'

There were gasps of astonishment in the courtroom. The journalists and jury had not been aware of these allegations before. Clarke waited for the crowd to settle down before continuing his questioning.

'I am aware of that allegation,' said Mrs Steele, her mouth tightening in creases of agitation.

'Can you tell the court whether this allegation is true or false?' said Clarke.

'It is totally false,' said Mrs Steele, free to give full expression to her long-suppressed anger. 'It is an evil, malicious lie. I have no idea how she could have formed such a warped idea. I don't even particularly like Captain O'Shea,' she added, as though that detail would put the matter beyond doubt.

'Could you suggest any reason why Mrs O'Shea could have made such an allegation, Mrs Steele?' asked Clarke.

'No, I can't,' said Mrs Steele. 'The only thing I can think is that one evening many years ago, Captain O'Shea discovered Mr Parnell staying at Wonersh Lodge without his knowledge and he came over to my house late at night, in some distress, to talk about it.'

'And what did you say to him?'

'I merely listened.'

'When was this?' asked Clarke.

'July 1881,' said Mrs Steele quickly.

'Was this around the time that Captain O'Shea challenged Mr Parnell to a duel?'

'Yes, it was,' said Mrs Steele, 'and I had to try to talk him out of it.'

'And did that incident affect your relationship with Mrs O'Shea?' said Clarke.

'Of course,' said Mrs Steele. 'Mrs O'Shea was suspicious of why Captain O'Shea had gone to my house and she was angry that I now knew of her liaison with Mr Parnell.'

'Why was she angry about that?' asked Clarke, affecting surprise.

'Because I told her it was wrong and that it would bring scandal on all the family,' said Mrs Steele, 'which it has.'

There were no further questions, and Mrs Steele left the witness box. I rubbed my face with my hands, scarcely believing the nightmare I was witnessing. If Katharine really believed Mrs Steele had had such a liaison with O'Shea, she should have come to give evidence. If not, she should have withdrawn the allegation. She did neither and, instead, allowed the allegations be made and refuted. Now it looked as if there were no measures she would not take to protect her own reputation and destroy that of others, including her own sister.

✎✎✎

More and more damning evidence of the sordid details of Parnell's private life was relayed to the gawping journalists by each successive witness. As the evidence for the day drew to a close, the judge rose and the journalists streamed out of the courtroom. I stayed behind to discuss the case with Lockwood.

'A bad day's work, Harrison,' he said.

'Devastating,' I said.

We walked out of the court and down the long, polished corridor, past groups of journalists, laughing among themselves, recounting the day's evidence.

'Should he have come today?' I asked Lockwood, as we got back to the robing-room.

'Yes – if he wanted to fight the case,' said Lockwood, 'but he clearly did not. Strange fellow, Parnell. Never met anyone like him. I can understand how he fell for Mrs O'Shea, though. She is charming.'

I passed no comment on that, but gloomily removed my collar and tabs.

'I'm going to Brighton now to see them,' I said. 'I don't quite know what to tell them.'

Lockwood looked at me in the mirror as he fixed his collar and necktie.

'Don't say too much in front of Mrs O'Shea,' he said, 'and make sure she doesn't see the papers tomorrow or Monday.'

I looked at him in surprise.

'Why do you say that?'

'Tell *him* everything in detail,' continued Lockwood, 'witness by witness. He will need to know the details to decide his response. But I think he didn't fight it today because he wanted to protect her from the …' – he paused to find the right words – 'the savagery of this place. The Divorce Court is no place for a lady like Mrs O'Shea. What a tragedy for her that she married a reprobate like O'Shea. No honour at all. Fellow should be horsewhipped.'

He put on his coat and gloves.

'Well, good evening, Harrison. I will see you on Monday.'

'Will you be here?' I asked.

'Yes, I think I will. Professional curiosity.' He nodded and walked off.

Fifty-Four

Hounds Unleashed

I PUT ON my own collar and necktie, grabbed my coat and walked quickly out of the Law Courts. It was a cold November afternoon, almost dark by this time and the Strand was crowded with people and horses and carriages. After the stuffiness of court, I welcomed the cold, bracing air and walked to the station to catch the train.

All the way down to Brighton, I pondered Lockwood's words. If Parnell had refused to fight so as to protect Katharine, then he had surely sacrificed his name, his reputation and his position for her. I shuddered at the thought of what the papers would write on Monday and after the Pigott forgeries, *The Times*, in particular, would have no mercy.

When I got to Walsingham Terrace, I climbed the seven or eight granite steps and knocked on the front door, with some dread. The housemaid showed me into the drawing-room, where Parnell and Katharine, Clare and Katie were sitting around the fireplace. Parnell and Katharine both stood up to greet me and the girls welcomed their 'Uncle James'.

'Is it over?' asked Katharine, after she had ushered the children out of the room. She looked pale and worried. 'Is it over?'

'I'm afraid not, Katharine,' I said, as softly as I could. 'The worst is over, I would say, but the case is not finished yet.'

She stifled a sob.

'But it will be finished on Monday,' I said, trying to be cheerful. 'I think all the evidence is in, so Clarke will make his closing speech, the judge will give his direction to the jury and the jury will decide. So the worst is definitely over.'

'And Willie,' she said. 'What did he say?'

'A tissue of lies, Katharine,' I said. 'He doesn't know the truth from lies any more.'

'And Anna?' she said.

'I think she was angry with you,' I said

'You must be hungry,' intervened Parnell. 'We waited for you for dinner.'

We talked of nothing else over dinner. I tried to give as complete a picture as I could of all the witnesses – without recounting the more humiliating details of their evidence. Even if Lockwood had not warned me, I doubt if I could have brought myself to recount the evidence of the intimate details which had been so cruelly exposed to the world that afternoon.

After dinner, Katharine excused herself and retired. Parnell and I went back into the drawing-room.

'There's more, isn't there?' he said.

I nodded.

'You might need a brandy,' I said.

'That's a good idea.' He stood up and went over to the cabinet. 'Sounds like you might, too.'

'A large one,' I replied.

'Cigarette?' he asked. He had recently taken to smoking cigarettes rather than cigars. He opened a rosewood box, with his name engraved in silver on the top, which I admired.

'Katharine gave it to me as a gift last month,' he said proudly, 'to celebrate our tenth anniversary.'

'Ten years?' I was amazed.

'Yes, October 1880,' said Parnell. 'You remember, I missed Roscommon.'

'Yes, I do.' I started to laugh. 'So that's where you were.'

He smiled also, and suddenly – incongruously – to relieve the unbearable tension of the day, we both began to laugh at the memories of that week so long ago.

'You shaved your beard off,' I said.

'I was afraid someone might recognise me,' said Parnell. 'I needed a disguise.'

'Well, it was effective,' I said.

'I realised that when you didn't recognise me,' said Parnell.

Over brandies, I recounted to him the dreadful business of the day, witness by witness, the whole gory mess. He listened carefully throughout, staring into the fire.

'I was right not to put Katharine through such an ordeal.'

'Lockwood thought that's why you didn't contest it,' I said.

'Why would I contest it?' said Parnell. 'I've wanted her to divorce O'Shea for years, but she wanted to wait until her Aunt Ben died. So we waited.'

'There might have been less of a scandal ten years ago,' I said.

'Maybe, maybe not,' said Parnell. 'I was still leader of the Party.'

'Yes,' I mused, 'there really was no good time in the last ten years.'

'But after Kilmainham, after Sophie died, I made a decision that I would never leave Katharine again and I never shall,' said Parnell.

'The papers will be terrible,' I said, after a moment. 'Lockwood said not to let Katharine read them.'

'I told her the same,' said Parnell. 'I don't think she wants to read them, anyway.'

'So O'Shea will get his divorce, whilst destroying you in the process.'

'Yes,' said Parnell, 'I am afraid so. Helped, no doubt, by Chamberlain.'

'Chamberlain?' I was surprised to hear his name.

'Chamberlain is behind it,' said Parnell. 'I'm sure of it. Who else has the means to pay O'Shea's lawyers' – Parnell extended one finger in the air – 'and has a motive for destroying me?' He extended his second finger.

'Charles, there is no shortage of people who want to destroy you,' I said.

'And who has access to O'Shea's secrets?' A third finger extended. 'And who is friendly with O'Shea?' A fourth finger extended.

'But why would Chamberlain want to destroy you?' I asked.

Parnell looked at me as if that question barely merited a reply.

'If I fall, then Gladstone will also fall. If that happens, then Home Rule will fall. Chamberlain will become leader and push through his central board scheme. He destroyed our Home Rule bill because he thought it would destroy Gladstone – not because he's opposed to Home Rule. Now, to destroy Gladstone, he is trying to destroy me.'

'And you think Chamberlain hates you as much as that?' I asked.

'I don't think he hates me at all,' said Parnell. 'I'm an obstacle to him – just like Gladstone.'

'But why now?' I asked. 'Just after your victory with *The Times*. I would not have thought this was a good time.'

'It is the perfect time,' said Parnell. 'It's at least another year to the election. It will be a lot easier for Chamberlain to force Gladstone out whilst he's in opposition than if he were Prime Minister.'

I exhaled a long sigh, thinking of the unseen forces which lay behind these events. The relentless ambition of lesser men to overthrow greater men; the inexorable law of the jungle which is political life.

'What will you do now?' I asked.

'I don't know yet,' said Parnell. 'We have spoken about going away. Switzerland, maybe, or France.'

'What, leaving England altogether?' I exclaimed. 'Retire! What about Home Rule?'

'It depends on what happens,' said Parnell pensively. 'I have given Ireland everything I have to give, but my private life will never belong to her. It belongs to me and to Katharine. All I have done is love her and if this is what results, then I will go somewhere where we can live in peace. They will not have me, body and soul. They will not.'

'There will be a terrible outcry in Ireland when the newspapers are out,' I said.

'I know,' he said, 'there will be howls. The howls of hypocrites.' He paused for a moment. 'Well, perhaps not all of them are hypocrites. Maybe some of them do actually believe their puny creeds can govern their lives. Maybe that is right for them ...'

He looked into the fire.

'They are like children, looking to the Church for rules. But it is not right for me. I will decide such matters for myself. I would rather appear to be dishonourable than to be dishonourable.'

His voice grew increasingly cold and harsh.

'I have told these children what they want and they clamour for it. If they will let me, I will get it for them.'

He looked over at me.

'But the Irish are addicted to defeat,' he said balefully. 'They are so accustomed to losing, they have no hope that someday they might win. For them, the struggle is everything. They never consider victory. They never think how to achieve it. I do. All the time.'

He paused for a moment.

'And if they turn away from me, it doesn't matter at all in the end. What the government of Ireland will be is settled. It will be so. And what my share in the work has been, and is to be, is also settled.'

I did not respond and we lapsed into one of those silences which were common and comfortable between us.

The following afternoon, I left Brighton to return to London and on Monday I returned to court for the conclusion of the trial.

More evidence was given on the day. More tawdry, embarrassing evidence of Parnell's and Katharine's daily lives together, now viewed through the prism of a hostile courtroom.

Clarke was scathing in his closing speech.

'We know quite well why Mr Parnell has not been here these last two days,' he said. 'It is because he is afraid of perjuring himself. He knows very well these allegations are true, so he will not come in here and lie on oath. He could be jailed for perjury and Mr Parnell has had his fill of gaols. He does not want to add a criminal offence to those offences of adultery and falsehood which he has committed over the last number of years, betraying a good friend.'

It was hard to listen to Parnell being so publicly humiliated.

In the early afternoon, the judge commenced his summing up and his direction to the jury, but before he started, the foreman of the jury put up his hand to speak.

'Yes, sir,' said Judge Butt, 'have you a question?'

'I have, Your Honour,' said the foreman.

'And what is that question?' said Mr Justice Butt.

'We are puzzled by some of Captain O'Shea's evidence,' said the foreman.

A low murmur could be heard in the courtroom, as the journalists exchanged comments among themselves.

'Would you like Captain O'Shea to be recalled?' asked Judge Butt.

'We would, Your Honour,' said the foreman. 'We discussed the matter over lunch in the jury-room and that is our unanimous wish.'

'Very well,' said the judge and then, turning to Clarke, he said: 'Mr Clarke, you heard what the jury have said. Have you any difficulty in recalling Captain O'Shea?'

'None whatsoever, My Lord,' said Clarke unctuously and he turned back to O'Shea and nodded to him to return to the witness box.

O'Shea took a seat once more. The judge leaned over to him.

'Captain O'Shea,' he said, 'I need not remind you that you are still under oath. Is that clear?'

O'Shea nodded solemnly.

'You may proceed,' said His Lordship to the jury foreman, who had remained standing.

'Thank you, My Lord.' He bowed. Then, turning to Captain O'Shea, he asked: 'Captain O'Shea, you said that you had been living on perfectly normal terms with your wife?'

'Yes, that is correct,' said O'Shea.

'But you were living separately from her in London for many years?'

'That's true, but I needed to live in London because of my parliamentary duties.'

'But you said in your evidence that you started living in London in 1878.'

'That is correct.'

'But you were only elected as a Member of Parliament in 1880.'

O'Shea shifted uneasily in his seat.

'That is true. But before I was elected to Parliament, I had business interests in London.'

'But I thought you said these business interests were in Madrid?' the foreman pressed.

'Madrid ... and London,' said O'Shea hesitantly.

'And how often, during those ten years, did Mrs O'Shea stay with you at your apartments in London?'

'I usually stayed with her at Eltham,' countered O'Shea.

'So she never stayed with you at your apartments?'

'Not very often,' admitted O'Shea.

'How often?' the foreman persisted.

'I can't really say,' said O'Shea.

'Ever?' persisted the foreman.

'I can't really remember,' O'Shea lied.

'And the children, did they ever stay with you in London?' asked the foreman.

'No,' said O'Shea, 'but they often came to see me in Albert Mansions if they could, if they were in London for the day.'

'You see, Captain O'Shea,' – the foreman scratched his face in puzzlement – 'what troubles us in the jury when we are discussing the case is that Mrs O'Shea says that you neglected her …'

'That's not true!' cried O'Shea.

'And that you knew about her liaison with Mr Parnell and that you connived at it.'

'That's not true,' repeated O'Shea.

'Well, if it's not true,' asked the foreman, in a disbelieving voice, 'why did you challenge Mr Parnell to a duel, unless you knew he was betraying you with your wife?'

'I thought he was,' said O'Shea, 'but I was wrong.'

'But how did you come to think he was?' The foreman's persistence was admirable and I watched as O'Shea tried to squirm out of his uncomfortable position.

'I had heard that he had stayed at Eltham on a number of occasions without my knowledge.'

'Who told you that?'

'The children,' said O'Shea. 'Gerard, my eldest boy. And I asked some of the maids and they told me so too.'

'So why, then, did you withdraw from the duel?'

'I didn't withdraw,' said O'Shea angrily – conscious now that the newspapers might seek to portray him as a coward. 'It was explained to me that I had made too much of it … I was assured by my wife that there was nothing to worry about.'

The foreman scratched his head dubiously and then looked around at the other jury members to see if they had any other questions. They shook their heads.

'Thank you, Your Honour,' he said and sat down.

The judge dismissed O'Shea and then turned to the jury, in a stern manner.

'Now, members of the jury,' he said, 'you have heard the evidence. All the evidence. Captain O'Shea has brought this case against his wife. He has alleged that she committed adultery and he has named the man with whom she was, and still is, in an adulterous relationship, as Mr Charles Stewart Parnell. Captain O'Shea has given detailed evidence of this adultery, as have numerous other witnesses, with specific details of places and dates. It is of no consequence that Captain O'Shea cannot give evidence as to when he believed the affair started ... That is of no relevance.'

The judge looked down at the notes which he had written. He turned one or two pages and then addressed the jury again.

'Now, I must emphasise to you,' he resumed, 'that all the evidence which has been given by Captain O'Shea and his witnesses is uncontroverted ... that is to say, there is no evidence given to the contrary by either Mrs O'Shea or Mr Parnell. So you must take it to be true.'

He paused and looked at the rows of jurymen.

'Moreover, Mrs O'Shea has seen fit to give no evidence – whatsoever – about her allegations against her husband and so you must consider *her* allegations in her pleadings to be entirely without foundation and untrue. Likewise, Mr Parnell, for his own good reasons, has also seen fit not to challenge the evidence of Captain O'Shea and that also – Mr Clarke urges upon me, and I now urge upon you – demonstrates the truth of Captain O'Shea's evidence ...'

He looked at the jurymen directly and deliberately.

'So, whatever doubts you may entertain about Captain O'Shea's evidence, there are no grounds for those doubts. So perhaps I could now ask you to retire and consider your verdict.'

The jury rose solemnly and were led out of the court. The judge rose and returned to his chambers behind the courtroom. The newspaper reporters went out into the corridor, talking noisily among themselves.

I leaned over the bench to have a word with Lockwood.

'What do you think?' I asked.

'The jury have to come back for O'Shea,' he said, 'but he's lying through his teeth.'

'You think so too?' I asked.

'Of course,' said Lockwood airily. 'I'm only sorry I didn't get a chance to cross-examine him.'

'You think you could have broken him down?' I asked.

Lockwood looked at me with an eyebrow raised, as if wondering how I had the temerity to doubt him.

'I should think so. I'm not sure I could get him to blow his brains out – like Russell did to Pigott.' He chuckled at the comparison. 'I gather that was quite a cross-examination.'

'It certainly was,' I said.

'You've been in two of the great trials of the decade, Harrison,' said Lockwood. 'Talk about beginner's luck! They will make your reputation.'

Within an hour, the jury were back and the reporters shuffled back noisily into the courtroom.

'Have you a verdict?' asked the judge, when they had all resumed their seats.

The foreman rose. 'We have, Your Honour.'

'What is that verdict?' asked the judge.

The foreman of the jury read from a note in front of him.

'We find the allegations of adultery proven, Your Honour.'

Many in the court gasped at the simple, damning finality of the verdict. Some members of the press dashed for the door and the early editions.

'Thank you, members of the jury,' said the judge. He turned to Clarke.

'I assume I should make the usual Order, Mr Clarke.'

'Yes indeed, My Lord.' Clarke leapt to his feet. 'An Order of Divorce Nisi in favour of the applicant Captain O'Shea against his wife.'

'Very well,' said the judge.

'And I would also apply for my costs,' said Clarke.

'You're entitled to your costs,' said Judge Butt. 'Very well then. The court will rise,' and, so saying, he stood and bowed to the court and returned to his chambers.

Lockwood looked back at me and shrugged.

'There will be all hell to pay for this in Ireland,' I said.

'Not only in Ireland, I should imagine,' Lockwood replied.

I waited behind until the registrar had drawn up the court order and I took it away with me. That evening, I again took the train to Brighton, to tell Parnell and Katharine the news in person.

'It's all over, Katharine,' I said. I reached into my briefcase and handed her the divorce decree.

She read it over, and I thought she would have burst into tears, had not Parnell taken it gently out of her hands to read it himself.

'We shall have this framed tomorrow and put on the wall,' he said, in high spirits.

Katharine began to laugh at his exuberance.

'Now that I have been set free, you might decide you want to marry someone else,' she teased.

He turned to her and drew her close to him.

'Don't say such terrible things,' he said, 'not even in jest.'

He went over to the cabinet and took out three crystal glasses and a bottle of champagne.

'I've had this in readiness,' he said, 'for quite some time.'

He popped the cork and poured champagne for each of us.

'To my darling wife,' he said, raising his glass to her.

'To my darling King,' she responded.

The newspapers seemed to cover nothing else that week. *The Times*, desperate to avenge itself on Parnell, had sent no less than three journalists to report every shred of evidence in the proceedings. Column after column went out in every newspaper, every day that week. The most devastating intimacies and deceits of Parnell's private life were laid bare, before the whole world. Hearing them in court was difficult but, somehow, seeing the details in cold, hostile newsprint made them seem more sordid, more deceitful, more shocking. I read the papers with a mounting sense of unease. Just as not a word had been said in his defence at the trial, so not a word in his defence was printed in the newspapers.

The jury verdict had been given and the court had pronounced its judgment. Parnell was guilty of adultery and there were few greater sins in the England of the day. This meant, in the eyes of right-thinking members of society, that he was a man of immoral character. Such a man had no reputation to defend. And if he had no reputation to defend, he could not be libelled by the newspapers. They could write what they liked about him, without any fear of a libel trial. And so the pent-up fury of fourteen years of British anger was unleashed against him, and it spewed forth in wave after wave after wave of bile, day after day after day, in newspapers and journals. It was the most sensational story of the year. It was shocking, shocking, shocking.

Fifty-Five

A Vote of Confidence

THE IRISH NEWSPAPERS also printed the stories in excruciating detail but, for the moment, declined to moralise,
holding their breath to see how the country would respond.
By coincidence, a public meeting had been arranged at Leinster Hall
in Dublin, for Thursday just two days after the divorce trial had
ended. This would be the barometer.

Parnell asked me to attend and so I caught the night sailing on
Wednesday evening and arrived into Dublin early on Thursday
morning – a miserable, wet, dark and dreary November morning.
I went straight to my home to sleep for a few hours and after lunch
met Justin McCarthy, Sexton and others. They were in a state of
despair. They had, of course, all known of Parnell's connection
with Katharine for years; it had been an open secret. But it was one
thing to know of a secret affair; it was quite another to read the
grossest details in the newspapers. Moreover, many Irish Members
of Parliament were Catholic. They did not have Parnell's lofty
disregard for moral conventions.

Healy, the arch-Catholic, would, I thought, be especially critical
of Parnell. This was now his great opportunity. However, he was
laid low with typhus and so, we thought, would be unable to attend
the meeting.

McCarthy, Sexton and I called to Healy's house on our way to
the meeting to see what message he wished us to pass on. To our
surprise, we found him up, dressed and waiting. He was coming
with us.

His skin was waxen; he had lost a lot of weight and seemed
nothing but skin and bone.

'Ah, Harrison,' he rasped. 'You were in the court for the full hearing, I believe.'

I nodded.

'Was it as bad in court as it seems in the papers?' he asked.

'Nothing you hear in court seems quite as bad as when you read it the next day,' I said.

He understood all too well.

'How is Parnell?' he asked.

'Bearing up,' I said, 'considering ...'

'Considering the abuse being heaped on him by those English rags,' snapped Healy. 'I've been reading them in bed for the last two days. It makes my blood boil. The English have been waiting to do him down for years and he's given them the perfect opportunity.'

I was surprised by this support from an unexpected quarter. Indeed, Healy was determined not only to come to the meeting, but also to speak out early, lest he should feel unwell later in the evening.

By the time we arrived, a great crowd had already assembled in the Leinster Hall and I counted over twenty members of the parliamentary party on the platform.

Justin McCarthy spoke first, as vice-chairman of the Party.

'We must let Mr Parnell know,' he said, to great cheers from the crowds, 'that he possesses the full confidence of the Irish nation and we are not going to change our leader just because there is a great cry against him.'

He paused, measuring his words.

'It may well be,' he continued, 'that Mr Parnell did not contest this divorce for reasons of chivalry and gentlemanly conduct, and if so, we should respect that decision. I dare say if O'Shea had been cross-examined, like Pigott, we might have got a very different story.'

'With the same ending,' shouted a voice from the crowd.

'Are we going to change the greatest Irish leader since Daniel O'Connell,' shouted McCarthy, 'just because some Liberal newspapers say we must?'

There were huge shouts of 'No, no!' and 'God save Parnell!'

Healy rose to speak. His voice was weak at first, but soon gained strength from his moral fervour and his anger.

'My friends, we know that for Irishmen everywhere, Mr Parnell is not just a man ... he is an institution.'

Great cheers and laughter greeted this opening line.

'And if he resigns his seat in Cork tomorrow, he will be instantly re-elected the following day. But I support Mr Parnell, not only for his sake but for Ireland's. I remember – not even ten years ago – when Ireland stood ragged and distressed, begging at the Gate of Nations, when Irish members used the House of Commons as an auction mart to barter their constituencies for a position in Government and I will never forget who it was who changed all that.'

He stopped and leaned on the table, breathing laboriously, before gathering his strength for one last shout of loyalty.

'And I will say this. At a time of crisis and storms, I say, like sailors everywhere in a storm, do not disturb the man at the wheel.'

There was a tremendous roar of support for Healy at these words and he slumped back onto his seat.

But behind that public façade of support, there were other forces at work. I sensed an air of disquiet at the meeting and afterwards, when we were back at Morrison's, having a drink, McCarthy pulled me over to an alcove in the foyer.

'Harrison,' he said quietly, 'I have been speaking to a number of our friends. They all say the same thing: Parnell should step down as leader – if only for a few months – and when all this has blown over, he can be re-elected.'

I was not in the least surprised. It was what I had expected and what I had come to Dublin to hear. I had wondered if there was a Brutus or Cassius in the Party. Healy might be a Cassius, but I was surprised by his support. The mild-mannered McCarthy could never be a Brutus but he was carrying a message.

'Do you mean that he should resign the leadership, or also resign his seat?' I had taken on the character of a negotiator.

'Well, the greater the contrition, the better,' said McCarthy, 'even if it is only apparent contrition.'

'Do you think he should resign his seat?' I persisted.

'Yes, I do,' said McCarthy, 'but he should immediately seek re-election. In that way, the gesture will have been made.'

'And the leadership?' I asked.

'He should also resign that for a year or so,' said McCarthy, 'and when this is all over, he will be re-elected. After all, it's not as if he's in the Commons every day. And he has time. The election is at least another year away.'

'Which is it, McCarthy, for a few months, or for a year or so?' I asked. 'You must be clear.'

'Well, for a few months, perhaps up to a year,' replied McCarthy hesitatingly. 'It depends on the situation.'

I had no doubt that McCarthy's views were genuine and widely shared. I also thought they were correct. Some gesture had to be made by Parnell. He might even welcome the opportunity to lay down the burden for a number of years.

'I shall tell him,' I said to McCarthy, 'and I shall let you know his view. When are you returning to London?'

'I shall be travelling on Sunday,' replied McCarthy.

'Well, then, I shall meet you in the House of Commons on Monday morning.'

I returned to London on Friday, and went directly to Brighton to tell Parnell what had happened. He had read the reports in the *Freeman's Journal* of the meeting and he was encouraged by the vote of confidence. I told him of McCarthy's suggestion – which I said represented the views of many members – that he should resign.

'I shall not resign – not even for a single day,' he said. 'If I did that, I would never return.'

He looked at me directly.

'You understand that, don't you?' he said.

'I'm not sure I do, Charles,' I said hesitantly.

'If I were to resign, it would mean that I accept that I have done something wrong – which I have not. The O'Sheas' marriage was ended long before I ...' He left the sentence unfinished.

'I know that, Charles,' I said, 'but it had not ended in the eyes of the law.'

'I shall not resign,' he said quietly, 'not for a single day. I shall fight it out and if I am beaten, then so be it. The Irish can get Home Rule without me.'

I rubbed my face with my hands. I could sense the storm gathering.

On Monday morning, I met Parnell at the Westminster Hotel at eleven o'clock and walked with him over to the House of Commons. I had rarely seen him in such good humour. The burden of his terrible secret must have worn heavily on his spirits for many years; now that it was in the open, the worst had been written, and he was, if not elated, certainly ebullient. As we walked through the lobbies, he actually greeted people he knew – unlike former times, when he would have kept his head bowed and walked straight through to the Chamber.

Just before we went into the meeting, McCarthy asked for a quiet word with Parnell and me.

'Parnell,' McCarthy said, 'I met with Gladstone yesterday.'

Parnell was surprised.

'How did that happen?' he asked.

'He wrote to me,' said McCarthy. 'He asked me to meet him in Carlton Gardens.'

'And?' Parnell asked quizzically.

'He wanted me to pass a message to you, that he thought it would be difficult now for the Liberals to win the next election,' said McCarthy, 'and that he wondered, at his age, whether he might still be here to fight the next one.'

Parnell smiled. 'Gladstone will live to be a hundred years old,' he said. 'I thought he might have sent you a message that he expected me to resign.'

'Oh, he was quite careful not to express any view on that,' said McCarthy. 'He said it was entirely a matter for the Irish party.'

Parnell nodded and we joined the throng of Irish members who filled Committee Room 15. As Parnell walked in, he was greeted with loud cheers of support and many sought to shake his hand as he made his way to the chair.

Sexton stood immediately and proposed Parnell's re-election as leader of the Party. It was voted on immediately, unanimously and amidst great applause.

Parnell responded, saying that in a few months time, when the real truth came out, he would be shown to have done no wrong. He sought to draw parallels between *The Times*' articles and his later vindication in the Special Commission. It was, it seemed to me, a blatant confidence trick. There were no parallels. There was no appeal pending in the divorce case and there would be no second hearing at which he would be vindicated – but no one wished to press him. Finally, Parnell said a few final words of thanks, drew the meeting to a close and, as was his custom, stood up from his chair and quickly left the room. I remained behind, to talk to some friends whom I had not seen for some months, but I soon became aware of hushed voices and a certain unease in the room. It was evident in the downcast faces and low tones of my colleagues.

I went over to Justin McCarthy, who looked at me with a frown.

'You did tell Parnell what I said to you in Dublin?' he asked.

'To the last word,' I said, 'and that I thought you were speaking for quite a number of members.'

'And what was his response?' asked McCarthy.

'He refused to countenance it,' I said. 'He said he wouldn't resign for a single day, that it would be an admission of wrongdoing on his part which would be unacceptable to him.'

McCarthy was silent.

Sexton came over to join us.

'Well, that was a surprise,' he said to me.

'In what way?' I asked, puzzled.

'We all thought he was going to resign,' said Sexton. 'I thought that was the whole idea of the meeting, that we would unanimously vote our confidence in him, to show our unity, and that he would then resign, for a short time, for the good of the Party and for the good of the cause.'

'Well, no one told him that,' I said, 'or me, for that matter.'

I looked over at McCarthy.

'No,' he said hesitantly, 'I didn't put it in those terms. I didn't think I needed to. I just assumed Parnell would realise he had to resign – if only for a short period. His position is untenable, and so now is ours!'

He looked down gloomily at the floor.

I quickly realised that McCarthy's and Sexton's views were those of the majority. Most members had, indeed, expected Parnell to resign at the meeting.

Fifty-Six

The Gladstone Letter

FTER A SHORT time, McCarthy and I left the room to look for Parnell. We did not have far to go. We saw him at the end of the corridor, deep in conversation with John Morley, a close associate of Gladstone's. As we approached, Parnell beckoned us to join them.

Morley nodded to us as we joined him. He was a man of slight build, with sharp features and a cold look.

'I was just telling Parnell ...' Morley began.

'Apparently there's a letter from Gladstone,' Parnell cut in, 'which Morley was supposed to show me before the meeting.'

'I wasn't able to find you,' stammered Morley.

'You knew perfectly well I would be at the Party meeting,' said Parnell sharply.

'What does the letter say?' I asked.

Parnell handed it to me and I opened it. McCarthy stood by my shoulder, so we could read it together.

Having regard to its devastating consequences, I think it is of some importance to set out much of its contents.

My dear Morley,
While clinging to the hope of communication from Mr Parnell, to whomsoever addressed, I thought it necessary, viewing the arrangements for the commencement of the session tomorrow, to acquaint Mr McCarthy with the conclusion at which, after using all the means of observation and reflection in my power, I have myself arrived. It was that, notwithstanding the splendid services rendered by Mr Parnell to his country, his continuance at the present moment in

the leadership would be productive of consequences disastrous in the highest degree to the cause of Ireland. I think I may be warranted in asking you so far to expand the conclusion I have given above as to add that the continuance I speak of would not only place many hearty and effective friends of the Irish cause in a position of great embarrassment, but would render my retention of the leadership of the Liberal party, based as it has been mainly upon the contribution to the Irish cause, almost a nullity. This expansion of my views I begged Mr McCarthy to regard as confidential and not intended for his colleagues generally if he found that Mr Parnell contemplated spontaneous action. But I also begged that he would make known to the Irish party, at their meeting tomorrow afternoon, that such was my conclusion, if he should find that Mr Parnell had not in contemplation any step of the nature indicated.

Believe me sincerely yours,
W.E. Gladstone.

I read through the letter with increasing dismay. It was an ultimatum. If Parnell remained as leader, Gladstone would resign. If Parnell resigned, then Gladstone would remain and there would still be a chance for Home Rule. I looked at McCarthy, who was stroking his beard pensively.

'This is much, much stronger than what Mr Gladstone said to me directly,' said McCarthy.

'Tell me again,' said Parnell, 'exactly what he said to you.'

'As I said, Parnell,' said McCarthy, 'he told me he thought the next election would be lost and he was unsure whether he would still be alive for the following one.'

Morley looked at McCarthy, aghast.

'You mean, you had also failed to tell Mr Parnell of Mr Gladstone's views on the subject before the meeting?'

'Yes,' said McCarthy. 'But I didn't know what they were – beyond what I told Mr Parnell.'

'And neither, it appears, did you,' I said sharply to Morley.

Morley looked crestfallen.

'I have let both of you down,' he said to Parnell.

It seemed extraordinary that such a critical message had failed to be delivered to Parnell at such a critical time. Was it really possible, I wondered, that history could turn on such mistakes?

'I had no intention of resigning,' said Parnell.

We stood around for a moment in silence.

'Gladstone must decide what to do for the Liberal party,' Parnell continued. 'I shall decide what to do for the Irish party.'

'But Parnell,' said McCarthy, 'this changes everything. If Gladstone says he will resign, then there will be no Home Rule bill.'

Parnell walked over to the window by the corridor, and looked out over the Thames. Then, half-turning to us, he said in a quiet voice: 'If I resign the leadership, even for a day, I shall never return.'

He looked directly at McCarthy.

'You can tell them that, McCarthy. Once I let it go, that will be it forever.'

'But Parnell, Parnell,' – McCarthy sought to remonstrate with him – 'we need to discuss this further. I think many of our colleagues expected you to resign.'

As McCarthy sought to continue, Parnell said to Morley: 'Will you excuse us, please?'

Morley withdrew.

'What do you mean, expected me to resign?' said Parnell sharply. 'They have just re-elected me unanimously.'

'I know,' said McCarthy, 'but most of us ...'

'Us!' exclaimed Parnell.

'Yes,' said McCarthy. 'I include myself. I believe you should resign, even if only for a short time.'

'What is a short time, McCarthy?' replied Parnell. 'A day, a month, six months?'

'Well, six months, at least,' said McCarthy.

'And if the election is not called in six months,' said Parnell coldly, 'what happens then?'

'Well, until after the election, then, Parnell,' said McCarthy.

'So my leadership is now at Salisbury's whim,' said Parnell sarcastically, 'for six months, a year, maybe more.'

'But you could come back after the election,' pleaded McCarthy.

'Back as what?' said Parnell. 'A leader who had refused to fight an election as leader of his party. Hiding behind your skirts, McCarthy, over some ludicrous English sense of honour. Don't be so stupid.'

He spoke sharply, cruelly even.

'And if I came back after the election, don't you think there would be a hue and cry that the people had been tricked by Gladstone, tricked by the Irish party, that the Irish party was a Trojan horse and that I was the wolf dressed up in sheep's clothes as an ordinary Irish Member of Parliament? Because that's what you all are. Sheep!'

There was a shocked silence, as Parnell's words seemed to echo in the high-ceilinged corridors of Westminster. I waited for him to withdraw the remark, but he did not.

'Parnell, I beg of you,' said McCarthy. 'Please reconsider this. We need to reconvene the Party and consider this matter again.'

'Absolutely not,' said Parnell firmly, 'the Party has made its decision. Just one hour ago. I am not going to allow a daily vote on my leadership. I was unanimously re-elected. We shall deal with Gladstone on another day. Good day.'

He nodded to us both and strode off down the corridor.

McCarthy and I walked back towards the meeting-room. Several members of our party were standing in twos and threes in the corridor outside the room, leaning against the wall or putting a foot up on the low window sill, gossiping and chatting about the situation. McCarthy shepherded them back into the Committee Room and asked for quiet.

'There has been a … development,' said McCarthy. He paused. 'Gladstone has sent Morley a letter …'

He proceeded to tell the members about his meeting with Gladstone and Gladstone's message to him and he read out Gladstone's letter to Morley. He explained how Parnell had not been told about it before the meeting.

'But this changes everything,' cried Sexton.

'That is exactly what I said,' agreed McCarthy. 'I asked Parnell for another meeting, but he refused to have one.'

'Well, we have to have one,' said Sexton. 'We can requisition another meeting if a quarter of the members request it in writing.' He looked around the room. 'We easily have that here.'

A piece of paper was immediately put down and Sexton wrote out the necessary resolution and signed it. The note then went around the room and all present signed it. It came back to me. I counted thirty-one signatures.

'Are you going to sign it?' asked McCarthy.

'You know very well I am not,' I said.

'I understand,' said McCarthy kindly. 'In any event, we have enough signatures. Now, as vice-chairman of the Party I am calling this meeting for tomorrow, in this room. Would you please spread the word?'

Later that evening, I told Parnell about the meeting. He was silent for a time.

'If thirty-one members signed for a meeting, then thirty-one members will vote for me to resign,' he said. 'The die is cast.'

The next day, the English press excoriated Parnell for not resigning and excoriated the Irish party for not forcing him to resign. If the Irish chose an immoral adulterer to be their leader, they clearly were not capable of self-government: this was the general line. Parnell dealt with days like this by doing what he had often done before: refusing to read the papers. This had the advantage that he saved himself a scourging, but it also meant that he became increasingly adrift from the mood of the party – a factor which became more significant as the days went by.

Fifty-Seven

A Manifesto to the Irish People

GLADSTONE'S LETTER WAS published in the newspapers
the next day. It was another fateful error.

The lobbies and tea-rooms in the Commons were feverish
with rumours and conjecture about what Parnell would do in reply.

I heard rumours that Healy, although still suffering from the
fatigues of typhus, had travelled over to London at the weekend
and was now going to demand Parnell's resignation.

The Party reconvened just before two o'clock, but we quickly
agreed that we needed more time to consider matters and adjourned
until the following Monday.

Later, I joined McCarthy in the tea-rooms, as he beckoned me
over.

'Have you heard what Davitt said?' he asked me.

'No,' I said, surprised. 'I thought Davitt was in America.'

'He is,' said McCarthy gloomily, 'but he has given an interview to
the *New York Herald*. I just read it a few moments ago.'

He took the newspaper up from the table.

'I won't read it all,' said McCarthy, 'you can read it yourself – but
listen to this paragraph.'

He adjusted his spectacles and read aloud:

When I first heard of the divorce case I came over from Dublin
expressly to see Mr Parnell in London. Parnell then told me: "Davitt,
I want you to go back to Ireland to tell our friends that I am going to
get out of this without the slightest stain on my name or reputation".
I fully believed and I think he intended me to believe, by those words
that he was entirely innocent of the charge made against him ... I told

my friends that I had never known Parnell to lie to me and that until the charge had been proved at his trial I would believe implicitly in his innocence.

No matter what the issue may be on Monday next I will have nothing more whatever to do with him as long as he lives.'

I shook my head in disbelief.

'He hasn't even heard Parnell's side of the story,' I said.

'Well, isn't that just it?' said McCarthy. 'No one has. He's not prepared to talk about it. He just bristles if anyone tries to discuss it.'

'That's true,' I replied. 'He said it's an entirely private matter and no one's business except his.'

'And I can understand that,' said McCarthy, 'but his personal life has now interfered with his political life – with our political ambitions – he must see that, surely.'

'This story will blow over,' I said. 'We should not exacerbate the situation, as Davitt is doing, by saying things which can't be unsaid.'

McCarthy looked mournful.

'Would that it were so simple,' he said.

⁂

On Friday, I met Parnell in the House of Commons library – a place in which he was rarely seen – working on a lengthy memorandum. He seemed to be in unreasonably good spirits, given Gladstone's ultimatum, Davitt's denunciation, and the rumours that Healy intended for call for his resignation.

'If Healy thinks I intend to leave myself open to his mercies, then he's a bigger fool than I think he is,' he said feverishly. 'This is a matter for the Irish people and for them alone. I want you to read this and tell me what you think.'

He handed me a large bundle of sheets of House of Commons stationery, covered with his handwriting.

I began to read out loud. 'A Manifesto to the People of Ireland.'

It was difficult to read even the first page. There were words and whole sentences crossed out and other sentences written in crabbed handwriting above the deletions. It looked haphazard and confused.

'I can't read it,' I said. 'I can't follow your handwriting.'

'Give it to me,' said Parnell impatiently. 'I'll read it to you.'

He snatched the sheets back from me and began to read quickly.

'The integrity and independence of a section of the Irish parliamentary party having been sapped and destroyed by the wire pullers of the English Liberal party ...'

'You can't write that, Parnell!' I exclaimed.

He looked at me. 'Why not?' he asked coldly.

'It's too ... intemperate,' I said.

He ignored me and continued reading. 'It has become necessary for me as the leader of the Irish Nation to take counsel with you and to ask your judgment upon a matter which now solely devolves upon you to decide.'

He proceeded to read out loud the rest of this inflammatory document, in which he revealed all the confidential discussions he had had with Gladstone at Hawarden one year earlier and stated in increasingly violent language that Gladstone was now trying to decide who would be the leader of the Irish party. The more he read, the more dismayed I became. Revealing Gladstone's confidences would destroy forever his relationship not only with Gladstone himself, but with any other Liberal leader. No one would trust him in future.

'What do you think of it?' he said, when he had finished.

'You cannot issue that,' I said, with some force. 'It's ... it's just wrong. You cannot reveal such confidences. It will only inflame the situation. It will destroy your relationship with Gladstone.'

'That was destroyed long ago – when he put me in Kilmainham and let me rot there, while my daughter lay dying,' he said bitterly. 'Now he has called for my resignation. What is there to save?'

'This will not help,' I said.

'I disagree,' said Parnell defiantly and, gathering up all his papers, he swept out of the room to find a journalist from the *Freeman's Journal*.

✧

The next day, Saturday, the *Freeman's Journal* published his Manifesto in full. As I expected, the reaction was calamitous.

I was in the Commons for most of Saturday and many Members of Parliament came over to ask me if Parnell was suffering from some kind of mental disturbance. Even McCarthy wondered quietly whether Parnell had lost his mind.

Worse was to follow. After the publication of the Manifesto, John Dillon and William O'Brien sent a telegram from America to the newspapers, saying they would never again serve under a man who could issue such a manifesto and that Parnell's continued leadership of the Irish party was now impossible.

Parnell had now lost Davitt, Dillon and O'Brien and the meeting had not even begun.

Fifty-Eight

Committee Room 15

O N MONDAY MORNING, I waited with Parnell in the Westminster Hotel for Justin McCarthy, who had said he would try to discuss the matter further with Gladstone. Within moments of our arrival, McCarthy came in and greeted us cordially.

Parnell, without greeting him, said abruptly, almost rudely: 'Well, what answer have you brought from your shuffling friend?'

'I will tell you in a moment, Parnell,' replied McCarthy.

'I will hear it with no shuffling,' said Parnell.

'Please, Parnell,' implored McCarthy, 'let me tell it to you. Without interruption, and with good breeding.'

'I have more good breeding than you,' Parnell said tartly.

'I have spoken to Gladstone,' said McCarthy, ignoring this comment. 'He told me he could no longer deal with you, but only with the Irish party.'

'Very well,' said Parnell, 'we will continue with our meeting,' and he walked away, shoving McCarthy out of his way.

'Is he out of his mind?' asked McCarthy, when Parnell had left. He was utterly bewildered, as indeed was I, by Parnell's behaviour.

As we walked across to the House, a reporter from the *Freeman's Journal* shouted over to Parnell to ask whether he would remain leader. Parnell, without checking his stride, beckoned to the journalist to walk alongside him.

'You can tell them,' he said, 'that I will fight to the end.'

The reporter tried to scribble down Parnell's words on his notepad, as he walked along beside him.

'You and your colleagues should attend this meeting,' said Parnell. 'The Irish people need to know the truth.'

The young journalist could not believe his good fortune.

'We'll be there,' he said.

Parnell nodded grimly to him and strode on, into the House, across the lobby and up the wide oak stairs to the first-floor corridor. When we went into Committee Room 15, the room was almost full. Every member who could be there was there. The only absentees were Dillon, T.P. O'Connor and William O'Brien, who were in America, and the O'Gorman Mahon, who was ill. I could not remember a Party meeting so crowded.

Committee Room 15, our home for the next six days, was a large, high-ceilinged room with dark oak rafters, two enormous casement windows, which looked out over the Thames, and high oak wainscoting along the walls.

As I walked into the room, I saw Healy, hunched up in a chair so close to the fire that one of its legs was practically in the grate. He was buried in his overcoat and scarf, shivering with cold and fever, trying to get warm. Parnell ignored him entirely.

In the centre of the room was a large, dark, oak table, shaped like an elongated horseshoe. Parnell sat at the head of the table, with me on his left. Immediately on his right was Justin McCarthy; then Thomas Sexton, then Healy, who had limped slowly over to take his place; and then other members of the Party, all of whom, I had come to realise over the last few days, opposed Parnell's leadership. On my left were John Redmond, James O'Kelly, William Redmond and others. And so it started: Parnell's opponents all on his right and his supporters on his left. In the open space of the horseshoe – between both sides of the table – sat two or three reporters from the *Freeman's Journal*, their chairs pulled close so they could lean on the table as they wrote, copying down proceedings in shorthand. Behind the persons sitting at the table, another row of chairs filled up with supporters of either side and behind them stood more members, leaning against the walls.

Parnell took the chair, called the meeting to order and, as arranged, asked me to read all the telegrams which had been received. Over 200 telegrams of support for Parnell had been received from all over

Ireland: city corporations, county councils, constituencies, regional groups of the National League.

This brought about the first row.

'These telegrams are all supporting you, Mr Parnell,' Sexton said. 'Why don't you read Dillon's telegram from America criticising you?'

'Have you got it there?' said Parnell. 'If you put the original in my hands, I will read it.'

Sexton looked at him in surprise.

'The original?' he said. 'You know perfectly well the original was sent to the newspapers.'

'If you do not have the original telegram, it cannot be read,' Parnell insisted.

'This is ridiculous', said Sexton. 'It has been published in all the newspapers. I will read it from the newspapers.'

'You will do nothing of the sort, Sexton,' said Parnell sharply. 'If you do not have the original, it will not be read. How are we to know the newspapers have not twisted its meaning? We have had experience of that recently. Or have you forgotten?'

Parnell glared at Sexton and asked me to continue reading the telegrams of support. When I had finished, he said: 'Now, we will consider any resolutions which are properly before this meeting. At present, there is only one resolution before this meeting and that is what we shall debate: the resolution is that this meeting be adjourned until Friday.'

He looked up at the members in the room.

Sexton said, with some surprise in his voice: 'Mr Parnell, that motion refers to last Friday. As you know very well. We met on Wednesday, considered adjourning to Friday and now we meet today.'

'That is not clear at all,' said Parnell. 'This is the only motion before me and that is the motion we will debate, that we should adjourn until Friday.'

Abraham, the Member of Parliament for Limerick, cut in.

'I move that the resolution before this meeting should be: that the members of the Irish party do declare that Mr Parnell's tenure as chairman of this party is hereby terminated.'

There was a stunned silence. Abraham had, for the first time, given voice to what many of us believed was unutterable, impossible to conceive, let alone articulate.

'This is not an amendment to the current resolution before the meeting,' said Parnell coolly. 'It is an entirely separate resolution and therefore will not be taken at this time.'

'How are we to decide what is an amendment or not?' asked Sexton.

'I shall decide that,' said Parnell, 'as chairman.'

'I want to second Abraham's amendment,' said Sexton.

'You cannot second it,' said Parnell. 'It is not an amendment; it is an entirely separate resolution.'

'Then I wish that resolution to be put to the meeting,' cried Sexton.

'As I said, it cannot be put,' said Parnell patiently. 'There is another resolution before the meeting and that will be discussed first.'

'What is that resolution?' said Sexton.

'That this meeting adjourns until Friday,' repeated Parnell.

'This is like *Alice in Wonderland*, Parnell,' intervened Healy, for the first time.

'You will not argue with rulings from the chair,' said Parnell. 'Otherwise, no progress will be made.'

'Let us have a vote on it, then,' said Healy.

'There will be no vote on a point of order,' said Parnell. 'These are matters for the chair.'

Captain Nolan then intervened.

'Chairman, if I may,' he said, 'I have an amendment to the resolution. May I read it?'

Parnell nodded.

Nolan read out the amendment he had earlier agreed with Parnell.

'That the question of the leadership of the Party be postponed until members have had an opportunity of consulting their constituencies in Ireland on the matter,' he read.

'That is an entirely proper amendment to the resolution,' said Parnell, 'and I shall put this to the meeting.'

He looked around.

'Anyone who wishes to speak should address themselves to this motion. Captain Nolan, you may speak first.'

Nolan, who spoke rarely enough in the Chamber, seemed to find an easy eloquence in Committee Room 15.

'I can only say,' Nolan said, 'that the real question here is whether we should decide this question ourselves in this room, or whether we should – more correctly, in my view – consult our constituencies about it. It will hardly take too much time – a matter of two or three weeks – no more – and on any issue as large as this, we should take our time to discuss it fully and thoroughly, all over the country.'

Sexton was the first of Parnell's opponents to rise. He was sombre.

'Mr Parnell,' he said, 'I deeply regret that I find it impossible to vote for Nolan's amendment. This matter is now urgent. We cannot afford any more delay. We have already delayed for nearly two weeks and great damage has been done in that time to our alliance with the Liberals. They are now opposed to you, sir. We have heard it from their members in this House and we have heard it from Gladstone himself in his letter to Morley.'

He stood, solid and calm, looking around the room.

'This is not a matter for the people of Ireland,' he continued. 'This is a matter for us, here, as Members of Parliament. We are a body of representative men, trained to judge these public questions. This is a case for the calm and firm exercise of our independent judgment. And I tell you, gentlemen,' – he looked around the room and gestured with his open hand to Parnell – 'I need no reminders from anyone here about Mr Parnell's great services to Ireland. I have good cause to know them. I stood with him in the struggle to form the Party. I stood with him at the State trials in Dublin. I shared his imprisonment in Kilmainham and I have sat by his side these eleven years in the House of Commons.'

There were cries of 'Hear, hear' around the room.

'But, gentlemen,' – Sexton raised his voice, even though he commanded the room – 'no service by any leader entitles him to ruin his cause or his country's cause, and that is what will happen if Mr Parnell stays. Our last hope of Home Rule is the alliance with the Liberals and, if Mr Parnell remains, that alliance is lost. Now Mr Parnell, in his Manifesto to the Irish People, has said that any of us who have sought his resignation have had their integrity destroyed.'

'You are part of the conspiracy, Sexton,' said Parnell angrily.

'I am not, sir.' Sexton was stung by the sudden accusation.

'You are, sir,' said Parnell, rising to his feet and leaning his hands on the table. 'There is a section of this party – you and your like – who ought to know better, who are engaged in a conspiracy to put me out of my position.'

Sexton tried to speak, but Parnell continued.

'This conspiracy of yours has been going on now for days – in every hole and corner of this House – and I would not have issued this Manifesto to the Irish People, if I had not felt that I had to let them know what was going on behind their backs.'

Parnell sat down again.

'I have to declare to you, sir,' said Sexton, his voice beginning to break with emotion, 'that you are unjust. I have not entered into any conspiracy with any man against you, nor would I. The men who are urging you to retire are the very same men who have stood immediately around you over the past eleven years, during these terrible parliamentary fights.'

There were further cries of 'Hear, hear'.

'But our integrity is not the unconditional acceptance of the views of any one man; independence is not submission. We are your colleagues, sir, but we are not your slaves.'

He paused and, pressing his hands on the table, leaned forward to draw breath. We waited for him to continue.

'But,' – Sexton turned to his colleagues again – 'the question, the urgent question, is between the leader – whom we can never forget, and whom we have loved – and the cause. If the leader is retained, the cause is lost. If the cause is to be won, it is essential that the leader should retire.'

Loud cheers interrupted Sexton again, but he waved them down.

'But I wish to say to you, sir,' he said, looking at Parnell, 'that I never can have a leader whom I love and regard as I have loved and regarded you.'

Sexton resumed his seat, to great applause from everyone in the room – including Parnell.

John Redmond was next to speak – called on by Parnell as a supporter.

'This is not a matter, sir,' he said, addressing himself to Sexton, 'just for our party and our party alone. If Mr Parnell were just a party leader, then of course it would be a matter for the Party alone to decide, but he is not. He is the leader of the Irish nation, and only the Irish nation can depose him. Not us.'

'Hear, hear,' said Parnell, somewhat incongruously, I thought.

'Moreover,' – Redmond was warming to his theme – 'Mr Sexton says we must throw over Mr Parnell to preserve our alliance with the Liberals. But what is that alliance? What is it worth? What will they give us in return? If we are asked to sell our leader to preserve the alliance, then we should enquire what are we getting for the price we are paying.'

Parnell intervened.

'Indeed. Don't sell me for nothing. If you get my value, you may change me tomorrow,' he said, to loud cheers from his supporters.

'Because, gentlemen, make no mistake,' – Redmond turned his face towards his opponents – 'we are not only selling Mr Parnell to preserve the Liberal alliance, we are also selling – irrevocably – the independence of our party. Because, before Mr Parnell, every Irish party went the same way, selling and bartering its independence, and, if we sell Mr Parnell, our independence as a party is at an end. Does anyone believe that if Mr Parnell were thrown over, Gladstone would listen to our views on Home Rule? Of course he would not. He would have the Party in the hollow of his hands, and he could do with us as he liked.'

'Hear, hear,' shouted his supporters.

'And,' said Redmond, 'remember this: this party unanimously re-elected Mr Parnell last Tuesday – when the full details of his divorce trial were known. What has changed in the last week? It is Gladstone's letter to Morley, saying he would resign. That is all. And if Gladstone wishes to resign, let him! Gladstone may wish to trample you into the ground, sir,' – Redmond turned to face Parnell – 'but I want you to know, sir, that whoever wishes to trample you into the ground, I will take no part in that transaction.'

Redmond paused.

'I will say one thing more, Mr Parnell.' He looked down at the table, as if trying to control his emotion. 'It is true that I have a feeling of great loyalty to you.'

Parnell nodded graciously, in acknowledgement.

'It is also true that you have been my friend and I think this is no time in which a man who has been once your friend should turn against you. But I would sacrifice my liberty, I would sacrifice my life, for the sake of the independence of my country. And, therefore, I would sacrifice my leader ... But I believe your presence is essential to the success of our cause.'

Redmond sat down, to the great applause of all – including Sexton and Healy – just as Sexton had done before him.

Despite Healy's torpor of a few hours earlier, he now rose to his feet. The conflict seemed to have given him energy and he would have his say.

'I must say, gentlemen,' he said, 'that I have never found a greater occasion to admire and respect my colleagues than I have over the last number of days. And I will say this: whatever happens, this party shall remain united and unbroken.'

There were further cries of 'Hear, hear'.

'But I am amazed,' he continued vehemently, 'that Sexton should have tolerated that allegation of conspiracy from Parnell with so much patience and forbearance. I doubt if any such allegation were made against me that I should be so patient.'

He paused, perhaps to dare Parnell make a similar allegation against him, but Parnell would not be drawn.

'But to speak to the resolution before us,' Healy continued, 'I say there is no need to adjourn this matter any longer. Why should we? Parnell has put out all his arguments in his Manifesto. We have heard them all. There are no new arguments for him to make.'

Healy had about him some newspaper cuttings, which he placed on the table.

'How can we trust Parnell any more,' said Healy, tapping his finger on the table for emphasis, 'when he says in his Manifesto that Gladstone refused to give him his assurances in Hawarden when ...' He adjusted his glasses, picked up one of the cuttings and began to read.

'... when a few days after meeting Gladstone at Hawarden Mr Parnell spoke at a meeting in Liverpool in which he said: "My countrymen recognise and join with me in recognising that we are on the safe path to our freedom".'

Healy threw the paper carelessly back on to the table.

'Now, Parnell, were you misleading the Irish people with these words?'

He picked up another piece of newspaper. 'I have here another sheaf of newspaper reports, in which Parnell gave speech after speech praising Gladstone and saying that his policy was the correct policy. So, Parnell,' – Healy turned towards Parnell – 'either your Manifesto is false, or your speeches after Hawarden were false.'

Parnell looked thunderous.

'I will not stand for any accusation of falsehood from you, Healy,' he said angrily. 'You will withdraw that remark.'

Healy, realising perhaps that he had overstepped the mark, said: 'Very well. Out of respect for the chair, I withdraw the accusation.' He paused. 'But let me say this. I went to the Dublin meeting and I stood up to support Parnell. Even in the face of the English clamour and the clamour of the bulls of Rome, I stood up for him – even after what had become evident in the divorce courts – and if Parnell had any insight into our hearts he would have – in the passionate declarations made in his favour that night – the greatest evidence of the sacrifice that people were prepared to make for him.'

He looked around the room defiantly.

'But that has now changed. It is now clear that Parnell has alienated all of the Liberal party. All of them. He has no foothold anymore in that party and his Manifesto last Saturday was the final straw. Why do I defer to English opinion, you may ask? Why did we defer to it in 1886? Why were we willing to do so then, when passion and hatred animated our nation against the English? We were willing to do so because we were led by Charles Stewart Parnell.'

He jabbed his finger at Parnell.

'And he was able to abate that passion so as to ensure this acceptance by every representative of the Irish nation. Ireland possessed neither armies nor fleets. Having neither, we are bound to rely – bound to rely – upon constitutional and parliamentary methods. There was no hope for Ireland until Mr Parnell succeeded in obtaining the promise of a Home Rule settlement. He did this in consultation with English opinion and reduced many of our demands. And now he has alienated that English opinion and the Liberals have deserted him. I wish it were not so. I wish we had no such dissension, but that is the hard necessity of the case. It would have been better if Parnell had resigned last Tuesday. He should have done so.'

We listened in silence as Healy continued, his singsong voice in full flow, like a river surging after great rains. He had a torrent of words in him which he needed to speak out.

'We have been maintaining Mr Parnell for years. Not only on account of his great parliamentary services, but because of the great value of his name. He was a magnet and a centre for Irish patriotism, but I say this to Mr Parnell. Sir, your power is gone. You derived your power from the people. We are the representatives of the people. If you place an iron bar in a coil and electrize that coil, the iron bar becomes magnetic.'

Healy gestured dismissively at Parnell with his thumb.

'There stands the iron bar. This party is the electric action. The electricity is gone and the magnetism with it, when our support withers away.'

'You're a bitter man, Healy,' cried Nolan across the table.

'If I am,' retorted Healy swiftly, 'it is because of the bitter reality that we now face. But I say now …'

Healy looked back at Parnell and paused.

'All men are ephemeral,' he said quietly. 'Men pass away – but causes remain, and the Irish cause will always remain. And I now declare that my vote shall be for the deposition of the chairman of the Party …'

My heart sank. We had now lost Sexton and Healy.

Parnell rose to his feet, looked over at Healy and pointed towards him.

'Mr Healy has been well trained in this type of warfare,' he said, 'but I am not surprised. Who trained him? Who saw his genius? Who gave him his chance, his first opportunity? Who got his seat in Parliament for him? That Healy is here today to destroy me is due to myself.'

Parnell paused, his breathing laboured.

'But why then did Healy support me in Dublin?' he continued. 'Why did Sexton do so? Why did McCarthy do so? Why did you all do so? Why did you encourage me to come forward and maintain my leadership in the face of the world, if you were not going to stand by me now, a week later?'

It was an unanswerable point and more and more faces gazed down at the floor, unable to look Parnell in the eye.

'Why did my officers encourage me,' continued Parnell, 'to come forward and take my position on the bridge if they were going to act as traitors … ?'

There were cries of 'Shame, shame' but Parnell would not be stopped.

'Yes – to act as traitors and, as traitors, to hand me over to the opposing commander in chief.'

There was a deathly silence as the full weight of this taunt filled the room.

'I did not ask for your support in Dublin,' said Parnell venomously. 'You gave it to me and Healy – the leader-killer – now sharpens his poniard to stab me – just as he stabbed the old lion, Isaac Butt, in days gone by – and I allowed that old man to go down, honoured, to his grave, rather than seek to step into the shoes of a politician who, however many his faults, had created a great movement.'

There was an intense silence in the room.

'But,' continued Parnell, 'if you want to vote for my deposition then you should be sure you are getting the value of it. Can you do that? If you can do better than I did with Gladstone, then do so. Will Healy get any better? Or Sexton? Or McCarthy?'

His tone grew increasingly cold and contemptuous.

'If they can, let them do it. Go to Gladstone now! Because if you are to get something better for Ireland than I did, I would like to see it.'

He sighed deeply.

'I should like – and this is not an unfair thing for me to ask – that I should come within sight of the promised land.'

There was a long silence after Parnell sat down, but eventually McCarthy stood up to speak, nervously fingering his spectacles in his hands.

'I do not know, Parnell,' he said disconsolately, 'why you felt you had to keep the Hawarden talks a secret from us.'

'I told you why, McCarthy,' said Parnell harshly. 'Gladstone had expressly requested me to and I had given him my word.'

'That I can understand,' said McCarthy, 'but why then go on a public platform and praise Gladstone, when you knew his proposals would be so unacceptable? And if it was so important that confidentiality be maintained, then why did you break that bond and reveal those details in your Manifesto last Friday?'

McCarthy looked hard at Parnell.

'That was a vital error of judgment,' he said, 'and that error of judgment has and must imperil your leadership. Your secret was revealed at the wrong time.'

Another supporter of Parnell's, John O'Connor, demanded to be heard.

'Mr Parnell,' he said, 'I have listened with very great attention to the speeches of your opponents and they try to place us in a false position. They say it is a matter of choosing between you and the country. Well, I will not have it so. I am as anxious to act in the best interests of our country as they are. And I will not have it said otherwise. But we know well what the condition of our party was in the past. It is you – and you alone – who have reconciled the conflicting elements in which you have found Irish politics and I fear that once your guiding hand is removed, once your cementing genius is withdrawn, Irish politics will resolve themselves again into those conflicting elements.'

There were further cries of 'Hear, hear' from Parnell's supporters.

O'Connor continued.

'The Liberal alliance will survive this setback. I remember that this alliance was forged at a time – as we all remember, sir – when you were charged with conniving at murder.'

O'Connor thumped his fist on the table.

'A far more serious allegation than is now being laid at your door and we remained independent, sir, as we always have been, under your leadership.'

And so it went on, hour after agonising hour, the debate ebbing and flowing, sometimes in favour of Parnell but mostly against. As the afternoon drifted into the early evening and the light faded, a gloom descended upon the room and the lamps were lit, casting a deathly glow. The debates and discussions and arguments went on until it was almost midnight, when there was a call to adjourn the meeting until the following day.

Fifty-Nine

The Battle Raging

THE MEETING RECOMMENCED the following day at midday. Parnell arrived early, unusually for him, and was in the chairman's seat before anyone else arrived. He seemed to be in high spirits, which was all the more remarkable given that I could not see how he could remain as leader beyond today.

'Now,' said Parnell, 'the motion before the Party is that we adjourn to let the people of Ireland consider this matter.'

'Then let us vote on that now,' said Healy.

'No,' said Parnell. 'You have spoken, Mr Healy, but there are plenty of others who have yet to make their contributions.'

'There is no point in continuing this discussion,' cried Healy. 'I have for you, Mr Parnell, if you will permit me to say, the highest personal respect, for the dignity with which you have conducted these proceedings and the gentlemanly character of your whole temper yesterday, notwithstanding the very painful position in which you found yourself.'

Healy turned to speak to the other members in the room.

'And I say that, whatever opinion anyone may have of Mr Parnell, they must all regard him as a man of enormous parliamentary ability and reputation. But Mr Parnell should not be allowed to obstruct the business of this meeting.'

'This business will not end in this room or in this House, Healy,' said O'Kelly angrily, in his first intervention. 'If you drive Parnell from the Party, you will begin a civil war.'

There was a shocked silence in the room, as O'Kelly's words lingered in the air.

'If the people decide, then we will all accept their verdict,' O'Kelly continued. 'If the Party decides, then we will look as if we were forced to the decision by pressure from an English statesman. And we should not let that happen. What Healy is suggesting is that we should place our trust in Mr Gladstone! Why should we do that? We know the English are not to be trusted – ever,' he roared, 'and we know it not only from our history, but from our own experience.'

He thumped his fist on the table.

'What we must do is keep ourselves united under our leader. Mr Parnell is the standard around which the whole Irish race is ranged, and if we pull down that standard, we will find that our battalions will disperse in every direction. If Parnell falls, then the statue of Irish liberty will be smashed to pieces.'

Parnell, agitated by the emotion of this speech, bowed his head.

'I will leave the room for a moment,' he said, in a subdued voice. 'Perhaps, McCarthy, you could take the chair.'

Parnell rose and left the room, and McCarthy moved to take his seat.

Arthur O'Connor spoke next.

'Gentlemen, this situation is distressing and heartrending in the extreme,' he said earnestly. 'It is intolerable to ourselves and to Mr Parnell to prolong it. We must decide it now and I vote we request Mr Parnell to resign.'

'I agree,' said Healy.

Some moments later, Parnell came back and resumed his seat, but neither Healy nor O'Connor acted on their words.

As the day wore on, everyone who wanted to had spoken and Parnell was eventually obliged to put the matter to a vote.

'I shall insist that the names of each member be taken down and their vote recorded,' Parnell said. 'Now, the resolution is, that all questions touching on the leadership of the Party be postponed until the members ascertain the views of their constituents. All those in favour, please raise one hand.'

Tellers were appointed to count the votes and to write down our colleagues' names.

'All those against.'

The vote was called, the names were written down and the votes were counted: twenty-nine members in favour and forty-four members against. The majority did not want the meeting adjourned: they wanted to decide the leadership there and then.

An eerie silence filled the room, as all members held their breath to see what Parnell would do next.

'Very well,' said Parnell, 'we shall resume tomorrow afternoon at two o'clock,' and, standing up, he immediately left the room.

∽◦◦◦∽

Parnell returned the next day, again in good spirits, and took the chair, as if normal parliamentary business was being discussed.

'I intend to leave the room for a few moments, gentlemen,' said Parnell, to the surprise of many, 'as I believe that Clancy has a proposal to put to you.'

He rose and swiftly left the Committee Room.

'What is your proposal, Clancy?' asked Sexton, in some surprise.

'Or is it just another of Parnell's delaying tactics?' said Healy suspiciously.

'I suggest that we consult with Mr Gladstone,' said Clancy. 'Mr Gladstone has the answers. We will not accept Home Rule without control of the police, nor without control of our land laws. And now, when we ask him to give us guarantees on these matters, he throws his hands in the air and says he couldn't possibly interfere in our affairs. He has already interfered. And it is imperative that this matter be settled once and for all. What will Gladstone give us, that is the question. If Gladstone can give us satisfactory guarantees that the next Home Rule bill will grant control over the police and the land laws to the Irish parliament, I believe that Mr Parnell will retire.'

There were loud cheers from Healy's side of the table, and Healy rose to request that Parnell be immediately sent for. I stepped outside to see Parnell at the end of the corridor, leaning against a window casement and gazing out at the rain on the Thames. Even at this terrible crisis in his own affairs, he had about him a natural and resolute calm.

He returned to the room and resumed his seat. Healy stood to speak.

'We have heard from Mr Clancy a proposal, Mr Parnell,' he said.

'Which did not emanate from me,' said Parnell.

'Which, if it was agreed to by you,' continued Healy, 'would allow us a resolution of our predicament.'

Healy summarised the elements of Clancy's proposal.

'And if I may say, Mr Parnell,' said Healy, almost tearfully, 'if this comes to pass, my voice would be the first to call you back to your proper place as the leader of the Irish race.'

Parnell was in no mood to listen to Healy's sentimentalism.

'What is the question?' he asked sharply.

'Sir,' said Sexton, 'if Gladstone offers us satisfactory guarantees that the police and the land laws will be contained in the next Home Rule bill, will you retire from your position as leader?'

Parnell brought his hands together and placed them under his chin, and seemed almost to close his eyes.

'That, Mr Sexton, is a sudden question,' he said, raising his hand and looking at him. 'I would like to reflect on that for twenty-four hours.'

'Very well,' said Sexton. 'I propose we adjourn until tomorrow at twelve o'clock.'

This was unanimously carried, and Wednesday's meeting was adjourned.

∽✑∾

But the clouds, which had seemed to be lifting, darkened ominously that afternoon when the Catholic Church chose that moment to intervene. Every cardinal, archbishop and bishop in Ireland had been meeting at Maynooth for days, to consider Parnell's divorce case. We read their views the following morning in the *Freeman's Journal*:

> The question is who is to be the leader of the Irish people or rather who is not to be their leader. Without hesitation or doubt and in the plainest possible terms we give it as our unanimous judgment that whoever else is fit to fill that highly responsible post, Mr Parnell decidedly is not.
>
> After the verdict given in the divorce court we cannot regard Mr Parnell in any other light than as a man convicted of one of the gravest offences known to religion and society aggravated in his case

by almost every circumstance that could possibly attach to it so as to give it a scandalous pre-eminence in guilt and shame.

It was a savage blow of the crozier, delivered in the most violent and unambiguous manner.

∽◦◦◦∽

On Thursday, we re-assembled in Committee Room 15 to await Parnell's answer. He had not discussed the matter with me at all, except to ask me to bring along more telegrams of support. Again, Parnell took the chair and, to my surprise, asked me to continue reading out the telegrams. This caused an immediate outcry.

'What is the point of this farce, Mr Parnell?' cried Sexton firmly. 'Tell us of your decision.'

'My decision on what?' said Parnell disingenuously.

'You know very well,' said Healy, 'on whether you will retire from the leadership.'

'Oh, yes,' said Parnell absentmindedly. 'Yes. I have considered that matter overnight and my reply is that my responsibility is derived from you, to a large part.' He opened his hands to gesture to the parliamentary party. 'But it is also derived from a long train of circumstances and events, in which many of you have had no share. My position has been granted to me not because I am the mere leader of a parliamentary party, but because I am the leader of the Irish nation.'

There were gasps of astonishment as members listened to his reply. Parnell had no intention of going at all!

'And I am the leader of the Irish nation,' continued Parnell calmly, 'because I have built up this party, I have kept the discordant elements of our race within the bounds of moderation, and you, gentlemen, know that there is no man living, if I am gone, who could succeed me, in persuading the Irish people to accept the lesser provisions of this Home Rule bill.'

Healy rose to speak, but Parnell gestured that he had not yet finished.

'But I want to say more: my recollection of what happened at Hawarden has been challenged by Gladstone, but he has not said in what respect exactly I was wrong. Well, let him do so now. We have not been informed by him that he will grant us a constabulary. So let us ask, or rather, you can ask him; ask him these straight questions. But I can tell you, gentlemen, that I have been negotiating with Gladstone since 1880 and I have never yet succeeded in getting a single straight answer to a single straight question from him. The man is an unrivalled sophist. But if you think you can do better ...' He shrugged his shoulders. 'But I will say,' he resumed, 'that if you go to Gladstone and get clear answers on these two questions, the police and land laws, then I shall retire as leader.'

It was difficult to follow the tortuous and labyrinthine workings of his mind and Healy's patience was wearing thin.

'What on earth are you saying, Mr Parnell?' he said. 'Will you resign or won't you?'

'You will speak, Mr Healy, to the resolution before the meeting,' said Parnell imperturbably.

'I am doing that,' said Healy angrily. 'Forget about Gladstone. We can't get a straight answer out of you.'

'I have given you my answer,' said Parnell.

'You have given us two answers,' said Healy. 'One said you would retire and the other said you would not. Do you take us for children?'

'It is my answer,' said Parnell coldly. 'It is my answer to the question Sexton put to me and upon that answer I will stand or fall before the country.'

'Then, sir,' said Healy sharply, 'you will fall.'

'Away with him, away with him,' Healy's supporters began to shout out.

'Crucify him, crucify him,' someone shouted, also from Healy's side.

Healy spun around.

'You will not use such blasphemous language here,' he said furiously to the unknown speaker.

He turned back to Parnell, indignantly.

'You see, Parnell,' he said, 'the divisions you are now causing in the Party.'

There were shouts from the other side of the table for Healy to withdraw his remarks, but Healy ignored them.

'You said, Parnell, that the time has come when the Irish party should enter into an alliance with the Liberal party.'

'I did,' said Parnell.

'And now we have that great alliance.'

'Agreed,' said Parnell.

'And now it has been broken,' said Healy.

'Yes. By Gladstone,' said Parnell.

'No,' said Healy coldly. 'It has perished in the stench of the divorce court.'

He said this with such contempt, as if the very sight of Parnell was repugnant to him. Parnell rose quickly, as if he had been struck and glared at Healy. The two men glowered at each other, with only Sexton and McCarthy between them.

'Sit down, Healy,' shouted Redmond, getting to his feet, red-faced and angry. 'You should be ashamed of yourself. Your speech is one insult after another, the worst-tempered, most hysterical speech ever delivered in this party. The only hope for Ireland is that Mr Parnell remains at his post.'

Sexton intervened, to calm matters down.

'Gentlemen, gentlemen, we do not need to resort to this. I respect every man's argument, every man's motives. We have fought too long together to fight against one another now.'

Our colleagues all resumed their seats.

'But again,' said Sexton, 'I ask you, Mr Parnell, if we obtain those assurances from Gladstone and a majority of the Party are satisfied with them, will you resign?'

'You know my answer, Mr Sexton,' said Parnell. 'I shall.'

'Very well,' said Sexton, 'then let us appoint some among us to go to Gladstone and ask for his response.'

~⁂~

On Friday, Sexton and Healy, Redmond and I – two from each side – went to meet Gladstone at Carlton Gardens.

We were shown into an elegant drawing-room, with three large sofas arranged round a fireplace in which, even though it was just after midday, the fire was already crackling. Redmond and I sat on one sofa, with Sexton and Healy across from us. There was an awkward silence between us, punctuated only by the startling gunshots of the dry wood on the fire. After some moments, I got up and walked over to the bookcases to read the titles in Gladstone's library.

'You must give me a copy of your memoirs, Mr Harrison, which I can add to my library,' said Gladstone genially, as he came into the room to greet us.

'Which I have just been admiring, sir,' I said, turning around.

Gladstone came in and shook hands with us all, his grip resolute, his grey eyes clear.

'Your memoirs should make interesting reading, Mr Harrison,' said Gladstone, as he sat in the middle sofa, facing the fireplace. A maid had followed him in to offer us tea. 'I have to rely on the newspaper accounts, but by all accounts you are having a rather trying time.'

'That is certainly true, sir,' I said, 'which is why we are here.'

'But, if I may,' continued Gladstone, 'I do not wish anything I have to say to have a bearing on your dispute. What I say, I say for the Liberal party, no more. I have no desire to meddle in the affairs of the Irish party.'

His demeanour appeared sincere, but as I watched him I doubted it was the full truth. He had been outmanoeuvred in Parliament and in Ireland by Parnell, during the Land League years; he had put Parnell in gaol and Parnell had put him in and out of Government almost at will. They were both public men, hewn out of rock, who led their parties and their nations effortlessly. It would only be natural for Gladstone to look at Parnell's standing after the divorce case and to decide that now was the best time to remove this meddlesome, troublesome rival entirely from the stage. I, for one, did not doubt that Gladstone was engaged in a wholly Machiavellian attempt to remove Parnell from the scene once and for all.

Sexton opened the discussion.

'The reason we are here, Mr Gladstone,' he began, 'is to ask whether in the event that a new Home Rule bill is introduced by you ...'

'You seem to forget, Mr Sexton, that I am only the Leader of the Opposition,' interrupted Gladstone, with a smile. 'You mean, if I am ever Prime Minister again.'

'Indeed,' smiled Sexton, 'but, assuming you will be, whether you will permit an Irish parliament to have control over its own police and over its own land laws.'

'I shall not discuss the Hawarden proposals,' said Gladstone serenely. 'Those are a matter between myself and Mr Parnell. I shall not re-open that dispute.'

'I quite understand, sir,' said Sexton, 'but this is a matter which touches vitally on the Home Rule bill, and in which the Irish party need a clear indication from you.'

'Indeed,' said Gladstone. 'I am happy to talk freely with you about matters pertaining to the Irish police. But I had understood from the newspaper accounts of your meeting yesterday that you are here to discuss the disagreement about Hawarden, and that, I am afraid, I cannot discuss. Except to say that I rely entirely on my version of events.'

'If the Party requested us to discuss matters of Home Rule policy,' said Redmond, 'would you discuss it?'

'It would depend on the request,' said Gladstone, 'as to how I would respond.'

And so the discussion went on, in an intricate and polite but ever-evasive manner.

We put all our questions to him, but we received delphic replies to all of them; he would be happy, he said, to discuss the questions of the police and the land question with the Irish party, but as these issues had now become linked with the leadership, it would be inappropriate to deal with them until the leadership question was resolved. He said he would look forward to discussing it with us at that time.

'What did I tell you?' said Parnell triumphantly, as I reported on events to him. 'The arch-sophist! He will devour you all.'

Sixty

The Split

WE MET AGAIN, on Saturday, the sixth day, in Committee Room 15.

'So, gentlemen.' Parnell was confident as he surveyed the room. 'A deputation from this group has spoken to Mr Gladstone, and we shall receive their report.'

'What report?' asked Healy.

'The full report of your conference with Mr Gladstone,' said Parnell serenely.

'We have minutes of our meeting with him,' said Healy, 'and all our correspondence. What more do we need?'

'There should be a full report,' insisted Parnell, 'with dates and times and letters.'

'But you have seen all the letters,' said Healy, in exasperation. 'You have them all there.'

'Of course, I have everything that is here,' said Parnell, to laughter. 'but I don't have your report.'

'Don't be ridiculous,' said Healy angrily. 'We can report on it here and now.'

'It should be in writing, Mr Healy,' said Parnell, with exaggerated calmness and patience, 'with a list of all pieces of correspondence and the reason for each one, and then your comments.'

'But you have it all,' insisted Healy. 'If I took all these documents and stuck a pin through them to keep them all together, you would have them.'

'There is no blame attaching to you, Mr Healy,' said Parnell imperturbably. 'You only got Gladstone's reply late last night. But the delegates need to consider your report.'

'This is just another waste of time, Parnell,' said Healy.

'I agree,' said Sexton. 'Everyone is here. We can give our report verbally to the meeting.'

'No, you will not,' said Parnell firmly. 'You should all agree it in writing. It will be used to communicate matters to the Irish people.'

Healy sighed heavily. 'Pure obstructionism … I will not stand for any more of this.'

He moved his chair back, as if to leave the room.

'Sit down, Healy,' roared Harrington, from the other side. 'You are doing everything to ruin this party.'

Healy turned back to the table.

'That is an outrageous slur, Harrington, and I reject it completely.'

'You can do the report in ten minutes, Healy,' said Harrington, 'so do it.'

'This report is not the real question,' said Sexton. 'Day by day, we are being led entirely away from the main issue which we have to decide.'

'Hear, hear,' said Healy.

'And, I may say, I will say, we have made up our minds that these intolerable proceedings will be brought to a close today,' continued Sexton.

He glared around the room.

'And if they cannot be brought to a close today by a motion from the chair, then they must be determined in some other way. There is no need for a formal written report. We can tell you what happened in our meeting with Gladstone. We have a written record of it, signed by all four of us who were there. A request for more is pure obscurantism. I cannot, I will not, endure this one day longer, nor will the country.'

Parnell intervened.

'Mr Sexton, I call on you to withdraw with your colleagues to prepare that report.'

'We shall not,' cried Healy, 'because even if we did, you would simply propose another obstructive resolution about the report.'

'Don't impute motives to me which you cannot substantiate,' said Parnell.

'Very well,' said Healy. 'I propose that all the letters and communications of our meeting be read.'

Parnell agreed to this, and so I read out our note of the meeting and all the letters to our members. When this had ended, Abrahams and O'Connor both stood up at the same time.

'I have a resolution to put,' Abrahams said loudly, 'that this party votes to depose Mr Parnell as leader.'

'Sit down, Abrahams,' shouted Parnell. 'Mr O'Connor, you have the floor.'

There was uproar on Healy's side, as they all shouted down O'Connor and demanded that Abrahams' resolution be heard.

'I have this resolution in writing,' shouted Abrahams, 'proposed and seconded as it should be, and I propose to give it to the vice-chairman, Mr McCarthy.'

Abrahams leaned over the table to pass the piece of paper to McCarthy, who took it in his hand. As McCarthy was about to open it, Parnell stood up, leaned over towards him and snatched the paper out of his hand.

'This resolution is out of order,' said Parnell, 'and I will not hear it.' He crumpled the piece of paper fiercely in his hand and gripped it tightly.

There were shouts of dismay and anger from all over the room.

'Until this party deposes me from the chair, I am the leader,' he said.

'You are not our leader any longer,' someone cried.

'Give us back our document, Parnell,' shouted Healy.

'You're a dirty trickster, Healy,' roared Harrington in reply.

'Order, order,' shouted Parnell, slapping his hand repeatedly on the table.

The meeting was now descending into chaos, as members began shouting at one another and at Parnell or at Healy.

Parnell, still standing, said: 'I am still your chairman – until you depose me.'

'Well, allow us to depose you,' said Healy fiercely.

'I shall call on Mr Abrahams shortly,' said Parnell. 'But Mr O'Connor had a prior resolution.'

But before O'Connor could speak, Justin McCarthy rose and looked around the room. His quiet dignity restored silence to the meeting.

'I have to say, sir,' he said to Parnell, in a quiet voice, 'I had a resolution given to me and you struck it out of my hand.'

'I took it out of your hand,' corrected Parnell.

'No, sir,' said McCarthy quietly, 'you struck it out of my hand.'

'You were about to put Abrahams' resolution to the meeting,' said Parnell. 'You were trying to usurp my functions as chairman.'

'Indeed I was not,' continued McCarthy, in his quiet, dignified voice.

'I assumed that was what you were going to do,' said Parnell.

'You could have asked me,' said McCarthy. 'I would have expected that courtesy of you.'

'I move that Mr Abrahams' resolution be heard,' shouted Healy.

'That motion is entirely out of order,' said Parnell.

'Put the motion,' roared Healy, 'put it now.'

'I will not,' said Parnell.

'Then I will put it myself,' shouted Healy, standing up.

'You will not, Healy,' said Parnell, standing also and glaring at him. 'I am the master of this party.'

Healy paused for a moment and glared bitterly at Parnell, his lip curling into a sneer.

'And who, then, is the mistress of this party?' he roared.

There was a stunned silence in the room, as the ugliness of Healy's taunt sank in. Parnell could contain himself no longer.

'You scoundrel, Healy!' he roared and, with a cry of anger and rage, he launched himself across the table at Healy, his hands outstretched as if he would choke Healy to death with his bare hands, his eyes wild with fury.

Healy started and jumped back, his chair falling behind him in the tumult.

Had it not been for the two or three people between them, Parnell would surely have struck Healy there and then. There were roars of anger from all sides of the room.

I leaped up and tried to hold Parnell back.

'Charles, Charles, not like this,' I said, but to no avail. He was like a man possessed, his clothes askew and hair dishevelled, in his effort to attack Healy.

'I appeal to the chairman,' cried a voice.

'Better appeal to that cowardly scoundrel there,' said Parnell, pointing a finger at Healy, 'who, in an assembly of Irishmen, dares to insult a woman.'

There were cheers of support and cheers of derision from both sides of the room.

Justin McCarthy rose again and, gesturing with his hands for people to calm down, asked all persons to be silent.

'The time has come, my friends, when we ought to bring this debate to a dignified end,' he said quietly.

There were shouts of 'Hear, hear' and the sound of hands thumping on the table.

'I do not want to say one word more to increase the bitterness of this crisis. I had hoped that our chairman would have helped us out of this terrible calamity.' He paused. 'But I feel we would be wasting our time in further controversy. The door has been closed to the final settlement of the controversy in this room today.'

He took out a handkerchief and, taking off his glasses, wiped them clean. I could see there were tears in his eyes and his voice shook with emotion.

'We have all come so far, my friends, and I am proud to have been a part of this great group of men. But now, I must ask all those who think as I do, at this grave crisis, to withdraw with me from the room.'

He pushed his chair back and, looking neither right nor left, walked out of the room. There was a sudden hush and then I heard the sound of chairs being pushed back from the table and I watched as many of my colleagues and friends, with grim expressions on their faces, in total silence, and without a sidelong look at Parnell, rose from their seats and filtered out of Committee Room 15.

When they had left, a strange quietness filled the room.

I rose and closed the door behind them. Those members who had been sitting on the window ledges walked over to take up the empty chairs, but no one righted Healy's chair – it stayed where it had fallen.

Redmond was the first to break the silence.

'I shall never be a member of any party whose leader is chosen by Gladstone. I am with you, sir, to the end,' he said quietly.

'I thank you, Mr Redmond,' said Parnell, nodding graciously to him, 'and I will say this, gentlemen. We have won today.' He looked around the room. 'Although our ranks are reduced in numbers, I still hold the chair.'

There were some muted cheers, but they lacked conviction, and Parnell smiled his wintry smile.

'Although many of our comrades have left us, Ireland will fill their ranks again ... Our friends have left this room because their position was no longer tenable, and they stand today in that most contemptible of positions – of men who, having taken pledges to be true to their party, to their leader and to their country, have been false to those pledges. We shall return to Ireland next week and we shall continue the battle there.'

With these words, Parnell brought the meeting to an end, and we left Committee Room 15 for the last time.

In truth, it did not feel like a victory; it felt more like a death. I felt as soldiers must do on returning from a terrible battle. We may have been in command of the battlefield, but so many of our greatest friends and fellow soldiers had fallen that victory had a bitter taste.

After a time, I walked downstairs and waited in the lobby. The porter told me that McCarthy and the others had all gone to a conference-room and that they were still there. I told him I would wait in the smoking-room. In about an hour, he came over to say that the first members had left the meeting. I managed to speak to McCarthy on his way out. Forty-five members had left the Party – a majority, as McCarthy pointed out to me; he had been elected chairman, and they had passed a resolution that Parnell's position as leader of the Party was now terminated.

'How has it come to this, McCarthy?' I said sadly.

'You know how,' he said. 'But it is a sad day for Ireland and a sad day for all of us.'

He put his hand on my shoulder, as if to lean on me.

'Are you all right?' I asked.

'No, I am not, Harrison,' he said, looking at me with tears in his eyes. 'My heart is broken.' He took a handkerchief from his pocket. 'He is our most gallant leader, but he will not bend with the storm. He would prefer to be broken and uprooted rather than bend to the prevailing winds.'

'He was ever thus,' I murmured.

'Tell him …' – McCarthy looked at me through his tears – 'tell him he still has my greatest regard and affection.'

I promised that I would and we parted in the palace yard and went our separate ways.

Sixty-One

Invictus

B Y AN ACCIDENT of unfortunate timing, there was a by-election due to be held in North Kilkenny the following week.
   On Tuesday evening, Parnell and I left for Dublin on the night train from Euston.

The following morning, we arrived in Dublin to a huge welcome; Parnell was cheered from Kingstown to Dawson Street. But over breakfast in Morrison's, we heard that the United Ireland offices had been taken over by our opponents and that they had barricaded the front door. Parnell's response was immediate: he rose from the table and, without even fetching his overcoat, dashed onto Dawson Street and hailed a cab for Sackville Street. I gulped down my tea and followed him out.

'Twice the fare if you make it in five minutes,' Parnell urged the cabbie.

The horse was whipped almost into a gallop and the cab weaved its way in and out of the traffic at breakneck speed. As we approached the offices, Parnell shouted at the cabbie to stop suddenly and the cabbie pulled on the reins so hard that the poor brute of a horse almost fell over.

Outside the newspaper offices, a crowd of people were shoving and jostling before the front door, which was locked against them. Parnell pushed through and, seeing a pickaxe in a man's hand, snatched it from him and shouted at everyone to stand back. Then, raising the axe behind his shoulder, he brought it down on the front door with a resounding crash. The door shuddered but held firm. Three more huge blows from Parnell and a large panel above the lock was broken through. Another man, armed with a crowbar, shoved it between the door and the door jamb, and a group of men leaned on it to jemmy the door open. Suddenly there was the sound of breaking wood, and the crowd, pushing past Parnell's shoulder, charged at the door. It gave way, suddenly, and a small number fell through onto the floor. Parnell clambered over them, dashed up the stairs, two at a time, to the offices on the first floor and, finding them empty, opened the window and leaned out to salute the crowds below. There were great cheers when they saw him, axe in hand, breathing heavily, frock coat and clothing dishevelled, dusty with the fragments of wood.

'They have fled,' he shouted down. 'Like the cowards that they are. The paper is ours. Dublin is ours and Dublin is true. What Dublin says today, Ireland will say tomorrow.'

There was another rousing cheer from the crowds. Within moments, Parnell reappeared downstairs and, flinging the axe down in the hall, walked quickly through the front door, strode back to the cabbie – who had witnessed the whole drama open-mouthed – and ordered him to return to the hotel.

'I will fight them wherever I see them,' he muttered to no one in particular, and he never said another word until he was back at Morrison's, where he called for fresh tea and breakfast.

'I am as hungry as a hawk,' he said and resumed his breakfast as if nothing had happened.

The following day, we travelled to Castlecomer, where Parnell was to address another gathering. But as he walked towards the platform, a man emptied a bag of lime over him, covering his head and shoulders, blinding him with its terrible acidic dust. I immediately took Parnell off and guided him to the nearest hotel, where he washed off as much he could. But one of his eyes was stinging badly and we summoned a doctor, who doused the eye with an antiseptic ointment and bandaged it up. When it was done, Parnell insisted on returning to the platform to give his speech, but by then it was almost dark and most of the crowd had dispersed. Parnell persisted, however, and spoke to a small crowd of curious onlookers in that by now familiar declamatory style. Soon it began to drizzle, and a fellow speaker passed Parnell a deerstalker to protect him against the rain. The image was too tempting for a local artist, and his impromptu sketch of Parnell with a white bandage around his head, his one eye staring out wildly at the crowd and a deerstalker on his head, was published in all the newspapers.

This illustration and reports of his assault on the United Ireland offices with the axe, made him appear off-balance, frenzied, almost unhinged.

That first campaign of our divided party was difficult to endure and at times it was almost more than I could bear as I watched and listened to my former friends with great eloquence, which they had mastered after years in the Commons or in campaigns led by Parnell, turning on him to accuse him of being the great obstacle to Home Rule.

In the end, the result was inevitable: our candidate was defeated by over 1,100 votes, a humiliating result.

I urged Parnell to return to Brighton to rest, as he was exhausted and increasingly prone to errors in what he said and in what he did. He had taken to smoking cigarettes incessantly now, the ash gathering on the cigarette, untipped, until it fell onto his jacket or his waistcoat; he seemed increasingly careless of his appearance or his clothing, his eyes staring into the distance, glassy, unfocused, almost past caring. He was fighting now for something in which he no longer believed, fighting to regain the ascendancy he had once so effortlessly achieved. The tide was going out against him and, although he was on his feet, wading back towards the shore, it took all his energy not to be swept out to sea. I stayed by his side until I had brought him safely home, as he was prone to falling into a deep sleep, almost an unconsciousness, and if he were left on his own I feared he could end up in Scotland instead of Brighton.

After some weeks of rest, he seemed more at ease when I next visited him. He had received a letter from Dillon suggesting a meeting – in Boulogne, as Dillon feared he would be arrested in England.

'They want to surrender,' Parnell told me when he received the proposal, but I doubted that judgment, as I doubted many of his judgments at that time.

Within days, Parnell and I travelled to Boulogne and met Dillon and William O'Brien, but, as I had suspected, they did not want to surrender; they merely wanted to negotiate a compromise similar to that offered in Committee Room 15. If Parnell resigned, even for a short time, then the price would have been paid and he could return as leader after a short interval. But it was too late now for compromise. The daggers had been unsheathed. The issue was no longer the divorce or the independence of the Party, or the Liberal alliance or even Home Rule. The issues had now been transmuted into one irreducible element: Parnell. Were you with him or against him? I tried, delicately, to modify Parnell's position, but he was impervious to advice or suggestion. It was not a battle he had wanted, but it was brought to him, and he never shirked a battle. He fought it all the way, as he had done with obstruction in the House of Commons, with the Land League in the country, with *The Times* in the courts. Why were we surprised that he would now fight with members of his own party, with the Church, with the whole country?

We chatted with our old friends over dinner, without rancour, but we could not mend the tear. It was like a rendezvous between lovers whose affair is over, and yet who meet one more time to see if it can be rekindled, and who, on finding that it cannot, part from one another more disillusioned than before.

By now, Healy had become the leader of the anti-Parnellites, the chief hater and the chief baiter. He spewed out a daily dose of anti-Parnell invective in his articles and speeches; a concoction of bile and venom to rival anything ever published in England. He would have no dealings with Parnell, he said, he would have no compromise with him, he would hunt him down wherever he showed his face. It was a stark message of hatred and bitterness, wholly disproportionate to the issues. But Healy was nothing if not an incendiary, and burning bridges was his greatest political strength. Healy wished to destroy Parnell and if, in so doing, he destroyed the cause of Home Rule, so be it. On Sundays, Healy and The National Press took its day of rest and on that day the Church took up the fight, its croziers beating Parnell down in pulpit after pulpit, throughout the country. Such violent verbal assaults inflamed matters even further and eventually Healy was attacked in Cork, punched in the face, and had his glasses smashed. Some splinters of glass lodged in his eye. After the lime in Castlecomer, it had now become an eye for an eye. When, I wondered, would it become a life for a life?

❧

Months later, there was a second by-election in North Sligo. Parnell campaigned hard, but the result was the same: we lost heavily. He seemed to be in constant motion at this time: leaving Brighton on Monday, travelling to London, to Holyhead, to Dublin, to Sligo, travelling all around Sligo and then on Friday back to Dublin, to Holyhead, to London and back to Brighton, back to Katharine for a day's rest, before beginning the next week's journey. He was utterly exhausted, but he refused all offers of help and all requests to rest.

❧

In June, the long wait for the divorce decree to be finalised was over and Parnell and Katharine were married in a registry office near Brighton. In the quietness and dignity of the service, it seemed extraordinary that their love affair should have so shunted the affairs of our country.

Parnell, however, only had a few days of honeymoon – spent with Katharine at Brighton – before he travelled back to Ireland to campaign at a third by-election in Carlow. His marriage to Katharine inflamed his opponents. It showed them Parnell paid no heed whatsoever to their criticisms, their sermons or their moralising cant. He had waited eleven years to marry Katharine, and he married her the moment she was free from the bonds of her previous marriage. The Church, stung by his indifference to its criticism, increased its attacks. I campaigned every day with him in Carlow, but it was a dispiriting experience; priests who had shared a platform with Parnell to support his agitation, in earlier days, now patrolled the squares to drive away anyone who might attend.

As the days passed, Parnell's great hold over the Irish people appeared to dissolve. He still spoke with great power and dignity, but the people no longer appeared to listen. He had lost the country.

Curiously, he greeted the Carlow campaign with great good humour. I scarcely remember seeing him so elated. Defeats never wounded him, the battle was all. It was a glorious last campaign, fought in a glorious Irish summer. I see him still, talking to small knots of people in town squares, outside hotels, at crossroads, exhorting them to vote for his candidate, to keep Gladstone's hands off the Party, to keep the Party independent at all costs.

I remarked one evening that if Salisbury called a general election, there was a real possibility we might only win two or three seats.

'Then,' he said laughing, 'it's back to where I started and we build again. I am a young man and I can wait. Gladstone is over eighty. We'll see him off. Then Healy. Then all the others. Mark my words.'

In the final days of the campaign, on a Saturday evening in Carlow Town, after the sun had gone down but while it was still bright, I leaned against the grey limestone pillar of the hotel on Main Street and watched as Healy spoke, standing on the back of a hay cart, holding a crowd enthralled as he pilloried Parnell and Katharine in one of his most vitriolic speeches, his voice carrying easily across the street on that quiet, balmy evening.

'… we had Home Rule in the palm of our hands' – Healy's voice had become almost a shriek, such was his level of indignation – 'but Parnell did not bother to attend the House of Commons. Instead of looking after Irish affairs, he was looking after his own affair.'

His humour was too biting, too acidic, to generate a laugh, as he accused Parnell of selling his seat in the House of Commons to O'Shea, 'for the price of his wife'. If Katharine had been Healy's wife, one might have understood such bitterness, but it seemed too intense to be merely a political emnity.

'I don't like talking about Mrs O'Shea,' he said sneeringly. 'Mrs "Katharine O'Shea".'

'Kitty,' a voice shouted from the crowd.

'Aye, Kitty,' responded Healy, 'our great national leader trapped by a Kitty.'

The bawdy and vulgar innuendo was picked up and laughed at by the bawdy and vulgar crowd.

An unknown supporter called out: 'Leave her alone.'

'Leave her alone!' exclaimed Healy. 'Why didn't Parnell leave her alone? If he had, none of this would have happened. But no, he had to run to her, a British prostitute ...'

I saw Healy looking over at me, as if he were addressing his remarks directly to me.

'Aye, I say, there goes Parnell, consorting with prostitutes and prostituting the great national cause for her. Prostituting the seat of Galway for her husband ...'

I could hear no more. Shaking my head in despair, I turned my back on Healy, walked back to my carriage and left the town.

∾≋∾

The rain fell incessantly in Ireland that autumn. Throughout August and September and early October, Parnell travelled throughout the country without rest, wherever he was invited to speak: from Westport to Wexford, from Dublin to Galway. At a meeting in Cabinteely, he got wet through and suffered a feverish cold; the following morning we travelled to Roscommon, where he spoke to a small crowd in the pouring rain and, again, got soaked through. He began to suffer now from pains in his joints, his elbows, his knees, and he could not shake off the chill.

On our way back to Dublin, our train braked suddenly, jerking us all forward in the carriage. As I leaned out of the window, I saw a group of people rushing to the front of the train. When I enquired what had happened, I was told that a young man had fallen from the platform and had been crushed to death. When Parnell heard this, he went completely pale.

'It is a portent,' he said, looking gloomily out the window. 'Something always happens to me in October.'

We returned to Dublin that evening and travelled to England the following day. Parnell seemed to have caught another cold and was complaining of pains in his knee and in his arm.

'Come back with me for dinner,' he said. 'Katharine would like to see you.'

We travelled back together to Brighton one more time. When he arrived home to Katharine, she nursed him tenderly and put him in front of a warm fire and arranged supper for us. In a matter of hours, he seemed greatly restored.

The following day – Saturday – he seemed in good spirits and I left after breakfast to return to London.

On Wednesday morning, in the blackness of the hours before dawn, I heard a loud banging on my front door. It was a telegram boy, with a telegram from Katharine urging me to come immediately, saying that something terrible had happened. Within the hour, I was dressed and on the first train to Brighton and thence I went by cab to Walsingham Terrace.

I knocked on the door; a maid answered and showed me in, but before I could ask any questions Katharine appeared, coming down the stairs. When she saw me she collapsed into my arms, sobbing so much she was hardly able to breathe.

'He's dead, James,' she cried, her shock and grief choking her words. 'Charles is dead.'

At first I thought I must have misheard her.

'He died during the night,' she continued, trying to speak between her sobs. 'I don't know what happened to him. Something happened to him. I don't know.'

As I stood in the hall, too stunned to react, a local doctor, whom I did not know, appeared down the stairs and nodded solemnly to confirm what Katharine had said.

'But what happened?' I heard myself asking him.

'It's hard to be sure,' said the doctor.

'Can I see him?' I asked.

The doctor nodded and led the way back up the stairs. I held Katharine as we went, as I thought she might faint from shock and grief. We went into the bedroom and I looked at Parnell, who looked pale and careworn but otherwise as if he were only asleep. Katharine sat on his bed, cradling his head, touching his face, his cheeks, moving her hands through his hair, rocking back and forth and crying out in great gasps of shock and pain, tears running freely down her face. I looked back at the doctor, who stood at the door.

'What happened?' I asked, stupefied. 'When I left him he seemed rested, recovered.'

The doctor beckoned to me to come outside for a moment.

'He took ill again on Sunday,' he said. 'I came over to see him and he was in considerable pain. Rheumatic fever. He was exhausted, poor man. Quite worn out. That's what did for him in the end. He had no reserves to deal with the cold, the fevers. I think he may have had a thrombosis, a coronary thrombosis. But it's difficult to be sure.'

I looked back on Parnell and Katharine, absolutely bewildered, the scene framed by the door-case, captured in my mind forever. I felt numb, shocked and numb, at the suddenness, the unexpectedness of his death. I sat for hours with Katharine, hardly conscious of anything and yet all the memories of that terrible day are as fresh in my mind as if it happened only yesterday.

Several days later, Parnell began his final journey back to Ireland. As his coffin left their home, I looked back at Katharine, standing at the door utterly forlorn, broken by grief, her two children clutched to her side. She could go no further to accompany him on his journey. She had never visited Ireland with him whilst he was alive and she could not visit it with him now, in death. I promised her I would stay with him to the end. I followed the coffin by carriage to the station, and then by special train to Holyhead, and then on his final voyage across the Irish Sea.

It was a stormy crossing that night and it was raining hard when we arrived in Kingstown, early on Sunday morning. A small crowd, sombre and silent, awaited the arrival of his coffin. They watched, without a sound, as the funeral attendants moved the coffin from the ship onto the Dublin train and shortly afterwards we set off on the short journey to Westland Row.

It was, they said afterwards, the most extraordinary funeral the country had ever seen. Hundreds of thousands of people stood in the streets, watching in silence as his coffin passed, heads bowed, many praying in silence, others with tears openly streaming down their faces. From Westland Row, the procession made its way to the old Parliament building – where it stopped for a moment to recall Parnell's speech to the crowds so many years earlier, on the eve of his imprisonment; thence to St Michan's Church, where the funeral service was held; thence to City Hall, where he lay at the feet of the statue of Daniel O'Connell.

For hour after hour, thousands of people passed before him, muttered a silent prayer before his coffin, blessed themselves and moved on.

By late afternoon, the rain had stopped. The coffin was placed back on the carriage, barely visible beneath all the wreaths, and, with members of our party marching on both sides and the mourning coaches and brass bands behind, it set off for its final procession across the city to Glasnevin Cemetery.

Healy, wisely, did not attend.

It was early evening when the last prayers were read and Parnell's coffin was finally lowered into his grave. As the people walked away and the wreaths were being arranged for the last time, I saw a great, bright light blaze across the darkening sky. It was, I discovered later, a scientific fact that a brilliant meteor had fallen across Ireland at half-past six in the evening on that Sunday in October 1891.

It was, as Parnell himself would have said, a portent.

Epilogue

I RETURNED TO London several days later, subdued by sorrow and depressed in spirit. Aimlessly and almost without thinking, I went walking along friendly and familiar streets, until I found myself close to the House of Commons. It was mid-October now, a still, autumnal afternoon. I passed the House and crossed the bridge, where I stood for some moments in a reverie, looking back across the river at the Houses of Parliament. As I did so, I remembered the first time I had seen this great palace: that first evening I had been in London, when I had walked with Fanny and Parnell across Westminster Bridge; when Fanny had laughed to be on the arms of two such handsome men; when I, in my youthful love for her, had been too shy, too timorous, to repay the compliment; when Parnell had hoped he would be the last Parnell to be elected there; when, in our youth and excitement, we had looked forward to our great adventure together.

And, as I stood gazing across the river, I remembered all the times I had spent with Parnell over the last sixteen tumultuous years. I remembered the laughter of Biggar, Parnell and myself, as comrades-in-arms in the early days of obstruction; I remembered the terrible scenes of the starving tenants in Westport and thought once again of my poor dying mother; I remembered Parnell's great speeches during the days of the Land League campaign; I remembered the bone-chilling cold of the gaol in Kilmainham; I remembered Parnell's grief as he returned to prison on the day he buried his daughter; I remembered the great triumph of the Land Act, our anticipation in the House of Commons when Gladstone introduced his Home Rule bill and our devastation when it failed;

I remembered the scheming lies of Pigott at the Special Commission, the malicious lies of O'Shea in the divorce court and the vile diatribes of Healy in Committee Room 15 and in the final campaign in Ireland.

All these and all my other memories crowded in upon me and I wept. I wept for my mother who had died in the famine so many years ago, lost and unknown; I wept for the boy who had never known her; I wept for Fanny who had died so needlessly and so far away; I wept for Katharine who had lost her husband; I wept for Clare and Katie who had lost their father; I wept for my country which had lost its great leader; but, most of all, I wept for the death of a great and remarkable man who had been my friend.

About the Author

B RIAN CREGAN was born in Dublin and educated at Gonzaga College, University College Dublin and St John's College Oxford. He has been a practicing barrister for over twenty years. *Parnell – A Novel* is his first novel.